Blackhorse Road

Merida Johns

Coffee Cup Press

Copyright © 2020 Merida Johns

The moral right of the author has been asserted.

All rights reserved.
No part of this publication may be reproduced, stored in a retrieval system, or transmitted, in any form or by any means, without the prior permission in writing of the publisher, except in the case of brief quotations used in critical articles or reviews, nor be otherwise circulated in any form of binding or cover other than that in which it is published and without a similar condition including this condition being imposed on the subsequent purchaser.

For information, address Coffee Cup Press Publisher, PO Box 1143, Huntley, IL 60142.

This book is a work of fiction. All events, dialogue, and characters are the product of the author's imagination and are not to be construed as real. Though the mention of some characters, events, or places are based on the historical record, the work as a whole is a work of fiction.

FIRST EDITION

Designed by Rena Hoberman Cover Quill

Published by Coffee Cup Press

ISBN 978-1-7332790-0-0

Typesetting services by BOOKOW.COM

To my family members and those of past generations who have shared with me the value of memory making and memory keeping.

ACKNOWLEDGMENTS

No acknowledgment is sufficient to express my gratitude to my husband, Russell, for his loving support and insight, and his continued confirmation of the worthiness of this effort. Our daily discussions over morning coffee were a welcome venue to refine the plot, sharpen the characters, and have fun with metaphors and similes. My appreciation to my sisters, nieces, and close friends whose encouragement drowned out any inner critic that might dare to lurk in the shadows and threaten the completion of the work. Thank you to my many friends who have followed the creation of this story via social media and whose expectations have kept me accountable for completing this work. Finally, sincere thanks to Megan Gregan, my developmental editor, who kept rooting for me and challenging and coaching me in creating a better story. Many thanks to Kim Bookless, my copyeditor, Pat Hertel, my professional proofreader, and Rena, my book cover designer from Coverquill.com. Special thanks to Denise Marie, Jennifer, Marian, Sue, Carol, Laurel, and Lalani who are the best cheerleading and critique squad an author could have.

PROLOGUE

The cranky engine revved as the driver shifted gears, and the military bus crawled forward exiting the air force base. Along a narrow and dark roadway, the vehicle increased its speed and left the MPs at the gate standing immobile and mute in the glow of the rising moon. Drifting through the open windows, the Southern California desert air blew like pixie dust across the faces of the thirty young women headed home. A few hours ago, they were preening and adjusting their bouffant hairdos, reapplying creamy pink lipstick, and placing the last twirls of mascara on their eyelashes to prepare for a street dance with cadets from the elite Air Force Academy. Then, the atmosphere buzzed with gossip, chatter, laughter, and anticipation. Now, the glimmering night sky created the perfect backdrop that lulled each into a contented silence to fantasize about the handsome men they had met.

Luci Bartolino closed her eyes and rested her head against the vehicle's window frame. As the driver navigated the empty highway, the herbal desert smells floating on the dry air wafted into Luci's thoughts. June 10, 1966. Like a butterfly's transformation from a cocoon, the routine day had metamorphosed into an enchanted evening, leaving Luci feeling like Cinderella. Although the night heat permeated the bus, emotional chills skipped across Luci's arms as she daydreamed of the cadet with the electric blue eyes. She sighed, and a smile of wonderment and gratitude danced across her face. *Thank you, Lucinda McCormick, for giving me the courage to conquer my self-doubt.*

Part I

1966-1967

CHAPTER 1

Lucinda

Luci felt a unique connection with her great-grandmother, Lucinda. An Irish immigrant to Canada, Lucinda McCormick was the ideal by which her female descendants measured themselves. They admired her courage, culture, beauty, and perseverance, and her death in the prime of life intensified her mystique in family lore. As her great-grandmother's namesake, Luci believed she had high standards to meet, but she sometimes questioned whether she had the grit to meet the challenge.

During summer vacations in Canada, Luci spent sultry evenings on her grandmother Geneviève's front porch. There she listened, riveted by the Lucinda stories her aunts and uncles told. They recounted the McCormicks' prosperity as linen merchants and their social standing in Northern Ireland. The McCormicks, they said, had a beautiful home, servants, and the means to send their children to England for formal education. But the Irish potato famine and stiff competition from cotton manufacturing merged to upend the family. It sent them whirling into a financial downfall, causing them to lose their income, home, and other resources.

Their friends the Blakes and McMahons had settled in Canada and urged the family to immigrate there. Both families took jobs in the Ottawa Valley as laborers constructing the Rideau Canal linking Montreal to Kingston, Ontario. After the project finished, they migrated further west and chose a little mercantile and farming village on the Detroit River to call home. As they prospered, they sent messages of hope back to Ireland. Their encouragement bolstered the McCormicks' decision to gamble that an uncertain future in Canada was better than the bleak one in their homeland.

Facing a harrowing transatlantic trip, the McCormicks, like other immigrants, left Ireland on a "coffin ship." These vessels were overcrowded and unsanitary, lacked adequate food and ventilation, and were rampant with typhus, dysentery, and cholera. Allowed a mere ten square feet per passenger, the eight members of the McCormick family huddled with two hundred other immigrants in claustrophobic and filthy conditions for the two-month voyage. In most cases, these deplorable ships reached their destinations with ill and weakened passengers, and many times, more people died than lived through these journeys. Luci shuddered at the account and asked herself, *How did they survive it? What caused their resilience?* Her forebearers' incredible grit burned an image into her mind.

After eight weeks, the immigrant ship sailed into the Gulf of St. Lawrence, and the family anticipated an end to their grueling three-thousand-mile journey. But their luck did not hold out. Late that day, the ship went on alert when threatening weather brewed in the distance. The crew and passengers knew the gulf was more treacherous during gales than the open seas, and disasters were frequent. With shallow waters and shoals and few available harbors along its coast, the gulf was a dangerous place in the best of weather. From yellowed copies of Lucinda's journal that she had written as a young woman, Luci's relatives recited to her the harrowing story.

> *At two in the morning, a violent storm came up, the likes we had not seen before. The ship thrust from side to side. It was pitch black on the lower deck where we were, and people were falling over each other. Anything that wasn't nailed down got tossed in the air or thrown across the floor. Everywhere people were screaming, crying, and praying. I was trembling, sobbing, and hanging on to my mother. As the rocking and jolting got worse, pandemonium exploded. We were a desperate mob pushing our way up the narrow stairs trying to reach the upper deck. When we got there, the sleet was so forceful it stabbed our faces and froze our clothes to our bodies. I recall my father's haunted look when he saw the ship's rigging covered in ice from the freezing rain. At that moment, he understood our doomed prospects. Passengers panicked as they realized the crew was helpless in controlling the ship. The worst, though, was the grating sound I heard as our vessel's hull ran aground a shoal.*

> *There are no words to describe the dark feeling of hopelessness. In those few seconds, two hundred people lost all faith. We clung to the ship, but within a short time, it broke into pieces. Plunged into the icy water, all of us grabbed for remnants of the boat as the last possibility to stay afloat. There was an ice floe nearby, and with an enormous amount of difficulty, my father and brothers got all the family onto it. By then, we had lost our shoes and outer garments and had to huddle together like animals to stay warm. We feared that the bobbing patch of ice might crack and hurl us into the water again. At last, early the next morning help arrived. I remember thinking throughout it all,* What will it feel like to drown?

Against the odds, all the family lived through the harrowing ordeal. A horrifying scene the next morning, however, shattered their hopeful mood. Strewn along the beach were the bodies of eighty immigrant women, men, and children. Luci questioned how Lucinda, a child of five, endured memories of such a terrifying trauma. Family members told her the hellish episode plagued the McCormick children, and they relived it in nightmares and traumatic flashbacks throughout their lives.

The compassionate French community near Cap-des-Rosiers, where the ship had foundered, took in the McCormicks and the other survivors. A few weeks later, they boarded a vessel to Grosse-Île, a small island community in the St. Lawrence River not far from Quebec. There, the government quarantined immigrants for the evaluation of typhoid and other contagious diseases. As the McCormicks' ship approached the island, it was forced to halt. The migration was so massive that vessels waiting to unload their passengers created a line several miles long. Having few choices, government officials issued a fifteen-day general quarantine for all ships.

In a heartbreaking turn of events, Lucinda's mother, Ellen, contracted typhoid fever during the delay and died in the ship's lice-infested hold. Her grief-stricken family watched in distress as the ship's crew committed their mother's body for burial in the St. Lawrence River. Those who died on land fared worse interment, the family learned, their bodies stacked like cordwood and buried in mass graves.

As her descendants recounted, life's transitory nature made a lasting impression on little Lucinda. Her father and siblings, dealing with their loss, did what they could to comfort her and to serve as a surrogate mother.

Still, they could not compensate for Lucinda's heartache or feelings of insecurity and abandonment. After all, Ellen was closest to her youngest child. She was the one who hugged, clothed, and praised Lucinda, kissed her scrapes and bruises, and made her feel safe in the world.

It was some time before Lucinda came to grips with the knowledge that her mother would never return. She and her siblings faced a fundamental choice: continue to live in emotional pain or adjust to a world in which their mother was no longer part. Later in life, in a letter to her sister Mary, Lucinda confided her feelings of insignificance, fear, and guilt during that troubling time.

> *Somehow, I felt I was responsible for our mother's death. I know now it was an irrational fear. Even so, I thought she would still be with us if I had not fussed and sobbed so much. I believed God was punishing me. I thought if I stopped whining and crying, our mother would return. From my child's eyes, everyone was going on with their lives, and I felt invisible. I didn't think I was important anymore.*

While Lucinda could never eradicate her sorrow, she decreased her emotional pain by including Ellen in her life in different ways and wrote about these in her journal years later as a young woman.

> *The heaviness I endured made my heart as cold as stone, leaving it devoid of feeling. But in me, the flicker of love and yearning for my mother triumphed. Through remembrances and symbols, I fueled the ember until the stone turned warm and emitted a healing glow throughout me. I remembered the songs my mother sang to me. I held her prayer book during church services, knowing I was fingering the pages she had touched. I took one of her delicate, laced handkerchiefs and safely tucked it among my belongings. Just as a locket of hair comforts a lover, this tiny piece of cloth consoles me.*

This experience influenced Lucinda's life philosophy that she confided in her journal:

> *I can never reconcile the concept of a merciful God with my mother's cruel demise. If death can suddenly strike down someone who is as*

vigorous as my mother, then safety is an illusion and faith a crutch. What defines a person are not one's financial or physical attributes or beliefs. Instead, it's the choices that one makes in surmounting life's challenges.

* * *

After the quarantine, the McCormicks took passage on an open-air barge, and five days later they arrived at Amherstburg, a small town at the confluence of the Detroit River and Lake Erie. Disembarking at the town dock, their old friends the Blakes and McMahans welcomed them with open arms.

Lucinda's father, Felix, established himself as a merchant in the small river town. Most of his children, however, moved to a section of Detroit called Corktown, where Irish immigrants had made their home since the 1830s. A bustling industrial and commercial center, Detroit promised economic opportunity, and Felix McCormick's children were hungry for advancement. After a few years, they distinguished themselves and prospered in the metropolis referred to as "Boomtown."

Lucinda frequented her sisters' homes in Detroit as much as possible. She found the city exciting and alive, giving her access to a full circle of people and a world of new ideas. It was true Detroit had its seedy and dangerous areas with taverns and brothels. For the most part, the merchant class and fashionable citizens, including Lucinda's family, avoided or ignored these. Horse-drawn streetcars transporting people and crisscrossing the city's broad and business-lined thoroughfares created a buzz that energized Lucinda. Magnificent public buildings and parks dotted the town, and there were plenty of literary and social activities to occupy and charm a young woman of the era. Detroit was on its way as a cultural center. It was a place to live it up, and Lucinda exploited its advantages.

As Lucinda matured into an accomplished and self-reliant young woman, friends and acquaintances admired her presence and her intellect. She was slender, and her tall figure enhanced her elegant comportment. Her flawless complexion, violet-blue eyes, and thick, wavy, raven hair complemented her gregarious disposition. At parties, Lucinda delighted the guests with her musical talents. On the piano, she played pieces by ear, and her mezzo-soprano voice added to the gaiety of every evening. Lucinda's pleasant brogue and impeccable social graces ingratiated her with

Irish matrons on both sides of the border. It was not long before a steady stream of beaus from Detroit and the local Canadian village appeared on the scene.

Lucinda held her suitors at arm's length; her ambition for autonomy outweighed any marriage proposal. A decade younger than her siblings, Lucinda grew up on the cusp of the industrial revolution. The era brought a change in the role of women. Positions outside the home increasingly replaced domestic work. Opportunities for women to fulfill themselves beyond household responsibilities excited Lucinda, and she repelled the thought of a census taker listing her occupation as "keeping house."

She was an avid reader, and early feminist writers influenced her life view. A favorite was Margaret Fuller, whose book *Woman in the Nineteenth Century* declared the equality of women and men. To her family, Lucinda explained her decision to pursue independence using paraphrases of the author's words. "Why should women restrain their spirits? Why would God give women spirit and not expect them to fulfill it? Women should work according to their spirit. The past should not bind women's destiny and freedom." Attitudes were slow to change, and Lucinda's family resisted her views. They were not convinced that the radical idea of individualism should supersede social conformity.

Teaching and nursing were the few professions open to single women who desired careers to control their destiny. It was Lucinda's love of learning that spurred her to study at a provincial institution dedicated to teacher preparation. The Toronto Normal School, standing on the impressive St. James Square, was an imposing three-story brick complex. In an entry in her journal, Lucinda described the school's poignant first impact on her sentiments.

> *I felt humbled walking into the largest building in the Americas committed to training future teachers. The school and the cultural opportunities of Toronto are fruit on a tree that is ready to be picked and enjoyed. It's here where my destiny as an independent woman begins.*

Felix had humored his daughter and had given his blessing for her to attend the Normal School. Still, he held out hope that she would not have the determination to make teaching a career. To his dismay, after her graduation, Lucinda accepted a teaching post in a country school a few miles from Amherstburg. Lucinda's siblings pressured her to stay home and to abandon her idea of a career. After all, as the youngest child, it is your responsibility to care for your aging parent without complaining, they told her. This was especially true, they thought, for an unmarried daughter.

Steadfast, Lucinda pursued her career and defied her family's wishes. She had a hunger for learning and a passion for instilling the desire in others. "Being a teacher," Lucinda argued to her siblings, "is in harmony with our religious belief of caring for one another. It is as equal to the good works of the saints that we honor. My life's purpose is to help others prosper."

Lucinda saw the hardships of immigrants in Detroit and knew that a lack of education limited their opportunities and choices. She recounted to her students the harsh lives of the newcomers who had little training. "They live in overcrowded and poor housing. Many times, an entire family lives in one small room. Along with low pay, they endure unhealthy working conditions. With little legal protection, they are the prey for unscrupulous landlords, employers, and others. Unable to read or write the language of their new country, it is difficult for them to progress, and they end up on the bottom of society. My family was fortunate because we could read and write, and my father had a trade. Literacy makes you free. Shouldn't everyone have freedom?" she challenged her little charges.

One summer in her grandmother's basement, Luci discovered a battered shoebox filled with old letters. Tucked among these was one that caught her attention. It was a note to Lucinda from her sister Kate, and it confirmed the family's opposition to Lucinda's career choice.

Detroit. August 15, 1871

My dear Lucinda,

Your very welcome letter I received and read with genuine pleasure. It seems a lifetime since you favored poor me with a note. I must congratulate you on your success in your continued studies in music and literature. But I do not, my dear Lucinda, bless your idea of being a teacher, decidedly not! I would not do it were I in your place. You ought to remain with Papa and thus enable him to enjoy the short length of life that now remains for him. You know how sad it would be for Papa to have his remaining daughter absent herself from home. Stay close to Papa, dear child, and make him as happy as you can, and you will receive heaven's rewards.

Your loving sister, Kate

After reading the letter's contents, Luci's admiration for her great-grandmother's courage heightened. *Considering the guilt her family laid on her, who wouldn't acknowledge Lucinda's bravery in resisting their pressures*, Luci thought.

* * *

In the fall of 1871, Lucinda assumed the post as the schoolmistress of a one-room school located in the French Canadian community of Vereker. Ten years before Lucinda's employment, females made up less than twenty-five percent of the teaching force in the country, and within the seven-county area where she lived, there were only forty-one female trailblazers. Luci believed that in choosing a career, her great-grandmother was an example of heroism in continuing the cause of women's equality.

As was the custom, schoolmistresses boarded with a local family. While most shared a room and bed with the younger children in the home, Lucinda's family, the Réaumes, provided her with private and comfortable accommodations. Communities of the era held rural teachers in high esteem, and in this regard, Lucinda was no exception. But she garnered more than respect in her community. Her down-to-earth attitude and engaging personality endeared her to the adult population as well as to her fourteen charges who adored their pretty dark-haired teacher. Within a few weeks, Lucinda was an integral part of their life, and soon she had a long line of male admirers.

When a handsome French Canadian caught her eye at the autumn harvest dance, Lucinda's life unpredictably changed. Antoine Desjardins had broad shoulders and a muscular build, honed through years of physical labor. His lake-blue eyes contrasted with a ruddy complexion, handsome face, and a splendid mop of thick, curly black hair. His physical features, flirtatious smile, and jovial nature stirred Lucinda's emotions, and he proved too tempting for her to ignore.

Antoine's forefathers were early French settlers to Canada, who arrived in Quebec City in the 1630s. Over the generations, his family moved up the St. Lawrence River, and in the early 1700s, they settled on the northern banks of Lake Erie. By many standards, Antoine's family was prosperous. Most were farmers and tradesmen, and a few were wealthy lumber barons. Unlike his flourishing father and uncles, though, Antoine owned a small farm, and most of the community agreed he was larger on personality than ambition. His goal in life was not to be the wealthiest person but the happiest. Antoine took pride in his heritage of the famed *coureur de bois*, the adventurous, freedom-loving French explorers of early Canada. Antoine celebrated these men as heroes, and he emulated their attitude and hot-blooded temperament.

Lucinda captivated Antoine. He saw in her beauty and culture, but she had a quality he admired more: her spunk. Strict social constraints of the time meant limited opportunities for courting. During winter evenings, Antoine called on Lucinda but always under the watchful eyes of the Réaumes. When spring arrived, the couple slipped away and took long walks alone along the lakefront in the chilly afternoons. Warm embraces and secret kisses threw them into a whirlwind of passion, and early the following summer, the church announced their marriage bans.

On a crisp October day under a canopy of autumn color, they married in Sainte Jean Baptiste church on the anniversary of their first meeting at the harvest dance. For Lucinda, the event was bittersweet. Her marriage outside her Irish community raised an eyebrow among her siblings, and her change in marital status meant relinquishing the autonomy she had worked so hard to achieve. Unlike their male counterparts, women were forced by regulation to resign their teaching positions after they married. But Lucinda had determination. Against convention, she petitioned the board of trustees, asking to remain in her position. In the end, she was allowed to retain her job, but only until the end of the academic year—in the era, there was one choice, either career or marriage.

* * *

As the years went by, Lucinda sometimes questioned the choice of exchanging her self-sufficiency for marriage to a bigger-than-life personality. She endured the hardships of a farmer's wife and often craved the intellectual life she had enjoyed as a single woman. In an excerpt from a letter written to her sister in May 1880, she reflected:

I often think that if I had bent to your will and had not married, my life would be more comfortable. Still, I question if the measure of a good life lies with luxuries and leisure, or something more? I find comfort in Thoreau's words that "Merely to come into the world the heir of a fortune is not to be born but to be still-born." Is that, dear sister, not as true for those who would bend to conform with society and marry or not for comfort or a fortune?

If not driven, Antoine had other qualities. His zest was infectious, and with Antoine, Lucinda lived life as an adventure. He was jovial and delighted in telling jokes, teasing, and playing pranks. Easygoing, Antoine believed that the world was a good place, and no matter what the challenge, life would work out in his favor. Antoine's love for Lucinda was unquestionable, and above all, he was a kind, attentive, and supportive husband and companion.

Lucinda's six children were born in quick succession. Tending to the needs of a household that was miles from city conveniences, made her days long and tedious. There was incessant dust, and odors of sour milk and barnyard animals permeated the house. Lacking simple privacies drove her to desperation at times. Writing in her journal was an emotional outlet that made her feel renewed. Securely placed in the back of a dresser drawer, the journal was her constant listener. *It allows me to empty my heart without judging or advising,* she wrote. Sometimes her entries were reflections in prose or poetry. Other times, they chronicled her feelings and reactions to the day's events. Lucinda was grateful to her journal for concealing what she called her dark times. Typical of these was an entry in early June 1878:

June 14, 1878
The dark times steal upon me. Is it wicked to despair in strife?
Cruelly my memories haunt me. For what is the real profit in life?
The dark times slip over me. Is it wicked to be so lithe?
Cruelly my memories haunt me. For what is the real profit in life?

Though she had regrets and the dark times were recurrent companions, Lucinda worked to balance these with being grateful. She avoided obsessing over past actions she could not control. Heeding the advice of Thoreau, she embraced the present as the pathway to her future and impressed this principle on her children. To remind herself to live these values, she scribed a daily contemplation in the front of her journal:

Acknowledge the goodness in life for there you will find happiness
Live in the present for there is the path to a worthwhile life
Seek out your options for there you will discover the best choice

Lucinda prized reading and writing, and she took joy in cultivating a similar appreciation in her children. She often snatched moments to engage in her passion, stealing away to the lakeshore near the farm. There, Lucinda sketched the quiet scenes of the lake islands and, using her imagination, created stories and poems. When she daydreamed, her fingers unconsciously doodled drawings of the rose of Sharon, and she wrote in her journal about her relationship to the beloved flower:

I take pleasure in thinking the rose of Sharon and I are alike. My blossoms are delicate, but they are not fragile. My branches are willowy, but they are not weak. My roots are intricate, but they are not frail.

As she worked, she hummed lyrical Irish ballads that lifted the day's burdens. She retained her freedom of spirit, and she flourished, seeing a continuum between herself and the future. What she did and how she lived in the present would last beyond her, she believed. Enriching her family with these values fueled Lucinda's life's meaning, and she trusted these would pass to her progeny for many generations. Poignantly, her last journal entry considered what her purpose and place in the continuity of life might be:

In the end, what have I given? A flower begins by receiving a seed from one that has gone before, and at its end, it gives a seed so another can start. The purpose of the flower is not to receive or to give. Its meaning is in the quality of the bloom that it nurtures to beautify the world. I have received, and I have given, but the essence of my life is the bloom that I have become.

* * *

In 1886, cool breezes and sun-filled days announced the start of preparations for planting crops on the Lake Erie northern shore. Awaiting the arrival of her seventh child, Lucinda treated April 7 like any other day. Waking early, she crawled from under the feather blanket and glanced with affection at a sleeping Antoine. Shivering from the cold, Lucinda dressed quickly then stepped into the hallway and closed the bedroom door without making a sound. She tiptoed through the central corridor to the kitchen and, hovering over the cast-iron stove, stoked the fire. The warmth from the fading embers comforted her in the few peaceful moments she had before starting the day's chores.

As the dawn light reflected on the crystallized dew and danced through the window, Lucinda took a deep breath and drank in the moment. She knew that the new baby would be born soon, and while she was happy, she was also troubled. Even though Lucinda's babies had been delivered unaided and with no complications, maternal and infant mortality was a reality; pregnancy in 1886 was a dangerous event for mother and baby.

The nascent fire sputtered, and a lone bird whistled from the tree limb outside the kitchen window. Listening to the early morning sounds, Lucinda prayed for a safe birth and a healthy newborn.

Later, as she cleaned up from the noonday supper of her brood, Lucinda's labor pains began. She had made the preparations for the birth in advance. Lying-in clothes were washed and placed folded on the dresser top. Laundered sheets and a fresh nightgown for herself and swaddling clothes for the baby were ready. She had tied a cotton blanket to the upper bedpost so she could pull on it to help mitigate the birth pain. Hot water from the kitchen cookstove reservoir and clean rags were all she needed to gather.

By midafternoon, Lucinda recognized that the labor pains today were different from those before. These were more intense, and she knew the birth was not progressing as it should. Her hands shaking and chest tingling, Lucinda went to the back door and called out to her eldest son, Luc. "Go fetch your father. Hurry, hurry," she hollered.

Luc ran to the back of the farm's sixty acres where Antoine was plowing the field. Flushed and out of breath, Antoine arrived at the house where he found Lucinda in backbreaking pain. Distressed, he harnessed the horse to the buggy and rushed three miles to his brother's farm for help. In less than an hour, Antoine arrived back with his sister-in-law to aid Lucinda.

After several hours, it was evident the birth was breech. Antoine rushed to town for the doctor, but the physician was several miles away in Dube Corners delivering another baby. It was well into the late evening before the doctor arrived. Shortly after midnight on April 8, Lucinda gave birth to a healthy baby girl that she and Antoine named Geneviève.

After the delivery, Lucinda found it impossible to tend to the needs of the baby, her six other children, and her domestic chores. With the other births, her strength came back, and within a day, she resumed her usual work. But this time was different; she was sluggish and had bouts of fever and chills and stomach and back pain. Six days after Geneviève's birth, the family was alarmed when Lucinda's condition worsened, and she began to fall in and out of delirium. In whispers, her relatives agonized: childbed fever.

Lucinda lay in the one piece of expensive furniture she and Antoine owned and eyed the intricate, carved flowers of the bed's headboard. As the hours of fever continued, hallucinations overcame Lucinda. In her delusion, the delicate flowers on the headboard turned into her most beloved blossom, the exquisite rose of Sharon. Imagining the bloom was her final comfort before she slipped away.

All the community gathered for Lucinda's funeral at Sainte Jean Baptiste, the church where she and Antoine married. Mourning, Antoine and the children dissolved in tears during the funeral service. As Luci's relatives recounted to her, Lucinda's sudden and tragic death haunted Antoine for the rest of his life. He second-guessed his choices: *What if we had fewer children? Would she have lived if the doctor had come earlier? Would she have recovered if she had more help? What if I had been a better provider?*

Suffering through his grief, Antoine ensured Lucinda's legacy. He kept her memory alive through anecdotes about her wisdom and beauty. He described her spunk in stories of her spirit and perseverance. He nurtured the tradition of retelling "Lucinda stories" to his children, and they passed on the chronicles to the next generation. Beyond the memories and tales, Antoine solidified the continuation of Lucinda's purpose. He donated land and underwrote the cost of a new school in Vereker, the place where Lucinda captured his heart.

* * *

Eighty years later, on muggy summer evenings on her grandmother's front porch, Luci listened to the family stories. Relatives reminded her that there was no talent as great, no mind as bright, and no character as determined as Lucinda's. Her great-grandmother's unorthodox choices fueled the fascination surrounding her legacy, and they were fodder for conversation and debate. Despite her positive characteristics, a dark undertone accompanied the adulation of Lucinda for those inclined to conformity. They whispered that Lucinda had too much of an independent streak. She espoused feminist ideas about the place of women in society and cultivated these ideas in her children. She sought a career beyond a home keeper, and she married outside her cultural community.

More upsetting to some was Lucinda's break in the tradition, as the youngest child, of caring for her aged parent. "Pure stubbornness and selfishness," her sister Kate often remarked. In the final analysis, they questioned whether pursuing change was worth the frustration, anxiety, and backlash it might produce. The cynics' unspoken lesson was that there is a price to pay if you go against the norm. Follow the rules; it makes life easier, they believed.

But there were others, Luci among them, who did not buy that message. They argued that the skeptics misunderstood the importance of choice. Conformity may make life seem more comfortable. But blind obedience, in time, frustrates and disappoints us. It is conformity that robs us of our hope and deprives us of improving ourselves and creating a better and fairer world, they challenged.

Luci protested that it was because Lucinda's nature went against the grain that her life was an example of virtuousness and courage. "Lucinda was thankful for the good things given to her. Gratefulness diminished her fear and increased her courage to act from her heart and on her convictions. I don't want to live a life of conformity at the expense of living a fulfilled and honest one," Luci asserted. Time would determine whether Luci had the strength to live up to that conviction.

CHAPTER 2

Family Ties

UPBEAT and optimistic, that was Sam Bartolino, a man who chose hopefulness and perseverance over complacency and fantasy. To his daughter Luci and her three sisters, he stressed, "You have three options when you hit a brick wall and can't get what you want. You can accept the situation and endure it. You can live in a fantasy world and pretend everything is fine. Or you can persist and find a way around the wall." A twinkle in Sam's eyes, synchronized with two raised eyebrows, left no doubt as to which alternative he thought best.

Born in 1901 in northern Italy, Sam was orphaned at four years old when his parents died from cholera. While his maternal grandparents and extended family cared for him and met his physical needs, it was not enough. "As much as they tried, their attentions weren't the unconditional love and the bonding that a mother and father provide," Sam confided to his wife and daughters.

Sam's grandparents had financial means. They owned a profitable flour mill, lived in a large home, and had a social standing in the small town where they lived. At the time, industrialization and modernization of infrastructure were taking over the area's larger cities, and the expansion of railroads connected Sam's community to industrial centers across Europe. With better transportation and innovations in agriculture, profits grew for Sam's family.

World War I, though, shattered their promising future. The war was devastating on many levels, and for Sam, it cut his childhood short. With his uncles conscripted into military service, Sam had to leave school to undertake their work at the family's mill. "Terminating my education was a hard blow, and having learning ripped from me made me value it more.

A lack of education is a disadvantage that impedes a person's prospects for business and social success," Sam told his children. His experience explained why he championed a college education for each of his daughters.

When the Peace Treaty of Versailles ended the hostilities in Europe in 1919, Sam looked for a better future than war-torn Italy's poorly performing economy could provide. He was eighteen years old, yearning for adventure and a fresh start. A decade earlier, an older cousin, Emilio, immigrated to Ontario, Canada. His entrepreneurial spirit and hard work paid off, and by 1920, he had a thriving business as a fruit and meat merchant. "The population of this city," Emilio wrote, "is exploding. The place is overflowing with jobs with the expanding automobile industry here. There's a lot to offer a resourceful young man."

Sam needed no encouragement to join Emilio. In the spring of 1920, in a departure that was hopeful but painful, Sam left his family and beloved Po Valley region and had no expectation of seeing either again. With little money, he boarded a steamship in Antwerp as a third-class passenger, and although the vessel was not as horrific as the Irish coffin ships, his accommodations were minimal. Sam knew his place as a steerage traveler and never forgot the humiliation of affluent passengers on the upper deck promenades peering down and pointing at him as if he were less than human. *That will never happen again,* he vowed.

After a ten-day journey, he arrived in Quebec and then traveled five hundred miles by train to Windsor, Canada's southernmost city. The expansiveness of the Canadian territory, with its rivers, lakes, forests, lush valleys, and farmlands, surprised him and made Europe seem a miniature landscape. *How can one travel so far without crossing a border or having to show a passport?* he wondered.

In Windsor, Sam worked selling vegetables from a street cart for Emilio. But he desired more than Emilio's neighborhood of Little Italy—Sam wanted to assimilate into Canadian culture. After a year, he moved away from the familiarity of the immigrant community, found a job in the construction trade, and settled in a diverse district. Through his new work, Sam made Canadian friends, learned their customs, and took vocational evening courses to perfect his English. Eight years later, he and a friend established what was to become a thriving masonry business in southwestern Ontario.

* * *

At twenty-eight, Sam had promising prospects and was ready to settle down as a family man. In 1929, at a New Year's Eve party, he met Marie, a pretty and vivacious elementary school teacher of French Canadian and Irish descent. Marie's roots reached back to the early 1600s when her French relations first arrived in Quebec. Her lineage and family standing were important to Sam. In his mind, marrying into one of the most established families in the county would be the epitome of assimilation and the culmination of a dream. "Her relatives include prosperous businessmen and farmers who have city streets named after them," Sam boastfully wrote to his family in Italy.

At first, Sam was unaware of Marie's complex disposition built on internal conflicts she had battled since her mid-teen years. As a young girl, tales of her grandmother, Lucinda, mesmerized Marie. She fantasized resisting convention like her grandmother, a behavior at odds with her rigid upbringing. The battle between autonomy and conformity produced a whirlwind of contradictions and self-doubt that Marie adeptly concealed from others.

Adding to her internal conflict, Marie entered her teenage years during the height of the Roaring Twenties. It was an age of rebellion against Victorian norms and a time for women to break with tradition. Marie thought she had the boldness to join in the resistance and reap the era's advantages. Detroit's seductiveness sucked in Marie, and she visited her Irish cousins there as often as possible, going to parties, dances, and movies and taking in cultural events, symphonies, and plays. Her relatives in the States were more freewheeling than her Canadian family. They embraced the notion of the flapper girl whose dress and behaviors portrayed a woman who knew what she wanted and went after it. Jazz music excited them, as did dances like the Fox Trot and Charleston. The glamour of liquor and speakeasies defined their lifestyle.

Marie's stateside relations were wealthier and better educated than those in Canada. For seventy years, they had worked hard and persevered, and their political cleverness propelled them from Corktown to the highest echelons of society. Marie's Irish American relatives were not shy in asserting their status. They lived in large and elegant homes along Woodward Avenue, the Detroit boulevard that announced, *You've made it.* Higher education and money commingled on the American side of the river. Marie's male and female cousins graduated from four-year colleges and universities that provided them the social and political access they needed for prosperous careers and elevated status.

In Detroit, Marie played the role of a flapper as much as she dared. Her periodic forays, though, were not enough to free her from the traditional bounds of her home life. While Marie admired her Irish relations, their wealth and education intimidated her, and Marie's inner critic kept her from feeling that she measured up to them.

Nonetheless, she ached to be part of the exciting upheaval in societal norms. Marie read the literary works portraying the radical notions of the time, consuming the works of F. Scott Fitzgerald, Eugene O'Neill, and Edna St. Vincent Millay. The novels, plays, and poems intensified and fed her urgency to seek independence and not lose out on the action. She indulged her talent and love for drawing, sitting for hours at the lakeshore, illustrating the region's landscape in her sketchbook and imagining being a university student in a bustling city. But Marie's desire to study art, philosophy, and literature wasn't an opportunity within reach for middle-class women like her. Females made up a small proportion of the five percent of the university-aged population enrolled in higher education. With these odds, Marie's aspiration was more a pipe dream than reality.

Increasing the impediments to her dream, Marie's relatives scoffed at her idea of becoming an artist. "What a frivolous notion for a woman from a working-class background," her aunt commented. "How do you think you can establish yourself in a field dominated by men?" an uncle asked. "Privileged women of means have time for such fancy preoccupations—not you!" another said. "Attend teacher's training school and be happy with it. It has more prestige than a salesclerk or secretary," her father stated. Marie walked up to the nonconformist line, but she lacked the nerve to cross it. In the end, she traded her artisan dream for teacher training college.

Captivated by all things Rudolpf Valentino, Marie fell hard for the charismatic Italian she met at a New Year's Eve party. With a shock of chestnut-brown wavy hair, a deep smooth voice, and milk-chocolate brown eyes, Sam Bartolino lit Marie's romantic fantasies that gave her the courage to buck one norm—marrying within her social group. But she harbored doubts over her decision. She was not only taking an Italian immigrant as a husband, but she was also giving up a career. Even in the early 1930s, regulations required that she resign from her teaching position because of her marital status. *Is the short-lived thrill of seduction worth the cost of losing self-determination and social status?* she often wondered.

* * *

Although the Great Depression unsheathed its claws and tore at the construction industry, Sam and his sweetheart married in the fall of 1931. Like everyone, they faced tough financial times. Canada got walloped by unemployment that reached thirty percent in 1933, and the Depression left a trail of devastation across the country. Farmers and small businessmen, no matter the region, got knocked down during the "Dirty Thirties." But Sam ran on optimism, and he never considered a problem existed that he couldn't solve. His philosophy of three choices was his motivational fall-back: succumb, live in fantasy, or act. Sam cobbled together construction jobs, but beating the bad economy required ambitious ideas. With Emilio, he hatched a high-risk plan to bootleg whiskey to the United States. But getting Marie to commit to the revenue-generating scheme, Sam knew, would be another matter.

In Canada, unlike in the United States, distilling and exporting whiskey were not illegal. Still, Sam knew he would come close to crossing an ethical boundary by rum-running. *Although my actions aren't banned here, they are shady. If I tell Marie the plan, she becomes involved. But if I try to hide it, aren't I being dishonest with her?* For several weeks, the dilemma of sharing or not sharing his plan tumbled in Sam's mind. *The foundation of a marriage is trust and honesty. Lying once makes it easier to do it the next time and the time after that. Deceit has a funny way of propagating until it finally destroys the thing it was attempting to protect.*

Determining that honesty was the best option, one evening after dinner, Sam disclosed the plan to his wife. He ended his defense with a vivid picture of the thirsty Americans. "They have parched throats, and their tongues are swollen and hanging out of their mouths like panting dogs. There's good money in liquor, and we can distribute it within the law."

Marie laughed and shook her head. "What a picture! Sam, you have learned your way around the English language, but you're going to have to do better to convince me. It's not the legality I'm concerned about, Sam. It's the kind of people you'd be dealing with–thugs and gangsters. It's not safe."

Sam turned on his salesman persona, his eyes growing prominent and focused. "Believe me, Marie, the danger is minimal. With Emilio's business, we have a ready distribution system and crew in place. In our province alone, there are at least forty distilleries where we can get the stuff. And Detroit, on the other side of the river, is a stone's throw away."

Marie shot her husband a guarded look. "I've read the newspaper accounts about the hoodlums, Sam. My relatives down the river have dabbled in rum-running for years. They say if it isn't an American gang, it's a Canadian religious do-gooder that you must fear. Both are ruthless."

"I don't deny there are bad people on both sides of the river," Sam said. "But Emilio and our crew are tough, and we are ready. We can deal with the thugs." Then he turned and pointed his finger toward Detroit. "What I don't want, Marie, is to look out our front window and see bootleggers crossing that river and scarfing up the money I could make. I don't want to lose our home or our car or go hungry because I was afraid of some ruffians or concerned about breaking the idiotic laws in the States."

Her head whirling and eyes tearing, Marie understood her husband's reasoning; his worries were real. They had friends who divided their homes into semi-apartments and rented these out to strangers to eke out enough money for food and to pay the mortgage. Moreover, the people they rented to had lost their own homes. It was a vicious circle of one person profiting from another's misery. Marie despised it, and she felt helpless. She recognized there were choices, and this was the one that Sam had picked.

"Sam, these are hard times. But is this the way? In the long run, is it worth risking turning hard by this venture? To go as low as the people with whom you must deal? I couldn't bear to watch that. Can you promise me that won't happen?" she pleaded, tears flowing down her cheeks.

Taking his wife in his arms, Sam pledged, "I won't lose my humanity, Marie. I promise I'll quit before that happens."

* * *

Sam kept his commitment. After a year, the bootlegging seeded him enough money to augment the earnings from the construction jobs he scraped together. Despite this, Sam and Marie's financial worries did not end. They still improvised to maintain the bare necessities and to keep their home from foreclosure. If they needed fuel, Sam went to the rail yard and gathered coal that had fallen along the tracks from passing trains. If they were short on household cash, Marie made and sold home-baked goods. If they needed money for doctor bills, Sam always found a way. They were proud of making it through desperate times without the repossession of their automobile or home. A prevalent motto of the Depression was, "Use it up, wear it out, make it do, or do without." Sam put a positive spin on the saying: "Be grateful that you can use it up, wear it out, make it do, or do without." He frequently said, "I survived the Depression by being hopeful and grateful. These are the two most powerful virtues a person can have to get through life."

In 1939, Canada entered World War II, and Sam's finances made a turnaround. With the nation's war efforts depending upon the construction industry, federal money became available and boosted the building trades. There was plenty of building going on: armed services housing, training schools, factories, and airplane hangars. By the end of 1942, Sam and Marie were finding their financial footing. They also had a growing family: nine-year-old Adele, eight-year-old Darla, and baby Aimee.

* * *

After the war, construction boomed in Southern California, and with optimism and an eye for an opportunity, Sam saw a better future for his family in the Golden State. "I want a bite of that *California Dream* for us," he told his wife. But Marie was wary. She was not inclined to move her family over two thousand miles from her ancestral home for her husband's daydream.

In early February 1951, Sam came home from work and announced, "No more living in the cold, snow, and ice. It's bad for business, and it's bad for me." Sam's Emilia-Romagna birthplace was more temperate than the Great Lakes' bitter winters. Middle-aged and having lived through a quarter of a century of icy winters, Sam made up his mind to leave Canada.

At first, Marie thought this was wishful thinking, but as the weeks passed, she saw that Sam was unwavering in his desire to move the family. One afternoon in mid-April, Sam told the family that he was striking out for California in his new red pickup truck to go out and "look around." His spur-of-the-moment trip frustrated Marie. She felt Sam's actions brushed away her concerns and diminished her control of the family's destiny. Arguments with Sam over his impulsiveness resulted, but Marie was unable to prevail.

Six weeks after the start of his trip, Sam arrived home from California and made a stunning announcement to Marie. "I've purchased a small construction business in a rural town in the San Bernardino Valley."

Marie stood shell-shocked. "You were going out there to scout, not to buy a business. You don't get it, Sam, do you? You are not a single man! It may be an adventure for you, but it's a disruption for the rest of us."

"Marie, this is God's country. Its geography is like my birthplace; it draws me to it like a magnet. Snowcapped mountain peaks, extending skyward up to ten thousand feet, surround vast citrus groves and vineyards, and the Pacific Ocean is an hour's drive away. It looks like Hollywood in the movies." And he was right; the area could model as a picture postcard.

But seeing Marie's hard stare, Sam knew she remained unconvinced. "There's no lack of water. Rivers rampaging down the mountains skirting the Valley provide limitless water for irrigation to the booming agricultural industries in the area."

"If it's a rampaging river you want, we have one right here! Look out our window, Sam. It's called the Detroit River."

"How can I convince you, Marie?" Sam asked, throwing his hands in the air. "The town has a prosperous future for us. It's close to the industrial boom areas, and it has a new steel mill, one of the largest in the nation. With work and perseverance and the right political connections, I can turn the construction business into a thriving venture."

Success, Sam knew, required cultivating those with influence. Once he decided to buy the business, he put his charismatic personality to work. Like his masonry, Sam laid the groundwork brick by brick to establish his presence in the community, and he bragged about it to his family. "I took the mayor to dinner, made friends with the editor of the local paper, and lunched with the head of the chamber of commerce. People of power in that little town know that Sam Bartolino has arrived. We're going to cash in on the California Booming Fifties," he pronounced to his wife and wide-eyed daughters.

Cashing in or not, Marie was furious with Sam for making such a life-changing decision on a whim. She felt betrayed by a man who she had trusted and to whom she had given her total loyalty. Relocating with their three-year-old toddler, Luci, and uprooting their three other daughters from their community and heritage was something Marie could not fathom. The thought of leaving her social and family network and a place that held cherished memories made her feel that she was in the middle of an unending nightmare. Heartbroken, Marie had frequent anxiety attacks, believing the world was closing in on her and that there were no options. To save face with friends and relatives, Marie outwardly embraced the relocation to *The Land of Sam's Nirvana,* as she called it. Inwardly, however, she felt broken and never forgave Sam for what she considered his selfishness and disloyalty.

Over the years, Marie chose to think about what she had lost rather than what she had gained. Hers was the sickness of regret, manifesting itself through low self-esteem, lack of confidence, and depression. A world of self-scolding for not measuring up plagued Marie, and she subjected her family to common refrains of doubt and self-rebuke. "I should have attended the university. I wasn't good enough to marry into society. I should have pursued being an artist. I could have done better." Marie laid out a roadmap of insecurities for herself, and given her example, her daughters, in varying degrees, followed the same path too.

Marie's insecurities made it essential that others saw her as significant and influential, and she used various tactics to secure their regard. She hyperbolized her family's successes. She flaunted living in the *right* neighborhood. She overcommitted to service, church, and community organizations. A scrapbook of newspaper clippings that showcased her achievements became a prized possession, and it provided Marie the ego reinforcement she craved. Despite these devices, her insecurity intensified with the family's move to California.

Leaving her ancestral home was difficult. Separation from her family and friends left Marie feeling disconnected. "Who can I confide in here? There are no traditions here. I miss all my familiar places," were phrases Marie used that unveiled her anxiety. But her misgivings went beyond herself. In large part, Marie blamed the troubles of her two older daughters on the relocation. Often, she upbraided her husband. "Sam, we left a tight-knit group. Communities like that give people a sense of place, set boundaries, and check people's actions. You think twice before breaking the rules."

Adele, the oldest, broke the rules by marrying a divorced man with a bad-boy reputation. But a few months after her wedding, Adele recognized her husband was all wrong for her. He drank to excess, found it difficult to hold a job, and abused her emotionally through insults, threats, and intimidation. But for Adele, admitting the union was a mistake would require owning the responsibility for her decision. Instead of achieving the autonomy she sought by fleeing Marie's controlling behaviors, Adele's ego played havoc against her self-interest. For several years, saving face with her mother became an end in itself.

Darla, the second oldest daughter, had a romantic relationship with a Catholic priest that resulted in her pregnancy. Being unwed and pregnant was shocking enough in the 1950s. But for Marie, Darla's situation was revolting and disgraceful. She believed that her daughter was at fault for the affair; Darla was too flirty, too irresponsible, too self-absorbed, and too irreligious. For Sam, the situation hardened an already cynical view of the religious. To his disappointment, he lost the chance to bare his knuckles and rough up the cleric when the priest was speedily transferred to an undisclosed location by his superiors.

As an unmarried and pregnant woman of the era, Darla faced limited options—stay at home or be sent far from where she lived to have the baby. Darla went to Los Angeles, and like many women in her situation, she lived in a place with the euphemistic title of "maternity home." In a letter Darla wrote to her sister, Adele, she described the institution as large, impersonal, and having no semblance of a compassionate or loving environment. "Many of the girls have registered under an assumed name, and I'm not even sure when I talk with someone whether she is using a manufactured or real name. I'm so happy that I refused to be stripped of my identity like so many of the others. At least I have that comfort. You can't believe how the staff shames us and pressures us to give up our babies for adoption. Most of the girls are surrendering their newborns, even though that's not their wish. I'm so thankful that Pop supported my decision to keep the baby, even though it wasn't what Mother wanted."

Sam believed his daughters made choices that would last their lifetimes. But unlike other parents, he would not add to their burdens by holding back his love or abandoning or shaming them. Sam gave Darla his emotional and financial support during her pregnancy and afterward as she faced her new role as a single mother. Beyond that, he encouraged her to continue her education. "Get a career, Darla. Be independent," he said. Darla took her father's advice, and Sam provided the resources she needed to pursue a career in nursing. A few years later, she fell in love with and married a high school teacher.

Marie, in contrast, was unforgiving of both daughters and used bullying and recrimination to humiliate them. "If you hadn't been so headstrong, you wouldn't be in this predicament," she would say to Adele. Other times, to Darla, it was, "You made your bed; now you can lie in it." Marie took pains not to let her daughters' disgrace reflect on her. She maintained her social status, like many other parents of the era, by lying about her daughters' circumstances to her circle of friends. "Oh, Darla? She's away at college in Santa Clara. And did you know she has a straight-A record? We're so proud of her." And for Adele, she might say, "Her husband is so successful. Did you know he's a chief engineer on the Feather River Project?"

Marie's insecurity and irrational guilt fanned her actions. Her inner critic fueled her perfectionism, accusing her of failing in the moral formation of her children. In Canada, Marie had sought a spiritual adviser to help her with her obsessive concerns. Marie's consultation of a confessor puzzled her husband. Sam could not reconcile how his wife's dread of eternal retribution squared with a God whom she said she believed to be all-merciful.

Her husband's indifference to religion stressed Marie, but for Sam, there was little connection between morality and religion. He believed that one could be a moral person without being religious. He put all creeds in the same basket and subscribed to none. "Some of the greatest atrocities in history have occurred in the name of religion," Sam preached to his daughters. "Following the beliefs and rules of a specific faith is not what matters. What counts is how people morally conduct their lives."

Sam believed in living a life of purpose beyond oneself and being honest, trustworthy, and principled in one's decisions. To live these values, one did not need a spiritual adviser, Sam reasoned. He pitied his wife and others who let their bias prevent them from seeing a person's worth and character beyond religious or cultural rules. Sam attended church each Sunday to avoid Marie's pestering, but his religious practice stopped there. Although his lack of religiosity caused his wife additional anxiety, Sam did not alter his behavior. He believed he must be true to himself and his values first. Anything less, he thought, was hypocritical.

While Marie's older daughters' transgressions increased her humiliation, she held out hope for the younger two. Aimee, the third child, was a parent's dream. She practiced her religion, stayed out of trouble, excelled in school, and was studying to become a physician. A raw spot, however, was that Aimee was a student at Berkeley. "Den of oddballs," Marie often said, referring to the university.

Luci, the youngest, was Marie's last chance to even up the odds in fulfilling her duty for the moral preparation of her children. Luci, like Aimee, stayed clear of trouble, was a good student, and practiced her faith. Luci's concerns were with social justice issues and not with relationships with boys. Nonetheless, failure with Luci was not an option for Marie, and she felt compelled to hold the reins tight on her youngest daughter.

While the move to California was adverse in some ways for Marie, it was positive in others. Relocation freed her to grab some of the autonomy she had denied herself in the past. Marie threw off the teacher's yoke in favor of creative endeavors, and she dedicated a room within her home where she could sketch and paint, and she christened it Artspace.

Besides Artspace, Marie set up a studio getaway in a little desert town sixty miles from her home. There she established herself in a small but thriving artisan community. Harking back to her Detroit days of fun and exploration, Marie joined the playground of the 1960s entertainment set in Palm Springs. With her artist friends, she kicked up her heels and frequented art galleries and nightspots like the famous Starlight Room.

Her transition posed a certain irony that her daughters noted. Years later, Adele summed up her reflections to her sisters. "Mother never learned from her frustrating experiences. Instead, she replicated them with us. She intensified the behaviors that stymied her autonomy and self-determination. In the end, Mother couldn't break the family's cycle of control. Had she thought to balance her disappointments with the positive things in her life, she would have been a lot happier."

Chapter 3

Grit and Courage

Sam flipped on the light switch in his daughter's bedroom. "Rise and shine. All sailors on deck!" he roared.

There is no escaping the inevitable, Luci figured, knowing her father would not stop repeating the annoying phrase until she got out of bed. Sam was never a sailor, so it baffled Luci why he bellowed out the greeting every weekday morning. She shook her head. *Some things are not worth the effort to try to comprehend.*

It was Friday, June 10, 1966, a week after her high school graduation. Luci pushed back the covers and rolled out of her bed, happy to be free of the regimentation of school. By the time she removed her curlers and styled her hair and dressed, her father had a tempting breakfast ready. Sam loved to cook, preferring his meals to any of those his wife prepared. "Life revolves around mealtime," Sam said, and this was why each meal he made was an appetizing creation.

"What's up today?" Sam asked Luci as she sat down to a concoction of eggs with Italian cheeses, sausage, and toast.

"Not much, Pop. I'm taking the four-year-old children over to the Weston ranch to see the chickens. Mr. Weston is setting up an egg hunt, and his wife is making the cookies the kids go crazy over. After that, I'm planning to cut out early, right after lunch."

For the past two years, Luci had been working part-time at a local nursery school. Sam believed the job was a good fit for his daughter, giving Luci pocket money and making her feel independent. But Marie did not approve, thinking it allowed Luci too much freedom. "How can we track what she does with the money she earns? Look at the stuff these kids buy these days: cigarettes, drugs, alcohol, and who knows what else," she complained.

When Marie jumped into a tirade about monitoring Luci, Sam warned, "You put the bridle on too tight, Marie, and the horse refuses to go forward." Then, he hoped his wife would listen.

"What about plans for this evening?" Sam asked.

"Nothing yet," Luci murmured, undecided about her options. She thought she might go with her school chum, Shelia, and Shelia's brother, Sean, and his two pals, Chris and Paul, to the drive-in movies. The weekly forays hanging out with these politically liberal college boys were better than staying at home on a Friday evening. In truth, she preferred their cerebral discussions to the childish antics of most of the high school boys she knew. Steve, the one boy she excluded from the juvenile category, had not called her for a date that evening.

For the Nerds, as Shelia referred to her brother and his friends, Friday evening was guys'night out. But the young men didn't mind Shelia and Luci palling around with them. Showing off their intellectual prowess to the girls without the strain of any sexual tension boosted the boys' egos. But as entertaining as these evenings were, Luci longed for something other than watching movies interspersed with Vietnam War critiques among the young men. Listening to debates over what topics to include in the next issue of the *Pink Sheet*, the underground anti-war college newspaper the guys surreptitiously published, got a little old.

Luci finished her breakfast, and by eight o'clock, she was on the job at the nursery school. Once there, things went as expected. Ralph pooped his pants by eight thirty; Rickie, crying up a storm, had separation anxiety and needed cuddling, and Daryl had fallen, skinning both knees. Despite this, by nine thirty, Luci had a small group of children lined up and ready for the short walk to the Weston ranch. In the 1920s, the fertile valley was a model for the back-to-the-land, anti-urban movements. Scattered across thousands of acres were small, family-run agricultural enterprises that included citrus and walnut groves and chicken ranches and vineyards as far as the eye could see. The region was an idealist vision of a pastoral America where cooperation among all and opportunities for everyone flourished. By the 1960s, the Weston ranch was among the few remaining chicken farms dotting the area that harkened back to that kinder era.

Luci got a kick from seeing the children scurry around the vacant chicken coops with small baskets, squealing at the discovery of each egg.

Little did the youngsters know that Mr. Weston placed their prizes for easy detection. After an hour visit and stuffed with Mrs. Weston's chocolate chip cookies, the troop reluctantly said farewell. Dragging their feet, they returned to the preschool under Luci's watchful eye. As she helped the children wash up for lunch, Luci had no clue of the life-changing event that was awaiting her around the corner.

* * *

"I hope Mom isn't around," Luci mumbled as she turned the key to unlock the front door to her home. She tiptoed into the house and crept down the hallway. *I don't want to hear her grouch about the evil person of the day or her complaints about the women's club or church committee.* Luci's luck held; Marie was in her Artspace studio working on a Cubist painting.

Slipping into her bedroom and closing the door, Luci tuned her radio to KMEN-129. She flopped on her back across her bed and stretched, letting the strains of the Beach Boys, Beatles, and Dave Clark Five fill the room with pleasant memories from her senior prom with Steve, three weeks before. Luci had met her handsome boyfriend a few months earlier at the party of a mutual friend. Steve had smoke-gray eyes, a hulking build, and a smile that could light a fire. Adding to his allure, he was on the high school football team from neighboring Riverside. Because of his muscular build and easygoing personality, Luci gave him the nickname, BTB, Big Teddy Bear.

Luci smiled as she thought about how she had blown the minds of her catty classmates from St. Anne's Catholic girl's high school when she arrived at the prom with handsome Steve. Most of her fellow students came to the dance in boring family cars, but she had arrived in Steve's flashy artesian-blue Turbo-Jet 427 Impala convertible.

At school, Luci's peers admired her intellect, effervescent personality, and her attractive looks. With her large, deep-brown eyes, delicate features, shapely figure, and full lips, many thought she resembled some of the famous Italian actresses at the time. These qualities, however, were either not enough, or too much, for membership in the stuffy in-crowd. Sweeping into the prom on the arm of good-looking Steve, and walking by the cadre of snobby girls, though, turned out to be the sweetest retribution Luci could have imagined for being excluded from the inner circle.

Marie's stipulation—"No solo dates until the last year in high school" —limited Luci's social life. During the past school year, Steve was the boy Luci dated the most. While visiting in Canada the previous summer, she had had a fling with Brian, who was cute, Canadian-nice, and spontaneous. There might have been a lasting relationship if not for the couple's young age and the geographical distance between them. In the end, they did not have the maturity or the time to explore the kinds of mutual interests that make for a long-lasting bond. Nonetheless, the couple made the most of their teenage romance, going to outdoor concerts, dances, and movies and necking on lovers' lanes.

***

Luci's daydreaming abruptly ended. "Luci, get up!" her mother blasted while banging on the bedroom door. Not waiting for a response, Marie barged in. "Get up, Luci! Get up! Sister Mary Catherine is on the phone and wants to talk with you. What could your high school principal want after you have graduated?" she asked, jumping to the conclusion that Luci might have been into some troublemaking.

Luci got to her feet so fast that her head began to float. Catching her balance and shaking herself awake, she hurried down the hallway to the kitchen. Picking up the phone receiver from the kitchen counter, she wondered, *What on earth could this be about? Some of the perky in-crowd girls get phone calls from the nuns, but certainly not me!*

Luci had been a good student, but she did not shine enough to be a teacher's pet. She had chalked up a list of yearbook entries: junior class president, student body secretary, school newspaper reporter, yearbook staff, and member of the French club. She had made the semester honor roll seven times, but disappointingly, it was not enough for her to garner the prized National Merit scholar gold cord at graduation. One incident, though, humiliated Luci more than any other and darkened her self-confidence. At the beginning of her junior year, she was shocked to learn she had been denied enrollment in the third-year mathematics course. She asked the reason from Sister Mary Catherine, and the nun barked, "Luci, you are too stupid to do Algebra II." Apart from embarrassing Luci before her classmates, the trauma ate at Luci's confidence and made her question her scholastic and intellectual abilities.

Luci picked up the phone. "Good afternoon, Sister," she said. Nibbling her lip while waiting for a reply, she feared that the call must be about something ominous.

The nun got right to the point. "Luci, do you have plans for this evening?"

Oh lord! She's not inviting me to a religious ceremony on a Friday night, is she? Luci's mouth went dry, and in her mind, she ticked off the pros, cons, and potential consequences of telling the truth. Clearing her throat, she responded, "No, sister, I have no plans for tonight." As soon as the words slipped from her mouth, Luci chastised herself. *Man, she was right. I am stupid! Now, she'll drop the bombshell and ask me to attend a ridiculous religious ritual!*

"Good," stated the nun. "You know about the formal dances the next two Saturday evenings for the Air Force Academy cadets. You responded to the invitations, is that right?"

"Um, yes, sister," Luci answered. *Are the dances canceled? Or maybe she's taking the invitation back,* she worried, expecting the worse.

"I thought you had," the nun said, and not stopping to take a breath, she went on. "There is an impromptu street dance tonight at the air force base, and there are not enough girls for the event. You are invited. Be at the school parking lot at five thirty sharp, and a military bus will be waiting to take you and the other St. Anne's girls to the dance. Even though this is short notice, I know you won't let me down." Clunk! The sound of the dial tone blared Luci's ear.

Replacing the phone receiver, Luci tensed. *Just like Sister,* she thought, shaking her head. *The fact that I wouldn't want to accept the invitation wasn't a factor in Sister's mind. She didn't consider it would disgust me to be part of a contingent of impromptu girls for an impromptu dance. Guess this means the teachers' pets had a full calendar for the evening. Otherwise, Sister would never have contacted me.*

The Air Force Academy saga had begun one morning in May when Sister Mary Catherine flew into homeroom rip-roaring mad. The principal of St. Joseph's, the Catholic boy's high school in town, had slighted Sister or St. Anne's in some way. *Holy cow, Sister is going overboard today,* thought Luci as the nun paced back and forth at the front of the room and launched into a tirade. Sister's temper flares were frequent, but this one looked destined for the record book. The nun railed in incoherent sentences, and Luci wondered, *What the heck brought this on?* She glanced over at Shelia, who was rolling her eyes.

During the past year, differences between the two school principals erupted for reasons unknown to both student bodies. Nonetheless, it made for salacious gossip. Perhaps, the students surmised, the nun and priest were having a love spat or some St. Joe's boy did something improper with a St. Anne's girl. All noxious scandalmongering, Luci believed. Today, though, the insult was specified: St. Joe's did not invite the St. Anne's girls to an important social event.

In a huff, the nun laid out her position to the homeroom students. "If Father Brennen doesn't think our St. Anne's girls are good enough for his St. Joe's boys, then I will show him a thing or two! Our girls can get invitations to affairs from schools better than St. Joe's," she said, the vein in her forehead engorged. The word "affair" brought on suppressed giggles from the girls, Luci and Shelia among them. Their snickers produced a stern look: the nun's raised eyebrow, furrowed forehead, and peering eyes behind her wire-rimmed glasses never failed to stop her charges in their tracks.

Undistracted, the principal continued with an announcement. "Colonel Bates is inviting the St Anne's senior girls to two cotillions in June honoring the Air Force Academy cadets visiting the air force base. Submit your name if you want an invitation, and I will contact you if you are selected." Then the nun turned, and as fast as a tornado, she exited the room, her floor-length black habit flying behind her like a car's exhaust, and the rosary beads at her side banging together as loud as cracking knuckles.

Receiving the invitation was not surprising. Many of the St. Anne's student body had fathers who were officers at the base. Being asked was not, as Sister suggested, because other better schools were beating down a path for the company of St. Anne's girls. It was that St. Anne's had connections and was one venue for securing young women for the dances.

Luci knew nothing about the Air Force Academy but soon learned. Across campus, the invitations created a buzz, and girls in the know tittered and shared factual as well as fanciful stories concerning the cadets. Within a few days, Luci and her friends realized the significance of securing an invitation to dances with this elite group of young men.

Luci's negative inner voice tore at her. *Should I or should I not submit my name? Sister gave an open offer to everyone, but I am sure she doesn't have me in mind. I hate to submit my name and be embarrassed if I'm turned down. Like, why would I get picked?*

Luci's intimidation stemmed, in part, from not belonging to what she and her friends termed the *Sodality Princesses.* These girls made up the leadership of a religious sorority, called the Sodality, and they caught the eye and approval of the nuns by leveraging their all-American girl looks and conforming behaviors. Outwardly, they submitted to the norms and regulations of St. Anne's. But for many, beneath the pretense lay a darker world of alcohol, experimentation with drugs and sex, and inner conflict. Luci had no problem with people making choices that challenged the status quo. What she did not like was duplicity. *What great actresses, but at what expense?* While Luci reasoned that such ploys were emotionally unhealthy, being excluded from the nuns' inner circle still hurt.

"What the heck, I have nothing to lose," Luci told Shelia. "I don't expect to receive an invitation anyway."

In the back of Luci's mind, however, lay another concern. *What will my Friday night pals think about me going to dances with military cadets? The Nerds argue against the military and the war, but all I know is what I hear from them. Shouldn't I get another perspective and listen to the thoughts of those who chose a military career?*

* * *

Hovering close throughout the call, Marie could not gather much from the one-sided exchange. Arms folded, she waited for an explanation after Luci hung up the phone. "Well, what did Sister want?" she pressed, frowning.

"She expects me to go to a street dance tonight at the air base. It's with those cadets from the Air Force Academy. There's a bus that will be waiting at school at five thirty to take the other girls and me to the dance."

Marie curled her lip. "What? I thought the dance is tomorrow evening!"

Aware of her mother's bias against her daughters dating soldiers, Luci realized that Marie might be a hard obstacle to overcome. *Remain calm and explain.* With a reporter's lack of emotion, Luci gave her mother the facts once more and let them speak for themselves.

Marie gave Luci a dismissive wave of her hand. "She calls this late and expects you to drop your plans and go to some frivolous event? And you said yes? Why did you do that? How on earth do you plan to get there?"

Marie's challenges made Luci feel stupid, but she knew it was dangerous to argue when her mother was in a keyed-up state. *Technically, I didn't say yes. I didn't say anything,* Luci sighed and then chastised herself. *I should have asked some questions and not stayed silent. What's wrong with me?*

With a rising sense of panic, Luci processed the phone call with Sister Mary Catherine. *Good grief, how am I going to get to St. Anne's when I don't have a car to drive?* she wondered. Sam would not be home from work until six o'clock. The family's second vehicle was in the repair shop, and taking her father's beloved T-Bird sports car was off-limits. With no public transportation, there were few options. *I should have stood up for myself. I've made a commitment that I may not be able to keep.* That thought unleashed an avalanche of worries. *If I'm a no-show, then what? Why didn't I get Sister's phone number?* At that moment, the phone rang, and Luci jumped. *Is it Sister again?* she fretted. She picked up the receiver, happy to hear Shelia's voice.

"Hey, Luci, did you get a call from Sister Mary Catherine about a dance tonight?" her friend bubbled. Shelia's breathless excitement was hard to miss.

"Yes," Luci answered. "Are you going?"

"Are you kidding?" Shelia asked. "I wouldn't miss this for anything. Sean and the guys will have a fit. You know how they feel about the military, but I don't care. There are going to be ninety cadets and forty-five girls. That's a number I can dig. What time should I pick you up?"

Luci hung up and heaved a sigh of relief. For the next two hours, she was in a whirlwind, like Dorothy leaving for the Land of Oz. *What is a street dance? What do I wear to it?* Rummaging through her closet, Luci tossed potential dress selections across her bed in a heap. Facing her floor-length mirror, she held up one outfit after another then reevaluated each again. She finally chose a Jackie Kennedy-like sleeveless white sheath, complemented by pearl earrings, a matching necklace, and white flat shoes, *Too formal? Oh, heck! White goes everywhere.*

She gave her fashionable bouffant flip an extra teasing and assessed her makeup options. Deciding that her flawless skin needed no foundation, she highlighted her dramatic eyes. She dusted blue shadow on her eyelids and applied a thin line of black eyeliner and added black mascara to accentuate her thick, long lashes. A few strokes of rose blush and a creamy pastel pink lipstick on her full lips finalized her look. As the last touch, she took her bottle of Wind Song perfume and misted her wrists and neck. As she breathed in the scent, it brought back delightful memories of prom night and kisses with Steve. *This is for good luck and confidence,* Luci promised herself.

* * *

When Luci and Shelia arrived at St. Anne's, a blue military bus was waiting. As they stepped into the vehicle and walked to seats at the back, they shouted greetings to animated former classmates. To say the bus was no-frills transportation was an understatement. *What a drag! Hard seats covered in a putrid-green vinyl and no air conditioning,* Shelia thought. Jesting with each other, the girls wondered whether the spartan interior foreshadowed what the evening might hold. It was Shelia, though, who revived a slew of jokes the group often told when they traveled together on buses to intramural basketball games. While the girls hollered these out to one another as they waited to leave, the bus driver, a young airman, pretended to ignore the corny puns, but a smile tugging at his lips gave him away.

Promptly at five thirty, the bus pulled from the school parking lot. The late-afternoon sun made the inside of the vehicle feel like a sizzling oven, and everyone was relieved when the bus picked up speed, and a breeze circulated through the open windows. After traveling through desert-like terrain for forty minutes, they arrived at the air base main gate, and the bus was waved through by the MPs standing guard. For several blocks, the boxy vehicle crept along featureless streets before the driver stopped, pulled the noisy hand brake, and parked the bus in front of a massive green lawn.

An audible "Wow!" sprang in unity from the girls' mouths as they viewed the scene before them. The enormity of the park-like, manicured parade ground wasn't what they had expected. More jolting, however, was the ocean of handsome young men dressed in sky-blue shirts and deep-blue trousers awaiting them. Luci blinked. *Shelia was right. It's an oasis of guys!*

Looking through the window beside her, the sea of men turned into a line of luscious-looking cadets standing in a single file. Their hair was short and meticulously groomed, and Luci could smell a squeaky-clean scent floating through the air. This was a lot different from her Friday night buddies. Being charitable in describing her friends, they were scruffy, with disheveled hair and a uniform of faded jeans and T-shirts. Seeing the crisp blue line from her window made a smile dance on Luci's lips: *Hmm, I sort of like the change.*

Scanning the parade green, Luci saw the band and heard it warming up. Beyond them, festive paper lanterns, strung from lamppost to lamppost across the street, swung gently with the breeze. *It is so magical and dreamy, like in the movies. It's giving me goosebumps,* Luci thought as she rubbed her hands over her arms. The words to the romantic theme, "A Summer Place," and thoughts of Troy Donahue swirled in Luci's mind, making her feel gushy.

While Luci's companions giggled and jostled one another to be first to leave the vehicle and be met by a cadet, a sick feeling rose in Luci's stomach. She sat immobilized, feeling a wave of panic rushing in. *What if I get paired with someone who doesn't like me and feels obligated to be polite?* Luci wondered. In her Jackie Kennedy sleekness, she now felt out of place. Eyeing the other girls wearing casual, easy-care poplin sheaths in psychedelic colors, she realized she had overdressed for a street dance. Her mind raced. *How will my outfit appear to these cadets dressed in their short sleeve blues? Will I seem stuck up and unapproachable?*

Marie's role modeling of self-doubt infiltrated Luci's psyche. From her window seat, she watched the blue line advance, and her breathing became faster. *What do you say to guys like this? These cadets are supposed to be so smart, with all kinds of academic and other achievements.* Luci's brooding and failing confidence made her too frightened to move, and her inner critic went to work. *Each of the boys I know, Brian, Steve, and the Nerds, is an average Joe with no stellar accomplishments. How can my dates with them prepare me for this moment? How can I measure up?*

Luci's subconscious flashed back to sultry summer evenings on her grandmother's porch and the stories about Lucinda McCormick. *That girl had grit and courage*, she thought, pursing her lips, irritated at her lack of self-confidence. Luci's eyes blazed, and she turned resolute. *These crazy doubts won't stop me from having a good time this evening! They are not in control—I am!* she whispered as she marched down the aisle, the last girl to leave the bus.

CHAPTER 4

Street Dance

SEEING the line of girls getting shorter, Barry Callahan elbowed his way ahead of the other cadets, determined to have a date for the evening. Barry had an all-American look that could have matched the young men in Norman Rockwell's illustration on the cover of *Boy's Life* magazine. With sandy blond hair, electric blue eyes, and a broad smile, Barry could charm the meanest rattlesnake. A sports injury when he was a senior in high school delayed his entry for a year to the Air Force Academy. As an entering cadet, he was a year older than his classmates, and his maturity and self-assured presence were unmistakable. He walked with a spring in his step, head high, shoulders back, and confidently made eye contact with any passerby.

At the front of the line of cadets, Barry stretched to his full six-foot height to see who the last girl would be, and in a flash, he sized her up. Watching Luci descend from the bus, his instinct cried, *Wow, this one was worth the wait.* Here was a dark-haired young woman about five feet six inches tall with a model-like figure. The simple outfit she wore added to her allure and screamed sophistication that separated her from the rest of the group. Her natural Mediterranean coloring, enhanced by a suntan, created an earthy and alluring contrast to her chic white sheath. Barry's eyes widened; he loved what he saw. *God, she looks like Pier Angeli!* He knew the girls were new high school graduates, *but this one has the confidence of someone older than her years*, he thought.

Luci reached the last step of the doorway and stopped. Faster than the click of a camera shutter, she captured a picture of the cadet standing before her. He was attractive but not in a polished, movie star sort of way. His good looks went beyond being clean-cut, with a wide smile and broad shoulders. Barry instantly drew Luci in, and her curiosity meter went sky high. *There's something cool about this guy!*

Reaching for his hand, Luci stepped from the bus and fixed on the cadet's dazzling eyes. She shot him a smile that met his and playfully introduced herself. "Hi. I'm Luci with an i."

Drawing in a long breath, Barry's heart raced like a plane on takeoff, but he found his wits to follow her cue. "Hi, Luci with an i. I'm Barry with a y." The jocular introduction broke an awkward blind date silence, and they chuckled in unison at their silliness.

Barry could not decide if his parched throat was due to the desert air or from feeling flustered in the presence of the girl he had met. "Hey, there are some refreshments over there. Would you like something to drink?"

Luci flinched. *Ugh! Stilted first meeting language!* "Sure, I'd love something," she replied.

They walked toward the refreshment area, and while Barry retrieved the cold drinks, Luci noticed a few courageous couples venturing out to the street and doing the twist as the music started. *Hmm, I wonder if this Barry with a y is any good at dancing?*

Jolted from her thoughts when Barry came to her side, Luci reached for the drink he offered. "Thanks," she said, before taking a sip. Letting the tingling liquid trickle down her throat helped to cool down the heat coming from her excitement before she relieved the uncomfortable pause. "So, Barry with a y, where are you from?"

"If you mean where did I live before coming to the academy, then that would be Buffalo, New York. Have you been to Buffalo?" he blurted out, anxious to fill the space.

Luci smiled. "No, I haven't, as it happens. Tell me about it."

Standing with Luci and sipping his drink, Barry regained his composure by falling back into familiar storytelling territory. He started with his family, telling Luci about his parents, his three brothers and one sister, and noting his Irish background.

"You're Irish?" Luci asked.

Barry's brows pinched. No girl had been impressed with his background before. *What's that about?* he wondered. A swift manufactured brogue rolled off his tongue. "I'm one hundred percent Callahan. What about you? Are you Irish?"

Hmm, Callahan! So Irish, Luci thought as the stranger beside her raised her interest. "I'm named after my Irish great-grandmother, Lucinda McCormick. Perhaps we could be kissing cousins," Luci said, coyly.

"Cousins? Probably not! Kissing? Maybe yes," was Barry's quick comeback.

Luci gave him a half shrug. "We'll see about that."

Barry grinned, her response heightening his expectations for the evening.

"I've always wondered if the mystique the Beach Boys created about you California girls was real," Barry commented.

"Aah, do I look unreal to you?" Luci shot back.

"Now that you asked, yeah, you do, but in a good way."

"And I will take that as a compliment," Luci responded. "So what do you want to know about surfer girls?"

Barry's questions were like the ones Luci received from teenagers she met during her summer visits to Canada. Answering them got wearisome and prompted a nagging inner voice making her wonder if her attraction was more about where she lived than about her qualities. Luci recited the customary responses to Barry's questions about Doheney, Newport, and Huntington Beaches, surfing, and endless summer fun. "My friends and I go to the beach, but I'm not into surfing," Luci confessed. "I like hanging out, lying in the sun, and looking cute."

"Oh, and that wouldn't be hard!"

Snapping her head toward him, Luci teased, "What wouldn't? Hanging out, lying in the sun, or looking cute?"

Barry's blue eyes flashed. *Sassy—I like that*, he thought. Barry knew what he had meant. "Lying in the sun and looking cute, of course."

Luci laughed. "Good reply. I guess you cadets *are* as smart as they say."

"The ones from Buffalo are!" he joked, and then changed the focus to Luci. "So you're not a surfer. But have you always been a California girl?"

Luci gave Barry a quick summary: born in Canada, mostly French and Italian heritage, father in construction, mother an artist, and three older sisters.

Born in Canada, not something I expected, but French and Italian ancestry, not surprised, Barry thought, unable to keep his eyes off Luci.

Luci liked the look of this cadet with a splash of freckles across his nose. *Those penetrating cornflower blue eyes are a challenge to Paul Newman*, she thought. *I like his humor, and with such a shit-eating grin, he is worthy of an Irish last name like Callahan. Mom would be impressed.*

Barry took Luci's hand as the band started a Stones tune, and the two crowded in with the hundred dancers on the street. As they rocked to the frenzy of "Get Off of My Cloud," Luci took in the moment. *So Disneyesque. Glowing, colorful paper lanterns swaying in the desert breeze and a handsome guy smiling and staring into my eyes. Nothing could be more mesmerizing!*

At the start of their second dance, a cadet tapped Barry on the shoulder and cut in. Thrown off base, Luci looked from side to side at both boys, wondering what would happen next. *Oh, my God! Cutting in happens in 1940s movies, not to me!* Barry shrugged and stepped aside and let the cadet take his place. *This attention is flattering. But I would prefer being in Barry's arms for this slow dance,* Luci thought as she watched the cadet with the electric blue eyes evaporate into the crowd.

Taller than Barry's six feet, Luci's new dance partner had reddish-blond hair, dull blue eyes, and a pale complexion. Together his features gave him a washed-out look. Circling his arms around Luci, he wasted no time talking about himself. His name was Tom Fisher, and he was from Philadelphia. He was obsessed with engineering, and he planned to be the best officer in the history of the air force. The young cadet was so self-absorbed that he didn't think to ask Luci her name until the song ended. With a slight pause between tunes, the band slid into another number. *This dude is giving me the heebie-jeebies with his self-talk, but at least this is not another slow dance,* Luci thought with a heavy sigh.

From the corner of her eye, Luci searched for Barry. But between the maze of dancers on the street and those on the sidelines, he was impossible to spot. Barry, though, kept Luci within eyeshot, and before the song finished, he swooped in from behind and cut in on the dance. Tom stepped aside, his eyes narrowing, and he lingered close by. Letting a few bars play, Tom cut in on Barry again. Not considering she had the allure to grab the attention of two boys, Luci mulled, *What is the history between these two, anyway? This competitiveness is getting silly!*

Again, the band did not break but led into another slow dance, and Tom picked up talking about himself. Like a sports broadcaster, he ticked off the highlights he wanted Luci to hear. He graduated from a Jesuit high school, lettered in three sports, got outstanding grades, and was student body president.

As the cadet droned on, Luci, exasperated by Tom's self-absorption, fretted, *What a neurotic and self-centered child. If I want this, I can have it with the St. Joe's boys.* Luci felt the heat creeping up her neck. Her frustration boiling over, she pulled back and interrupted the narcissistic cadet. "And am I supposed to be impressed by all of this?" she snapped.

Tom's wishy-washy blue eyes bulged, looking like they might pop from his head. For a second, he was perplexed, but then he recovered. "Plucky," he said, adding a snarky grin. "I like a gutsy girl."

Luci bit the inside of her mouth. *Good grief! I'm dancing with an idiot!*

As if telegraphed of her annoyance, Barry appeared, and dispensing with a gentlemanly tap on Tom's shoulder, he pushed his fellow cadet aside and cut in. Barry gripped Luci so close there was not a breath of air between them. Putting his cheek against hers, he asked softly, "Want to go on a walk and ditch this place?" The sensual touch of Barry's face made Luci feel like jelly inside. Without a second's hesitation, she replied, "You bet!"

* * *

The two navigated the web of couples and moved away from the dance area, free from Tom Fisher and the wailing sound of the band playing a surfer number. Walking down the street, they found themselves in a quiet residential neighborhood that housed married officers and their families. Barry took Luci's hand and placed it in the curve of his folded arm. She thought the gesture was old-fashioned but liked the feel of her fingers landing on Barry's warm skin. Luci noted that Barry walked on the curb side of the sidewalk. The mark of a gentleman, her father would say.

The San Bernardino Valley held in the oppressive heat that had reached ninety degrees earlier in the day. Though it was near dusk, Luci felt the sidewalk heat seeping through her thin-soled shoes, and she saw a few small beads of dampness on Barry's brow. The uncomfortable temperature was no match, though, for the rising heat from Barry and Luci's growing infatuation with each other.

As they strolled through streets bordered by majestic palms and lined with Spanish-style homes with stucco walls, red-tiled-roofs, and manicured, green lawns, Luci mused about her surroundings. *What beautiful housing.*

Reading her mind, Barry intruded on her thoughts, nodding toward the houses. "One day, my family will live in orderly quarters like this, in Germany, Spain, or Japan."

"Is that so? So what else are you planning?" she asked. "I mean like career-wise, of course."

Barry grinned, thinking he caught Luci's double entendre. "It's a good thing you added career-wise, or I would have to go to confession after telling you what I had in mind," he kidded. They both laughed, a little uneasy, but not much.

"Seriously, I'd like to be a pilot like my father. He flew in the army air corps during World War II. If I can come close to being as open-minded, fair, and forthright as him, I will be satisfied with my life." As he spoke, Barry's eyes brightened, showing his words matched his emotions for his parent. Luci thought Barry's relationship with his father might be like the one she shared with Sam. *What a refreshing change from that vain Tom*, she thought.

"So Luci, what are your ambitions? What do you want to do in life?"

Not expecting such a probing question, Luci faltered. "Well, let's see. I'm starting school at a state college in the area, and I'll be living at home," she began. "It's a commuter college out in the middle of nowhere that is opening this fall. It's so cool because I am part of the first admitted freshman class." Aware she was babbling, she hoped that Barry would not notice or ask many questions about the school. Luci did not dare to reveal her embarrassment that the college was not her first choice. Her favored school rejected her because she lacked the third-year math class denied her by Sister Mary Catherine. Luci hastened to let Barry know she had plans past the small state college. "In the long run, I want to pursue a graduate degree in public administration or foreign affairs."

Barry chewed on her last statement, finding it unusual for an eighteen-year-old to have such definite plans. "What would you do with that kind of a degree?"

"I'd like to work in a career related to social justice. Law school, maybe," she added.

Now, Barry was curious. What grabbed his attention was not the law degree; it was the social justice angle. The top priority for most people in his crowd was not advocating for equality but was having fun. "Why social service?" he asked.

"I've learned a lot from observing my father's business dealings and know the power politicians wield. Sometimes their intentions serve the public interest; often, they are self-serving."

He agreed with Luci's statement about power, but his companion's assertion surprised him. *What does she mean by the business dealings of her father and knowing politicians? What the heck does her father do, beyond construction?*

"My dream," Luci pressed on, "is to challenge the status quo. I want to promote change. You know, start at the local level and then move to the national or international arenas. Foreign service or politics has entered my mind."

Barry looked ahead and didn't respond.

Did I blow his mind talking about resisting the status quo? After all, he is in a status quo organization. Luci took in a deep breath and an uneasy swallow. "You're quiet, Barry. Does a disruptor in your midst bother you?" she asked.

His sparkling eyes and wide grin told her he was amused. "Not at all! You've got my attention. I want to hear about your plans for troublemaking."

Unsure if he were serious, Luci eyeballed Barry, letting him know that patronizing behavior would not make points.

Catching her look, Barry replied, "No, seriously, I'm curious."

"Okay, I'll tell you then. Last year, I volunteered for a nonprofit organization that provides services in an impoverished section of the county. That experience opened my eyes and made me realize that not all people enjoy the same middle-class prospects like me. They don't have a good education. They have inadequate housing, and many times don't have enough to eat. There's not a level playing field to achieve the American Dream, and I don't think that's right."

Barry pursed his lips, and Luci took this as a sign to elaborate.

"Beyond this, I have a group of friends who have broadened my view. Friday evenings, we go to the drive-in movies, but besides watching the film, we end up discussing civil rights, Johnson's Great Society programs, and the Vietnam War. We also debate questions closer to home like issues of migrant workers and the recent Fair Housing Act."

Barry's nod showed that he understood, but in the back of his mind, he wondered about her group of friends and whether a boyfriend was among them. Putting that thought aside, Barry considered his conflict over his career direction. He was unwilling, however, to reveal his confusion to someone he barely knew. Instead, he felt more comfortable sharing his viewpoint on social justice.

"I've thought about being at the forefront of change to make society better too. I think there's an urgent need for civil and women's rights and equality. Two years ago, I volunteered and worked with my church's outreach program in Appalachia, not far from Buffalo. This experience, like yours, opened my eyes."

Luci lifted an eyebrow. *The Nerd group sits around and talks about activism, but they don't do much about it.* She wanted to hear more. "Appalachia, that's near your home? I thought West Virginia, Kentucky, and more southern states were considered Appalachia."

A smile pulled at Barry's lips; many people had a similar misconception. "You're right; it includes those areas, but it's more expansive than that. Southern New York State and large parts of Pennsylvania and Ohio are in the region. It's a huge geographical area."

"So what did you do in this outreach program that opened your eyes?"

"I was sort of a gofer. I worked in a food pantry collecting, stocking, and inventorying the goods. Most people came to get food. But we also had a counselor who helped folks get connected to the right resources, like medical care."

"Seriously? I never thought of a counselor at a food pantry."

"Oh, yeah. She mostly referred people to a doctor who didn't charge for his services or took payment in barter, like chicken eggs or venison. I met him several times. He was a young guy, and I thought that he was inspirational."

"So how were your eyes opened? What did you mean by that?"

"Those sound like questions a shrink might ask," he said.

"So?" Luci asked, ignoring Barry's reference to a psychoanalyst.

Lowering his eyes, he waited a few moments, and Luci let the silence lay. "It's hard to say in a nutshell, but summing it up, I learned that I don't know much about people who aren't as well off as I am. Luci, I never imagined what life is like for them. I saw how hard it is for them to find good jobs or go to a decent school. I saw how so many people who were sick couldn't afford to go to the doctor. I learned that poverty is another label we attach to people so we can make excuses for not trying to make things better."

"That's kinda heavy! So what's the answer?"

A hint of a frown crossed Barry's face. "Well, bits and pieces won't solve the problems I saw. It's nice my church has a program to support these folks, but it's not the answer. There are lots of reasons for our messed up system, and it's going to take a major change to get it fixed. Big reform, like Medicare and Medicaid. These changes scare the hell out of some people, but it's the best way to resolve stuff like this."

Luci saw that the handsome young man standing beside her had thought a lot about the topic. Nodding her agreement, she asked, "So what about the big 'C' and 'S' labels people are attaching to those programs now?"

Barry lifted his shoulders in a full shrug and shook his head. "Oh, you mean communism and socialism? Hogwash! That's an excuse for not trying to change things."

Luci's eyes flashed. "Bingo! It sounds like you are a disruptor too!"

Barry chuckled, half acceding to the disruptor label and interpreting Luci's observation as a green light to keep going. "I think American democracy is a work in progress, not a destination. Circumstances in the world require we defend it more than ever. Besides being inspired by my dad to go into military service, an address given by President Kennedy to West Point's 1962 graduating class motivated me."

Luci eyed Barry. "What did Kennedy say that was so moving?"

"Kennedy's vision," Barry began, "was that the military has a responsibility to deter war, as well as to fight it. He said this generation of academy graduates has the greatest opportunity for defending freedom by the military taking on a broader role as an arm of American diplomacy. I see this as a powerful and transforming idea, Luci. I see the military as a way to defend democratic principles around the world."

What a perspective, Luci thought. *Sean, Chris, and Paul sure don't see the military's role this way.* The Nerds believed that the army in Vietnam was being used to defend an overblown theory of domino aggression. "There isn't enough evidence to show if one country in a region falls to communism, then the surrounding ones will capitulate too," Sean had argued. The war's motivation, the group believed, was to protect natural resources and corporate financial interests not to stop the spread of communism and defend democracy. Noncombatant casualties of men, women, and children resulting from the military search and destroy missions were upsetting. "Is it right for the United States to be involved in a country's civil war?" Paul questioned.

Luci knew that the difference in these perspectives needed resolving if she were to have a future with Barry. *Can I have a serious relationship with someone whose views are so different from mine?* She decided to empty her mind of such concerns for the time being. *Tonight is not the time to ponder this. Pause. Listen and learn, and recognize and respect differences before making a judgment,* she told herself.

Beyond the similarity between their ethnic and religious backgrounds, Barry had applauded the election of John Kennedy because he believed in Kennedy's promotion of public service and civil rights. "The assassination of Kennedy was a bleak day. I felt it was the end of the world. My older brother and I and some of our friends made the trek by train from Buffalo to New York City and then down to Washington, DC, for the funeral. We felt we had to be part of that history."

Luci weighed Barry's words. Her feelings about the assassination, which had occurred three years earlier, were the same. "It seems like Kennedy's death happened yesterday, but it also feels like an eternity ago," Luci said under her breath. "The evening after the assassination, I felt alone and unsafe. I know it was irrational, but all I could think about was the Russian threat, and I worried whether President Johnson could keep us safe."

Their conversation found its way to topics about the faith they shared. Eating no meat on Fridays, keeping holy days of obligation, making an Easter duty, and splitting hairs between venial and mortal sins, Barry thought, were silly rules. The similarity of Barry's opinions with her own made Luci shiver, despite the warm evening.

Luci had grown up within strict religious boundaries, and she saw how these constraints blinded family, friends, and clergy in considering ideas outside their faith. She agreed with Barry that the list of restrictions was absurd and endless. Do not attend a Protestant service. Do not marry outside the faith. Do not get a divorce or marry a divorced person. Luci understood her religion was not alone in constructing walls. As a Catholic, she experienced prejudice too. Nativist bias, fears, and conspiracies like the Pope will rule the country if a Catholic is elected president or the misbelief that Catholics worship statues reached far back in history. *I won't be tied to a person who uses religion to outstrip common sense or to target people who don't have the same beliefs,* she vowed.

When Barry clutched her hand and occasionally nudged her, Luci found there was more to like about him than his religious beliefs and politics. The sound of his baritone voice, the sweep of his breath across her face, and the subtle fragrance of his cologne brought a swarm of butterflies to Luci's stomach. *Good grief, I've known the guy for twenty minutes, and my hormones are going haywire!*

* * *

"Hey, Luci, what's with these palm trees?" Barry asked. "I've seen them in pictures, but, man, those photos never gave me a perspective of their height or beauty."

Living in Southern California, palm trees were so integral to Luci's life that she never thought about how they may appear to someone else. She accommodated Barry's curiosity, explaining that palm trees came in many varieties. "Some produce dates and others don't. There are sleek tall ones and shorter husky types. I think these, with the large crown of fan-shaped leaves at the top and that beautiful thatch underneath, are California fan palms," she informed him.

"Hmm. I'm wondering," Barry stated, "if I could climb that one over there?"

Luci chuckled. "Well, I've seen it done at the Indio Date Festival, but I don't think you'll get far with the shoes you have on," Luci pointed out, directing her gaze toward his feet.

"Why not? My brothers call me the tree-climbing champion." *What a chance to impress her!* he thought as he approached a tree, examining it. "I bet I could get a foothold on these scales on the trunk," Barry said and started climbing. But after a few feet, he began slipping back, scraping his wrists as he fell. Biting her lower lip, Luci looked at him with folded arms. Not dissuaded, Barry grinned and tried climbing again and failed once more. Throwing in the towel, he winked at Luci. "My chance to dazzle you is defeated by a pair of shoes!"

Luci shook her head. "It's not the shoes that are the problem," she teased.

"Okay, add that I'm a dumb shit, too."

With a cocked eyebrow, Luci hit back, adding to his embarrassment. "I won't comment further."

"Fair enough," Barry conceded. To cover his humiliation, he took Luci's hand, placed it on his folded arm, and while they walked together, he moved to another topic. "So how did you happen to come to the dance tonight?"

Luci gave Barry an abbreviated account of Sister Mary Catherine's phone call. Embellishing the story, she added a "white lie" that she had skipped her regular Friday night drive-in movie outing to attend the dance. *Well, that would have been accurate if Shelia had not come to the dance*, she justified.

"And how did you show up here?" Luci asked.

Barry shared that the visiting cadets were to have dinner with an officer's family, but it turned out there were fewer hosts than cadets for the evening. "So someone dreamt up the dance option, and I'm sure glad they did. What a cool coincidence that we met," he said, flashing his blue eyes at her.

Luci threw her companion a slight smile, not yet ready to accept his remark about a coincidence.

Changing the subject, Barry teased, "And what are you doing during your summer vacation besides lying out in the sun and looking cute?"

Luci rolled her eyes and gave a heavy sigh. "Well, as it turns out, I've got a lot more planned. I go to Canada every summer. At first, my mother, sisters, and I made the trips, and Pop stayed home taking care of his business. But since my sisters have lives of their own now, my mother and I are the ones who make the yearly trek."

Luci described the itineraries that took her to places Barry had never imagined seeing: San Francisco, Seattle, Vancouver Island, the Canadian Rockies, New Orleans, and Chicago. "On one trip, we were adventurous and sidetracked to the Hudson Bay wilderness and the little village of Churchill. That's where I saw polar bears, dog sled teams, and visited fur-trading posts. The ruggedness of that country blew me away! This year we're planning to repeat the Canadian Rockies trip."

"Wow! My family vacations seem tame in comparison to that. Except for a few forays into Washington, DC, New York City, or Philadelphia, I've spent most summers at the southern shores of Lake Ontario or at our family cabin in the wilds of western New York State."

The mention of western New York State piqued Luci's curiosity. Since reading *Drums Along the Mohawk* and *The Last of the Mohicans*, New York State had captivated Luci. In her enthusiasm, she showered Barry with questions about the area. "Are the gorges and waterfalls that beautiful?"

"Oh, yes! Everyone knows Niagara Falls, of course. But there are so many other sites. We even have a place called the 'Grand Canyon of the East' because it is so spectacular."

"Is it true that there are tons of snow in the winter?"

"You bet! It piles as high as the telephone wires."

"What is the Mohawk River like?"

"It's big and wild, and during the spring thaw, the ice, big as boulders, jams the river."

"And what about your family's cabin?"

Luci unknowingly had led Barry into a happy zone. The cadet with electric blue eyes couldn't talk fast enough, telling her about what he considered was the most charming mountain and lake region in the world. "My family's A-frame summer cabin is my favorite place. It sits about three miles outside this cool little village called Alfred, about one hundred miles south of Buffalo. From the village, we have to drive up a steep and twisting dirt road through dense forest before getting to the top of Hartsville Hill and our cabin."

"Hartsville Hill? Is that a small village too?"

Barry grinned. "Well, no, not a village of people. "Hart" is an old English word for deer, and believe me, Hartsville Hill is a village populated by a lot of whitetail deer. We have deer that come right up to the cabin munching on the wildflowers and grasses. Every season we identify specific deer and give them names."

"You've got to be kidding!" Luci said, her eyes expanding.

"Nope. There's Camille, Maybelline, and Dorothy, and of course, big Buck."

Luci gave a quizzical smile, and Barry stopped walking, turned, and peered into Luci's eyes as he described the breathtaking views from the cabin's porch. "I feel I'm on top of the world when I'm there. In the summer, the shades of green that dot the landscape make the rolling hills look like a velvet carpet. And in fall, the trees, with their brilliant red, orange, and yellow leaves weaving through the valleys, turn the panorama into a kaleidoscope."

As a child, Barry spent summer days sitting on a swing attached to a sturdy tree in front of the cabin. Gazing at the countryside, he imagined what life would have been like in a typical Iroquois longhouse. He pictured community activities, fires stoked, and simmering corn soup. He thought about Native American braves hunting and running through the woods from village to village. This was the land of Hiawatha, the legendary leader who united the Seneca, Cayuga, Onondaga, Oneida, and Mohawk tribes. Barry sensed Hiawatha's power and that of the formidable Iroquois Confederacy he devised. Out in the woods listening to the forest sounds, Barry felt he was not alone. Among the hum of the woodland species, he thought the forest retained the energy and whispers of phantoms of generations past. "It's mystical," Barry told Luci.

"The Native Americans have several legends about western New York State. Since you like the land of the Mohicans, do you want to hear the one I like best?" he asked as the two resumed strolling.

Luci lifted an eyebrow and played along. "Okay."

"Once upon a time," he began, "there was a beautiful Indian maiden named Lelawala. Her chieftain father promised her in marriage to a warrior, but Lelawala despised this man. Over time, she became more depressed about her approaching marriage and agonized over what she should do. She was torn between obeying her father and following her heart. Pledging herself to someone she detested, she believed, would destroy her spirit, but disobedience would disgrace her family and herself. Feeling trapped, Lelawala thought that she had no choice but to bow to fate."

Barry paused, and Luci threw him a "What bullshit is this?" look. Then, she reconsidered. *Is this a more than a pickup line?* The word "choice" stood out in her mind.

The corners of Barry's lips turned up in a self-pleased look. Not daunted by Luci's skepticism, he resumed. "Late one afternoon, Lelawala walked away from the village. Alone in the forest, she laid down in a clearing, closed her eyes, and went into a dreamlike state. When she awoke, she was lighthearted, and she gathered summer flowers to make a wreath for her hair." Barry halted for a dramatic pause.

Bemused, Luci shrugged her shoulders. "Okay, Mr. Storyteller, you've got my attention. I'm hooked. What happens next?"

"Before dawn the next day, Lelawala put on a white doeskin cape, placed the flower garland in her hair, and then slipped away to the river. She climbed into a canoe, and the rushing water swept her downstream toward a place named 'A point of land cut in two' that today we call Niagara Falls."

Luci's interest spiked as Barry paused once more. *What was Lelawala up to? Was she running away?* she wondered.

Looking into Luci's eyes, Barry resumed in a lower voice. "As she came closer to the falls, Lelawala couldn't control the canoe, and it crashed on the sharp rocks jutting from the frothing water. The roar of the approaching falls was frightening, but when she reached them, her courage returned. She opened her arms and began chanting a death song as the canoe fell through the cloud of silver mist over the edge."

Barry waited to gauge Luci's reaction. Observing her expected shock, he resumed in a whisper. "Thunder God, who lived in a cave behind the falls, saw Lelawala falling. Before she reached the crashing waters, he reached out and caught her in his arms. As he clutched her, Lelawala raised her head and opened her eyes and saw the warrior's compassion and love. When they were in the safety of the cave, and the cascading water a distant melody, Thunder God whispered to Lelawala, 'Your fears are yesterday's distress, and your hopes are today's fulfillment.' Today, the spirits of Thunder God and Lelawala live together in the refuge behind the falls."

Luci looked in the distance and deliberated. *I bet he uses this with every girl he meets!* Nonetheless, she tried piecing the story together. *Does it have an underlying message?*

Uncertain what to make of Luci's stillness, Barry brought his head close to hers and asked, "What are you thinking?"

Luci held back, still gazing ahead. She turned and drilled into Barry's blue eyes. "I guess, using an Irish term, I could say, 'What a bunch of malarkey!'" She drew back her lips in a saucy grin and weighed his reaction.

Luci's response was unarming but charming. Barry laughed. "No one has ever told me in such a nice way that I'm full of bullshit."

"Well, I guess there's that!" Luci chuckled, then turned thoughtful. "Putting the 'BS' aside, I'd say the story is about choices, not a lovestruck fairy tale. It's about risks and consequences and being true to your values. It's about living who you are and not how someone else expects you to live."

Luci had turned the tables on Barry. No other girl understood what he believed was the tale's underlying message. Some were appalled to think Lelawala attempted suicide. Others interpreted it as a rescue by a handsome, brawny, and powerful man. For several, the legend enthralled them with its fairy-tale and happily-ever-after ending, and a few thought it was a juvenile pickup ploy on Barry's part. *This girl is different, and she's the one I am going to marry,* he thought, stunned at himself.

Barry squeezed Luci's hand and, leaning over, surprised her by giving her a gentle kiss on the cheek. Without hesitating, she looked into Barry's eyes and said, "And I bet you've told that story to at least a hundred other girls and got a kiss out of it too!"

Barry threw back his head and laughed. "Nah, not a chance."

Luci staged a fake frown of disbelief.

"Okay, you've found me out," Barry admitted, "but not a hundred girls —maybe ninety-nine!"

They laughed that Barry got caught in his scheme. Then Luci challenged him. "And what do you think the story means, clever cadet?"

"Hmm, I think it's about time to return to the dance. It sounds like things are wrapping up, and they are playing some slow dances. I don't want to miss the chance to play Thunder God and to take you into my arms."

Luci's eyes flashed. "How corny! And I suppose you have a nice dark cave we can go into as well."

"Don't tempt me," Barry said, taking Luci's hand.

* * *

It was magic when they arrived back at the dance party. Night had fallen, and the neon-colored paper lanterns twirled in response to the beat of the music. Barry was right. *The band is ending with slow dances*, Luci observed with pleasure.

An Everly Brothers ballad started, and Barry wrapped his arms around Luci's waist. She responded and put her arms around his neck. Raising her head, Luci found herself gazing once again into Barry's alluring eyes. She saw youth, passion, and longing as well as maturity, coolness, and caring.

Barry smiled down at Luci, lost in her brown eyes. He saw a beautiful and delicate face, as well as intelligence, spirit, and compassion. Swaying to the music and pulling Luci closer to him, Barry whispered the lyrics of the song into her ear. His breath floated down her neck and made her skin tingle. Luci felt she was in a fairy tale, being swept away by a knight in shining armor. *I'm falling movie-film madly in love with the man of my dreams.*

A whiff of Barry's cologne saturated Luci's senses. It blended with the summer breeze and the melodic ballad, making her feel dizzy. Luci's cheek touched Barry's. He turned his face slightly, and for the second time, he sneaked a passing kiss on her cheek.

After the song ended, the band moved into an emotionally charged finale of "When a Man Loves a Woman." Laying his hand on the small of Luci's back, Barry responded to the lyrics with a firmer embrace. Allowing Barry to bring her closer, Luci melted into his embrace, engulfed in the heat from his body and the sound of his breath. Laying her head on Barry's shoulder, she fantasized, *If I could make time stop, this would be the moment.*

When the music ended, Luci felt unsteady, like awakening from a dream. Barry took her hand and placed it again in the curve of his arm, and the two ambled across the parade green toward the bus, bewitched. "Hey, Luci with an i, when will I see you again? You are coming to the formal dance tomorrow night?" Barry stated as much as asked.

Luci was tangled in a twist of emotions. A niggling voice told her to keep her feelings in balance. *After all, I don't want to gush over a guy I met three hours ago.* On the other hand, her instincts told her that Barry was something different than other boys she had known. *He doesn't deserve a flippant remark,* she thought. "Yes, Barry with a y, and I'll be anticipating a few more of those Everly Brothers' dances with you," she added, with a coy grin.

"Okay, it's a date. I'll look for you tomorrow night, and I promise to be your Thunder God," Barry teased.

Luci stepped into the bus, walked down the aisle, took a window seat towards the back, and sat alone. As the vehicle lurched away, she saw Barry standing under the glow of the parade green lights, waving to her. Embracing the moment, Luci threw Barry a kiss through the window, and the vehicle pulled away, leaving the cadet with the electric blue eyes standing in the shadows.

CHAPTER 5

Irony

THE bus arrived at St. Anne's, and the calm of the night ride exploded into a gaggle of animated voices and giggles. As they walked toward their cars, the girls circulated stories about the *delicious* cadets they met.

"He was the most groovy guy I ever saw! "

"He had the cutest dimples and the most dreamy voice."

"Wow! He was hot!"

"Did I have a ball tonight," Shelia said as she and Luci slid into the car. "I was with the cutest guy. He's from some weird place. I think it was Ohio. Where is Ohio, anyway? Who cares? It doesn't matter, because could that guy kiss!"

"You mean better than Bob?" Luci asked.

Shelia raised an eyebrow, and a slight smile gave her away.

"Okay, can the great kissing of a guy from Ohio change your mind about going to the formal dance tomorrow?"

"Nah, I can't go. I have a date with Bob, and well, you know," Shelia said, letting the sentence hang in midair.

Luci rolled her eyes and used the expression she and Shelia exchanged when they did not agree. "You're entitled to your choice even if it is wrong."

Shelia's hormones were in the driver's seat when it came to Bob. Pursuing the conversation to change her friend's mind, Luci knew, was useless. Bob was Shelia's new heartthrob, and other than making out, Luci wondered if the two had more in common. It wasn't that Luci never parked in a lovers' lane or made out with a date, but. . . "Jeez, Shelia, don't you want more? Like a real relationship and doing other fun stuff together?" she had asked.

"What could be more fun?" Sheila always asked with a shrug.

Bob, four years older than Shelia, had moved to the area the previous year from Georgia. He was nice looking, in an Elvis sort of way, with a deep voice, a southern accent, and a quick wit. Shelia met him the past September at the local supermarket, where he worked as an assistant manager on the evening shift. Thinking he was cute, Shelia used the opportunity to pick up an item of food the family needed whenever she knew that Bob was working.

Most weekday evenings, Shelia and Luci went to the public library to do their homework. But instead of studying, they used the outings as a ruse to have fun by cruising and hanging out. At the library, they looked for any cute senior high school or freshman college boy who had a sense of humor and was not going steady. If no one met that standard, they moved on to the fast-food drive-ins to hang around with other high schoolers. Their hope was that any encounter might turn into an invitation to a party or a date. After Shelia met Bob, the girls added the grocery store to the list of cruise stops. Flirting between Bob and Shelia at the checkout counter escalated until Bob asked Shelia out. Since then, they were a twosome every Saturday night. For Shelia, dating Bob and being escorted by a twenty-two-year-old to the senior prom was the pinnacle of showing off to her classmates.

"Meet anyone interesting?" Shelia asked as they headed home on old Route 66. "I thought I saw you take off with a cute guy with blond hair."

Luci giggled. "Yes, I did," and then she dished up the juicy high points.

"Ugh!" Shelia groaned. "Talking about Native American legends is such a lame come-on. Attempting to climb a palm tree is so like junior high school! And you swallowed the line about Lilly-whatever-her-name was in that story? He sounds like a weirdo and as clueless as my brother and his pals," Shelia scoffed.

"So you think Sean, Chris, and Paul are clueless? Hmm, who thought Paul was so cool a few months ago?"

Shelia flipped her long hair behind her shoulder, dismissing Luci's observation with a shrug. "Oh, that was puppy love. Bob's the real deal who knows how to make a girl feel *steamy*."

"Tell me again the way Bob makes you feel hot and bothered," Luci ribbed her friend.

Shelia tossed her head back, laughing. Then she launched into a jingle about the ins and outs of going to first and second and on to third base with Bob. Both girls snickered at the hyperboles and asked out loud in unison, "Do you think that's a mortal sin? Should you go to confession?"

Putting the jokes aside, Luci remained unconvinced by Shelia's glibness. She wondered whether her friend couldn't figure a way out of the relationship or a superficial romance was all Shelia wanted. And then again, Luci did not understand why her friend gave Paul the brush off. When she had raised the topic with Shelia, Luci thought her friend's excuse was half-baked. "Paul flirts, but he never follows through with anything romantic," Shelia sniffed.

Luci's mouth fell open. "Good grief, Shelia! First, you snap at Paul every time he teases you. If you don't flirt back, what do you expect? Second, your brother is sitting right there in the car. Paul isn't going to make moves on you in front of Sean." Shelia brushed aside her chum's observations, but Luci thought, *Paul is one cute dude. Why Shelia doesn't play along with him is a mystery to me!*

* * *

It was close to eleven o'clock when Luci turned the key to the front door of her home and walked down the hallway to the kitchen. She heard the television from the living room and figured her father was watching the ending of a *Man from U.N.C.L.E.* episode. Sam got a kick from the tongue-in-cheek drama and those of *Batman* and the *Wild, Wild West,* whose exaggerations of good guys fighting bad ones provided a reprieve from his business dealings.

Marie loathed her husband's choices in TV shows. When she opined about them as stupid, Sam feigned the look of a sixth-grader in trouble. Then he would tease his wife, "But sweetheart, a little fantasy is good for the soul. If we lived in reality all of the time, we'd go raving mad." Marie would scoff and shake her head at her husband's preposterous notion. Then she would turn and walk away, smothering a half-smile. Sam knew his wife well, and her trick did not fool him. He knew Marie was amused.

Luci dropped her purse on the kitchen table and went to the fridge for a soda. She pulled out a bottle and went to join Sam, who had turned on the late news. Luci found the headlines unsettling most evenings. A tornado had devastated Topeka, Kansas, earlier in the day. Now, there were more shocking details of young lives lost in Vietnam. The war was more real to Luci than it was to most of her classmates. Sean, Chris, and

Paul were college juniors and would face the army draft soon. For the close-knit Friday evening group, the thought of one of them having to fight in Vietnam was a reality and a fear that lived in the back of their minds.

Hearing the Vietnam news, Luci recalled the day in 1964 when a profound sadness about the war touched her. Riding home from school on the public bus, no one seemed to notice the young soldier wearing a green beret sitting in the seat ahead of her. The previous evening, a TV news show reporting the terrible loss of several Green Berets heightened Luci's consciousness of the war. Sitting a few feet from the soldier, who was not much older than she, a wrenching sorrowfulness struck Luci. People's lack of interest and awareness of the war and its consequences fueled her gloom. Even her parents seemed inoculated against the reality of what was happening to young men in the army. Those in the mainstream wrote off anti-war celebrities, like Pete Seeger and Joan Baez, and student protestors as a lunatic fringe. It appeared to Luci that most Americans chose to treat these soldiers as if they were shadows and something to be ignored. The image of the invisible soldier haunted Luci, and she pledged not to forget the Green Beret who sat in front of her that day.

"Looks like you're tired," Sam remarked when Luci walked in and fell into a big rocker next to him. "But I can see by the sparkle in your eyes that you had a good time." Luci never could hide her feelings from Sam. He read her like a book, and worst of all, he could detect the smallest of white lies.

Sam got up to lower the volume on the television and returned to his favorite recliner. "Hey," he said, clapping his hands. "I want to hear what these cadets are like that you met tonight. What do you think? Are they as smart as they're touted to be?"

Sam knew the best way to get Luci to reveal her thoughts was to pose a question requiring an opinion. He recognized Luci's growing emotional maturity and was proud of his daughter's self-confidence and her commitment to a more tolerant world. He also welcomed her ideas and encouraged her to debate with him, believing it honed her judgment and decision-making. Often, Sam would ask Luci her thoughts about a political matter or seek her advice in sizing up a business problem. Allowing her to express herself in a secure environment, Sam believed, helped his daughter build self-esteem.

One of his biggest regrets was failing to devote the same attention to his older girls. He could provide good reasons for his neglect. He worked day and night to survive the Depression. Or afterward, reestablishing his finances depleted his time, energy, and emotional reserves. *Reasons*, he criticized himself, *are no excuses for lacking the will to do better. Perhaps, things for Adele and Darla would have been different if I had not turned so many reasons into excuses.*

Luci threw her father some bait. "What would you say about a guy who tried to climb a palm tree with his uniform and street shoes on in ninety-degree heat?"

Sam frowned. *Holy crap! Climbing palm trees? What kind of a jerk does that? This generation of American boys is brainless about impressing women!* "Humph," he let out with an exasperated sigh. "Before offering judgment, I need the answer to three questions. Question number one: Is this young man alone in the middle of a hot, desolate desert?" Sam paused for effect and let the question hang heavy. Question number two: Is the young man starving and without other resources for food? And question number three," Sam said, raising his eyebrows with his voice, "Is it a date palm?"

Luci smiled while Sam stopped to let the logical flow of his questions become apparent. "If the answer to all these questions is yes, the young man is a survivor. If any of the answers is no, this fellow is a *coglione*," Sam bellowed and added a time-honored Italian hand motion.

Luci choked on the last of her soda and doubled up laughing. It was a good thing Marie was not there to witness her husband's theatrical display. Marie hated Sam using the word *coglione*, thinking it was vulgar and common. Sam's standard response was, "Well, Marie, why are you so upset? The word means nothing more than a nut!" Then he would let out his hearty laugh, and Marie would walk away, shaking her head in disgust.

"Well, Pop, you've answered your question. For sure, the young man was not in a desert; he was not starving and was not climbing a date palm. I'd say that's terrible news for the cadets," Luci joked. Not wanting to divulge more details of the evening, Luci got up and went over and kissed the back of Sam's head. "It's been a long day, and I'd better find Mom and say goodnight."

Watching his daughter leave the room, Sam thought that there was more to find out about this palm-tree-climbing cadet, and he planned to learn it in due time.

* * *

When Luci entered her mother's studio, Marie looked up from the sketch she was drawing and glanced at the clock. Satisfied that her daughter had made her midnight curfew, Marie lifted and turned her head for a kiss on the cheek and received it. "A street dance in this stifling temperature?" she asked. "I can't imagine you had a good time. Don't these people have any sense?"

Her mother's remarks took Luci off guard. Uncertain, at first, how to respond, she decided that flippancy would get her nowhere. "You're right, Mom, it was hot, but I had a nice time. I'll tell you all about it tomorrow."

Marie nodded and returned to her drawing. *What could have happened at a chaperoned dance lasting a few hours?*

Luci hung her head as she left the room. *One minute she's all over me about what I'm up to, and the next she couldn't care less.* After the exchange, Luci wanted more than ever to be alone in her room. Her parents had given her the freedom to design her bedroom, and Luci had made it into a personal refuge. She decorated it with beige-colored walls, a dramatic aqua-colored carpet, and an antique brass bed. One of her most cherished items was an oversized bulletin board Sam had installed. It was five feet long and three feet high and covered the middle of one wall and provided room for Luci's posters and other memorabilia, like her prom picture with Steve and her high school graduation program.

Her favorite souvenir, though, was an oversized psychedelic peace print. She had acquired the trippy piece of art on one of her weekend trips to Santa Monica when she and Shelia visited Shelia's older sister, Colleen. These occasional weekend adventures gave Luci a taste of a swinging twenty-seven-year-old woman's lifestyle in the mid-1960s. During the day on those outings, Luci and Shelia dallied on the Santa Monica pier and sunbathed on the beach. But the evenings opened Luci's eyes to a diverse population of exciting people. Frequenting Eastern European and Jewish folk dancing groups made up some of Colleen's nightlife. But the most intriguing places were coffeehouses where hippies, artists, and Hollywood B-movie actors and television personalities hung out. Dark and claustrophobic, the sites buzzed with ordinary and eccentric characters and live folk music playing in the background. These nightspots and their patrons provided a sense of a forbidden, secretive, and dissident underground that exhilarated Luci, making her feel a little sinful. *Hmm, is this what Lucinda might have felt in Detroit?* she wondered.

Sharing a table with a personality she had seen in a television show or a movie thrilled Luci. She and Shelia flirted with the free-spirited and brawny young men, with exotic names like Baruch and Amir, who taught them folk dances. Marie was unaware of this part of Luci's weekends in Santa Monica. Had she known, she would have halted the trips at once, even though under Colleen's watchful eye, Luci's reputation and safety were not at risk.

Luci sat on her double bed, gazing at the peace poster. *Tonight's experience is worlds away from either the Santa Monica coffeehouses or my high school life,* she thought. Slipping out of the white sheath so purposely chosen a few hours earlier, the scent of Wind Song was still on her wrists and drifted through the air, igniting her senses. As she took a deep breath, memories of the evening gave her a pleasant chill, and Luci knew that the fragrance would always be linked with June 10, 1966.

Her thoughts were interrupted by the neighboring Johnson girls' chatter that bubbled through her open window. They had arrived home from attending a dance at Fort Irwin, an army base about fifty miles away. *I could have been with them had Mother allowed it,* Luci thought.

But a few weeks before, Marie vetoed Luci attending the dances, her fears two-fold. Lurking in the recesses of Marie's psyche rested the adage, "What goes around comes around." Her daughter forming a relationship with a military man, Marie thought, could be equivalent to a sentence of geographic separation from her child in the same way as her mother, Geneviève, had lost her. Marie's fear overwhelmed her consideration that her husband had nothing to do with the military but uprooted her life nonetheless. Her second trepidation, though, was the one she expressed to Luci. "Servicemen are too worldly. They will corrupt you and lead you astray." Luci knew that her mother's jargon was code for her fear of Luci having premarital sex.

Luci thought Marie's worry unfounded. *After all,* she reasoned, *I could be corrupted by any group.* Many times, Luci and her drive-in buddies debated the role that fear played in politics. On the one hand, they argued, appropriate alarm creates caution. It allows a closer examination of a potentially dangerous situation. But fear is also used as a means to exploit and control. Governments, religions, communities, peer groups, and even parents secure power by manipulating this basic human instinct. "Making people anxious through irrational fear," Sean said, "diverts their attention from real problems. Such tactics allow authoritative people to take actions that many times are not in peoples' best interests."

Luci witnessed how unfounded fears held back her oldest sisters, Adele and Darla, from achieving their potential. Subconscious voices screamed like hurricanes in their heads. "You're not good enough. You can't do it. You might fail. You will embarrass yourself." Doubt, fueled by their lack of self-belief, drove the poor choices they made in relationships. It kept them from discovering their talents and flourishing. Even this evening, Luci had almost given in to the destructive power of that kind of a word storm.

Given her mother's reluctance to permit her to socialize with the soldiers, Marie's permission to allow her to attend the Air Force Academy dances surprised Luci. *Is there a double standard here? Maybe the difference is because Sister Mary Catherine sanctioned these events. More likely, it is about social status for Mother. She thinks academy cadets are elite and a better group of people.* That thought turned Luci's stomach.

Lying awake in bed, Luci considered the legend of Lelawala. *Through facing her fear, she opened herself to freedom.* Luci sighed and smiled to herself in the comforting blanket of darkness. *At the beginning of the evening, I was fearful. Then, like Lucinda, I faced my fear. Look at the adventure I would have missed had I fallen prey to my doubts.* Thinking of Barry, Luci felt she was floating on a cloud. Sam counseled his wife and daughters, "Have gratitude. Be thankful. It changes your world." *I am thankful, thankful, thankful!* Luci screamed to herself and then turned to her side and hugged her pillow. *If Mother had allowed me to go to the dance at Ft. Irwin, I would never have met the cadet for the electric blue eyes. What irony!* Luci thought before dozing off to sleep.

CHAPTER 6

Shanghaied

SATURDAY morning, June 11. Except for the robin's song floating through Luci's open bedroom window, everything was still. The pleasant smell of percolating coffee wafted through the house, and Luci's senses were charged as she stretched in bed. In spectacular detail, every aspect of the previous evening flashed through her mind. Each movement, word, smell, and touch synchronized throughout her body. She found it an odd, heightened, and vibrant sensation. Lyrics from a current pop song *about good things coming her way* played in her mind.

Luci rolled from her bed, anxious to start the day. She threw on a short sleeve cotton top, denim Capri jeans, and yellow slide-on sandals, washed her face and combed her hair, and walked down the hall into the kitchen. Sam, as usual, was cooking a hearty breakfast, and this morning, it was one of his pancake concoctions.

"Blueberry season," he said, looking up as Luci entered the room. "I'm going to make you the best blueberry pancakes you've ever had. Nothing more than my little girl deserves." But even as Sam greeted his daughter, his eagle eye assessed signs of any secrets his daughter might be keeping about the previous evening's dance.

In short order, Sam had a tempting breakfast on the table, and besides the pancakes, there were side dishes of sausage and scrambled eggs finished off with fresh-squeezed orange juice. On Saturdays, Marie was a late sleeper, so Sam and Luci took the time by themselves to share updates about family, friends, political issues, or Sam's business. But the pieces Luci liked best, juicy tidbits of town gossip, her father would leave till last.

Sam's pipeline kept him up-to-date about the community's latest political deals, business transactions, and even domestic troubles. He surprised Luci the previous week, describing why Frankie Ferrara took a shotgun and chased his son-in-law, Rickie, down the street. "Oh, that Rickie has a wandering eye. He ran around on his wife, and running around on his daughter didn't sit well with Frankie. You can bet, Rickie won't be coming back to town if he knows what is good for him," Sam said and chuckled, almost snorting.

Luci had met Rickie's wife, a professional woman who worked in an attorney's office in town. *Unreal! What was Rickie thinking? How stupid to risk a reputation and hurt a family that way. Choices*, Luci remembered Sam telling her. *There are always choices.*

Sam made it a point to be on a first-name basis with city and county politicians and some state ones, as well, ensuring a prominent business profile. Italians made up a large proportion of the small community, and Sam, having held every office in the local Italian-American club, seemed to know all the Italians in town. Although he never ran for public office, Luci understood that behind closed doors, her father pulled big strings. Among others, his support had assured Joe Russo the local postmaster's position and Vic Gallo the job of district fire chief.

This morning, Sam confirmed his influence and shared another piece of small-town tittle-tattle while he finished his second cup of coffee. "Luci, guess who came up to me yesterday and asked if I would support him for mayor?"

As the tangy taste of the tart blueberries balanced by the sweet maple syrup glided across her palate, Luci pondered the question. "I don't have a clue, Pop, but I bet you're going to let me in on the secret." Luci's curiosity climbed, knowing her father was going to share a hush-hush bit of news.

"I was walking across Arrow Boulevard yesterday afternoon and who comes sauntering up to me but Dominic Parenti. We took a walk through the park, and we chitchatted about this and that, but I already know what Dom wants before he asks!"

Not surprising, Luci thought.

Sam gave a little shrug, and his jaw tightened. He waited a moment before continuing. Leaning in across the table, he said in a hushed tone, "Bambina, I know he wants to be mayor."

Luci's eyes doubled in size, imagining what was to come. Sam astonished her by knowing about things before they happened, and this episode once again confirmed her father had an elaborate, spider-webbed communication network. Luci had no desire to know about Sam's sources or influence. But when local political positions opened, it was a sure bet that someone would be at Sam's door asking for his support. Now, it was Dominic.

Luci knew Dom, a sort of disheveled and rough-and-tumble guy, and it made her wonder how he could measure up to be mayor. "So why does Dominic think he should head up the city?"

Sam pounded his fist on the table, making the silverware jump. "Oh, you are so smart!" Then, raising his hand, he pointed his index finger upward. "Exactly, why should Dominic be mayor? That's the question! Since he's been the local union president, his head has outgrown his brains. He thinks he is *famoso* now!" Sam bellowed, using his native tongue.

Luci played along with her father. Now, it was her turn to lower her voice to a whisper. "And what did you tell him, Pop, when he asked for your support?"

Sam moved close to Luci as if he were sharing top secret information. "In no uncertain terms, I told him what I thought. I said, 'Dom, I won't support you.'"

Luci pulled back. "Whoa."

"Dom got fidgety, and it took the poor bastard a moment before he gathered his wits to ask why. I slammed the hammer down hard so he'd understand what I thought. I told him. 'Dom, you would make a lousy mayor.'"

Luci's speechless reaction was impossible to miss.

"I told him the truth, Luci. It may hurt for a while, but the truth is always best," Sam said.

The response confirmed Sam's reputation as a straight shooter. *Dom would be nuts to run now*, Luci supposed. "Do you think he'll throw in his hat anyway, Pop?"

Lounging back in his captain's chair, Sam replied cooly. "Oh, I doubt it. We talked a little more, and I explained the facts. I think he understood he should drop the notion. As I was leaving, I told him to remember that it's better to be *bello* than *famoso*," Sam said, chuckling at his remark.

Luci heard that line many times: "It's better to be good-looking than famous." It was Sam's way of warning someone not to cross a line. Luci knew with certainty that Dominic would not be the town's mayor whether he decided to run for office or not. Without a doubt, Sam and his friends had plans for who would fill the position, and Dominic was not a part of them.

But Sam had more on his mind than Dominic Parenti. Before Luci finished breakfast, he wanted to hear a full rendition of the previous evening's events. Sharing gossip created an instant bond with his daughter. Revealing secrets, Sam knew, cultivated camaraderie, and playing the confidant was a way to find out what was on people's minds. Disclosing intimacies established trust. Loyalty most often followed and resulted in a reciprocal sharing of confidences. Sam was adept at using this tactic in business and political situations; if required, he also used it with his family. Now, he was priming the pump, making it comfortable for Luci to confide in him.

After seeing her father in action for eighteen years, Luci was on to him. Even so, she liked confiding in Sam because he did not rush to judgment about her ideas or even behaviors. Unlike Marie, Sam knew that judgmental thinking, arguments, strong-armed tactics, and excessive control drive children away from their parents and instill defiance not cooperation. Rebellion, due to Marie's controlling and intrusive behaviors, Sam thought, was one factor that explained his two older daughters' poor life choices. "Given the relevant facts and the chance to think things through, most people are smart, creative, and resourceful enough to make the right decisions," he said many times. Thus, Sam enjoyed the trust of his daughters, and each of them knew whatever the situation, he would stand by them.

"So Luci, do you have something else to tell your Pop about last night? You know he likes a good story," Sam stated, his sharp eyes suggesting there was plenty to learn.

"Oh, you do this all the time! You put questions in the third person, and it makes it difficult to refuse you. But it doesn't camouflage your nosiness," Luci said. Then she rolled her eyes and feigned surrender to his demand. Luci gave Sam an abridged account of the previous evening: the bus trip in a tin can of a vehicle, the beautiful officer's quarters and the manicured yards, the lanterns sparkling over the street dance, and the thrill of two handsome boys noticing her.

Sam sat still. He listened, nodded, and smiled at the appropriate places as the synapses in his brain registered every detail Luci was telling him. His daughter seemed oblivious to her good looks and charisma, but to him, it wasn't a mystery why young men would pursue Luci. Sam had his sources about Luci's boyfriends, her weekday evening library larks, and the goings-on in Santa Monica. He felt that these were innocent teenage exploits, and he never asked Luci about them. But if they ever became concerns, Sam would have the means to end them, and none of the family would be the wiser.

Luci slurped down the last of her orange juice, knowing that nothing less than the full scoop about the evening would satisfy Sam. So she gave her father what she knew he wanted to know. "I thought the boy I spent the most time with was cool."

Cool! The expressions these kids come up with these days! "Whadda you mean by 'cool'?" Sam asked.

"Barry is smart, has a sense of humor, and his worldviews agree with mine."

"Oh, and I suppose he was the ugliest boy there last night too. You have to be ugly to be cool, don't you?"

Luci wrinkled her nose as she cleared the breakfast dishes from the table. "Pop, please. No, Barry is not ugly. He's cute."

"Aah, I see I've hit a nerve," Sam teased. "Come here and tell your Pop more about this boy that you're going to see tonight." That statement took Luci off guard. *How did he know I planned to see Barry tonight?*

Knowing that Sam was like a dog with a bone, Luci poured herself another glass of juice and rejoined her father at the table. Giving him a sideways look and one of her practiced raised eyebrows, she asked, "And how did you find out I was going to meet Barry tonight?"

"Because if this boy is as cool as you say he is, he'd never want to lose a nice girl like you."

Luci rolled her eyes again and tried hiding a smile. "Okay, I confess! We agreed to meet tonight at the dance."

Sam slapped the side of his thigh in self-congratulation. "Okay, so he's cool. Does this Barry have a last name of any kind?"

"It's Callahan."

"Oh, Callahan! Well, Marie will be happy about that. Are you sure there isn't an 'O' in front of the name? That would make her happier, maybe even gleeful."

Luci laughed at the reference to Marie. In her mother's mind, as the family knew, the Irish were the salt of the earth. A question no one dared to ask, though, was whether Marie regretted marrying Sam in preference to one of her prosperous Irish cousins.

Luci playacted as if Barry's last name were a severe disappointment to her as well. "No, Pop, sadly, it's plain, underwhelming Callahan."

Without hesitating, Sam threw his daughter another curveball. "And I suppose this cute Irish boy is a Catholic as well?"

Luci saw the perfect storm gathering. Being a Catholic was even a higher prerequisite on Marie's list for a boyfriend than being of Irish descent. Decades of brainwashing withstood any attempt to remove her mother's bias. Dating or—God forbid—marrying someone who was not a Catholic, according to Marie, put one's soul in mortal jeopardy and on the road to perdition.

Sam, however, had different views on church beliefs. He saw them not as sound spiritual doctrine but as rules of the club and guardrails for protecting the church's propagation. His thinking was not restricted to one religion, though. In his view, most formalized denominations suffered from the same bias. Luci's requirements for a boyfriend were much different than her mother's and conformed to Sam's. The boy should have substance. He should be honest, fair, kind, and strive for a purpose in life greater than himself.

Sam roared, throwing back his head and clapping his hands. "Catholic too! Irish *and* Catholic! He is in like Flynn with your mother then. Too bad we can't slip an 'O' at the front of that name." Luci swirled her eyes at Sam, even though she had to agree that his assessment was correct about Marie's favoritism.

"What's this I hear? Something about an Irish Catholic boy?" Still groggy after getting out of bed, Marie had slipped into the kitchen and was grabbing a cup of coffee when she overheard Sam and Luci's conversation.

"Oh, it's nothing, Mom. It's about some guy I met at the dance last night, and Pop is making a mountain out of an anthill. It's not a big deal."

"Any time I hear it's not a big deal, I *know* it's a big deal!" Marie said. "You promised me last night you'd tell me about your evening. How *did* the dance go?"

Should I be evasive or candid? Sensing Marie's mood, Luci felt truthfulness mixed with caution was in her best interest. She concentrated on details appealing to Marie's pomposity: the street decorations, the officer family quarters, the immaculate yards, and the clean-cut cadets. She highlighted the part where one cadet then another kept cutting in, assuming

Marie would find it thrilling to live the event vicariously. But Luci left to the end the detail she knew her mother was fishing for most, an overview of Barry.

"His name is Barry Callahan. He is one of five children from an Irish Catholic, working-class family from Buffalo. His father served in World War II as a pilot. Barry's dream is to be a pilot like his father, and he has asked to see me at the formal dance this evening."

Marie remained silent as she stirred more cream in her coffee and quieted her negative inner voice. She was fatigued from always second-guessing situations. *This little adventure amounts to nothing more than ships passing in the night. This won't last. After all,* she reassured herself, *it's a silly dance*, and she let her concerns slide. "Well, that should be interesting," she remarked.

* * *

Typical of Saturday mornings, Luci spent most of the time helping with housecleaning, laundry, and ironing that Ida, Marie's housekeeper, had not completed during the week. On most Saturday afternoons, Luci and Marie made a trip into San Bernardino to the area's one major department store. Marie liked to go for a late lunch at the Café Madrid and afterward browse the racks of clothes and household items within the store's five floors. It was a recreational event more than a shopping one for Marie, but today, Luci was fortunate. Marie was too preoccupied to be torn away from finishing a watercolor painting to go rummaging through stacks of clothes.

Elated, Luci took the rest of the day to fantasize and prepare for the evening ahead. There was a whirlwind of decisions to make about what to wear for the dance. Throwing open her closet door, Luci gazed at the dresses, skirts, and blouses hanging in front of her. *I can't wear the same outfit as last evening. Is there anything in here that will blow Barry's mind*?

She flipped through her clothes in a frantic state, rejecting one outfit after another. At last, she settled on a beige taffeta sheath covered with white lace. Its length was perfect: above her knees. *Thank God! At least I don't have to follow St. Anne's stupid dress code anymore.* Gone were the days of kneeling in homeroom with the nun measuring the distance between the floor and the hem of each girl's dress. "Unroll that skirt!" the nun would yell if she caught a girl with the waist of her skirt rolled up to make the garment shorter. With no boys to impress at the all-girl school, Luci and her girlfriends pulled the caper, in part, to express their independence. But their bigger payback was witnessing Sister Emmanuel's face turn beet red with each scolding.

Late in the afternoon, Luci lounged in a bubble bath, daydreaming about the night ahead with Barry. Wiggling her toes in the frothy mounds and lowering her eyelids, she let the previous evening's romantic moments play over and over in her mind like a record stuck in a jukebox. *Hmmm,* she moaned. *I'm hoping for more hand-holding, whispers in my ear, slow dances, and kisses like last evening.* When the water turned tepid, she roused herself. Her body felt relaxed, but her emotions were in upheaval, and at dinner, her anticipation heightening, Luci's stomach felt like a butterfly reunion. *If I try to stuff down anymore, I'm going to be sick,* she told herself. Picking at her meal, she left the table with her plate half full and went to dress, style her hair, and apply her makeup.

Everyone says I look stunning in this lace dress, Luci persuaded herself, giving the outfit on the hanger a final once-over. To achieve the desired sophisticated effect, Luci chose small pearl earrings, beige pumps, and a clutch purse to complete the ensemble. She combed her hair in a dramatic style, puffing it into an upswept French twist held in place with a seed pearl comb. Feathery tendrils and bangs were the final touches and provided a wispy and—she hoped—sexy effect.

Black eyeliner and a thick coating of mascara complemented Luci's large dark chocolate eyes, making them a standout. She outlined her full lips in a dusky rose lipstick, filling them in with a light, creamy shade of pink. Looking in the three-way bathroom mirror, Luci judged herself, *spellbinding.* And, then, for good luck, she added the extra splash of Wind Song perfume to her wrists before slipping on her dress.

* * *

Peggy, Kitty, and Michelle, former classmates of Luci's, picked Luci up for the dance. Even though the four girls had attended grammar and high school together, they ran in different social circles. Peggy and Kitty were blond and perky and part of the Sodality princess group. Michelle was on the opposite end of the spectrum; she did not care a whit about status symbols and was sort of a group of one. She was spunky and petite with long, thick, sandy blond hair and had a fun-loving personality. Michelle focused less on grades and more on boys, reeling them in as if they were bass on the hook of a champion angler's line. Luci and Michelle liked each other because what you saw was what you got with both.

Luci slid into the backseat next to Michelle. "Groovy short dress and 'do, Luci," Peggy remarked, turning and staring at Luci over the front seat of the car.

"Yeah, cool, Luci," Kitty chimed in as she rolled her mother's Chevy out of the driveway, barely avoiding an oncoming vehicle on the street. Oblivious of the near accident, Kitty kept prattling. "I had a heck of a time figuring out what to wear, so I picked the shortest thing I had in the closet. Figured the guys wouldn't care too much about what I was wearing as long as they could get a good view of my cute, sexy legs all evening."

Luci cringed. *Oh, barf! I'm going to have to listen to this all the way to the dance. Sodality girls! Why didn't I drive myself?* Her thoughts, however, were disrupted. "Luci, you were there last night. What are these guys like?" Michelle piped up. Luci's seatmate was wearing a chartreuse-green sleeveless empire waist dress with a bow in the back flowing down its length. It would have been an ordinary-looking outfit except that it had a sexy keyhole cutout sitting between the shoulder blades. *Flirty Michelle is definitely going to have a good time this evening,* Luci thought.

"Hmmm," Luci began, trying to determine whether she should be serious or flippant. With this group, she settled on the second choice. "Delicious!" She let the word slowly escape her mouth, emphasizing the first two letters. Her reply incited the intended response, a squeal and clapping of hands in unison from all three.

Regaining her composure, Kitty pressed. "How delicious? I mean, like, what does that mean?"

"Oh, you're going to have to wait and see," Luci responded. Then she stuck out her tongue and ran it across her upper lip. That antic prompted another bombastic howl from the three girls that made Luci wince.

"Looks like we're in for a blast, tonight," Kitty burst out. "Hey, Sister Mary Catherine was so upset with me yesterday when I told her I couldn't make that street dance. But I had plans. I mean, like, I am booked for the rest of the month."

Michelle frowned. "Is that a fact?"

"Yes, Michelle, no kidding! Next week I'm going to Doheny for the week with Barb and her family. You gotta see the bikini I bought. I hid it from my mother. It's so skimpy, she'd throw a fit if she saw it," Kitty said, flinging her arms up in the air to illustrate her angry parent.

"Yikes!" Peggy screamed. "Can you dial it down, Kitty, and keep your hands on the steering wheel? We already had one near miss this evening."

"Oh, bug off!" Kitty replied. "You all are jealous of my great boobs." That statement made everyone roar since Kitty had a bra size that might approach an A cup.

"Skimpy? Like, how itsy and bitsy?" asked Michelle. On cue, the whole car broke into singing the lyrics from the popular song that celebrated the abbreviated swimsuit.

Avoiding the question, Kitty glanced up in the rearview mirror and looked at Michelle. "How'd you break free on a Saturday night? Aren't you going steady with Chuck?"

"Yep."

"So you aren't worried what Chuck might say about you going out like this?"

"I always say, what a guy doesn't know won't hurt him," Michelle replied, and that response produced another roar from Peggy and Kitty and a wink from Luci.

As they drove, the girls chattered about boyfriends, summer vacations, and what colleges they would be attending in the fall. Luci shared her plans of traversing the Canadian Rockies through the Prairie Provinces and on to her destination in western Ontario. Had Luci's carpoolers been more worldly, they might have been impressed. But what captivated the Sodality sisters were trips to the beach, boy watching, and determining who would be more daring in the latest renditions of swimsuits. While they twittered, Luci became lost in her thoughts, and her wishful glow made her nosy friends suspicious.

"Hey, what's up with you, Luci?" Peggy asked. "You're acting dreamy tonight. Are you holding secrets back from us?"

Luci threw Peggy a big smile. "Well, if I told you, I would have to kill you." That remark incited another roar from the girls.

The wheels in Kitty's mind whirled. "Oh, it must be Steve! Been in the back seat of his bitchin' Impala lately?"

Luci chuckled. "Me to know, you to find out." Her response raised the curiosity of Peggy and Kitty, and for the remainder of the drive, the two tried outdoing each other in describing the behaviors possible in the back seat of an Impala. Their remarks contesting what fell in the necking, petting, and heavy petting categories were too much, even for Michelle, who kept scrunching her nose at their comments. *Jeez Louise,* thought Luci, *I like a good time, but this is brain dead. The Nerd group has never looked better!*

* * *

When they arrived at the air force base, the MPs standing at the main gate directed them to a parking lot near a large, modern-looking structure. The girls' rollicking ceased when they left the car and treaded into unknown territory toward the building. Entering through massive glass doors, they were overwhelmed by the two-story atrium's size. None of the girls had been in a building so imposing. Two circular staircases on either side of the entrance led to a mezzanine level that offered a panorama of the entire valley through floor-to-ceiling windows. In a large room to the atrium's left, the girls saw appetizers arranged on decorated tables, and in an enormous ballroom to the right, they heard the strains of band music. As the foursome stood frozen gawking at the scene, a host approached and directed them through the atrium to an oversized outside patio. Once there, the girls' eyes sprung wide open. On their right stood hundreds of cadets in single file looking sumptuous in their dress blues, but to their disappointment, an equally long line of girls stood to their left.

"Crazy!" said Michelle, her eyes darting from line to line. "There must be five hundred cadets here. But bummer! Looks like there is the same number of girls!"

"Oh, no," Luci mumbled, seeing her hopes for locating Barry fading. Sizing up the situation, she groaned to her friends, "It looks like they are going to match us!"

"That's the pits," said Michelle, and rolling eyeballs between Kitty and Peggy showed they didn't care for the idea either.

With no other option, Luci and her pals went to the end of the line of girls. In parallel, the cadets and young women proceeded, and one by one, each was paired at the atrium entrance. Coming to her turn, Luci looked up and saw her partner. Her heart sank to the pit of her stomach in a wave of nausea. To her disbelief, Tom Fisher was facing her with a self-satisfied grin on his face.

"Hey, Luci, am I glad to see you!"

Oh crap! Luci grumbled under her breath.

In a formal gesture, like the cadets preceding him, Tom offered Luci his arm and escorted her to the ballroom. In less than sixty seconds, Tom was boring her with his self-absorption. On the brink of despair, Luci hoped that Barry would find her and cut in on Tom. But her escort, beaming, torpedoed her wish for a search and rescue. “Wow, what luck to get matched with you tonight; it would be a real drag getting stuck with a skag. And cutting in tonight is not allowed!” Tom said, wagging his finger back and forth and piggybacking the gesture with a sarcastic smile. “Orders are that we stay with the girl who we are paired with, and I couldn’t have a better partner.”

Oh great! I’ve been shanghaied by a dipshit, Luci lamented as she reluctantly began the first dance with Tom.

CHAPTER 7

Choices

THE evening's dance turned into a rant of hyperbole about the accomplishments of Tom Fisher. Tom graduated from a select private high school. Tom was the editor of the yearbook. Tom had lettered in football and basketball. Tom had a 1500 SAT score. Tom had a 4.0 GPA and more and more about Tom all evening. Most of his self-congratulation Luci learned the evening before. *Tom either has incredible short-term memory loss or he is the most egocentric asshole I've ever met,* Luci fumed.

Tom was the type of uptight boy Luci avoided. It was clear he had judgmental opinions as he described the personal failures of cadets who had washed out during their first year at the academy. His lack of empathy and gleeful depiction of every detail of these young men's missteps made Luci seethe.

"And I suppose you're perfect? Ever hear the phrase that people in glass houses shouldn't throw stones?" Luci asked, with a raised eyebrow and stare.

Tom blinked.

Luci's lips tightened in a smirk. *Lights on, but nobody home.*

Whenever Luci talked about issues important to her, such as civil rights and protests for equality, Tom became agitated and described the activists as "those lefty students at Berkeley." And unlike the cadets that he criticized, he didn't apply the same yardstick; instead, he rationalized his slipups. It wasn't his fault, he said, that he lost his temper during a recent family spat; it was his brother with the troublesome personality. Or he wasn't a poor driver; it was everyone else on the highway who was an idiot.

The longer the night wore on, the more Tom's immense ego ate at Luci until her shoulder muscles tightened in pain. *If I could figure a way to get home before the end of the dance, I'd split this place in a flash.*

Compounding the mind-numbing evening with Tom, the drive home with Peggy, Kitty, and Michelle was no less annoying. Her carmates, giggling about meeting their "eligible cadets" the next afternoon at Disneyland, added to Luci's despondency. Tom had mentioned there were several pre-planned recreational trips during the upcoming week, including the Disneyland trip on Sunday and a Dodgers baseball game on Monday. For the most part, however, Luci had tuned Tom out, hoping to discourage him from any thought of asking her to join him in these events.

"So why don't you have a date at Disneyland tomorrow?" Kitty asked.

Luci clenched her jaw. "Spending more time with that egomaniac would be the same as being tied to a stake in the middle of an anthill."

"You've been watching too many westerns!" Michelle said. Her comment lightened the moment, and everyone, including Luci, laughed at her quip. But it didn't temper the other girls' remarks.

"So I take it that Tom didn't ask you to join him?" pressed Peggy.

The implication was clear. Tempted to throw back a rebuke, Luci thought otherwise. *Don't piss her off and compromise your ride home.* Instead, Luci opted for a measured response and white lie. "The truth is, he wasn't available," Luci said. "He had an invitation for another outing. I think it was a golf thing. Since he was one of a few cadets chosen, Tom thought the invite was a better choice than going to Disneyland." Seeing the other girls mulling over her response, Luci embellished her remarks. "But he gave me his address and asked me to write to him." Luci's lies satisfied her carmates, and for the rest of the ride, they focused on themselves and what fun they would have the next day.

By eleven thirty, Marie was in a hand-wringing mode. Whenever Luci was out and her curfew hour approached, her mother kept a watch like a prison guard. And it wasn't beyond Marie to apply embarrassing tactics to keep her daughter in line. One evening Marie thought that Luci was taking too long to say good night to her date. Showing her displeasure, she released the family's Boston terrier, Zeppie, out the front door of the house. Going into overdrive, the dog barked at the kissing couple in the car and did not stop yapping until Luci went into the house.

"Give her a break, for Christ's sake," Sam said. "Luci is eighteen, and you're still trying to control her every move. You keep this up, and sooner than later, she's going to rebel like the other two. Stop talking about it! Allow her to have some independence!" he said and then went to bed.

"It will be a cold day in hell when I go to sleep before Luci comes home," Marie said under her breath after she joined Sam. When the front door key turned at ten minutes after midnight, Marie was satisfied and rolled over into her dream world, vowing she would quiz Luci the next day.

* * *

Luci shuffled into the kitchen, her head aching from the previous evening's disaster with Tom.

"Hi, Pop."

"Up so soon?" Sam asked, glancing at the clock.

Luci poured herself a cup of coffee, sat down at the kitchen table, and picked up the Sunday morning paper. A headline about the Catholic Church pressuring the Council of California Growers to recognize farm-workers' rights generally would have piqued Luci's interest. But even this could not distract her thoughts from the previous evening's disappointment.

Luci's silence permeated the room, and Sam didn't need a psychic to tell him that the dance had been a letdown. "So how was the Irishman at dancing last evening?" he offhandedly asked.

"I'm so bummed out. I'm never going to get my expectations up like that again." Sam's radar pinged, and he put aside the sports section of the paper he was reading and stared at his daughter.

Luci took another sip of her coffee. "I was stuck with the most boring jackass I've ever met. I had so much donkey crap on me that I'm surprised the smell of it didn't wake you up when I got home."

"Wow, that's an attitude change! Explain to me how someone could be so cool but within twenty-four hours turn into a crap-slinging jackass?"

"Oh, it wasn't Barry!" blurted Luci. "I got stuck with this creep named Tom Fisher." She filled Sam in on the details: the pairing of the girls and the cadets, getting matched with Tom and not Barry, and the insinuating remarks made by her carmates.

Sam saw through Luci's blustering and knew she was hurt, not angry. She was disappointed that she hadn't seen Barry, and her classmates' cattiness had bruised her ego. Pondering his next move, Sam didn't know whether he should be empathetic or challenge Luci to look at her options.

Believing where there is a will, there is a way, he made the latter choice. "So what are you going to do about it?"

Luci's mouth fell open. "What do you mean, do about it?" she asked. "The past is the past. I can't change it."

Sam shook his head and got up to fill his coffee cup while Luci silently fumed. "True enough, the past can't be changed. But what can you do in the present? The choice you make now drives your future."

Sitting down at the kitchen table across from Luci, Sam's brow grew tight, and his eyes fixed on his daughter. "Let me illustrate. Let's start here, in the present. Tell me, do you feel worse about the ego busting you got last night from your girlfriends or that you didn't see this Callahan chap?"

Whenever Luci was in a foul mood, she felt free to use light vulgarities with Sam. And Sam sometimes did the same with his daughter, but not when Marie was within earshot. Luci contemplated for a few moments. "I'm pissed at the girls for thinking something about me that's not true; that I'm not cute or sophisticated enough to get a date with a cadet. And I'm ticked off because I didn't see Barry. And what makes me super pissed is that I have no idea how to get in touch with him," Luci sounded off.

"But you haven't told me which one of these makes you feel worse," Sam said.

Pouring more cream into her coffee, Luci tried to sort out her feelings. "Not seeing Barry," she murmured. "After all, the girls' cattiness isn't my problem. I know they aren't right, and their stupid remarks show their insecurity, not mine. Their opinions don't impact my future. What matters is how I think of myself. So I can cross them off my pissed list and focus on what is important to me."

Sam leaned back in his chair, a relaxed smile crossing his face. "So, Luci, is seeing Barry again important to you?"

"Yes, Pop, it is! I had a great time with Barry. I felt so connected with him. I liked talking to him."

Sam rolled his tongue inside his cheek and considered Luci's response. "I take it the operative word here is 'I'? In other words, everything is about you? Where do the feelings of this Irishman fit? What's he think?"

Sam didn't allow Luci to respond. "You need some food to help you think better. Food makes solving problems easier. I'm making you some breakfast." Giving Luci time to consider his question, he got up and went to the stove and started to sauté onions, peppers, and mushrooms.

While her father whipped up the omelet, Luci considered, *Is this all about me? I accused Tom Fisher of self-absorption, but are my actions similar? Is this about status with my friends? Am I forcing an issue to be liked by them and to prove a point?*

Often, Luci reflected, she saw acquaintances pursuing a person when the attraction was a one-way street. It always turned out to be a waste of energy and time, ending in an emotional upheaval on the part of the pursuer. Those thoughts made her think of her neighbor, Christy.

In her high school junior year, Christy chased a guy named Danny. She knew Danny's hangouts and contrived to show up when he was there. She hung around with his circle of friends during school day breaks, hoping to get Danny's attention. Teasing and joking with Christy was Danny's way of giving her hope. After a year of this cat and mouse game, Christy grasped Danny was using her to prop up his ego. She was embarrassed and heartsick when she realized Danny's actions were a ploy and that she was one of many of his inside jokes. Her fall was hard with her self-confidence bruised, her self-esteem battered, and her pride wounded.

"Don't overthink it, Luci," Sam said as he placed the tempting omelet on the table in front of Luci. "Energy wasted on the past doesn't produce much for the future. Now, tell me more."

"You're right, Pop, before getting all jazzed over this, I need to understand why I want to see Barry."

"And?" asked Sam, dropping into a chair across the table from Luci. "Go on."

"Pop, I can say we had a great time together. We connected. We have the same interests and enjoyed talking with each other. I could see he was as comfortable with me as I was with him; we liked each other." And then another insight popped into Luci's mind. "And besides, Barry was the one who suggested meeting up again."

"Okay, that's settled. Let's start talking about the future. What do you want in your future where Cadet Callahan is concerned?"

"Jeez, Pop, I just met him! Why are you talking about the future?"

Sam wagged his finger. "Not good enough! You told me you're ticked off about not seeing this guy again. You've never said this about any other boy. How come?"

The spigot opened, and the truth came tumbling out. "Because, Pop, I think he could be more than a casual boyfriend. I think he could be a friend." She looked down, her cheeks turning pink, embarrassed at her rashness. She hesitated, trying to find the right words to express her thoughts. "There is something different about Barry than other guys I've dated." Looking up and still flushed, she saw the "Sam" look of skepticism: chin raised, mouth puckered, and eyes staring down on their target. "I know what you're thinking, Pop, and it is not all about sex!"

Sam threw back his head and laughed. "Oh, Luci, don't kid a kidder. At your age, it always involves hormones and sex!" He rubbed his fingers across his chin and shot his daughter another Sam look. "The question, Luci, is what choices do you have to create a future with this *cool* Irishman from Buffalo?"

CHAPTER 8

Cadet from Buffalo

BARRY sat in the lobby of the barracks waiting for a pickup game of basketball with other cadets. The previous evening was a bust, and Barry was in a lousy mood. He was matched with a girl who planned to enroll in a college near the academy in the fall. His date's *oohs* and *aahs* about military life and officers made it clear that her priority was to snag a cadet more than a college degree. While pretty in a Gidget sort of way, Barry had thought that she was self-centered, and he had been eager to figure out a way to extract himself. He had searched for Luci, but in the maze of one thousand people, she had been impossible to find.

Barry knew about the "cattle calls," a derogatory term some cadets gave to the arranged dances and the matching practice. *I should have specified a place beforehand to meet Luci*, he chastised himself over and over.

After an hour with the surfer girl wannabe, Barry had feigned illness, and he introduced her to a cadet who he saw was without a partner. Barry had felt sure the whimsical girl would captivate his classmate and that she would like her new date better too. Walking back to his quarters, Barry had admonished himself. *Stupid and foolish.* With no address or phone number for Luci, he realized that he might never see her again.

Waiting for the other cadets to show up, Barry thought of ways he might track down Luci. *Contact Luci's school and try to get her phone number? Lame idea! They would never give that information out. Persuade the school to pass my contact information to Luci? Didn't Luci say the principal arranged for the dance invitations? Her school might do that! She has an unusual last name; the telephone book would work. Oh hell! How does she spell her last name? Bertalino, Barolini, or was it Bartolino? Shit!*

An airman roused Barry from his thoughts. "Hey, I've got some girl on the phone who wants to speak to one of you cadets," he said, looking at Barry. "Do you know a Barry Callahan, by any chance?"

Startled, Barry replied, "Aah, that would be me." *Who the heck could be calling? I hope everything is okay at home.* Going into the barracks office, Barry took the offered phone receiver from the airman and, a little uncertain, said, "Hello?"

"Hi, this is Luci with an i. Am I speaking with Barry with a y, the Thunder God?" Luci asked.

Barry jolted upright, the phone receiver clutched to his ear. *Whoa! She's as alluring on the phone as she is in person.* Without a comeback, Barry blurted the obvious, "Luci, how the heck did you find me? I was just thinking about you!"

"It sure wasn't easy. It took about fifteen minutes. My call got shuffled from one person to another. I have to admit, though, there were a lot of nice airmen willing to help me out," Luci teased.

No doubt, with her sultry voice the flyboys were deliberately taking their time, Barry guessed. Barry cleared his throat, wondering what to say next. *Tell her the truth!*

"I was so bummed out that we didn't see each other last evening. I apologize. I should have known better and arranged a meeting place beforehand." After confessing this, Barry described his disappointing evening and how he terminated it early.

Luci wasn't ready to share the details of her lousy time with Tom Fisher. She figured calling Barry said plenty to raise his ego, and she got to the point of her phone call. "Since we sort of blew off last night, I thought why not try it again but do it right this time." Feeling she was losing her confidence, Luci blurted, "How about coming to dinner at my house tomorrow?"

Barry went silent, and Luci thought, *Yikes! Maybe he doesn't like me, after all.* But the invitation was more than Barry could have ever hoped. However, there was an obstacle.

"I've signed up for the Dodgers game tomorrow afternoon, and those in command frown on last-minute schedule changes. But heck, I'll find some cadet and pay him to go in my place. I'm not letting you get away again. Tell me where and what time." With arrangements made for Luci to pick him up at the main gate of the base the following afternoon, Barry's mood had turned 180 degrees.

Walking to the basketball court, Barry saw that the buses going to Disneyland were loading the cadets. While he was curious about the massive amusement park, he also thought that it wouldn't be much fun going there without having a girl by his side. In Buffalo, Barry and his older brother, Joe, often double-dated, and a favorite place to bring their girlfriends was the Crystal Beach amusement park in Fort Erie across the border in Canada. Taking the girls on the Comet, the park's super roller coaster and the midway Ferris wheel was a highlight for the two boys. During the rides, the girls hung on to the brothers for dear life, and behind their backs, Barry and Joe threw each other a wink and clutched the girls closer to them. And after a long day at Crystal Beach, there were dances in the evening and, still later, parking in a lovers' lane. This, to Barry, defined the ultimate trip to an amusement park.

In the searing heat of the San Bernardino Valley, Barry missed the hometown he thought was perfect. Barry's father often had said, "Time and place shape a person," and Barry thought about how his birthplace had molded him.

"Boost Buffalo. It's good for you!" touted a 1960s radio jingle that advertised the city as the finest hometown in the nation. The marketing, however, ignored that Buffalo was also one of the most racially segregated cities in the country. So, the ethnic areas of the city were celebrated—German Buffalo, Italian Buffalo, Polish Buffalo, and Irish Buffalo. This was the city Barry Callahan knew, and in the 1960s, Buffalo seemed to have it all: a modern expressway, the Thruway Mall, and ethnic festivals throughout the city. High-end downtown department stores contrasted with quintessential neighborhood bars, blue-collar bowling alleys, and restaurants that scattered popcorn and peanuts on the floor. Disc jockeys at WKBW, Buffalo's most powerful radio station, blasted out Top 40 hits and crazy antics. Eighteen-year-olds could drink in New York, and Iroquois beer was available and plentiful. Teens guzzled the brew in parking lots outside school auditoriums during sock hops, at drive-in movie theaters, and in parked cars at lovers' lanes that dotted the area. For sure, Buffalo was a hot town for the younger set.

Barry's ancestors arrived in Buffalo in 1825 and, similar to other Irish immigrants of the time, found employment constructing the Erie Canal. Like Luci's experience, handing down immigrant stories was a tradition in Barry's family. Listening to these accounts, Barry was proud of his forebearers' efforts—they built the transportation link that transformed a fledgling frontier village into a thriving commercial metropolis of three hundred thousand citizens by 1900.

The opening of the canal made commerce and shipping of goods possible from ports along the Great Lakes to New York City and beyond. Freighters from Cleveland, Toledo, and Detroit streamed across the Great Lakes into Buffalo's outer harbor, turning Buffalo into a bustling shipping port. Factories producing cement, copper, steam engines, and other materials flourished. Manufacturing plants provided jobs for current residents and attracted new waves of immigrants searching for economic opportunity. It was the melding of these different groups that gave Buffalo its hardworking and multiethnic culture.

Barry grew up in South Buffalo, where his family had lived and prospered for generations. After World War II, Barry's parents, Connor and Breana, considered moving the family to the suburbs that were popping up outside the city limits. They decided, though, that the benefits of raising their children in the old neighborhood outweighed those of suburbia. South Buffalo's bustling commercial district, well-maintained homes, and access to a tightly knit Catholic parish and Cazenovia Park were things that appealed to them. When it came down to it, Breana and Connor were products of South Buffalo, and they appreciated the feeling of place the community provided.

The family's foursquare frame and concrete two-story home and Barry's childhood memories were as entwined as vines on an arbor. The house was comfortable and typical of the Buffalo middle class and accommodated the seven-member family well. A massive front porch, perfect for lounging, spanned its width. The same as Luci's recollections of family get-togethers on sultry evenings, Barry recalled gatherings on the front porch with siblings and friends swapping baseball cards and playing cards and board games on sweltering summer days and nights.

From the porch, a large front door led to a small vestibule, and beyond, a living room welcomed guests. Oak pocket doors opened from the living room to a formal parlor turned into a playroom for the Callahan brood. During school terms, the children completed their homework seated around the large table in the middle of the room. But only when they finished their schoolwork did Breana allow them to read comic books, play games, or construct hobby airplanes and model cars. Television was not a distraction in the Callahan house during Barry's early years since the family did not purchase one until 1959.

The playroom opened to an expansive dining room. Behind it, there was a large kitchen with access to stairs leading to a basement. Barry had happy recollections of the smell of food being prepared by his mother in the cozy kitchen for Sunday and holiday meals. The dining room hosted milestone events like first communions, confirmations, and birthdays, and fun-filled and chaotic parties that included extended family members of grandparents, aunts, uncles, and cousins were regular affairs. One party stood out in Barry's mind. It was when he received a set of coveted Space Cadet walkie-talkies for his tenth birthday from his grandparents. Barry and his brothers created a commotion the entire morning playing hide-and-seek throughout the house with the contraptions. Much to Barry's and his sibling's disappointment, the phones were confiscated and banned at the dinner table.

Off the hall between the living room and kitchen, a carved oak staircase led to the second floor. The boys liked to commandeer its highly polished railing for sliding down to the first floor but never braved the venture when their parents were home. Most early twentieth-century houses had three bedrooms or fewer. But Barry's home had four, a luxury for the time, and the five Callahan siblings counted themselves lucky to have such spacious arrangements. Barry shared a room with Joe. His younger brothers, John and Robert, shared another room; his sister, Norah, enjoyed a bedroom to herself; and Connor and Breana took the largest of the four rooms. The second floor of the house had the home's one bathroom, making logistics in the morning and at bath time at night tricky. Although it was disgusting to their mother, the Callahan boys had no problem practicing pee shots in the toilet bowl together.

In the Callahan household, Sunday mornings were set aside for attending nine o'clock Mass at Holy Family Catholic church. Keeping with family tradition, Barry and his brothers served as altar boys, and Norah sang in the girls' choir. Unlike his brothers, though, Barry disliked altar boy duties. He thought the church rituals were outdated and had lost their meaning over time. For Barry, Sunday mornings were endured, not enjoyed. But after church services, a stop at Mangano's Donut World was a Callahan custom and a treat for the siblings. There, the family broke their communion fast and enjoyed the delights the bakery offered. Barry believed this was a sufficient tradeoff for suffering sixty minutes of religiosity.

Airplanes had fascinated Barry since childhood. In grade school, he enjoyed the popular Blackhawk comic series featuring a team of heroes who flew Grumman XF5F Skyrocket planes and fought against tyranny and domination. On school nights after completing his homework, Barry read accounts of World War II aviators. His favorite was Jerry Johnson, a US Army Air Forces ace in Europe and someone his father had known. Although Connor had flown as a pilot, he didn't share many war stories with Barry. Breana advised Barry not to press his father about his war days. "Stories about death, blood, and destruction remain a secret for a reason."

The study of aeronautics captivated Barry throughout junior and senior high school. He buried himself in books about aircraft mechanics and missile construction. Like other boys his age, he spent many Saturday mornings at Field's Hobby Center. There he browsed the shelves for airplane hobby models, and if he had enough money saved, he purchased a model kit and then spent hours at home constructing it.

Adding to the aeronautics repertoire during his junior high school years, Barry rode his bike to the Seneca Theater, known in the neighborhood as the "rat hole." There he saw aviation movies, and for a twenty-five-cent admission, he could spend two hours immersed in flying adventures. Among his favorites were *Twelve O'Clock High*, *The High and the Mighty*, and *The Bridges at Toko-Ri*. Barry considered the pilot in *Strategic Air Command* to be the epitome of an air force officer, principled and fearless.

Given his obsession with aviation, his family didn't question Barry's application to the Air Force Academy during his senior year in high school. Had he not applied to the new military aviation college in Colorado Springs, they would have been surprised.

To celebrate Barry's acceptance to the Air Force Academy, Conner took Barry and Joe to the Old Rhinebeck Aerodrome in Poughkeepsie. There, father and sons viewed demonstration flights of vintage planes, including a simulated dogfight between the fictional characters Sir Percy Goodfellow and the evil Black Baron of Rhinebeck. Connor surprised the boys by arranging a ride for them in a 1929 New Standard D-25 biplane. The staff outfitted the boys in a costume of goggles, leather helmets, and colorful scarves that hurled them almost four decades back in time. Strapped in the open passenger compartment in front of the cockpit, Barry felt the ride was as thrilling as the Comet roller coaster, except without rails. Barnstorming the countryside and soaring above the treetops, the wind was deafening as it rushed across the airplane wings, but the sights were spectacular. Barry could not help wondering what stories the plane could tell and what it would be like to fly a machine like that himself.

Beyond his passion for flying, though, Barry worshiped sports. In high school, he lettered in football and baseball, and of these, baseball was his favorite. "The difference between the two," he explained, "is in football, the team is first, and the individual is second. In baseball, it's the reverse. When I'm up to bat, the pressure is on, and I get an adrenaline rush. At that moment, I am accountable. The focus, strategy, and control are incredible. My teammates, the coach, and the fans are all depending on me to jump-start a successful chain reaction." Barry likened this experience to what he believed must be the relationship between crew and pilot.

Although Barry racked up eight semesters on the honor roll, academic pursuits didn't consume him. Barry Callahan was fun-loving with a quick wit, an extrovert who liked being with people. Many nights after Barry turned eighteen, he and his buddies played pool and darts and slugged down brewskies in neighborhood bars. Breana and Connor made clear to their sons, though, that getting drunk would not win any points with them. Barry's parents were not teetotalers, but both saw how excess alcohol destroyed the lives of family members, and they were hell-bent on preventing such a fate for their children. "Come home stumbling drunk and puking, and there will be consequences," Connor warned.

The boys didn't need convincing, and Barry thought getting more than buzzed was self-defeating. Observing how his friends acted when they were drunk, Barry thought that staying sober kept him and others safe—safe from bad decisions, accidents, altercations, and acting out. "I'd sooner have people laugh with me than laugh at me," was Barry's mantra, and he stuck to it.

Barry attracted young women with his good looks, but he maintained their interest with his optimistic and gregarious personality. His piercing blue eyes and great smile were his "chick magnets," as his friends called them. "I bring Barry to parties because he attracts lots of girls," his brother Joe often said. "I know there will always be enough great leftovers for me whenever I bring Barry along." The Callahan brothers were not afraid of sexual exploration with their dates either. The threat of committing a mortal sin over a French kiss that would send them straight to hell was little deterrent to the Callahan boys.

Connor didn't dispute the urges of teenage boys. Unlike many fathers, he was forthright about sex with his sons. He believed it was fruitless to advocate abstinence as a sole method of preventing unwanted pregnancy. No matter how many times a boy might curb his emotions, there would be a time he would drop his guard, and the consequences could be devastating. Conception outside marriage happened, a fact of life that Connor refused to deny. In his circle of acquaintances, he figured that at least twenty percent of the first babies arrived "early" after marriage. Far too often, Connor had seen people's lives and their dreams dashed due to a thirty-second sexual escapade. He determined, therefore, to do whatever he could to help his sons avoid the outcome of a poor choice.

On camping trips with the boys, they might tell naughty jokes and stories, but Connor made sure his sons understood their responsibilities. "Yes," he said, pointing his index finger at his sons. "It takes two, but you are the one in charge of the choices you make in your life. Don't blame your poor decision on someone else."

Connor made it clear he would not stand by his boys if they roughhoused, disrespected, or objectified a girl. "If you and a girl like each other enough and decide to go all the way, you'd better take precautions. Get a girl pregnant, and you are responsible for your baby, whether the girl wants to marry you or not. And remember this! I'll be the first to cut off an essential part of your anatomy if you don't assume your responsibility." The Callahan brothers always knew where their father kept the stash of rubbers.

CHAPTER 9

Facing Down the Gremlin

LUCI's heart fluttered when Barry agreed to dinner. After the phone conversation ended, she turned to Sam. "He took the bait!"

Sam flashed his daughter a triumphant grin. "As if there was any doubt!"

Feeling a rush of adrenaline, Luci gulped her breakfast and prattled about the logistics for the next evening. "Should there be appetizers? What should we have for dinner? How formal should we set the table?"

Sam saw his daughter's growing anxiety. Taking Luci's hand and using her pet name, he reassured her. "Not to worry about dinner tomorrow, Bambina. I have it covered, and I promise it will be perfect!"

Luci raised her eyebrows, challenging her father for specifics.

"I'll make a great antipasto. Then I'll prepare my special chicken cacciatore, a big salad, spaghetti, and cannoli for dessert. We'll show the Irish boy from Buffalo what a real meal is like!" Relieved, Luci threw her father a victory sign and gave him a hug.

Sam hated the North American diet loaded with sugar and red meat. "Poison, poison, poison," he would wail. Instead, Sam preferred a menu typical of his Italian culture. He wanted a meal of fresh vegetables, fruits, fish, beans, poultry, olive oil, and of course, lots of red wine. Consequently, the choice of who oversaw meal preparation was never in doubt. Marie, more interested in her social groups and art projects than battling her husband over dinner menus, relinquished the role of chef to Sam without complaint.

Swallowing the last bites of her breakfast, Luci stared at Sam and paled. "Oh, no! We didn't ask Mom about Barry coming to dinner! What happens if she has something else planned? What if she says Barry can't come?"

Sam bobbed his head and shrugged. "Don't worry, Bambina. I will take care of the matter. Your mother will be fine with the arrangements."

By design, Sam had not included Marie in the decision. Knowing her possible objection to a budding relationship between Luci and a soon-to-be airman, Sam believed it better to keep his wife out of the loop. He knew the depth of Luci's disappointment in not seeing Barry at the dance; he was not going to allow Marie's unrealistic control to add to his daughter's distress.

"Pull the cinch too tight and the horse bucks," Sam had said over the years to his wife, but to no avail. Control for Marie was like liquor to an alcoholic. She was a tormented soul, and her insecurities prevented her from accepting the difference between authoritative parenting and authoritarian behavior.

Sam's viewpoint was different. He believed in balancing dependence and independence in child-rearing. In his book, establishing emotional bonds with one's children, supporting their autonomy, and developing their sense of responsibility were vital to cultivating good relationships and happiness.

Sam loved his wife and understood her flaws, but he also loved his daughter and recognized her needs. He believed Marie's excessive control was harmful to Luci's well-being. Sam was adamant. Life is a series of choices, plain and simple. If pleading with his wife did not change her behavior, then he had a duty to protect Luci's autonomy.

Comforted that her father had matters under control, Luci glanced at the kitchen clock and saw she would be late for Mass if she did not hurry. She quickly dressed, then grabbed her purse, missal, and mantilla veil, and dashed to the car for the short drive to St. Mark's.

Marie put off attending Sunday Mass until evening services. She preferred lollygagging on weekend mornings, sleeping in and reading the newspaper at leisure. Sam was a reluctant churchgoer. "If rituals and chants make some happy, good for them," he would say, "but those aren't my taste." The longer Sam could postpone the Sunday duty, the better he liked it. Besides that, Sam observed that sermons from the pulpit at 5:30 p.m. were a lot shorter than those at morning Mass.

Driving through the residential streets, Luci marveled at her boldness. "Yikes! I did it! I did it!" she shouted, proud of her self-confidence, decision, and action. Her buoyancy did not last long. Turning into the church parking lot, Luci started ruminating about the next evening. Her negative voice had struck again, and the "what-ifs" made her brain feel on fire. *What if Barry decides not to come? What if Mom says no to the invitation? What if the dinner turns out to be a dud? What if Barry doesn't like me after all?*

Luci's inner critic always found a crack, no matter how small or convoluted, to wiggle into her unconscious and make itself at home. The undermining of her self-belief began with a nibble. A morsel here and bite there piled up and ground down the edges of her confidence until a broader vulnerability opened for deadlier attacks. Luci long ago recognized the crafty opponent. She even created a name and metaphor for it: Doris, the Cynical Intruder. Now, Luci faced a choice: control by Doris or autonomy. *Oh, shut up, Doris! No, I'm not rolling over and letting you have your way. No, I'm having none of that! I'm kicking you out! You are getting a one-way ticket to the moon.* Like a shot, Luci sent Doris into outer space. Once the gremlin entered orbit, Luci, unmarred by a deluge of unrealistic what-ifs, regained her freedom and confidence and set her sights on a fairy-tale date with Barry.

CHAPTER 10

Baptism by Fire

MONDAY, June 13, sizzled. With the temperature soaring to 105 degrees, Luci set out on the thirty-mile drive to the air force base in the family's new Mercury Montclair. Although not as upper crust as a Lincoln, the Mercury signified middle-class aspirations of the good life. Loaded with modern gadgets like air conditioning and power windows, steering, and brakes, the car was upscale, and Luci was proud to be driving the cream-colored vehicle.

Sam was lead-footed, and it explained the reason he had an eye-popping Lincoln motor installed in the new car. "To ensure," as he termed it, "we have some get up and go." Luci inherited her father's *fast* gene, and after navigating back roads, she weaved through the freeway rush-hour traffic, inching the speedometer beyond the legal limit.

Breezing past slower cars, she dialed the radio to KMEN-129 and increased the volume when the disc jockey played a Mindbenders tune. She giggled to herself. *Crazy! My first slow dance with Barry was to this song.* Now, listening to the lyrics of "A Groovy Kind of Love," Luci believed they were providential. *Man, if that ain't the truth! When he was close to me, I sure could hear his heartbeat, and it is undeniable that I could feel his breathing in my ear.* "Whoo Hoo!" Luci whooped as she pushed down hard on the accelerator.

With Doris silenced and floating somewhere in space, Luci was ready for a magical evening. She didn't worry about measuring up to someone else's expectations but focused on what she wanted to learn about Barry. "Don't make snap decisions, good or bad, about someone. Before forming an opinion, figure out what makes a person tick," Sam had counseled many times.

Questions buzzed in Luci's mind. *What does Barry like to do in his spare time? What are his favorite books? What is academy life like? Are his family and friends in Buffalo similar to mine? What are more of his views on politics, religion, and the future?*

"Understanding what motivates people," Sam always said, "is a circular process. Listen to what people say, observe their behaviors, ask them questions, then repeat the steps." Sam had used a spiral metaphor to explain the process in simple terms to his daughter. "Envision getting to the endpoint of a spiral, where the truth resides. The more you listen, observe, and ask people questions, the farther you go down the spiral. Even so," Sam had said, "acquiring that level of understanding takes time and persistence. Remember, Luci, patience is your friend."

Luci visualized her father's meaning in her way. *At the top, the opening is wide, containing all kinds of distractions, biases, and falsehoods that bury the truth. As you go down the spiral by listening, observing, and asking questions, the circles become smaller and tighter, and the extraneous junk drops away. The closer you go to the bottom of the spiral, the more you know about a person.*

Leaving the freeway, Luci steered onto State Highway 60 and a few miles later took the fork for Route 395. After ten minutes, she exited onto a desolate two-lane road toward the air force base where three evenings earlier her daydreams had begun. As Luci drove, she started to feel hiccups erupting in her stomach, and she steadied her nerves by noticing the things around her. Compared to the urban area a few miles away, with its lush lawns, tangles of wisteria, blooming oleanders, and rose gardens, the landscape here was arid. *Given an opportunity, the desert, in a blink of an eye, could reassert its supremacy over the fabricated city oasis. Mother Nature is in command,* Luci mused, noting, like Lucinda, life's transience. *Even more reason for me to be present and soak in the experience and my physical surroundings. Listen and absorb the sounds and smells around me. Be aware of my sensations and feelings. Most of all, be present to enjoy the process of "spiraling" with Barry.*

* * *

What an unusual-looking structure for an air force base, Luci thought as she approached the main gate. Preoccupied with either fear or anticipation during her last two visits, she had not noticed the 1950s contemporary architectural design. The entrance consisted of a large concrete canopy supported by steel poles with a guard station in the middle that separated incoming and outgoing air force base traffic. Emblazoned across the canopy façade in white capital letters several feet high were the words *March Air Force Base,* presenting an imposing image.

Luci slowed the car as she approached the security guard station, and a few feet beyond, she saw Barry waiting and flashing his big Irish smile. She stopped at the entrance, and Barry, his blue eyes twinkling, slid into the car. "Hi, Luci with an i. I'm your Thunder God!"

Seeing Barry in his dress uniform, made Luci's heart race. "Come rescue me, Thunder God," she greeted him. As the MPs waved her through the gate to make a U-turn to exit the base, Luci thought she noticed the barest of smiles—unusual for military police

"Hey, you look fabulous," said Barry, eyeballing Luci, who was dressed in a short, soft-pink lace sheath that showed off her great-looking legs. Like the evening they met, Luci's hair was styled in a bouffant flip that fell to the top of her shoulders, and the whiffs of Wind Song perfume intensified Barry's memories of the street dance.

"So what have you been up to today?" Barry asked as they left the base.

Luci's eyes flashed. "What do you think? I spent it thinking of you!"

"As you should!" Barry replied.

They both laughed at his response, but Barry hoped that Luci was being somewhat truthful. Since her phone call, he speculated a good-looking and fun-loving girl like Luci must have dozens of guys lined up for dates or may have a steady boyfriend. The latter, though, he dismissed. Luci didn't strike him as a girl who would two-time a guy.

Barry accepted that cheating was a habit for some. He knew cadets who had steady girlfriends back home but dated others when they were at the academy. Barry saw no issue with playing the field. What bothered him were people who made a commitment to someone and then reneged on their promise. For Barry, cheating—whether it involved finance, sports, or personal matters—was never worth it. Lies, he believed, caught up with a person one way or another. Barry's father was fond of quoting Mark Twain: "Always do what is right. It will gratify half of mankind and astound the other." Barry thought he couldn't go wrong following that advice.

As they drove, Barry scanned the panorama of the dusty and parched landscape. "Coming from Buffalo, it takes a while to get used to how barren it is around here," he remarked. "Still, it's lovely in its way."

No snap judgments or closed mind, like Tom Fisher and his tirade Saturday evening about the unattractiveness of the San Bernardino Valley, Luci thought.

"Look at those mountains! They must be thousands of feet high," Barry said, pointing to the summits around them. "The Appalachian chain south of Buffalo is beautiful but has nothing on these peaks when it comes to height. And is that snow on the tops of them?"

"Yes, and it's there most of the year. That peak you're looking at is about eleven thousand feet. Did you know that millions of years ago, the movements of earthquake faults that run through the area created the mountain range you see here?"

"Is that so? I've never been in an earthquake. Have you?"

"Yep, I've been through a few quakes. In some, there's been a deep rolling roar that accompanies it. In others, there's been a sharp shake with sounds of glasses tinkling or the house cracking. Then there's this odd feeling; it's not the same as being dizzy, but more like being off-balance. And you sway while seeing the building walls move from side to side."

"Wow, I bet that might be fun to experience."

Luci frowned. "Not on your life. Earthquakes aren't cool. They hurt and kill people, and they damage buildings and roads, not to mention screw up economies."

"Touché! I'm convinced!"

Luci slid her companion a guarded look. "Sure?"

"No more talk about earthquakes," Barry promised, recognizing defeat.

Even though Luci negotiated the freeway deftly, approaching eighty-five miles per hour was over the threshold even for Barry. "Hey, Luci with an i, do you worry that you might get a ticket?" Barry asked, looking over his shoulder.

Luci's eyes shot up at the rearview mirror. "Crap!" she said, letting her go-to swear word slip out. But, seeing no red lights, she tried to coverup a sigh of relief. "Well, I never thought about it, but I guess I could slow down. There's no rush, and how embarrassing to get a speeding ticket in front of you!"

"Well, I don't know about embarrassing, but it sure could be expensive! Even in my uniform, I don't think the cop would let you off," Barry replied.

"To use a favorite word of a cadet that I know, touché!" she answered.

Going slower, Luci played travel guide and pointed out a barren and rocky mountain jutting out from the surrounding flat land like a beacon. "That's Mount Rubidoux, and it has a remarkable history. In the beginning, it was part of the Rancho Jurupa, a large land grant given by the Mexican government to a guy named Juan Bandini sometime in the 1830s. Now, it is a tourist attraction where Easter sunrise services are held."

"So all this land belonged to Mexico at one time?"

"Oh, yeah. Spanish and Mexican history and culture in the valley are significant. Spanish explorers first came here in the late 1700s, and because it was so beautiful, they named the area the Valley of Paradise. Later, after the War of Mexican Independence, all the area became part of Mexico, and that's when Rancho Jurupa was created."

Barry kept throwing Luci questions, and their conversation segued into the founding of the Spanish missions in California and the general colonial history of the region. "Amazing," was all Barry could utter, astounded at his ignorance about his own country.

After exiting the freeway, they passed miles of citrus groves and vineyards. In his wildest imagination, Barry never guessed the expanse of either, and the fruit on the trees was the largest he had ever seen. On the two-lane road they were driving, the citrus groves were an arm's length away, and his mouth watered thinking of pulling fresh fruit from the trees with his own hands. "Look at those trees, loaded with lemons. Can we stop and pick a few?" he asked.

"You'll be getting up close and personal to some trees like those soon. My house is built on land that was a citrus grove, and we still have a lot of orange and lemon trees where it is safe to pick the fruit."

"It's dangerous picking lemons?"

Luci giggled, then nodded. "It can be! Citrus ranchers don't take kindly to folks picking their crops. It's technically theft, and it's grand theft if you pick fruit valued at over a certain amount."

"Aah, so, not a good idea," Barry said, surprised. *In that case, it would also be a violation of the academy's honor code*, he realized.

"As for vineyards, those can be dangerous too. I should know!" A glance with one perfectly raised eyebrow invited Barry to ask more, which he did.

"Yeah, one evening when my girlfriends and I were cruising, our car got stuck in a patch of mud in a vineyard."

Barry frowned. "Are you serious?"

"It's true! A car of guys we knew was chasing us, and we turned into the vineyard, but it's too complicated to go into. In the end, their car got stuck, but we maneuvered ours out."

Barry considered what he heard. *There is more spark in Luci than I imagined.*

* * *

Approaching Luci's hometown, Barry got the jitters. He was in unfamiliar territory—facing the parents of a girl he barely knew, far from his hometown neighborhood. *Baptism by fire*, he feared.

From what Luci had told him about her father, Barry figured Sam was a man who did not suffer fools and could size someone up in an eyeshot. From his Buffalo experience, Barry knew that Italian families were often close-knit. But Luci had assured him that her father didn't have an Italian ethnicity test for the boys she dated. "If he did, you wouldn't be here with me now. Besides, your Irish roots will score a lot of points with my mother."

I hope she's right, Barry thought as Luci turned into the hundred-foot-long secluded driveway that led to her home.

Ahead of him, Barry saw an attractive Western ranch-style house sitting, as Luci promised, among several orange and lemon trees. An edge of impeccably maintained low-growing flowers that enhanced the beauty of the home circled the manicured front lawn. The outside walls were beige stucco, and the roof was red tile similar to the officers' quarters at the air force base. A purple bougainvillea rambled on a trellis by the front door; fragrant and blooming desert willows bordered one side of the home and California sunflowers completed the edge on the other. Barry got the sense Luci's family, while not wealthy, had financial means.

"Wow, Luci, this looks like some kind of a resort," Barry said when he stepped from the car.

Luci stifled a smile as she unlatched the massive wood-carved front door and thought, *Everyone who visits for the first time has the same impression.* She led Barry into a long corridor, stretching at least forty feet, whose floor was covered with sienna-colored tiles. Barry's eyes widened as he realized that the curb view of the home belied its grandness.

They passed two bedrooms and a bath to the left of the corridor, but it was the hallway's right side that took him off guard. Floor-to-ceiling windows made up the entire wall and overlooked a large flagstone courtyard. The dwelling's enclosed patio in a Spanish-California U-configuration was breathtaking and made his eyes spin. Waterspouts gurgled from a narrow ornamental pool that spanned the length of the enclosure and dominated the near side of the court. Tubs of flowering plants interspersed with lounge chairs and tables gave the courtyard a relaxed and informal feel. Peering to the far side of the patio, Barry saw another inside corridor of windows leading to additional rooms.

Barry's head turned from side to side, and Luci grinned at her guest's amazement. "This is incredible! I've seen homes like this in magazines but not in real life," he confessed.

Luci suppressed a laugh. "Well, yeah, you might expect this. My dad is in the construction business!"

"Touché!" the cadet replied.

"Mom chose the floor plan from a rendering of an old Spanish hacienda in a book on Western ranch homes. She said if we were going to live the California lifestyle, she wanted a home that characterized the area's heritage."

The story, though, was not that simple. Marie had driven a hardnosed compromise in agreeing to move to California. As payback, she demanded a fashionable and luxurious home, and Sam willingly complied. Marie had combed through floor plans of Western architecture and settled on a five-thousand-square-foot layout. She stipulated it must include an enclosed courtyard and a studio for her artistic pursuits. Besides these requirements, Marie insisted that each bedroom have a private bath and that there be fireplaces in the dining and living rooms, library, and master bedroom. Sam had constructed a home that was an area showcase, and it made Marie happy.

As they walked down the corridor, Sam came out from the kitchen, heading them off. Wearing a white apron tied about his waist, he looked every bit an accomplished chef. He extended his large hand and gave the cadet an enthusiastic welcome. The powerful handshake was unmistakable, and Barry's broad smile became a half-wince as his hand crumbled within Sam's palm. Barry knew Luci's father had already sized him up. He hoped it was for the better.

"So," said Sam, "you're the young fellow from the East who likes to climb palm trees!" At her father's remark, Luci wanted to melt to the floor, but Barry took it in stride.

"Well, it wasn't my finest hour, sir," he said.

Sam shrugged. "We'll have lots of time to discuss your finest hours over dinner. I have the antipasto to finish up in there," he said, pointing to the kitchen. "Luci, take Barry around the house, and afterward, I'll be ready." Before returning to the kitchen, Sam turned and gave the cadet another once-over. Barry felt Sam's eyes on him, and a twinge of uneasiness reminded him who was in charge.

Leaving her father to his preparations, Luci took Barry for a tour of the rest of the house. As he entered the living room, the thirty-foot-long space with a vaulted wood ceiling and massive beams dazzled him. A brick fireplace flanked by full-length bookcases dominated the far side of the room. Another set of floor-to-ceiling windows gave a view of the manicured backyard, peppered with a half-dozen citrus trees. *My home in Buffalo is lovely, but this blows me away.*

"Oh, so this is the Irishman from Buffalo, I've heard about," Marie said, sneaking in behind Luci and Barry. As she gave Barry an examining glance, the blue uniform he wore made her squirm.

Startled, Barry turned to face Marie. "Yes, ma'am, all one hundred percent of me," he said with a broad smile. But Marie's pitch put Barry on alert. Feeling he might smooth the path for the evening, he added, "Luci says you have Irish roots too."

Clever was Marie's first thought. *Took me off guard* was her second one. *Trying to get the upper hand* was her third opinion.

Rudeness, though, was not Marie's way; she had craftier means of getting what she wanted. Marie returned a crooked smile as the phrase "two ships passing in the night" popped in her head again. She instinctively judged she was walking a tightrope and did not want to do anything to change the course of that idiom.

"Well, yes, that's right, Barry, and I want to hear all about your roots," she said, regaining control over the conversation.

Her impression was *clean-cut, good-looking, and Irish charm. Perfect if he would ditch the military career.* Marie had made her final judgment: handsome, Catholic, and Irish were not enough. She wanted all this plus a guarantee that Luci would never stray far from her. For Marie, Barry lost the battle for her acceptance before it began.

* * *

Sam bounded in and interrupted the conversation, announcing that the appetizers were ready. He led the trio into the courtyard, and showed them to a table displaying the tempting antipasto platter he had prepared—an array of cheeses, pickled meats, and olives was artistically laid out before them.

Bubbling waterspouts in the pool provided a relaxed backdrop for conversation, and after everyone was seated and oohed and aahed over the appetizers, Barry picked up the exchange started earlier with Marie. "Mrs. Bartolino, you asked me about my Irish background. My Callahan clan came to Buffalo in the 1820s and worked on the Erie Canal. And how about your Irish family? Did they immigrate to Canada at about the same time?"

A smart move was Sam's first analysis. Within the space of twenty-five words, Barry made a good impression. Sam mentally ticked off three positives. *One, he shows initiative and is not intimidated; most young men in this situation would have held back, waiting for a question. Two, it's clear the cadet listened to Marie earlier; he picked up on what was important to her, and most of all, he didn't forget it. Three, he's polite, using her married title; most young men are at cross-purposes in addressing their girlfriend's mother.*

Barry's question broke the ice, and Marie gushed as she shared stories about the McCormicks' immigration and her Irish relatives in Detroit before commenting about Barry's family. "Oh, I love your parents' Irish first names. And your name, Barry, isn't that derived from Gaelic? And you said your sister's name, Norah, is spelled with an 'h' at the end? And Callahan, what could be more Irish than that? Except for O'Callahan," she said with a smile.

When Sam shook Barry's hand, he had made a quick assessment but had reserved final judgment about the handsome cadet. Now, he sat silent, leaning back in his chair, looking nonchalant. From the corner of her eye, Luci glanced at her father and knew that he was anything but indifferent. Behind Sam's calm demeanor, Luci imagined that his mind was bubbling as fast as boiling water figuring out what made Barry tick.

As Sam listened and observed, Barry's enthusiasm about his family's Irish roots was evident. Sam also detected that Marie was softening up toward the young cadet. Her jaw became relaxed, and her eyes showed a spark of interest that disabled, to some extent, her explicit bias toward a military man. As Barry shared childhood and family stories of Irish immigration and neighborhoods, Marie found common ground with him.

Sam bided his time, eyeing Barry's body language and registering what the young cadet said during his discussions with Marie and Luci. Now, it was his turn to be the interrogator and release his first salvo. "Tell us about your mother, Barry. What's Breana like?" Coming from a culture that honored the mother and suffering the loss of maternal love as an orphan, the question was meaningful to him. "You know the quality and character of a man by the way he treats his mother," Sam frequently said to his daughters.

The question sat Barry back on his heels, and his mind raced. *Ask about my mother? Never in a million years would I think that someone would ask me that. She has so many qualities. How can I possibly categorize my mother?*

"To be honest, Mr. Bartolino, no one has asked me that. People usually want to know about my dad: what kind of job or hobbies he has, what sports he likes, or what my father and I do together. No one thinks to ask about my mother."

Sam listened and observed and let a pause signify the importance of his question before following up. "Why is that, do you suppose?"

Barry lowered his eyes and clenched his jaw. He was unwilling to admit society's truth about a woman's position. He swallowed hard. "I suppose it's because women's roles in our culture are so stereotyped that the question seems unimportant—even irrelevant—to many people."

If a pin had dropped on the patio flagstones, it would have been heard across the globe. Of those listening, the one mouth that did not fall open was Sam's; he knew how to mask his reactions. Luci's eyes widened in unison with parted lips. The first word that came to her was *bitchin'*, which she wanted to yell out but never would utter in front of her parents.

Marie, glancing over at Sam, raised an eyebrow and tightened her lips. *Insightful young man; too bad he is not from around here and that he wants a damn military career.*

"And to my question about your mother?" Sam asked.

Barry's mind whirled, searching for an example that could begin to describe the totality of Breana. Then he landed on the one he thought was right.

"To use an air force analogy, my mother is the commander of the Callahan squadron," he began. "My mother leads her team by setting an example of behavior, managing the resources, and laying down the rules, so we become a better unit."

Barry's creativity impressed Sam, his sensitivity swayed Luci, but his shrewdness struck Marie. In Sam's opinion, Luci's cadet measured up well. But he could detect by the tick in Marie's eyelid, that her fascination with the cadet did not outweigh her disapproval. *I hope she doesn't mess up things with Luci like she did with Adele and Darla.*

Sam and Marie continued to lob questions to Barry about his family, school, politics, and career until the group finished the appetizers. *Baptism by fire,* Barry thought again as the foursome returned into the house for dinner.

Whoa, this is as spectacular as the living room, Barry thought, entering the dining room. The room measured over twenty feet in length and had a massive fireplace against one wall. Like the entrance corridor, sienna-colored tiles covered the floor, and completing the decor was a large carved table that was set for a formal meal. At the end of the room, there was another bank of floor-to-ceiling windows. Through these, Barry saw a Spanish-style tiled fountain, which was encircled with containers of brightly colored flowers resting on flagstone, and provided a focal point for the secluded side garden.

As Sam had promised Luci, the dinner was fabulous, and Barry did the meal justice by finishing the large portions Sam dished out. "I like a man with a good appetite, particularly if it involves eating the food I prepare," Sam quipped.

While they ate, the conversation was lighthearted. Barry had learned from his father the value of curiosity and the importance of listening. "If you don't know people's experiences and what they are thinking and why, you can never learn how they feel or what matters to them. To have a real relationship with someone, you must understand them. To understand them, you must ask people questions and listen to their answers," Connor had said.

Barry asked questions and paid attention to the responses. He was curious about Sam's life in Italy as a young man, his immigrant journey, and how he became a successful businessman. He queried Luci's mother about her art interests and her French heritage. But, it may have been the look in her eyes or the use of too many superlatives that gave Marie's deception away. "Barry, have you had enough to eat? Oh, Barry, you were the quarterback on your high school's football team, how wonderful! Barry, you want to be a pilot—isn't that dangerous?"

Barry believed in the Mark Twain quote, "It ain't what you don't know that gets you into trouble. It's what you know for sure that just ain't so." Instead of prejudging Marie, he considered possible reasons for her shift between being stiff and friendly. *She could be an introvert and feel uneasy around people, or maybe she doesn't feel well tonight.* At the end of the evening, Barry still had reservations about Marie's feelings toward him. But staying true to Mark Twain, he gave her the benefit of the doubt.

Throughout the years, Marie had honed her skill in deception, evolving from low self-esteem and a need to control events. Pretending to like people disarmed them and avoided outright conflict. In this way, she could outwardly maintain positive relationships while using underhanded tactics to achieve her ends. She might pander to someone to secure favor but afterward deride the person. She would promise to advocate for someone but purposefully fail to do so. Her tactics were second nature. Pretending to like Barry avoided a clash with Luci. It bought her time to exercise control in other ways if she thought it necessary.

Sam was impressed with Barry's maturity and his knowledge of national and world events. His appraisal of Barry's family was as favorable: hard working with community roots. Sam had not served in War War II, but he admired those who did. Learning of Conner's war record, the reasons Barry might pursue an air force career were obvious.

Beyond these pluses, Sam enjoyed Barry's stories of fishing trips with his father and brothers. The sport was Sam's favorite. Barry's tales of catching lake trout and walleye delighted him, and Sam felt a tinge of jealousy over the bond between Connor and his sons. Sam longed for the companionship of a son, and envisioning fishing with a young man like Barry provided a temporary feeling of camaraderie.

With his experience limited to Lakes Erie and Ontario, Barry was as engrossed in Sam's deep-sea fishing accounts as Sam was in Barry's angling stories. "You come again, Barry, and we'll go catch us some albacore. Then you'll find out what real fishing is all about," Sam boasted.

Hmm, an invitation like this is a good sign, thought Barry.

As the dinner progressed to the dessert course, Barry's opinions began to take shape. *There is a lot of Sam in Luci but nothing of Marie in her daughter. Sam is not the hardest challenge facing me; it is Marie.*

CHAPTER 11

Coincidence

DOING cleanup after dinner was a habit for Barry at home, but Sam and Marie refused his help. For Marie, it would be snowing in July before she would invite dinner guests to clear the table or wash the dishes. For Sam, the reason was incontrovertible. *After all, Luci invited Barry so she could be with him, not with Marie or me.*

"Hey, Luci, why don't you take Barry for a ride in the Bird?" Sam suggested.

Luci blinked, stunned, hearing her father's offer. Sam treated his prized 1956 Thunderbird with kid gloves. He never let anyone take the snazzy two-seater, red and white convertible with a continental kit, out for a drive.

"Wow, Pop, are you sure?"

"What the heck! It is a beautiful summer evening. I took the top off this afternoon, so why not enjoy it?" Sam took the keys from his pocket and tossed them to Luci. From the description of the vehicle as the Bird, Barry hoped it was the classic sports car he was thinking about. He glanced at Luci, and the wink and the A-okay sign she flashed him confirmed Barry's suspicion. Biting his lip, he thought, *Man, I wish Dad and Joe were here to see this!*

The Bird had been a sore point between Luci's parents since the day Sam bought it a few months earlier. For a decade, owning the sporty Ford was one of Sam's biggest wishes. Marie, however, thought the idea was frivolous. She had tried to tamp down Sam's plan to buy a ten-year-old car as a useless outlay of money. Sam won out when he told himself one day, *It is now or never*, and he had the car in his garage that night.

But the classic did not bring Sam the happiness he had anticipated. After buying the vehicle, he discovered there was no one with whom he could enjoy it. Marie refused to ride in it, and Sam's friends were not predisposed either. "Sam," one said, "where do old farts like us go in a car like that without looking like we're having a midlife crisis? And anyway, it doesn't have room for fishing gear or golf clubs."

Collecting classic cars was not Sam's hobby, so there was no enjoyment gained from repairing or customizing the vehicle. Having driven the car fewer than half a dozen times in six months, the hard truth, Sam realized, was that fulfillment of a dream did not guarantee happiness. Marie's instincts, Sam reflected, were right all along.

Unable to control their smiles, Luci and Barry hopped into the car. Watching Luci drive the T-Bird down the driveway, Sam smiled and thought, *It's amazing how the smallest act of kindness can bring so much happiness.*

* * *

Now what? Where should we go? Luci wondered. It was early in the evening, and nothing would be happening at the regular teen hangouts. Even if those spots were an option, Luci wasn't going to waste precious time with Barry hanging around with the local group. "Hmm, what would you like to do?" she asked Barry.

"That's easy. Let's go somewhere where we can talk and walk together, get to know each other—and have fun," he said with a broad grin. Luci caught Barry's drift, and her lips curved into a smile.

"I know the place. But hold on, because we're going to go fast."

Barry squinted and looked to both sides as if scanning for a trooper, then reached over and squeezed her hand. "Bring it on, Luci."

Luci's choice was an oasis, a twenty-minute drive from her home. The famed landscape architects who had planned New York City's Central Park also designed two hundred acres of memory-making park in the middle of a semidesert. It had everything lovers desired for losing themselves in each other: a tranquil lake for gazing and dreaming, walking paths for strolling, park benches for cuddling, and a fairy-tale carousel for making time come to a standstill. In Luci's mind, this was a perfect pick for a romantic summer evening.

Luci pulled into the parking lot, and Barry once more was amazed at the San Bernardino Valley's secrets. In the distance, he saw the park's lake, circled by enormous cypress and palm trees, and a landscaped paradise beyond. Early evening brought out families cooling off from the day's heat, and younger teens were squeezing in adventures in one-person sailboats on the lake. He saw adults enjoying games of lawn bowling, and in the distance, the rousing music from a carousel's Artizan band organ signaled that jumping horses were giving children a whirlwind ride. White geese and Muscovy ducks were plentiful, and the spoiled beggars were unabashed in approaching strangers, expecting a handout.

Helping Luci from the car and taking her hand, the two strolled toward the lake's edge as Barry imagined a memorable evening. "This is perfect!" he said. "There's something about this park that makes me feel at home."

Luci turned toward Barry, a small frown on her face. "What gives you that impression?"

"My home in Buffalo is close to a big park that feels like this one. I mean, there are differences, of course. The one in Buffalo has greener vegetation, and naturally, there are no palm trees. Even so, it has a lake, open areas, and beautiful walking paths, like this park. It's called Cazenovia Park. It's a pretty big deal because the hotshot landscape architect named Olmstead who designed it also created Central Park in New York City."

Luci's eyes shot open. "Oh my gosh! Olmstead designed this one too!"

"Unbelievable," Barry said. "What a coincidence! No wonder it feels familiar. What do you think the odds are that you and I, living thousands of miles apart, both have Olmstead parks as a playground?"

Luci shrugged. "The odds are that any crazy event can happen."

"Oh, so you don't believe in coincidences. Don't believe in divine providence or anything like that?" Barry asked.

"Hmm," Luci murmured, leaving Barry confused.

The phenomenon of coincidence was a topic Luci's Friday evening buddies had thrashed about because it provided an endless circle of good-natured argument. "Coincidence is a random event," Chris had claimed one evening and backed up his assertion with mathematical probabilities and the law of huge numbers. Luci gave his shoulder a soft punch. "Oh, stop showing off with another example of stupid nerd-speak."

Her reproach, though, was like kindling to a fire. After a rant about statistical odds, Paul had taken the opposite position. He claimed that the synergy of events occurring with no explainable cause is fate like something pre-planned by the universe or God. With this reasoning, the conversation had moved to philosophy and a debate over the existence of a free will. The argument continued until Shelia told the guys to "Knock off your baloney." Having achieved their two-fold goal of annoying and impressing the girls, the Nerds stopped their antics until another dispute caught their attention.

"So what about it? About coincidence," Barry asked.

Luci had a well-thought-out response. "Okay, here's my perspective. If you take the position coincidences happen because any strange random event can occur, you relinquish the concept of free will. And if you believe that coincidences are something pre-planned or caused by fate, you abandon the idea of free will as well." Luci stopped to let Barry consider these thoughts.

"So what are you saying, Luci? Believing in coincidence is nonsense if you believe in free will? Sounds like a circular argument," Barry said, drawing an air circle with his index finger.

Luci slapped her palm to her forehead. "Exactly!" she said. "What I mean is that we shouldn't spend our energy wondering if hidden messages lurk in unexpected events or if they are random. Isn't it better to be curious about the event itself and not the why of it? Explore the novelty and the opportunities that something presents to you?"

Barry lowered his eyes, considering whether he should agree or disagree.

Luci saw his uncertainty and broke the silence. "Look. Tonight, for example, we could search for a hidden meaning about why both of us live near Olmstead-designed parks. Like, who cares? Wouldn't it be more interesting to learn about the similarities and differences between the parks? Even better, wouldn't it be more fun to discover and share some of the great memories of things we've done in the parks?"

Barry looked in the distance, considering her thoughts. As she waited, Luci hoped that he was on the verge of appreciating her theory that living in the present was a better option than prescribing a cause, random or otherwise, to an event. Then she pointed to a large white structure that looked like a warehouse. "Look over there across the lake, Barry. See that big building? That's the armory, and some of the best times of my life have been there."

Barry squinted and studied the structure. "No way! In an armory? How could an armory be fun?"

Luci drilled into Barry's sharp blue eyes. "Ever hear of Dick Dale and Del-Tones?"

Looking down, he tried to remember. "Oh, yeah, they're the Beach Boys before the Beach Boys, aren't they?"

Luci scrunched her nose. "Well, not quite. We make a big distinction here between the Del-Tone instrumentals that are actual surfing music and the Beach Boys songs that are music about surfing." To provide proof that the Del-Tones were the real deal, she playfully nudged Barry with her elbow and provided some surf music trivia. "You know it's the Del-Tones that performed the music hits in the Beach Party movies."

"Aah, no, that's news to me. So teach me more, little surfer girl," he said while putting his arm around Luci's shoulder.

Showing off, Luci instructed Barry on the subtler points of authentic surfing music, much of which she learned from the bantering between Sean and his friends.

Impressive, Barry thought. Her knowledge about acoustics, loudspeakers, and amplifiers solidified she was a real California girl, after all.

Determined to make her point that creating and sharing memories far surpassed thinking about coincidences, Luci hammered away. "Right in that armory, I've gone to Dick Dale stomps, and were they far out!" The thought of the dances fueled Luci's adrenaline pump, and her cheeks flushed. She wiggled out from Barry's arm and started to dramatize.

"Imagine this! The place is jammed. The fans are screaming and dancing. The guitars are squealing, and the drums are beating hard. The band never stops playing. One tune goes right into the next one. And when they play "King of the Surf" that mentions San Bernardino and Riverside, the crowd goes crazy stomping and yelling. There is nothing like it. You leave wired and a sweating mess," she said while dancing the Swim and imitating a surfer.

Barry laughed, and although self-conscious, he tried to dance and match Luci's depiction of Del-Tone fans. Afterward, he faced Luci and wrapping her in his arms, surprised her by stealing a kiss on the lips. "You're definitely right, Luci," he admitted, pulling back and looking in her eyes. "It's silly to wonder if something is a coincidence. What we do now counts more. So let's go and make memories together."

* * *

Over the next quarter-hour, they walked along the cypress tree-lined paths next to the lake. Clutching Barry's folded arm with his hand atop hers made Luci light-headed. She had held hands with boys so many times that she had lost count. This time, though, the sensation was different. The warmth and strength of Barry's hand across hers, his breath floating across her face, and a pleasant scent she could not categorize made her punchy. *Focus! Get your act together!* she told herself.

Luci turned up her curiosity and sidestepped the wave of emotions. "What is it like living at the academy? I don't know anything about a cadet's routine. It wasn't until Sister Catherine offered the dance invitations that the military academies crossed my mind."

Barry had given his family superficial accounts of academy life: the everyday grind, the courses, and field experiences. But he had held back sharing his emotions toward all of these, not even confiding in his brother Joe, his closest friend. Now, Barry felt he was walking on a tightrope, wondering if he should give Luci the usual trivia or divulge his deeper feelings. Luci's sincerity and sympathetic ear made Barry feel she would be a safe harbor for his feelings, and she would not judge him. Taking a deep breath, he took the risk to unburden himself. He steered Luci to a bench near the edge of the lake, and they sat down together. Holding her hand, Barry lowered his head, eyes scanning the ground.

"The past twelve months at the academy, Luci, have been physically and mentally challenging. To be honest, at times, I've wondered if I would make it through the year."

Luci felt Barry's unease as his hand unconsciously tightened around hers. "Fourth-class cadets are called 'doolies,' and we are the lowest in the pecking order at the academy. The word 'doolie' comes from the Greek, meaning a slave. From that definition, you get the picture of what life is like for first-year cadets." Barry's face softened, and looking into Luci's eyes, he felt assured that it was safe to confess what he had gone through the past year.

"Our day begins at five thirty in the morning with the upper-class cadets banging on our dorm room door and shouting at us to get up. From there on, the day is regimented. Even taking showers and eating are timed and disciplined. We get twenty-five minutes to eat, and we have to do it sitting at attention. That means sitting at the edge of the chair and looking down at the eagle emblem on the plate. To eat, we take the food from our plates scoop by scoop and replace our utensils on the table between bites. Then there's the chewing part of it all. We must chew each mouthful seven times before swallowing it."

Luci was familiar with stories of basic army training from her Friday night pals, but this side of academy life shocked her. She nodded. "Go on," she said.

"As doolies, we're required to memorize all kinds of stupid and unrelated facts. Any upperclassman can quiz us on these at any time. Those guys get right up in your face, like an inch away, and start shouting questions one after another at you. They are so close they spray their spit on you as they interrogate. If you don't give the correct answer, they discipline you with extra drills or calisthenics. I'd demonstrate the process, but it would scare the hell out of you."

"That sounds like torture. How does anyone cope with that? How did you cope?"

"The truth is a lot of cadets don't manage."

Luci got chills thinking back to Tom Fisher's remarks on Saturday evening. At the time, his criticism of the first-year cadets who had dropped out disgusted her, but now his disparaging words were even more repugnant.

Barry sighed, looked up, and gazed out across the lake. "A third of those admitted to the academy will never graduate. That is a fairly high attrition rate, and I didn't want to be part of it. I coped by focusing on surviving. *Get through another day,* I'd say to myself. I knew if I took one day at a time, I could endure, and afterward, I'd get the prize: becoming an air force officer." Barry paused. Admitting that survival was at the forefront of his mind for twelve months lifted a weight from his shoulders. Unconsciously, he believed it showed weakness on his part. By getting it out in the open to someone, he felt absolved and free.

"My dad gave me two good pieces of advice, Luci, before I left for the academy. First, he said to take every negative experience and find something positive about it. Thinking that way put me in a position of control. So when some bastard was screaming at me to remember a ridiculous fact, I didn't take it personally. Instead, my dad's counsel was whispering to me, and I took control by looking for the positive. I persuaded myself that the process was honing my skills for remembering details. I convinced myself that creating a habit of recalling facts could be critical in saving my life in combat someday."

Hearing the word "bastard," surprised Luci. While it revealed Barry's opinion of the upperclassman, she wondered if it disclosed something more. *Could Barry be finding that academy life is at odds with his values?*

Barry took his free hand and ran it unconsciously through his hair before continuing, and Luci tightened hers on his arm. "So Dad also told me to focus on what is essential and don't stress out about anything else. Studying, building relationships, doing your squadron duties, and being a good wingman to your roommate are the most important things. It's the cadets who can't separate the important from the trivial who feel they don't control a situation and who have difficulty coping."

Luci sat without saying a word. *Holy crap, what a life. My mother is controlling, but eating at attention and having to chew every bite of food seven times is going too far. But he chose to act and to take charge. We have choices when we hit a wall.*

"That's nuts! All that control freaks me out, but I sort of understand the way you've dealt with it. My father has given me similar advice."

"Seriously? Our fathers think alike? Another coincidence?"

Luci let the coincidence remark slide with a who-cares shrug. "But for real, Barry, Pop has a basic rule for success. If faced with a hurdle, he says a person always has three options. The first is that you can be complacent and suck up the situation. This option gives you no control, and chances are it will make you feel trapped and depressed. The second choice is you can live in a fantasy world and pretend everything is fine. In the long run, daydreaming like this depletes your energy and makes it impossible to succeed. The third choice is to be persistent and find a solution to get what you want. This puts you in control of your life. My dad says it's the way to believe in yourself and be successful. It sounds like you've found the solution to get what you want."

Barry nodded and raised an eyebrow. *I was right the first night I met her. She is amazing!* Then he threw Luci a flirtatious smile that made her blush. "Oh, yes, Luci, I have a plan on getting what I want. Who cares about coincidence? Right now it's time to make more memories with you!"

Chapter 12

Blackhorse Road

In memory-making mode, Barry and Luci wandered to a concession stand where Barry purchased cold drinks and added an order of French fries to give to the pesky geese and ducks. They found an empty picnic table and sat down, and while sipping their drinks and feeding the waterfowl, Barry told Luci more about his brothers and some of their high jinks. The Callahan boys were adventurous, but some of their escapades, like their activities on lovers' lanes, were best left untold.

"Yeah, the four of us can be immature," he said. "You know, doing a lot of goofy things. Sometimes when we're cruising around in the summer, we play a version of musical chairs by jumping out of the car at a stoplight and changing seats. It's kind of stupid, I know, but we have so much fun doing it. Unfortunately, doing stuff like that has given us a reputation in the neighborhood as the crazy Callahans."

Luci rolled her eyes. "Oh, I can imagine."

Barry loved his hometown area, and his words tumbled out as he described the large amusement park in Fort Erie that he and his family visited each summer and his memories of Cazenovia Park. "I'd love for you to visit me in Buffalo when I am on leave in a few weeks. You know, Buffalo isn't that far from where you'll be spending your vacation in Canada. It would be a blast to take you on the Crystal Beach roller coasters and to see my Olmstead park. You could spend a few days getting to know my family at our summer cabin in the foothills of the Alleghenies. We'd have a ball!"

Mother would keel over dead before allowing a visit like that, Luci thought.

"I'd love that, Barry," Luci replied. "But I'd have to do battle with my mother." After letting that nugget slip, Luci tried a softer response with a puppy-dog look. "What I mean is that she might be a little old-fashioned when it comes to her daughter visiting, well, a stranger's family."

Luci's fears were not unfounded. The discussion revived an uncomfortable memory of Marie's superordinate control two years earlier. While visiting in Canada, Marie put her foot down, objecting to Luci staying a few days with family friends on their farm in Northern Ontario. They had a daughter a year younger than Luci and four sons, two of whom were older but near Luci's age. Marie's imagination went into overdrive visualizing every possible illicit act that might occur between Luci and the boys. It was true Luci had a crush on one of them, but Marie's projections astounded her. It was that perverse thought that tipped the scale, making Luci determined to free herself from Marie. *If she has her way, I will be tied to her apron strings all my life. Adele and Darla are victims with messed up lives because of Mother's control. I will not be a casualty too,* Luci vowed.

Barry assessed what Luci told him, trying to find an angle out of the dilemma. "I've got it! What if my mother sent you an invitation and then spoke by phone with your mother and assured her you'd be in good hands?"

Luci glanced down, not answering.

"Don't you think that's an old-fashioned way to handle an old-fashioned problem?"

Luci gave Barry a shoulder nudge. "You wisecracker! But seriously, that might work." Still, Luci didn't believe his strategy had much of a chance, but she was too embarrassed to reveal the extent of Marie's control.

"Then we'll give it a try," Barry said. "I know my family will love you." But even as he was confident, Barry reminded himself of his initial wariness of Marie. *She's solicitous and friendly to your face, but what is in her heart?*

Luci switched the subject, asking Barry more questions about his family. His older brother, Joe, was attending a Catholic university in the Boston area and was in a navy ROTC program. "Joe and I kid around about the services. He thinks the navy is the best, and of course, I disagree with him," Barry said. "Joe will be graduating in a year, and then he will get his officer's commission. My next brother, John, is twelve months younger than me. He is the real family rabble-rouser." Barry shook his head and smiled. "He's a riot, but he didn't get the college genes. So he enlisted in the marines, and last December went to Vietnam."

The disclosure paralyzed Luci. *Oh, God. What a revelation!* Hearing it, she felt ashamed about her involvement, even though indirect, in the production of the *Pink Sheet* by her Friday night buddies.

"How do your parents feel about that?" she whispered.

Barry paused and looked aside. "Mom and dad put up a good front, but I know they worry. Dad, of course, understands what happens in war. He rarely talks about his army air forces service. Mom says there are good reasons why he doesn't and not to ask him about it. Late some nights, I've seen dad drinking alone and getting plowed. I know there are ghosts in his past that deal with the war, and it makes me sad because there is nothing I can do to help him."

Barry wavered, and Luci knew that this family dynamic was tricky and one that he did not want to talk about. Barry cleared his throat. "About Vietnam, my folks know they will have three sons in the military soon. With the draft, it doesn't matter if we all enlist or wait to get called up. If the war doesn't end soon, one way or the other, we'll all be in it. While mom and dad are patriotic, I know they question what we are doing there. Of course, they don't say much about it to us," Barry said, his voice trailing off. Gnawing in his mind were similar concerns, but he could not indulge these, given his current military service. Even talking with Luci about these was impossible.

Hearing about John's deployment, Luci was afraid that she might offend or hurt Barry by divulging details of the Nerd group's conversations. Even so, she knew young men who were fighting in Vietnam, and protesting the war did not diminish her friends. Instead, Luci and the Nerds opposed the politicians who created a policy that sent people to war without reasonable justification. After meeting Barry at the street dance, Luci knew she would have to resolve any differing perspectives about the military and the Vietnam War. *I have a choice. I can hold back and say nothing more on the subject or tell Barry what my friends and I mull over every Friday.*

Luci's brain whirled as if it were on a spindle trying to find its balance. *Trust builds relationships*, she reminded herself. *Trust requires openness. A personal bond involves sharing a set of values, but that doesn't mean there can't be differences of opinion. Undeniably, seeing different perspectives helps people increase their knowledge and tolerance. Respecting divergent viewpoints is as vital as having overlapping values in a relationship. Isn't this one reason the Nerds get along so well? The guys agree on most things. But on those they disagree, they don't hold back their opinions, and they listen to each other's arguments. Regardless of whether everyone agrees with each other or not, in the end, they have an improved outlook.*

Luci's anxiety rose, and her heart sped up as she told Barry about the Vietnam War debates among her Friday night pals. She explained the group's concerns about the war's motivation and stressed that they disagreed with the political policy, not with the men and women who were in harm's way. "All my friends say if drafted, they will go into the military," Luci said. "They aren't pacifists, and they have no intention of running off to Canada or making up some physical ailment to circumvent the draft."

Barry continued to hold her hand, but Luci squirmed with unease, waiting for his reaction.

"I like your friends, and I haven't even met them," he said.

Luci pulled back. Barry's statement was unexpected, but it proved that her impression of the Irishman from Buffalo was correct. *He is a person who sees life through a variety of prisms.* Luci took in a deep breath, anxious to hear what Barry would say next.

"I'm not informed enough to offer an opinion on some of the arguments you laid out. What I do know is that our country's freedom depends on people being able to express their opinions and ideas and to listen to those of others. I'm happy you have these kinds of discussions, Luci. Most of the girls I know aren't that concerned about what's happening in the country, much less the world. But you think about things that affect people's futures, like Vietnam and civil rights."

Luci sat with her eyes cast down. Barry's compliment left her speechless.

Leaning over, Barry whispered in Luci's ear, and he held her hand so tight that it made her breathless. "This is why I like you, Luci with an i. You're challenging me to think about these things and to be a better person."

I was right about him. He is something special, Luci thought, smiling to herself.

Barry cocked his head and gave Luci a grin. "Hey, how about us lightening up?"

Throwing the remaining French fries toward the ducks, he took Luci's hand and led her toward the carousel music. He bought cotton candy, and they pulled chunks of the warm gooey stuff off the stick like six-year-olds and stuffed it into each other's mouths. For half an hour, they rode the merry-go-round surrounded in a cloud of fantasy under a thousand twinkling lights. When the music stopped between rides, they practiced their version of musical chairs. They leapt among the thirty artistically carved horses and, like children, feigned a competition about who rode the best one. They laughed and bantered about nothing special, whirling in circles that brought them to the brink of dizziness as they gazed into each other's eyes.

Darkness descended before they realized it, and they grudgingly rode their last round on the carousel. The Artizan band organ played a Wurlitzer-style military march, a salute to Barry, thanks to the carousel operator. When the music stopped, Barry slid off Chief, a magnificently carved horse decorated with American flags and a patriotic theme. He looked up at Luci sitting on Mountain Dancer, a white horse with a flying mane and flashing eyes that was laden with flowers in gorgeous contrasting hues. "I wish I had a camera to take a picture. You look like a forest princess," he said. His hands gripping her waist, Barry lowered Luci from Mountain Dancer. "You are my Lelawala," Barry whispered in her ear as he nuzzled his face against her neck, making her flush and taking her breath away once again.

Before leaving the park, the lovers lingered, leaning against the car, immersed in drawn-out kisses and embraces. Luci's Wind Song perfume glided on the receding desert heat like the intoxicating power of alcohol, and Barry knew that the fragrance would always be associated with happy memories. He hoped, though, that the darkness camouflaged them sufficiently since this romantic behavior was out of bounds for a man in uniform. *Who the hell cares? It's worth a reprimand.*

* * *

With the convertible top down, Luci and Barry drove toward the base. Silence wrapped them in the calming comfort of a cozy blanket while the breeze rushed through their hair. "Look up there," Barry said, pointing to the bright, waning crescent moon peering down from a cloudless sky. "Do you know, Luci, what tonight's moon signifies in mythology?"

"I know a full moon is associated with the ocean tides and weird behavior patterns of animals and humans. And, oh yes, doesn't it have something to do with lovers too?" she asked with a wink. "But a crescent moon? It has a magical meaning?"

Barry cocked his head. "Kind of," he stated. "In mythology, tonight's moon signifies it is a time to think things over, throw off negative feelings, and prepare for something new. I know you don't believe in coincidence and that tonight's moon doesn't have a hidden meaning for us. But I'm making it have a meaning—for me, it's a beginning with you."

Barry leaned toward Luci, his hand gently falling on her thigh. His touch set tingles far above his stroke, and Luci returned a satisfied glance. "I'm taking this moment and folding it into the first act with you. Isn't that so much better than a coincidence?" she asked.

As they approached their destination, Barry removed his blue and white name tag from his uniform jacket. When they arrived at the main gate, the guards waved them through, and Luci drove Barry to his quarters. Before opening the car door, Barry leaned over and gave Luci a last, long kiss.

Pulling back, Barry gazed at Luci while pressing his name tag along with a small piece of paper into her hand. "I'd like you to write to me, Luci. Will you do that?" he whispered,

Luci felt her heart lodge in her throat. "I will, Barry."

"My home address is written on the paper I've given to you. I'll be there in about three weeks on a month's leave. I will write to you, too, and I will share all my deep, dark secrets and desires," he said, with a mischievous look in his eyes.

"But you don't have my address!"

"Oh, yes, I do! I memorized the house number as soon as we drove into your driveway this afternoon."

* * *

After arriving home and parking the car in the garage, Luci looked at the paper Barry had given her. Under her breath, she read aloud: 181 Blackhorse Road, Buffalo, NY. Closing her eyes, Luci dug back into her memories of Celtic tales retold to her on sultry evenings on her grandmother's porch. *The horse represents freedom, and a black horse signifies strength, wisdom, and maturity for overcoming life's obstacles. Perhaps there are coincidences, after all!*

CHAPTER 13

Barry Glow

FOR Marie, a young couple cruising in a T-Bird convertible at night was courting trouble, and she was furious with Sam for suggesting that Luci take the car. Sitting in their living room after Luci and Barry had left, Sam and Marie shared their critiques of Cadet Callahan. Marie, on her final glass of wine for the evening, was in a caustic mood. "He's handsome enough. But that's all I'm giving him."

"Oh, come on, Marie. He's smart, ambitious, has a solid future, and he's a Catholic and Irish, to boot. What else could you ask? It isn't as if this is permanent. It's a summer romance."

Marie shook her head, drained her glass of wine, and snapped, "You're a fool, Sam Bartolino," and then she got up from her chair and walked down the hall to her studio.

Marie sulked in her artisan sanctuary and was on alert for the sound of the T-Bird's engine. As soon as Luci walked through the front door, Marie materialized from her sanctum and started giving her daughter the third-degree. She barked questions and laid on a guilt trip without waiting for a reply.

"Where were you for four hours?"

"What did you do for so long?"

"Why didn't you say you were planning to be gone that long? I worried myself to death about you."

"Didn't you think your father and I wanted to visit more with Barry? Why didn't you bring him back here?"

"You drove home at night, by yourself, in a convertible? What were you thinking, Luci? And why did that cadet let you do it? Has he no sense?"

In an instant, the evening's romance was shattered. Luci felt her stomach churning and a nauseous feeling developing. Tears welled in her eyes, but bursting out crying, she knew, would result in more drama and make her a victim of her mother's hounding. *What have I ever done to merit a cross-examination like this? Being sassy won't accomplish anything. Engaging Mother while she is in a hissy fit precipitates a worse meltdown.*

Luci gave the one reply she knew to settle her mother down. "I'm sorry. I didn't consider the issues." Lowering her head, she tried to recall the barrage of questions her mother had wailed. Luci's brain felt like a bouncing scale trying to weigh her mother's concerns. To be generous, she thought it could be possible that her mother had real fears about her safety. Unfortunately, Marie was unable to meld her worry with sensitivity. As a first choice, Marie jumped to negative conclusions instead of considering positive alternatives.

Answer her and be truthful. It will quiet her down. I have done nothing wrong. Answer her questions.

"We went to Fairmont Park."

"I took Barry there because it was a place we could talk and walk together."

"Barry bought Cokes and fries, and we fed the ducks. We watched kids sail their small boats on the lake. We got cotton candy, and we rode the carousel."

"Time slipped away, and Barry had to return to the base. I'm sure he would have liked visiting more with you and Pop if I had planned better."

Marie's arms, bound across her chest, and her pursed lips warned Luci that her mother was still displeased.

Now, for sure, a trip to Buffalo is dead on arrival, Luci thought.

* * *

The "Barry Event" and "Barry Glow" were how Shelia dubbed Luci's new relationship and resulting effervescence. For kicks, Shelia labeled special occasions and items, and she was not letting Luci's tryst get away without a descriptive tag.

"You sound like a one-woman intelligence service," Luci told her friend many times. "I have the hardest time unscrambling your shortcuts."

Returning a James Bond Girl saucy look, Shelia would retort, "Duh! That's what code is supposed to do," and then the girls would laugh together.

"You're not getting off the hook," Shelia told Luci on the phone the morning after Luci's dinner date. "You will tell me every exquisite detail about the Barry Event. I'll pick you up tonight at seven. We'll go to the hangout, and you *will* tell me everything."

Luci's body buzzed like a hive, hungering to unload her feelings to someone who would understand her emotions. After all, Marie was unsympathetic, and Luci would never broach a discussion about her boyfriends with her mother. Furthermore, there were limitations to what Luci felt she could disclose to her father. *How can you ever tell your dad personal stuff, like that you French-kissed a guy!*

At seven o'clock, the girls drove to the hangout that was, in reality, a burger and root beer drive-in. In the 1950s, the place had a reputation as a Hell's Angels meeting place, hence the tag Shelia attached to it. Reformed by the mid-1960s, it was where teens congregated to check each other out and flirt. After ordering root beer floats over the drive-in speaker, Luci divulged her tale of the Barry Event to Shelia.

"Heck, Luci, you know more about Barry after one night than I know about Bob in four months!" Then, she shook her head and wagged a finger at Luci. "But I'm seriously disappointed in you for passing up the opportunity of doing some serious necking in that hot convertible."

Luci's skittishness in experimenting with sex piqued Shelia's curiosity, and she wondered, *Is Luci concealing a secret?* Shelia had heard rumors about one of Luci's older sisters but respected her friend's privacy too much to make a big deal out of uncovering the truth.

Her joking rebuke aside, Shelia admired Luci for taking control and asking Barry to dinner. "That was bold of you. I'm proud of you for doing that. I don't know if I would have the guts to track him down. What if he had said no?"

Luci took a long sip of her root beer float. "We take risks with guys, Shelia, but in different ways. You take them with sex. I take them with the possibility of getting my self-confidence slammed," she stated. "If Barry turned me down, what's the worst that would happen? For a couple of minutes, my pride is bruised. But then I wouldn't worry about other things, like getting pregnant, would I?"

"Luci, you need some serious sex education! Have you not heard of rubbers?" Shelia asked as if she were experienced in these matters.

"Point taken!" Luci conceded, deciding an argument wouldn't change Shelia's mind on the risks of going past third base.

It was still early, and tuning the radio to the familiar KMEN-129 station, the girls took off to cruise the streets to see who was available for flirting.

* * *

Four days after the Barry Event, even Luci's Friday night pals detected something different about her. "Hey, Luci, what's up with you?" Chris asked when the Nerds picked her up for their weekly movie outing. "It's like you are holding back a secret or something."

Chris, like Sean and Paul, had graduated from St. Joe's, but most of the high school student body judged them as dissidents for not meeting the school's profile of conventionality. Refusing to play the game of ingratiating themselves with the priests and other teachers, the three young men stood their ground on their values and challenged many of the religion's rules. Once Chris had quipped to one of the teachers that he was considering joining the Jesuit Order of priests, and the teacher snarled back, "Chris, even you're too radical for the Jesuits."

A few weeks before, the three Nerds had completed their junior year in college. Chris was majoring in chemistry, and he planned to work toward his doctorate after graduation. A personal mission fueled his interest in the field. His father had been a steelworker for two decades at the plant in town and died of cancer when Chris was sixteen. In the past five years, reports linked asbestos and the disease, and everyone knew that the fibrous insulating material swathed the local steel plant. Chris recollected his father often coming home from work with white sediment on his clothing and that his mother would comment that the stuff looked dreadful. "I get that gunk on me walking between the buildings at the plant. It comes down like snow some days. No big deal," his dad said and would shrug.

Having more of a concern for profits than lives, companies as early as the 1930s began concealing their knowledge of the connection between cancer and asbestos. In the past half decade, the local community saw a higher incidence of lung and kidney cancer, and a recent study reported that family members of asbestos workers were also at risk.

Corporations' unfettered greed angered and disgusted Chris. Since his father's death, he wanted to devote his life to finding a cancer cure. He saw the path to achieving his goal through pharmaceutical research. He was not naïve, though, about the interests of that industry either. Chris knew the checkered history of drug trials and human experimentation and the alarms about the increase in unethical behavior relating to pharmaceutical research. Like the asbestos and manufacturing companies, pharmaceutical firms and academic institutions were putting profits and promotions over human lives. Correcting breaches of ethical practice in research intensified Chris's desire to commit his life in service to protect people. But he feared his dream would have to be put on hold. Unlike some others, Chris was pessimistic about the Vietnam War ending and thought it was starting to heat up. He figured that the military would snag him in the draft long before he could go to graduate school.

Chris was hands-down handsome. Broad shouldered and over six feet tall with light-brown curly hair, a ruddy complexion, and intense brown eyes, there was no doubt that Chris DeLuca had magnetism. His perfect smile accentuated his easygoing personality, unusual for the nerd stereotype. No slouch in the romance department, he had his choice of any girl, and those he dated joyfully hoped for a permanent relationship with him. He never found, or perhaps looked for, the right emotional and intellectual balance with any of them, leaving him happy to play the field.

Chris had racked up a 3.8 grade point average through his first three years in college, and his academic achievement was rewarded by a full scholarship. That the funding came from a conservative nonprofit foundation made his anonymous editorship with Sean and Paul of the notorious college underground newspaper, the *Pink Sheet*, bizarre. "If my sponsor finds out about my left-leaning activities, I can say *ciao* to my tuition support," he often confided to his fellow accomplices.

"Okay, Luci," Chris pressed as the group drove to the drive-in theater. "You didn't answer my question. You seem, like, mysterious tonight. Hmm, could it be that you noticed, at last, how good-looking I am and are star-struck?"

Shelia, sitting in the third seat of the van, recoiled at Chris's attempt to be humorous. "Come off it, Chris! Luci has Barry Glow from the Barry Event last Monday evening."

Chris narrowed his eyes, throwing Shelia a suspicious glance, and then turned to Luci sitting next to him in the middle seat of the vehicle. "Barry Glow, what the hell is that?"

Luci was as oblivious to Chris's growing infatuation with her as Shelia was to Paul's, and thought Chris was more annoying than cute whenever he teased her. Luci scrunched her shoulders. "You know, Chris, it's Shelia's secret agent language. Ignore it."

Sitting in the front, Sean and Paul heard the crosstalk and gave each other a side-glance and stopped talking, wanting to overhear the backseat chatter. They knew about the cadet dances and had feigned indifference, not wanting the girls to discover their underlying curiosity.

His interest was raised, but Chris realized he wouldn't get Luci to give up any tidbits. Making a quarter turn in his seat, he looked toward Shelia. "Since you coined the phrase, I want to hear your definition of it."

Sheesh, I should have never opened my big trap, Shelia thought as Luci gave her friend a look that screamed, "I'm ticked off at you."

Wanting to stay on Luci's right side, Shelia gave Chris and the rest of the nosy group the highlights spattered with white lies. She described the saga of the cadet dances as boring. "Those cadets are stuffy and stuck up. Their hair is too short, and for me, they are zero on the romance scale."

Luci bit her tongue to hold back laughing at Sheila's last point. *After all,* she thought, *wasn't it an Ohioan who was such a great kisser?*

Chris stared at Sheila, waiting for more.

"Oh yeah. Luci decided to snare some guy from Buffalo by following the adage that the way to a man's heart is through his stomach." When Chris cocked his head at that remark, Shelia realized she had undermined her proposition that the cadets were duds. Undeterred, she then attempted to make Barry sound like a flake.

"So, Chris, Luci is basking in the glow of this cadet dude. This is a guy who likes to climb palm trees, tell silly stories about Native American maidens, and skips a Dodgers game to have dinner with her." Shelia's subterfuge turned out a miserable failure when Chris turned and shot Luci a sly smile.

"Jeez, Luci, I've got a stomach too, Don't you want to win my heart? I'd skip more than a baseball game to have dinner with you," Chris said, pantomiming his words by holding his hands over his heart.

Luckily, they had arrived at the drive-in, and the movie, *Harper*, was about to begin, stopping the teasing at the right time. As the opening movie credits rolled, though, Chris gazed in the semidarkness at Luci, feeling a slight lump in his throat. He realized he could no longer deny that his crush on her was heating up by degrees, and he found himself a little bit jealous of the "cadet dude."

* * *

The final academy dance was a ho-hum affair. Luci was close to begging off attending the event, but having committed, she felt compelled to carry through on her promise. Like the previous dance, the cadets and the invited girls stood in two lines and were matched one by one with each other. The arrangements were identical to the week before: the same band, food, and venue. With Tom Fisher long gone and her sanity safe, Luci spent the evening with Craig, who hailed from a small Illinois farming community. He was well-mannered, tall, nice looking with dark hair, and easygoing. Craig spent the evening talking about the 4-H, showing his prized sheep at the country fair, and about farming in general. It made Luci wonder why the strapping young man chose a career in the air force. *He's cute but certainly is no Barry Callahan,* Luci concluded.

Halfway through the evening, Craig hinted he would like to write to Luci. In the sweetest way possible, Luci said, "If someone hadn't beaten you to the punch last week, I would be head over heels for you."

Her response did not put her new beau off. "In case things don't work out with the other guy, here's my address," he said at the end of the evening and handed Luci his formal calling card with his address.

* * *

Late in the afternoon, ten days after the Barry Event, Luci came home from her part-time job yearning for the sanctuary of her bedroom. Sam would be back at five thirty, and Marie would return from a church meeting about the same time. Exhausted from working nine hours with high-energy preschoolers, Luci wanted to make the most of the sixty minutes she had to herself. She slipped off her sandals and threw herself across her bed and hugged her pillow. She had not received a letter from Barry, and it concerned her. *Don't panic! It's hardly over a week since we saw each other. If he's as busy as I am, it's no wonder he hasn't written*, she reasoned to quash her fears.

Closing her eyes, she took a deep breath and reveled in thoughts of June 13. Luci tried not to ruminate about past adverse events. *A waste of energy on things that cannot be changed,* she thought. Thinking of happy experiences, though, was a different ball game; recalling these intensified and prolonged the pleasure enjoyed at the time.

During these "savoring moments," as she called them, Luci visualized a gold gate before her. As she opened and stepped through it, a glowing pathway guided her through a dappled sunlit forest. At the end of the lane, the trees parted and revealed a verdant grassland bathed in the sunshine where she could enter and remember savored times. Her visualization presented infinite ways of reconstructing her experience. It gave her a refuge where she could create a potpourri of pleasing scents, textures, colors, breezes, skies, and sounds and recreate a cherished moment.

This afternoon, she unlatched the gold gate, and, unhurried, stepped onto the glimmering path. She danced in the rays of sunlight that stroked the forest pathway ahead. Going down the lane this afternoon was different from any before. Now, she saw herself as Barry's forest princess riding the carousel's white horse with the flying mane and flashing eyes and laden with flowers. Feeling a gentle breeze across her face gave her incredible pleasure. The trees responded to the zephyr's magic, too. Like graceful ballerinas, their shadows swayed and guided her toward the soft strains of carousel music.

Entering the lush meadowlands, she dismounted from her horse and lay down among the wildflowers, blissfully inhaling their sweet scents. She revived the intimacies she and Barry shared: stories of their families, philosophies of life, humor and giddiness, gentle touches, heartfelt embraces, sweet and tender kisses. Her spirit overflowed with gratitude, and the presence of the Wind Song fragrance cradled her in contentment as she dozed off.

* * *

Bing, bang! Luci woke to Sam making dinner in the kitchen and rattling pots and pans. She stretched, still feeling the afterglow of her memories, and rose to help her father with whatever wonderful meal he was creating.

"There's my hardworking Bambina. Still a little sleepy-eyed?" Sam asked Luci as she entered the kitchen.

Sam tried to acknowledge his children's achievements, believing success developed self-esteem and drove success. Luci working a summer job and taking extra hours to compensate for her upcoming vacation was worthy of a compliment. Many of his acquaintances' teenaged children chose to loaf during the summer. Consequently, Sam was proud of Luci's persistence in seeking a job and encouraged her independence.

Beyond financial security, Sam believed that independence was a mental characteristic. "People are foolish to assume that money makes one secure," Sam said. "Over and over, I see wealthy people revealing their insecurities. They are egotistical. They are jealous of others, and they exploit people no matter what the cost is to anyone else. Their weaknesses make them a target for flattery, easy manipulation, and extortion by unscrupulous people like themselves."

Sam often told his daughters that using money as the foundation for independence wouldn't save a person from downfall. "People who seek wealth for wealth's sake have it all wrong. You must turn the applecart upside down. Independence relies on a healthy sense of self, not money. If you know yourself, set your goals, and seek your vision following the cardinal virtues, then you are free." Sam extolled his philosophy whenever he found the occasion, and his daughters knew Aristotle's core virtues by heart: courage, self-control, prudence, and justice.

Friends and family might provide a circle of support and offer advice, but Sam's experiences formed his belief that well-being was a personal responsibility. "Life's a journey," Sam told his children. "You get to pick the highway, the destination, and transportation. You choose the provisions available on the way. You make the decisions. In the end, you are answerable for your actions, looking out for your best interests, and completing the journey."

Retrieving the dinner dishes from the cupboard, Luci peeked over Sam's shoulder. "Yum, chicken piccata, roasted yellow squash and zucchini, linguini, and salad. What could be better?"

"Well, how about dessert? I have that, too, but it is a surprise." Her father's sly look toward a bakery box revealed that he had brought home one of her favorites—almond cake.

While Luci was setting the table in the dining room, Sam hollered out from the kitchen, "Hey, I hear your sister Aimee is cutting up in San Francisco. She was in a protest march with that free speech group she's so fond of. She phoned your mother this afternoon and got her upset. And, of course, Marie had to call me and interrupt my work to tell me all about it!"

Aimee had done everything right in Marie's eyes and signaled her conformity to everything. She had been a Sodality princess in high school. She graduated summa cum laude from a Catholic women's college. She went on to medical school. Besides these accomplishments, Aimee was dating a Catholic boy who worked for a large accounting firm. Most importantly, Aimee was not unwed and pregnant.

What made Marie uneasy, though, was Aimee's occasional participation in protest groups. Luci considered her sister's behavior on the lower rung of Aristotle's virtue of courage, and she knew her mother's worries were unwarranted. *Aimee is hardly an activist in the Berkeley sense*, Luci judged. While concerned about social justice, Aimee made sure her association with liberal groups would never jeopardize her future career. *Then again, who might blame her? After all, who wants to be teargassed or arrested?*

Aimee's phone call was the center of dinner conversation, and Marie's pessimism and hysterics hit the roof. "Why does Aimee have to distress me with these antics? She has a great future ahead, and she is jeopardizing it by running around with a bunch of anarchists."

Luci stifled a chuckle at the stereotype. *Hardly the American Revolutionaries or Bolsheviks!*

Sam wanted to enjoy his dinner without acidic aftermath, so he kept calm in the wake of Marie's panic. He assured his wife that Aimee's involvement in a small protest would not implode her career or morals. "Think of it this way, Marie. Aimee wouldn't call you if this protest thing were that bad. She knows how you feel about that kind of stuff. Aimee wasn't calling to get your goat; she was excited to be involved in something that had a bigger impact beyond her. Think of it as good practice for dealing with all kinds of people in her career as a doctor."

Marie thought over Sam's argument and was settling down before Luci added, "Mom, face it. Aimee has too much sense—or to use Pop's term, prudence—to do anything that would damage her career or offend her uptight boyfriend."

Oops, thought Luci, after the words had tumbled from her mouth. *I shouldn't have let my feelings about Clark slip out that way.*

Focusing one of her elementary-school teacher stares at Luci, Marie got up from the table in a huff. "Speaking of boyfriends, I guess you neglected to see the letter on the hutch from that boy from Buffalo."

* * *

Luci felt her knees wobbling. She wanted to jump, skip, hug herself, and let out a squeal that would sound around the world, but she was embarrassed to let either of her parents see her teenage excitement. Allowing her anticipation to intensify, she cleared the table and did the dinner dishes before she went to the dining room and removed the letter from the sideboard shelf.

Clutching the note in her hand, she walked down the corridor to her bedroom, and once behind the closed door of her room, Luci hugged herself in a love lock. She fell across the bed, buried her head in her pillow, and let out a muffled scream that left her feeling delightfully light-headed. After the ten-second hyperkinetic thrill, Luci righted herself and sat on the edge of her bed and opened the letter. Separating the sealed flap from the rest of the envelope was as thrilling as removing the wrapping from a gift. Holding the folded note, the familiar feeling of butterflies swirled in her stomach. *What will Barry say? What will he share with me? How will his letter end? Will he sign it "Sincerely" or "Regards" or "With love"?*

Monday, June 19, 1966

Dear Luci,

Seven days ago, you called and asked me to dinner, and since then you have been on my mind even though every day has been jam-packed with activities since I've arrived at this base. During the day, I barely have a chance to breathe. But in the evenings, I have time to recall the memories we made together in Fairmont Park. The thoughts and fun we shared keep rumbling in my mind, and I hope that they mean as much to you as they do to me. You challenged some of my thinking, but most of all, I'm thankful for your humor and listening and caring. I'll never forget the carousel with its music, the cotton candy, and your zany acting out of surfing to Dick Dale and the Del-tones. And your kisses are perfect!

Luci, you brought humanness back into my life; you don't know how much I needed this after my grueling first year at the academy. There's a lot of talk about soul mates these days, and I'm wondering if I've met mine.

I'm now at an air force base near Sacramento. The countryside looks like that around the base in Riverside but without those beautiful mountains. And I don't think there's an Olmstead-designed park here either! About my routine, I'm doing what's called Ops AF—that's air force talk for Operations Air Force. During this assignment, I get to see how a base operates by rotating among the divisions and shadowing air force officers to see what they do. What has me psyched, though, is doing familiarization flights, flying in the different types of planes that are at the base. I'm scheduled on one tomorrow that will break the sound barrier, which should be thrilling!

I am invited to dinner at an officer's home tomorrow evening. They include these gatherings to help us understand air force family life and to try to give us a little feeling of home. But I can tell you it's no substitute for the real thing, and I can't wait to get back to good old Buffalo. I'm anticipating your visit when I get my three-week leave so we can make more memories (and so I can show you off to my family and friends). I'll need your Canadian address and phone number so my mom can write you a proper invitation to visit me. I hope your parents will say okay to your trip. Buffalo isn't that far from your grandmother's, but I guess we'll have to think about transportation to Buffalo for you. Perhaps a train or bus?

I can't wait to receive your first letter when I arrive home in a couple of weeks. Do you remember my address? 181 Blackhorse Road, Buffalo, NY

Was it just a week ago that my life changed because of you? Unquestionably you broke a few hearts last night at the final cadet dance. I sure hope another cadet hasn't stolen your heart. If he had, I'd pay any ransom to get it back. I can't get you out of my mind.

Completely in love with you, Barry

Reaching Barry's closing, Luci's heart took a long jump and leapt in her chest. The ending gave her chills of joy. She reread the letter several times, committing most of it to memory and treasuring Barry's expressions, feelings, and reminiscences. But the contrast between passages of tenderness and the description of daily activities posed more questions than they answered. *What does Barry mean by writing that the evening brought back humanness into his life? Was the first year at the academy so desensitizing that he thought he could lose his humanity?* She thought she understood the emotional challenges Barry faced, but apparently, she had not grasped their extent. *And what does he mean when he says I challenged some of his thinking? Is this about Vietnam, social justice issues, or something else?*

Luci was amused by his reference to another cadet stealing her heart. *No, Barry Callahan, I wouldn't allow any boy to steal my heart, including you.*

I will only give it freely to the one I genuinely love. Then Luci tenderly kissed the letter, refolded it, and placed it for safekeeping in the small Lane cedar-lined jewelry box on her dresser.

CHAPTER 14

Soul Mates and Revelations

ALTHOUGH the sunlight glimmered through the picture window in the living room, it could not overpower the darkening storm within. Marie paced back and forth. Eyebrows furrowing, she glowered at Sam, unable to control her ire. "Can you believe it, after the first date he says he is completely in love with Luci? What's this gushy stuff about memory making and perfect kisses? What were they up to in that stupid T-Bird of yours? Maybe they went to Freemont Park, but I assure you, they weren't feeding the damn ducks!"

"Marie, what's this?" Sam asked, his eyes widening and giving the paper that his wife had dropped in his lap a cursory look. "Is this Barry's letter to Luci?"

"Don't start with me!"

A veteran of Marie's melodramatic explosions, Sam was on the alert for the havoc they could wreak. His wife's rush to judgment and her meddling were often at the expense of others, and Sam knew he was in Marie's line of fire. In his wife's agitated state, Sam figured his best option was to listen without offering a critique. Arguing or suggesting she should calm down meant a verbal battle, and Sam would be the loser. Long ago, he realized the way to overcome one of Marie's tantrum storms was to give her space and time to work through her frustration.

"Marie, why does this letter have you so worked up?"

"Sam, you can't be serious! It's what that boy wrote in the damn letter that has me fired up," Marie said.

Sam believed that fear was at the root of most emotional outbursts and caused people to try to direct things beyond their control. Chastising Marie for reading Barry's letter and assailing Luci's privacy would not achieve much. Instead, identifying the underlying anxiety that caused his wife's frustration would work better. By showing her empathy, Sam hoped to reduce Marie's agitation. Guiding her to focus on changing what was within her limits, Sam believed, would dissuade her from destructive behaviors.

"Tell me, Marie, what exasperates you about a young man saying he is completely in love with your daughter? What makes you afraid of that romantic sentiment? After all, didn't I say something like that to you the night we first met?"

Marie rubbed her forehead with the tips of her fingers and ignored Sam's comparison to their relationship. "Don't you see?" she asked. "Luci has a sensitive disposition. She will fall for the crazy idea that she and this cadet are kindred souls. She'll limit her possibilities to know other people. She'll tie herself down before she understands who she is."

Sam nodded, keeping his eyes on Marie while fingering the letter in his hands and refusing to look at any more of its contents.

Marie continued with her harangue, her face blood red. "Luci is going to college in the fall and has the whole world before her. She's too young to be flirting with the thought of being completely in love, for Christ's sake! What does she know about love?"

Experience influenced Marie's objections. Since her marriage, she had often second-guessed her decision in accepting Sam's proposal. She relived the past, playing out should-haves and could-haves. She scolded herself for not feeling equal to her prosperous Irish cousins or entertaining their attention and likely marriage proposals. She put herself into a dizzying state, admonishing herself for straddling the line between the conventional and nonconventional. Her subconscious desire for control worked overtime, influenced by the examples of power exercised over her own life, and generated a cycle she found impossible to regulate or change. Marie's parental instinct may have been to protect Luci from a disappointing liaison, but her ambition to control events was stronger.

Sam shifted around in the seat of the Mission style rocker, tapping the fingers of his right hand on the chair's arm. *There's a lot to decode here, but to be fair, some of Marie's points have validity.* Sam, too, had concerns that his daughter, at eighteen years old, might get snarled into a long-distance and exclusive relationship with one person. Young sweethearts living happily ever after was a myth in Sam's experience. *Finding a companion to complete oneself is absolute rubbish; people fulfill themselves by being who they are and knowing and exploiting their strengths. My challenge isn't to discount Marie's concerns but to find a way to funnel them productively. Sneaking behind Luci's back and reading her letters will not end well.*

The finger tapping stopped, and Marie stared at Sam, knowing her husband had reached a conclusion. "Marie, I can't agree more with your concerns."

Marie stood frozen, pressing her lips into a fine line and studying her husband.

"Luci is young and impressionable," Sam said. "Barry is nice looking, has a good personality, attends a prestigious school, and, let's be honest, looks great in a uniform." Marie's glare softened, but she remained on alert. She flopped down in the chair opposite her husband, arms crossed over her chest, waiting to hear more.

"From the little I see here, Barry has a way with words—I'll give the boy that! It's too mushy for my taste, but to an eighteen-year-old girl, it's flattering. So, of course, Luci is fascinated by it."

Marie listened, her jaw still tense, suspicious of Sam's intentions. "So you agree with me on something! Now that we see eye to eye on this, we must find a way to tamp down this relationship, and the sooner, the better."

Sam's finger tapping resumed. He wasn't following his wife's logic why the relationship should end immediately, betting it would fizzle out on its own. *Pure puppy love!* Sam's immediate concern was that Marie's need for control was overtaking good judgment.

He stopped drumming his fingers and leaned back in the chair. "Marie, let's look at the positive side of the situation and at the options for solving the problem without stirring up unnecessary conflict. First, the romance may burn itself out. After all, Barry won't complete his training for three more years. By that time, both of them will have other experiences and will meet other people." He stopped speaking. As he pitched the rocker forward and backward, his foot brushing against the carpet was the only sound in the room.

The atmosphere was calming down. "Don't forget, Marie, Luci has a desire for independence. She doesn't like being tied down. My hunch is she won't choose to limit her freedom with an exclusive relationship."

Marie lowered her eyes and pinched the bridge of her nose. "You have a point, Sam," she said. "It would be a long-distance relationship, and those rarely last. But at the same time, I don't like leaving things to chance."

Rocking and closing his eyes, Sam tried to gather the right words. He knew that his wife's need for control still had the upper hand over judgment and trust. "Shouldn't we have some confidence in our daughter's judgment?" he asked. "She's seen the experiences of Adele and Darla and the ramifications of their impulsive decisions. Guiding Luci and putting faith in her good sense will achieve a better outcome than handing her an ultimatum or interfering."

Sam hoped these remarks would restrain Marie until the relationship had time to cool down of its own accord. Based on experience with his wife, though, he was pessimistic. Her concerns weren't altogether about Luci's protection, as she professed. Instead, Sam knew, they were more about controlling Luci's preference for someone of whom Marie did not approve; Marie needed to win.

Ignoring Sam's last statement, Marie's control machine revved up anew. "The trip to Buffalo won't happen. Luci's not going to be traipsing around the country and doing who knows what with that boy."

His wife's rationale for blocking Luci's trip to Buffalo mystified Sam. *What can Luci do in Buffalo that she couldn't do right here at home?* He'd give in to Marie's whim on the Buffalo trip with the hope that it was enough to curtail any future meddling she might have in mind.

* * *

Twenty-four hours after reading Barry's letter, Luci knew it was futile to entertain thoughts of visiting him in Buffalo. At first, she was overjoyed and wanted to shout out the prospect of the trip to the world. She was unaware that her mother had read Barry's letter, but Luci's sixth sense told her that Marie would never allow her to visit Buffalo.

How do I handle this situation? Luci debated with herself. *I could let things run their course, knowing Mom will refuse to let me go to Buffalo. Or I could make up a pretext for not being able to make the trip and tell Barry before he contacts his mother. Or before Barry's mother writes an invitation, I can be truthful with my parents and ask their permission to make the trip.*

Luci rejected the first two alternatives. Allowing Barry's mother to send a request and have Marie turn it down would be unfair and embarrassing to both her and Barry. To decline the invitation based on a made-up excuse would be untruthful. *Relationships are based on trust. Lying to Barry, even with good intentions, is not the right path. Being truthful with Pop, Mom, and Barry is the best choice.* Her decision made, Luci planned to present the idea of the Buffalo visit to her parents that evening and secure a response. *Whether it is negative or positive, I can truthfully accept or reject Barry's invitation.*

* * *

Thursday, June 23, 1966

Dear Barry,

I was so thrilled to receive your letter yesterday. I must admit your schedule seems as crazy as mine. I've been doing double the hours at the nursery school to make up for the time I will be on vacation. Eight hours with energetic three- and four-year-olds makes me want to collapse at the end of the day. I'm eager for the holiday in Canada, and I am getting things arranged for packing. We'll be leaving next Monday with stopovers in Vancouver and Lake Louise, and on July 5, we will arrive at my grandmother's home. I wish you were with me to make memories in the Canadian Rockies! But I'll write and give you all the details and make a note of things I think you'd enjoy.

Every night before I go to sleep, I keep replaying our evening together at the street dance, and then our memory making at Fairmont Park. I know that no matter what happens in the future, these will be meaningful times and ones that I will never forget. Someday, I will share with you my special meadow where I'm safeguarding all the memories we've made together.

I may have brought humanness back into your life, but you brought a lightning bolt into mine. You've given me new perspectives about the military. Before knowing you, my opinions were more cynical, framing the military in terms of Vietnam. My thought now is that rushing to judgments that support our underlying biases restricts our perspectives and reduces our opportunities for seeing and doing new things. I have decided to observe how many times I make decisions by jumping to conclusions instead of being open and curious about new things. I hope this will make me a better person, more sympathetic to others, and give me a deeper understanding of the world.

Your memories of our time together gave me goose bumps. Recalling how intense you were listening to my thoughts, my experiences, and my aspirations makes me feel valued. I'm glad that I brought humanness back into your life, but I'm also curious about what you mean by that. I know from our discussion that your year was challenging. I'm guessing there's more to tell—that there wasn't much room for you to be yourself at the academy. I hope I continue to bring humanness to your life and can support you in your dreams and being all that you want to be.

I have depressing news, though, to share with you about my visit to Buffalo. Knowing my mother's views, I thought it best to float the proposal to my parents before your mother wrote a formal invitation. I didn't want a negative response to embarrass you or your mother. As I expected, my mother said a visit was out of the question, and Pop backed her up. I'm so mortified and sad over my parents' response, although you knew I was skeptical that they would allow it. I don't have the resources to make the trip on my own, so for now, I don't see any alternatives for me coming to Buffalo this summer. I am crying myself to sleep tonight over it for so many reasons.

Do you honestly believe in soul mates, Barry? Like coincidences, I don't know if these exist. But given my pledge to hold my unconscious bias at bay, I'm leaving the gate WIDE open to explore that and more with you!

As I might say if I were writing to you in my French Canadian heritage: "Je vous donne un gros bec!" (I'm sending you a big kiss),

Luci

P.S. Unquestionably, I broke a few hearts at the last cadet dance, but nobody stole my heart. I won't allow any boy to take it; I will only give it freely to the one I genuinely love.

* * *

After writing the letter and sealing it with a sprinkle of Wind Song, Luci collapsed on her bed, verging on tears at the revelation she had to make to Barry. Turning down his invitation offset the happy emotions of writing to him. She felt her parents were unfair to be so strict. *What trouble could I have in Buffalo that I can't have in Fairmont Park? There are lots of possibilities for "occasions of sin" with Steve, Sean, Paul, or Chris or with the guys in Santa Monica. My parents don't object to me going out with any of them. Why do they consider the visit to Buffalo so different?*

Indeed, Luci was aware Shelia went more than halfway with Bob, and she knew girls who went all the way with their boyfriends. Premarital sex was a fact, wherever it happened. *My God*, she thought, *my own family is an example of that reality!*

Beyond Darla, it was true that girls got "in trouble" close to home; there was ample evidence of that in her neighborhood. Two unmarried girls had become pregnant in the past year. Like Darla, the women were sent secretly to a "home" for unwed mothers and were provided cover stories by their parents. In Stephanie's case, she was visiting her "aunt" in Washington State, and for Alice, she was attending "beauty school" in Pasadena. Unlike Darla, though, Stephanie and Alice surrendered their babies for adoption and returned home as if nothing had happened. Regardless of the guises, everyone knew the real story.

Luci detested the double standard that stigmatized unwed pregnant women as promiscuous but applauded male sexual escapades as daring and manly. *There's nothing courageous about not owning up to your responsibility to a child you've fathered*, Luci thought. Because of her family's experience, Luci understood the social victimization and emotional devastation unwed mothers went through and how it could affect the entire family. After Darla became pregnant, Marie forbade her to reveal or discuss the matter with other relatives or her closest friends. Even Luci's cousins were unaware of Darla's predicament. But when she married a few years later, and a new child "miraculously" appeared, everyone guessed the situation, anyway.

These experiences and their consequences guided Luci's thoughts: pregnancy outside marriage was something she wanted to avoid. This didn't mean, though, that she subscribed to the principle held by her religion that premarital sex was a sin. Sex before marriage was one of many topics associated with current social movements and issues addressed by Luci's Friday night pals. They argued that restricting sex to marriage wasn't based on a universal virtue. Instead, they reasoned, the phenomenon was cultural and often linked with religion. Having sex, married or not, they concurred, comes with a set of obligations and consequences like any decision. Respect for your sexual partner and taking precautions to avoid unwanted pregnancy and disease were among these responsibilities. *I'll make up my mind when it is right for me to have sex, and I will assume the responsibility for my decision.* One evening, Shelia had slipped Luci a couple of condoms, telling her, "Just in case!" and Luci accepted them without comment.

Shedding more tears would not overcome her parents' nixing the trip to Buffalo. And falling into depression was not going to change their decision or make her happy. *Wallowing in self-pity is a waste of energy. Pessimism robs people of their freedom. It closes your mind to possibilities and opportunities. It makes you a victim of your behavior,* she told herself. *I have a choice. I can weigh myself down being depressed, or I can change my mood.*

Thinking about the next evening with the Nerd group lifted Luci's spirits. It was true that Sean, Paul, and Chris went to nauseating cerebral extremes. Nevertheless, they were also humorous, creative, and fun. Yes, they were shameful when teasing Shelia and herself. But they never used their intellectual prowess to intimidate or disparage them or others. Taken as a whole, they were the best friends anyone could have, and Luci knew they would do anything for her. Before going to sleep, Luci took out a tiny notebook from the drawer of the bedside table. *I am thankful for having the Nerds in my life,* she wrote, *because they've opened a new world of freedom and thinking to me.* Smiling to herself, she replaced the journal and, in her meadow place, daydreamed about the memories she made with Barry and drifted off to sleep.

***

Early the next evening, Luci's friends picked her up for their weekly event. Shelia and the guys had planned a farewell celebration for Luci before she left on vacation, so they headed to San Bernardino to splurge on burgers and shakes before hitting the movies. With no air conditioning in the van, everyone was sweltering in the ninety-degree heat. "Jeez, Sean, can you put your foot on it and get this tin can moving so we can get some air through the windows?" Sheila commanded.

Sean looked up in the rearview mirror at his sister. "And who is going to pay for the ticket?"

"Don't be such a smart ass!"

"Wow! You've finally said it out loud—I'm smart."

The brother and sister banter went on for twenty minutes, with occasional inputs from the others in the van, until they arrived at the iconic diner noted for its fast preparation of hamburgers, fries, and milkshakes. It was a preferred hangout of the younger set, and even with the high temperature, the place was teeming with young adults looking for fun on a Friday evening.

Lingering in line at the outside order counter, Chris plastered on a smile as a couple of cute girls flirted with him. Not one to ignore attention, Chris ate up being in the spotlight while his two gal pals smirked.

"Shameless," Shelia said to Luci, adding, "What else would you expect from Chris Casanova?"

Out of the corner of her eye, Luci caught Chris's wink. *What a show-off,* she thought and then winked back at him.

After paying for their orders, the group moseyed to the van to eat their greasy food feast. "I don't know what the hell I'm thinking, going to summer school," Sean said, popping a fry drenched with ketchup into his mouth. "Taking these classes shortens my time to graduation, which means it shortens my time to getting drafted. Even if I go on for my master's degree, I hear rumblings that deferments for graduate school are being discontinued. Accelerating the completion of my degree may not be the most brilliant idea I've had."

The war was hitting closer to home every day. News stories of the deaths of area servicemen were becoming more common. Since March, eight area men were casualties of the Vietnam War. Two weeks earlier, the local paper headlined the explosion of a C-130 airplane on a wartime mission that resulted in the death of an airman from nearby Highland. With thirty-five thousand men drafted each month, the specter of military service hung like a dark, dense cloud over the group.

As he sipped his soft drink, Chris gradually lost his easygoing, girl-magnet charm and turned reserved. "We're all in the same crazy boat," he said. "You'll graduate a semester after me, Sean, but the way the war is going, I don't think it makes much of a difference."

"I've heard the same rumors about grad school," Paul said with a grim twist of his mouth.

Chris was steaming, but it was not from his encounter with the flirtatious girls or the sweltering heat in the van. "I hate the draft hanging over me and every day worrying if 'Greetings from Uncle Sam' have arrived in the mail. And I can't stand the notion of trying to figure out a workaround to avoid the draft. Faking a stupid injury or leaving the country to avoid being drafted is not a choice for me."

The air became close in the van. Realizing the effect his last statements had on the group, Chris attempted to lighten things up. "Besides all that, even marrying a cute girl no longer gets you a deferment," he said, looking toward Luci and throwing her a broad grin.

"Oh, gross! I thought you already graduated from junior high," Shelia said while hitting Chris playfully on the back.

"So what's the choice?" Paul asked.

Chris ran his fingers through his thick, curly hair. "I'm going to use Luci's three-choice-doctrine she's always yakking about. I can sit around, give in to it, and get depressed. I can pretend it's all an illusion, which is damn stupid. Or I can take action to control the events. Luci, you will be proud. I've decided on option three, take action," he said, giving his gal pal a nudge. "I'm going to enlist."

All five suspended what they were doing until Paul, after almost choking on his burger, found his voice. "You've got to be kidding. What the heck! What's gotten into your head? Are you crazy, man?"

It was soundless after Paul's outburst, and Luci felt as if she were viewing a silent movie in slow motion. *It can't be true! This is nuts! He's going to get himself killed.* On the verge of tears, Luci could not imagine Chris in a war zone.

Luci's face turned red. "This is one hell of a farewell celebration for me. Why would you even consider this, Chris?"

"Well, Luci, I hear you've been consorting with airmen, and that you like the looks of a man in uniform. I wanted to catch your attention," Chris said, trying humor to diffuse the situation.

Luci set her eyes on her target in a deadpan stare. "This is nothing to be glib about. Stop trying to be funny; it isn't working, and you are not amusing. You are walking on thin ice here, dude. This isn't teasing anymore; it's cruel."

Chris's posture stiffened, and he burned with embarrassment. "Jeez, Luci, I'm sorry," he said, squirming in his seat. "I didn't mean to get you all jazzed up."

With a steely gaze that made Chris want to crawl under the seat, Luci gave her friend another dose of grief. "If I could use the "F" word on you, Chris DeLuca, I would. Real friends, Chris, get upset if they think their buddies are making a mistake. Real friends tell you they are pissed-off at you for acting like a jerk," she said, poking her finger in Chris's shoulder. "Why on earth would you enlist? And why would you make a joke about it?" Luci asked, her voice quivering.

Everyone in the van shifted in their seats, and Shelia caught Sean and Paul rolling their eyes at each other.

"You're right, Luci. This is nothing to joke about, and I guess I did it because I'm a little nervous about the decision myself. I was trying to lighten things up. That was stupid of me. I shouldn't have sprung this on any of you," Chris said, scanning the face of each member of the group.

As the nominal leader, Sean took a calmer approach. "I get what you're saying, buddy. We all live with that black cloud looming over us. There isn't a one-size-fits-all decision. So what's the thinking behind your plan? I know there's more to it."

Everyone held their tongues, waiting for his reply. Chris took a deep breath, figuring he owed his pals an explanation.

"As I said, I see three options: sit back and worry, pretend this isn't real, or take matters into my own hands. I have no control over the probability that I am going to have to serve, but I do have control over how I will serve. I don't plan on ending up like our former classmate Gary. He gets drafted. Then on induction day, a sergeant goes down the line of the new recruits and pulls out every fourth one and says, 'You're going to the marines.' Gary has been in Vietnam for less than six months, and he already has two purple hearts. No, I don't want to be that situation. I want to have a choice," Chris said, his voice shaking.

No one responded. As the group took in their friend's words, Luci winced, thinking of her verbal explosion to Chris's announcement. *Crap! I just told Barry that I was going to stop jumping to conclusions. Now, look at what I've done. Instead of being open-minded, I ran right down the judging rabbit hole.*

Sean spoke up for his buddy. "Chris, I know you make sense out of the world by looking at things differently than all of us. And that's great; your perspective is one of your strengths. And you're not afraid of anything—you jump right in. Remember last summer at Doheny beach when you ran into the surf to save that kid, even though there were rip tides? That was real courage, man!"

Chris lifted an eyebrow. "Umm, Sean. I don't know. That example might have canceled your perspective on my perspective!" At this, everyone laughed, and the grave tone in the van broke. Chris scooted to the edge of his seat. "Here's the plan. I'll have this hotshot chemistry degree soon. You know my life's vision is to be *the mad scientist* who cracks the cure for cancer through pharmaceutical research, right?"

Picking up on Chris's humor, Shelia responded. Well, great balls of fire —if it isn't the mad scientist. What fiddle-faddle, dear! You have entertained us for years with that tale. What has this got to do with enlisting? Or should I say, procuring or maybe soliciting?" All of the group laughed, getting into the spirit of Shelia's humor and her silly portrayal of a 007 ingénue.

"That's shocking, my dear. Positively shocking," Chris declared, attempting to throw a self-satisfied, James Bond look in Shelia's direction. Luci caught his expression too. As if noticing his good looks for the first time, she thought, *Chris has it all over Sean Connery!*

Chris let out a heavy sigh. "Seriously, though, the medical corps has pharmacy technician positions open. I've talked with the recruiter about these. With my background in chemistry, I can try for that position. Of course, I'll have to enlist for three years, instead of serving two years as a draftee. But for me, the extra time in the service is worth it. I'll have my choice of work, and I'll be getting training in a field that will pay off later."

Everyone assessed Chris's reasoning. Then Paul threw his friend a curveball. "Aren't pharmacy technicians classified as medics?" The group remained quiet, understanding Paul's angle.

Chris grasped the implication. "Yes, they are."

"Chris, you get that being a medic puts you right in harm's way. Medics aren't only stationed at field hospitals. In this war, medics are armed, and they are not identified with red crosses on their helmets or armbands. They go out and live with the units they serve, and they're making up many of the casualties in this war," Paul said.

Chris chose his words deliberately. "I get that, Paul. The point is not whether I am in a combat zone; for me, it's about saving lives, not taking them."

Luci gazed out the van window with mist building in her eyes. *This evening I made a stupid, snap decision when it would have been better to listen and ask Chris why he was enlisting. Berating myself won't change what I did, but I must let Chris know as soon as I can that I understand and respect his choice.*

CHAPTER 15

Contingency Plan

THE kitchen sucked in the July heat like a magnet. *There never were more accurate words,* Luci thought, connecting with the lyrics blaring from the radio as she washed the noonday dishes. *This town is hot, and it sure is summer.*

Luci's grandmother, Geneviève, was old school: no air conditioning in her home! "Summer is the time to absorb the warmth and humidity. It thaws the bones and moistens the skin. If God had wanted summer to be cold, he would have made winter last all year," her grandmother asserted. As a result, the household sweltered through the dog days, and everyone within it felt as jumpy as frogs on hot concrete much of the time.

With her mother and grandmother on an all-day excursion to Windsor, Luci smiled, grateful for the solitude to let loose her daydreams. *What unexpected twists have happened during the past three weeks,* she thought. An amusing and chance encounter on her train trip had added to her collection of memories. But it was an unlikely alliance that warmed her heart and another surprise that made her spirit soar.

* * *

Showing the pandering side of her personality, Marie was an agreeable companion throughout the rail journey on the Western Coast of the United States and through the Canadian Rockies. She displayed a remarkable sense of humor with the train stewards, and she was tolerant of the small inconveniences that were inevitable on such a long trip. Fellow passengers found her friendly. She engaged them in lighthearted conversation and projected a *bon vivant* lifestyle that impressed people she'd never meet again. Luci didn't mind Marie playing the social matron; after all, it allowed her the freedom to pursue her own interests without her mother's supervision. Marie's ability to flip the personality switch with ease mystified Luci. *How can she be an accommodating, gregarious, free spirit at one time and so anxious and alienating at another?*

To describe her mother as a two-faced personality would be the most straightforward response. But instinctively, Luci knew better. She had overheard Sam telling Adele one time, "Your mother is a complex and troubled woman." Those words stuck in Luci's mind and begged the question, *Why is she troubled*? Untangling the web of Marie's behavior, however, was not easy for her eighteen-year-old daughter.

If there was one thing Marie knew how to do well, it was traveling in style. She booked first-class tickets on the Canadian Pacific Railway's premier passenger train, noted for its stylish accommodations, spectacular route, and dramatic scenery. Between Vancouver and Calgary, the dome car offered six hundred miles of unobstructed views of the rugged Rockies. Luci soaked in vistas of towering mountains and rushing torrents of waterway gorges like the mighty Kicking Horse River. Viewing and crossing engineering feats such as the Stoney Creek Bridge was the same as getting an extra dollop of whipped cream on an ice cream sundae.

Booking a two-day layover at the grand turn-of-the-century Chateau Lake Louise in the heart of the Canadian Rockies, Marie did not forgo extravagance. The hotel, situated at the foot of a pristine emerald-colored lake nestled among the soaring peaks of the Pipestone Range, had four hundred luxury guest rooms.

Entering the impressive Chateau lounge when they first arrived, Luci stood transfixed, overwhelmed by the view through the large floor-to-ceiling windows. The blend of the incandescent jeweled-colored lake, framed by glaciers of thickened ice and surrounded by forested mountains whose peaks stretched to the clouds, created a breathtaking panorama that gave Luci goose bumps.

Enhancing the vista was an expansive lawn with gardens of multihued Iceland poppies flowing like a magic carpet from the hotel to a roughly hewn log fence at the lake's edge. Beyond, a narrow footpath hugged the lake and invited guests into the surrounding wilderness.

On the second morning of her stay, Luci walked alone along the trail, and wide-eyed, she absorbed the incredible view surrounding her. Dense conifer forests edged one side of the footpath, and lake waters lapped hypnotically on the other. Closing her eyes momentarily, Luci inhaled the pristine pine-scented air. Holding its force in her expanded lungs, she slowly exhaled, envisioning the energy flowing through the length and breadth of her body. As she emptied extraneous thoughts from her mind, a cacophony of sounds from the world around her emerged: water rippling on the shore, tree limbs rustling in a gentle breeze, and birds emitting cheerful songs. "This is memory making," Luci whispered. Afterward, she couldn't contain her eagerness to convey her feelings to Barry. *The experience is incredible. It's a gift that cries out to be shared. Holding its force inside of me would stifle its beauty and meaning.*

At dusk that evening, Luci walked through the hotel's block-long enclosed loggia next to the main lobby, looking for a quiet place to write to Barry. Strolling slowing through the gallery, Luci spotted a small desk positioned at the end of the long colonnade. Secluded, it faced a window overlooking the inspiring scene she had experienced earlier that morning. Taking a seat at the writing table, Luci retrieved a sheet of the elegant Chateau stationery from the desk's drawer and then allowed her emotions and thoughts to rush like a river during a spring thaw.

Sunday, July 3, 1966 – Chateau Lake Louise

Dear Barry,

We arrived in Lake Louise on Dominion Day, July 1. This is Canada's celebration of becoming a self-governing dominion of Great Britain. It's sort of like our Fourth of July in the United States. We've been here two days, and there are no words I can find to describe the beauty of the Canadian Rockies and this place in particular.

Chateau Lake Louise, to be sure, lives up to its name. It sits at an altitude of over a mile, and it is the grandest hotel in which I have ever stayed. The views are dramatic. Our room overlooks the lake and beyond to the imposing 11,000-foot Mt. Victoria and its impressive glacier.

Towering, snowcapped mountains that seem to touch the clouds surround the Chateau. The lake in front of it sits at the bottom of the valley like a little teacup and is the most magnificent turquoise color I've ever seen. I'm told the hue is caused by the deposits from the glacial runoff of shards from a specific type of rock. Despite its smaller size, I've never seen such a distinctive and commanding lake. From time to time, I see couples gliding on the lake canoeing, looking as if they had no cares except to soak in the beauty of this place. I keep wondering what it might be like to make memories like that with you.

If these views weren't enough to make my spirit sing, an expansive lawn and terraced gardens surround the Chateau and slope to the water's edge. When I see that sprawling turf, I feel like a three-year-old and want to run like a bandit with my arms outstretched across all of it. Of course, I've restrained myself and didn't do this, but in my mind's eye, I experienced it regardless!

A big surprise was the gigantic outdoor swimming pool that is filled with warmed water from the glacier. I went swimming, but I didn't have many companions since the outside temperature wasn't even 60 degrees! Glass walls surrounding the pool, allowed a stunning vista to engulf me, and I felt as if I had become one with the scene. As I stepped out of the water, the cold air hit me like a thunderbolt. It felt like I would shiver to death, and I made a beeline to the dressing room to dry off and change into warm clothes. But still, my teeth continued chattering.

Today I had the most awe-inspiring walk along the small pathway around the lake. Barry, I devoured the moments and breathed in the energy of this mountain paradise. I let it consume me. The smell of the pine trees, the melodic lapping of the lake, the electric blue sky, and the jumbo-sized clouds playing hide-and-seek among the mountain peaks all came together, and it challenged my senses in the most incredible way. But there was more to come! I had stopped walking for a little while and closed my eyes to allow the moment to overtake me. When I opened them again, I saw that the lake was transformed into an enchanting mirror image of everything around it. As if it could be possible, the mountains, the conifer forests, the glacier, and the sky and clouds were duplicated, giving me unanticipated double pleasure. This is memory making! Just like you, the magic here that has put a spell on me and captured my heart! And I am so grateful for both. I know there is memory making in our future in this enchanted place.

Tomorrow we start for Toronto, but leaving this place is bitter-sweet. Like you, Lake Louise has captured my heart and is insepa-rable from me. Sharing the intoxication of this place with you has bound both together. Saying goodbye to one is the same as bidding farewell to the other.

We expect to arrive at my grandmother's home late Wednesday evening. I will be glad to reach our destination, not because it's been a long trip but because I know there will be a letter from you waiting for me. I still am bummed out that we can't get together on your leave. But I concentrate on our memories and recreate those in my meadow place, and that makes things right again.

Je t'envoie mille baisers, (I send you a thousand kisses), Luci

* * *

René Gagne materialized like a rainbow after a morning rain. Over six feet tall with a muscular physique, intense violet-blue eyes, a cleft in his chin, and the look of Gregory Peck, the young rail conductor had a captivating physical presence. A university student from Montreal, René had taken the railroad gig for the past two years during summer breaks. Luci turned his head when she boarded the train at the Lake Louise station, and he decided she was a girl he wanted to know better. René's winning smile and playful personality endeared him on the spot to Luci and Marie. When he welcomed the duo aboard with a French greeting, Marie responded, "*Bon-jour! Comment allez vous?*" Recognizing from Marie's accent that she was fluent in French, René engaged her in banter in his native language as he ushered mother and daughter to their first-class cabin. Turning to Luci, he asked, "*Et vous mademoiselle, parlez-vous aussi le français?*" It didn't take long for him to realize that Luci's speech was rudimentary, and René jumped at the chance to offer his help in perfecting her French language skills.

The first evening, after his work had slowed, René had escorted Luci to the end of the observation car to begin her first French lesson. Smiling at Luci and with an air of mischief, he said, "We won't go into boring verb conjugation."

Sitting down in the offered chair next to the one taken by René, Luci smiled back coyly. "Whew! Am I glad to hear that! But *what* did you have in mind, Monsieur Gagne?"

"Ah, *phrases a'mitié*," René said. Leaning in and gazing into her eyes, he took her hand then spoke in a muted tone, "*Puis, des phrases pour les amoureux*," and waited to see if Luci understood.

Hearing René enunciate the French words in dreamy tones made Luci feel like crumbling into pieces. Regaining her composure and not doubting he used this line as a regular pickup tactic, she giggled, signaling to René that she was on to his game. Returning his gaze, she confirmed, "So friendship phrases first, then phrases for lovers. *C'est bonne!* How do we start?" she asked, sitting up straight like an attentive student.

René threw his head back and laughed. He understood immediately that Luci wasn't a girl to be fooled by his romantic come-on. "*Commençons par devenir amis*," he suggested, eyes twinkling.

"Starting as friends, I like that," Luci agreed, flipping her shoulder-length hair behind her right ear, a gesture that René found enticing.

They progressed in lighthearted stages, huddled together, flirting with each other under the guise of developing Luci's French proficiency. He regaled her with words of friendship, requiring her to repeat them and then corrected her pronunciation. She, in turn, desired to experience the intensity of his gaze and hear his enchanting accent again. She played the coquette, and tilted her head toward him, lips upturned, and requested he restate a phrase.

Every now and again, René veered from friendship phrases and slipped in a romantic expression. Each time he attempted this, Luci chastised him as if he were a four-year-old. Wagging a finger in his face, she said to him, "*Mechant garcon!*" He would laugh, give her a hangdog expression, pretending he was a bad boy, and the cycle would start over.

Half an hour of playing cat and mouse was enough for Luci. "Okay, kindergarten is over! I want to hear about René." *If I am going to spend an entire evening with this dreamboat, I want more than flirting and teasing. I want to open his gift-wrapped exterior to see the stuff deeper inside of him.*

René didn't overlook an opportunity to tease. "If it's going to get you past friendship phrases, then *oui!*"

Luci, raising both hands to her cheeks, hurled him a look of mock disbelief. "*Ah, monsieur, peut-être!*" she said, fluttering her eyelashes, indicating *maybe*.

Luci was her father's daughter. She knew by asking someone a question and listening undistracted to the response, she made it easy for people to confide in her. Her technique worked with René, who, in no time, was telling Luci his hopes for the future.

He was studying business administration and wanted to secure a position in banking after graduation. Montreal, René reminded Luci, had always been the financial center of Canada. Even though it was being challenged by Toronto for the number-one position in Canada, he thought Montreal would become a world financial center.

Beyond these aspirations, René held the view of his immediate family of "Quebec first, Canada second," and he questioned whether a solution between the Francophile and Anglophile divide could be achieved. Luci had heard her relatives debate the issue of Quebec separatism during conversations in the evenings on her grandmother's front porch. She understood that the long history of war and conquest between the French and English would not be easily overcome. The motto *Je me souviens*, meaning a collective "We remember," rang in her ears and were words that she often heard her relatives use for keeping the history, traditions, and culture of Quebec alive.

Luci thought René would make a fun-loving boyfriend. He also had the *joie de vivre* that she supposed attracted her great-grandmother Lucinda to Antoine. René's quick humor and storytelling about fur trapping and moose hunting in northern Quebec left Luci no trouble envisioning him as a high-spirited and fearless *coureur de bois* of Canadian voyageur days. He mesmerized Luci with his rich baritone voice as he sang songs of the Voyageurs, all under the guise of improving her French. Their final evening together, René had the entire observation railcar joining in on the refrains of well-known French Canadian ballads. She began to understand how difficult it was to resist a nature like René's, not to mention how his French accent made a girl's heart turn to mush.

Even with these qualities, he can't compare to Barry, Luci thought. What Barry didn't possess in a rugged appearance or a rollicking personality was offset by inner strength and self-assurance. Barry's character wasn't measured by the intensity of his vibrant blue eyes, flashing smile, or handsome, chiseled features. And it wasn't his genuineness, subtle humor, and lightheartedness that made Barry tower over others in Luci's eyes—it was his belief that he served a purpose higher than himself. For two evenings, René was a nice distraction, but nothing more than that.

* * *

Luci and Marie arrived early in the evening at Geneviève's home. Tired, they dragged their suitcases up the narrow staircase to their separate rooms on the second floor before joining Geneviève on the screened-in front porch.

"Ma Bichette, I have your favorite iced drink, Vernor's ginger ale, ready for you," Geneviève said as Marie and Luci sat down. Luci's grandmother, or *grand-mère*, as her granddaughter called her, referred to Luci as "Ma Bichette." When Geneviève saw Luci after she was born, she was enthralled by her granddaughter's big, doe-like brown eyes. Thus, Ma Bichette stuck, and rarely did she call Luci by her given name.

Geneviève presided from her comfortable 1930s hickory rocking chair and sipped an iced brandy while enjoying Marie and Luci's tales of adventure. With a lively personality, thick salt-and-pepper hair coiffed in a modern bob, and her nails manicured a bright red, Geneviève's appearance belied her age of eighty years old.

"Oh, Chateau Lake Louise, so romantic, and Monsieur Gagne sounds wonderful," Geneviève twittered after Marie and Luci shared the high-points of their adventures.

Reciprocating with stories of her own, Geneviève dished out the latest gossip about relatives and friends. Locals referred to Geneviève as the social maven of the town, and this evening, she lived up to that title. "Do I have a calendar set up for the two of you! Dates are booking up fast with invitations for dinner and luncheons."

Giddy, Geneviève couldn't hold back sharing the schedule of events. "There's dinner with the Dumouchel sisters for this Saturday evening at that gorgeous summer home they have on the Detroit River. Lucille is planning on seeing us for Sunday dinner at her adorable cottage on Lake Erie. Vic and Lenore called and want to set up a date for dinner next week. Of course, Maurice and his housemate insist we set aside an evening with them at their home on the river. And, oh yes, Father D wants to take us to the supper club in Kingsville."

Luci displayed a wide grin as her grandmother ticked off dinner and luncheon dates. "Grand-mère, we might not have to make lunch or dinner for ourselves during the entire time we are here."

"That's the plan, Ma Bichette. That's the plan," she said with a Cheshire-cat smile.

Limitless visiting and cavorting with extended family and friends made up the summer tradition at Geneviève's house. The octogenarian had jet-propelled stamina, and Luci marveled at how her grandmother's endurance outlasted hers or Marie's. Relaxed conversations sprinkled with gossip, friendly banter, and expressions of concern and affection comprised the get-togethers. Dinner tables were decorated with fragrant garden flowers and overflowed with delicious homemade food. Impatient, everyone talked over each other. Without taking a breath, they shared the latest scuttlebutt and told stories of escapades that happened over a hundred years before to those in the present. These were times of memory sharing and memory making. For Luci, the gatherings represented the joy of being home and feeling accepted without any condition.

"Oh, Ma Bichette, I almost forgot! You have letters waiting from two admirers," Geneviève said. Jumping up from her chair, the old matron scurried to retrieve the envelopes from the dining room sideboard.

Marie bristled. *One of these must be from that cadet. But who might have written the other one? Or worse, are there two letters from that boy?*

"Who are these young men?" Geneviève asked as if she were Agatha Christie. Examining the envelopes before handing them over, she added, "I see from the return addresses one is named Barry, and the other is Chris. Oh, Ma Bichette, I need to hear all about them. Hurry, open them, and read them to me."

Marie gave Luci a deadpan stare. "Yes, read them to us, Luci. I'd like to hear what they have to say too."

Luci ignored her mother's comment and coyly smiled at Geneviève. "Grand-mère, who said these are from young men? They could be from older men, could they not?"

Geneviève sat straight up in her chair, eyes opened wide, half-believing her granddaughter.

"Either way, they are top secret," she said with a wink.

Geneviève chuckled and leaned closer to Luci. "Oh, now it's a mystery! Perhaps this is private from your mother, but not from your grand-mère? You can share them with me later. You know, your grand-mère relishes a good romance," she said, patting her granddaughter's hand.

Marie stiffened and fumed in silence. *Right when I was enjoying myself, mother inserts her busybody self between my daughter and me. She relishes a good romance, my ass! She never relished one when it involved me.*

What's in Barry's letter? Luci wondered, fidgeting in her chair. Holding the letters, every ticktock of the mantel clock made concentration on her grandmother's conversation more hopeless. While Marie babbled about the trip and the latest gallery showing of her paintings, Geneviève detected Luci's restlessness. Issuing a polite yawn and covering it with a delicate tap across her lips, Geneviève signaled that visiting time was over, and she rose from her chair.

Before going to her bedroom, Geneviève leaned over to kiss her granddaughter goodnight and whispered, "Happy dreams, dear." Luci understood the sentiment, and it confirmed that she and Geneviève were now in league with each other.

* * *

Dizzy with anticipation, Luci entered her room but stifled the urge to rip open the envelopes in her hand. *It would be typical of Mom to drop by while I am reading my letters and snoop.* Instead, Luci undressed, slipped into bed, and placed the letters under her pillow. Her instinct was correct. A few minutes later, Marie stopped at Luci's door but, seeing the light turned off, proceeded down the hall to her own room.

Waiting until Marie had fallen to sleep, Luci turned on the table lamp next to her bed. Removing the letters from under her pillow, she placed Chris's envelope on the top, deciding to read his first. *Wow, he wrote, after all,* Luci thought, recalling the promise Chris made to her the evening of her outburst over his planned army enlistment.

That night, walking with Chris to the refreshment stand during the movie intermission, Luci had hoped to rectify her impulsive behavior. Apprehensive, she began her apology. "Um, Chris, I don't know how to begin, so I will come straight out with it. I'm sorry for mouthing off at you this evening. I shouldn't have said the "F" word thing." Relieved to get the first sentences said, the rest of her words tumbled out. "Sean is right. You always have good judgment, Chris. I'm sorry I put my foot in my mouth like a jackass and totally dismissed you."

Chris stroked his chin, staring at Luci. He hadn't expected an apology, nor had he felt any was needed. It was true their small group got into heated debates arguing different sides on many topics. But these never changed the affection and esteem they held for each other. A wave of heat climbed up Chris's face. He respected and had a fondness for Luci, but with this expression of concern, both took on more meaning.

"Jeez, Luci, you didn't have to apologize for sounding off. You don't play games by saying things you think people want to hear. That's what I like about you." He paused to give his statement weight then reverted to his joking manner. "And of course, I never thought for a moment you were dismissing me! I mean, how could you reject a good-looking guy like me?" he asked, his eyes twinkling, catching the lights from the concession stand.

Luci punched his shoulder and gave him a side-glance. "Chris DeLuca, you are so full of yourself! Like, you think every girl should fall for your pretty face."

Chris chuckled. "Got that right!" he said, nudging her back.

Chris had admired Luci from afar. His feelings of affection had grown for her over the past year. Now he wasn't going to let the opportunity for a closer relationship slip through his fingertips. With Luci's apology and finding himself alone with her, Chris acted on an impulse and unloaded his feelings.

"For sure, Luci, this was a huge decision for me. To be honest, deep inside, I'm afraid. I'd be nuts if I weren't. But if I allow fear to rule my life, I will never feel the joy of experiencing or accomplishing anything."

"There's fear, and then there's risk. I don't think the two are the same," Luci challenged.

Chris weighed Luci's statement. "You're right; they are not the same. Not to get all nerdy on you, Luci, but there's this psychologist, Abraham Maslow. He says that life is a process, and every day we make decisions between safety and risk. If we always stay on the safe side, we stop growing and never fulfill our potential. You know, there's that old saying, 'Better safe than sorry,' but I like saying 'Safe but sorry.' I think my version is better. I don't want to end my life, Luci, dwelling on all the should-haves or could-haves that I didn't do because I was afraid."

Without constraint, Chris shared his aspirations and innermost thoughts with Luci. She knew these from the Nerd group discussions, but in this one-on-one exchange, they came across as more profound and personal. He believed real happiness was not found in fleeting pleasures like buying a new car or getting a new pair of shoes. "Lasting happiness comes from contributing to something bigger than yourself," he said.

Before they returned to the others, Chris took Luci's hand in his and met her eyes. "I want to be inspired in life—feel real stuff like love, joy, gratitude, and pride in my accomplishments. These are the things, Luci, that make a person happy."

Sharing his sentiments, not to mention clasping her hand, caught Luci speechless. The emotional intimacy Chris now felt between himself and Luci made him recognize that it had been a long time since he had confided in someone so openly. Feeling that Luci filled that void this evening, Chris acted on another impulse.

"Hey, Luci, I'd like to write to you while you're gone. You know, get in practice for when I'm a soldier boy," he said, lightening up the moment.

"Are you for real? Luci asked, feeling off-balance.

"You bet I am! After spouting out my feelings tonight, do you think I want to stop? After all, every guy needs a shoulder to cry on." Not wanting to scare Luci by thinking this was more than a pal-to-pal request, even though in his heart, it was, he added, "C'mon kid, what's your address in Canada?"

* * *

After reading Chris's letter, Luci reflected. *He sure can't be accused of being a romantic or emotional letter writer. Considering how he poured his heart out the last time we were together, I'm surprised he didn't express more of his feelings.*

Then again, the Chris that she knew was a matter-of-fact guy with an embedded sense of humor that revealed itself when least expected. His letter followed this form. He described a *Life* magazine article that focused on priests frustrated by blind obedience to dogma who advocated for shared authority and liberalizing the church.

> *Luci, the opinions of these clergy line up with what we believe. They are concerned with issues like civil rights, opposition to the war and celibacy, and support for artificial birth control. Remember my flippant remark to Father Vincent that I was considering being a Jesuit, and he shot back that I was even too liberal for that order! How funny, but he was damned right!*

Chris went on to describe the importance of a recent Supreme Court decision and later mixed in some stereotypical humor about the Canadian frontier.

The Miranda v. Arizona ruling is momentous! You might not have heard about it, up in the wild hinterland. The court upheld that people have Fifth Amendment protection against self-incrimination as soon as they are taken into custody. This means that police, before interrogating suspects, must warn them that anything they say can be held against them and that they have a right to have a lawyer present during questioning. This is big, Luci. This is the hallmark of real civil rights for everyone.

Although not capturing the entirety of the precedent-making decision, Luci could tell by Chris's fervor that this was significant.

Besides critiques of magazine articles and the last movie he and the Nerds saw, Chris ended the letter describing the mechanics for enlisting in the army. It was in the postscript placed at the bottom of the message, though, that his playfulness, and perhaps something more profound, emerged.

P.S. Be wary of those handsome Royal Canadian Mounted Police dressed in their flashy red dress uniforms. They're famous for getting their man and their girl! I don't want them stealing your heart and preventing you from returning to the guy who loves you most.

Luci reread his last lines several times. They made her heart skip a beat. *What an odd statement. What does he mean by the guy who loves me the most?* she pondered. She dared not assume it had any meaning beyond Chris's usual joking and put the remark out of her mind.

Barry's message was another matter. Opening the envelope, Luci saw it was written on July 3. *The same day that I wrote to Barry! Coincidence or ESP or perhaps both,* she mused, smiling to herself. His letter was short, but it left Luci reeling.

July 3, 1966

Dearest Luci,

Your letter was waiting for me when I arrived home. Even though I was thrilled to be back in Buffalo with my family, receiving your note topped even that!

I told my family all about you, and I shared your graduation picture with them that you sent to me in your letter. Joe says you are a dish. He's a flirt, and I'm not going to let him near you! I love my brother, but all is fair in love and war! Besides, he isn't as cute as me and doesn't have my great personality, so I doubt you'd fall for him, anyway. And oh yes, my little sister is crazy about the little-stuffed dog you gave me to give to her the evening I was at your home. She is dragging that poor toy everywhere she goes, including the bathroom!

I'm so disappointed that you can't visit me here in Buffalo. I had so many plans for what we would do. Of course, going to Cazenovia Park was first on the list, then Niagara Falls, the home of Thunder God, and also Crystal Beach across the border.

But all is not lost! I have a BIG surprise for you. A favorite motto of my dad is, "If you are going to get what you want in life, you have to have a contingency plan in your back pocket." So I had one ready in case you couldn't make the trip to Buffalo. The fallback is that I am coming to see you!

With a little arm-twisting and bribing, Joe agreed to lend me his car. It's about 250 miles from here to your grandmother's, and I figure I can make the trip from Buffalo in about five or six hours. Plan on me arriving on the afternoon of Friday, July 15. Unfortunately, I need to make the visit short and leave for home on Sunday. Joe's a great brother, but he has his limits when it comes to his car!

Don't worry about accommodations. Since this trip is so unexpected, I don't want to put anyone out, so I've found my own place to stay. I did a little checking around through the local business association in that area, and they recommended a place called the Blue Heron.

Luci, I can't wait to see you again. Did anyone ever tell you that you have a sultry voice and dazzling brown eyes? They captivate and take total control over me. I am spellbound when I'm with you. You make it easy for me to share my innermost feelings, even my worries, and my insecurities. I've never expressed myself like this to anyone before, much less put it all in writing. When we talk, you are right there with me, and your presence makes me feel understood and accepted. I am counting the hours, not the days, until I can hold you in my arms again: 282 hours, and it seems an eternity to wait and so unfair.

Still completely in love with you, Barry XO

* * *

Finished with drying the dishes, Luci replaced them in the cupboard. Afterward, she went to the open kitchen window and leaned her elbows on the sill, letting the breeze from the Detroit River rustle through her hair. She gazed dreamingly across the expansive front lawn of her grand-mère's home. *Forty-eight hours until Barry arrives.*

CHAPTER 16

Geneviève's Front Porch

"BUMMER," Barry mouthed as he tinkered with the mechanic's tools. *This car will never get me to Canada tomorrow.* The previous evening, the car, not the most reliable of vehicles, let out a grinding noise when Joe and Barry exited the parking lot of a local tavern. Unable to shift out of first gear, Joe couldn't get the car past fifteen miles per hour. *Damn!* Barry thought as they crawled home, and he tried to come up with options if the Bug proved unfixable. *Is there a bus or train I can take? Can I borrow a car from someone else? I could always hitchhike.* All the choices felt improbable. *Just my luck!*

When the sun cracked the horizon, Barry was up and making an all-out effort to fix the car parked outside his parents' home. Joe appeared two hours later, half-awake, a cup of coffee in hand, and chuckling when he saw Barry covered in grease up to his elbows. *It's obvious Joe does not get the immediacy of the situation*, Barry fumed looking at his brother.

"Ah, Joe, I've tried every trick I know. I can't fix the damn thing. It's got to go to the repair shop."

Joe assessed the situation and shaking his head, agreed with his brother. Knowing that time was slipping away and that Barry had few options, Joe figured that he had the upper hand. "Barry, you've got my permission slip to take it to the shop and pay for the repairs."

Barry's jaw dropped. "Dude, you've got to be nuts!"

"Yeah, right. You're the one getting the kisses and hugs from a cute California girl in that car this weekend, not me! Make out in my Bug, it's going to cost you!"

"And I'm not the one getting kisses and hugs in that car for the rest of the year."

"Your choice, bro," Joe said and shrugged his shoulders.

But after quibbling, the brothers agreed to split the repair bill. By the day's end, the mechanic had the offending clutch cable repaired, and Joe knew he had gotten the better part of the deal.

* * *

The accommodations for Barry's upcoming visit had become a sore spot between Marie and her mother. Over afternoon tea earlier in the week, their haggling started. "Marie, I think we should invite Barry to stay with us instead of at the Blue Heron. I hate to think of a friend of ours staying there when we have plenty of room here," Geneviève said.

"Mother, Barry is not a friend! He's an acquaintance of Luci's. If you think that boy is going to sleep in the room next to hers, you are mistaken. It's not happening, Mother, and don't bring it up again or discuss it with Luci."

Your damn automatic objections! How can you have so little trust in your daughter? And, really, threatening me? Geneviève had a backbone, and her daughter's ultimatum was not going to dissuade her. But she knew that boxing in Marie with an outright challenge would be pointless. *If you want to change people's behavior, it's best to give them a plausible option.*

"I understand your concerns, Marie. But do you think it is wise for Barry to have his own motel room where he and Luci can go to be alone at any time?" Geneviève let the thought weave a way through her daughter's distrustful mind then continued her pitch. "If he doesn't come here, then it might be better for him to stay with one of our relatives."

Marie stared at the wall beyond her mother, and her mouth turned dry. *Damn, she has a point!*

Geneviève struck while the iron was hot. She left the room and phoned Millie and Ross, who were Marie's cousins and also Luci's godparents. Confiding in them the hullabaloo over Barry's accommodations, Millie read the situation and, without hesitation, offered to host Barry.

Millie's sympathies rested with Luci. She and Ross had a soft spot for young romance, built on their own experience. When Ross was a seasonal farmhand for Millie's father, he fell hopelessly in love with Millie. A developing love affair simmered through the winter months, but after the Great Lakes shed their sheets of ice in the spring, Ross returned as a seaman through the autumn on lake freighters. If anyone proved the saying that absence makes the heart grow fonder, it was Ross and Millie. During their separation, their romance exploded. Love letters united the young couple, and the double entendre postcards they mailed to each other made the postman blush. Millie's parents believed the match was foolish and tried to stifle it. But the young lovers persisted. So at ages sixteen and nineteen on the first day of winter, Millie and Ross were married at the church of Sainte Jean Baptiste—the place most family marriages, baptisms, first communions, and funerals had occurred since the early 1800s.

While Millie and Ross maintained their romance despite the obstacles put in their way, they knew others who were not as fortunate. The couple saw the crushing effect that a broken love affair could have on a person's happiness over a lifetime, particularly when ended by parental interference. *These things are better left running their course without worrying about the result*, Millie thought.

But more than romance, Ross and Millie had a heartbreaking story. Their first child, a girl, died soon after her birth, and a son, born later, succumbed to pneumonia as a teenager. Having Luci's friend as a houseguest was a gift. Millie and Ross would be happy for a young person's energy to fill their home for a few days.

Geneviève put down the phone receiver and scurried back to the room. "Everything is set. Barry will stay with Millie and Ross, and they're going to throw a big dinner party on Saturday evening and invite everyone. Oh, it will be grand!"

Marie puckered her lips, unsure whether she was pleased or ticked off with her mother's meddling. "Yes, how grand, Mother. And I'll be the one telling Luci about the arrangements, not you."

At first, Millie's invitation frustrated Luci. With such a short visit, Luci had hoped she and Barry would have all of their time alone; that would be impossible now. But she reconsidered. Family get-togethers were happy and loud. Luci's relatives were experts at conducting several conversations at once. To an outsider, it might sound like a cacophony, but to the participants, it was a routine and lively exchange. Everyone teased each other, but they were never hurtful. Voicing their opinions, they could listen as well. They disagreed but were not disagreeable. They were competitive but not cutthroat. They respected each other's individuality without judgment and could pull together as a team when required.

If my relatives are their raucous selves, it will be an entertaining party. They will test and tease Barry, and it will be amusing to see if he is up for the challenge!

* * *

The morning before the day of Barry's arrival, Luci, Marie, and Geneviève drove along a winding, narrow road following the Detroit River to the farm of Millie and Ross. They planned on picking up fresh eggs, courtesy of the farm's cadre of Rhode Island Red hens, as well as gorging themselves on a breakfast feast complemented with harmless gossip and animated storytelling.

From the car's back seat, Luci watched the busy ship traffic clip by on the river. Mighty freighters, some over one thousand feet long, carried stone, coal, grain, oil, and other cargos. They traversed back and forth on the Great Lakes to the open sea through the engineering feat of the St. Lawrence Seaway, opened a few years before. At night, the forlorn sounds from the mighty ships' horns carried miles over the countryside and were comforting companions that lulled Luci to sleep.

After a few miles, the car turned onto a long dirt driveway that circled a small, stagnant pond shaded by a stand of weeping willows. As they approached the one-hundred-year-old stone home, the cousins' caramel-colored mix-breed dog, Sport, ran along the side of the car barking and wagging his tail, issuing a welcome that later his owners would surpass.

Hearing the dog, the expectant hosts rushed outside the house, waving frantically to greet their visitors. Geneviève parked the car, and when the three women clambered out, there were hugs and kisses all around with their hosts. Chattering, Millie and Ross escorted their guests through the side door into the expansive, well-equipped farmer's kitchen. Even though the home had sizeable formal living and dining rooms, the kitchen was where the action took place. A colorful cotton cloth and matching napkins dressed the massive table along with a bouquet of Queen Anne's lace and black-eyed Susan. The smells permeating the air and the bounty of food on the table were testimony to Millie's baking and cooking prowess. Freshly made chunky applesauce filled one bowl while homemade canned peaches filled another. There were baked muffins right out of the oven, scrambled eggs, and a slab of home-smoked ham, and if these goodies were not enough, a homemade cherry pie with a perfect lattice crust made Luci's mouth water.

Millie and Ross held a special place in Luci's heart. From family gossip, she knew bits and pieces of the love story that sustained their lifelong romance. Even at their advanced ages, the two still teased and flirted with each other as if they were teenagers. Their joyfulness, optimism, and love and respect for each other created a relationship that fulfilled both of their lives.

As everyone dived into the morning feast, Ross popped the question most on his mind. "What's this I hear, Luci? Millie tells me you have a boyfriend visiting this weekend from Buffalo, and best of all, he's going to be our houseguest. Is it true what the family telegraph says about this American?"

All eyes at the table instantly turned to Luci, and she knew her godfather was baiting her. *The best way to deal with Uncle Ross is to give back as good as he gives.* "Well, Uncle Ross, that depends on what messages are in those telegrams!"

Ross raised his eyebrows, signifying he might know more than what Luci suspected.

"When it comes to romance, nothing is classified around here! Your Uncle Ross and I know all about that," Millie said, landing a dig about her parents' interference in their affair. "When Marie told us that your friend had made plans to stay at the Blue Heron, we would have none of that! We have a large home with three empty bedrooms. There's no way our godchild's friend is going to stay at an old motel," Millie said.

Throughout breakfast, Luci's godparents bombarded her with questions about Barry. What mattered most was his heritage, religion, and family —in that order. What's his last name? Is he Catholic? What's his family like? How did you meet him? What is the Air Force Academy?

After combing through this background, their interest turned to other details about Barry. "Is he cute?" Millie asked. "Can he manage a tractor?" Ross wanted to know. "Can he take a joke?" the two asked in unison.

The friendly interrogation continued and made Ross's heart pump with happy memories as he looked toward Millie. "Thinking as the young man I once was, I know the excitement of romance, Luci. Isn't that true, Millie?" he asked with a wink. Returning a coy smile, Millie agreed from the other end of the table.

* * *

"Oh, Lord, am I ever stuffed," said Geneviève after returning home. "And now we have to go to lunch with Father D! I don't know how I can put another bite in my mouth."

Marie waved her mother off. "If you feel that way, you don't have to come with us. I don't understand why you had that piece of cherry pie along with all the other sweets Millie put out. You know eating like that isn't good for you, but you do it anyway. You'll get no sympathy from me."

Luci walked out of the room, seeking safety from the quibbling between the two. The longer Marie and Geneviève were together, the better the chance for verbal skirmishes between them. Sometimes Geneviève triggered an attack. At other times, it was Marie. The spoken assaults typically involved whose experience was worse or better than the other one. "I wish I had it so easy," Geneviève might exclaim, or "Life was simpler in your day," Marie might say. The tiffs never resulted in a lasting grievance. Still, the negative sentiments they whipped up put emotional distance and misunderstandings between the two that made everyone around them edgy.

While Grand-mère is emotionally close to me, she often is cold and disconnected with Mother, Luci observed. She noticed similar dynamics among her girlfriends and their mothers, not to mention her own relationship with Marie. *What is it between mothers and daughters? What causes toxic behavior and one-upmanship? Is it because the earlier generation had fewer opportunities and less freedom than the next? Or is the clash due to mothers trying to protect their daughters from making the same mistakes that they made?*

Confrontations between Marie and her daughters most often related to opposing views involving religion and relationships with men. For the most part, in Marie's generation, the expectation was blind obedience to religious cannon, and the reinterpretation of moral teachings was not tolerated. Fear of committing a mortal sin and going to hell or being excommunicated by the church were major deterrents that kept the faithful in line. Relations with the opposite sex were formal, with dating taking place in movie theaters and dance halls, not in lovers' lanes, at least for "good" girls. Public shows of affection were discouraged, and sex was supposed to be reserved for marriage.

Luci's generation contested these traditional views. They questioned the efficacy of rules they saw as superficial methods of control and obstacles to their freedom. *Is this why my mother is so overbearing? Perhaps it is a conflict between who is heard and who is not? Whose experience is valued more? Is the real reason a regret of freedom not realized?* Luci wondered.

Using this logic, Luci tried to refrain from judging her mother. *Instead of exasperation, I can observe and try to understand her. Being angry with her gives me a headache and gets me no place, anyway.* To maintain her own sanity, Luci pledged to frame her mother's control in a new way but knew it might be a difficult promise to keep.

* * *

Father Denis, affectionately called Father D, a longtime family friend, had grown up in the same community as Geneviève before he joined the Basilian Order of priests. After serving in various parishes, he became the pastor of the church where Marie and Sam's family worshiped in Windsor. Father Denis's mother was French Canadian, and his father Irish. Combining the two backgrounds contributed to his ready wit and talent for telling jokes, making him a favorite with his parishioners.

Luncheon with Father D at the Lakeside Terrace Hotel in nearby Kingsville was a highlight of every summer visit. Father D always made it a point to reserve the restaurant's best table that overlooked Lake Erie. Seated there and looking at a panoramic view that stretched to Pelee Island, the group feasted on delectable food selections served on delicate china arranged on starched white linen.

Luci admired the ability of the clergyman to lift people's spirits. He didn't have pretensions like most other priests she knew. Father D was down-to-earth and nonjudgmental about human foibles. He didn't expect perfection. Instead, he encouraged people to celebrate their personal strengths and use them to become better in leading a good life. Most of all, he acknowledged a person's self-worth and listened to them without having to give an opinion. *He's more a psychiatrist than a priest*, Luci thought.

The luncheon was as entertaining as everyone anticipated, dominated by a convivial atmosphere where both mother-daughter pairs were in a lighthearted mood. With Father D, there was no reason for competitiveness or self-aggrandizing, nor was he likely to tolerate such behavior. Underneath the cheerful personality, he was socially and self-aware, with a commanding presence that inspired like behavior from those around him. If nothing else, his Roman collar dictated decorum. Luci wished that Father D was a permanent fixture in their everyday lives. *If he were, there would be less control and more understanding,* she thought.

* * *

Dog-tired, the trio returned home late in the afternoon. But exhausted or not, Geneviève wasn't deterred from welcoming family and friends to visit in the evening. As long as she was sitting in her rocking chair on her screened-in front porch, visitors were welcome to drop by and be part of the newsiest night gathering place along Murray Street.

As dusk settled, a scattering of neighborhood friends relaxed in each other's company. Drinking cold drinks to avert the suffocating heat and humidity, they revealed every bit of gossip they knew. Like an unseen observer, Luci listened, absorbed, and untangled facts, meanings, and innuendos from the stories and secrets that were shared every evening.

"Oh, I had no idea Bob Hunt had been in the hospital. I saw the news today in the Cards of Thanks in the *Echo.* But the paper didn't give any specifics! Does anyone know more?" Geneviève's next-door neighbor, Dora, asked.

Others promptly chimed in. Combining the bits and pieces known between them, they developed a full-blown narrative of the old man's hypertension and congestive heart failure. *There sure aren't many secrets around here,* Luci thought while she sipped Vernor's ginger ale.

A turn of the century holdover in the village newspaper, the Cards of Thanks column published short narratives of appreciation. This week, besides the Hunt family's gratitude for prayers and flowers, there were several other expressions of thankfulness. One from the Lemays praised the local firefighters for saving their home. Another was a testimonial from Mrs. Kelly to Fathers Simpson and Brown and the nurses at Grace Hospital for their kindnesses. And another, written by the Tri-Community Boat Committee, recognized volunteers for assisting in a beach cleanup.

The *Echo* was a wealth of current news and historical facts. Upsetting the Hourglass, a time capsule of events occurring twenty to sixty years earlier, was a column Luci liked to read in each edition of the newspaper. Scanning the entries, Luci used it as a lens for understanding the life and times of her grandmother and mother in their younger years. Often, she found news reports about her own family. Whenever this happened, Luci probed her relatives for details about the accounts, and she looked for clues in their descriptions that might help her better unravel current family dynamics. This is how Luci came to realize that past events had the power to influence the present.

Two years before, the column mentioned a hunting accident that occurred in 1924 and involved the death of a seventeen-year-old boy who was shot by his twin brother. It was an upsetting story, and during one of the evening gatherings, Luci pushed to hear the circumstances. After Geneviève recounted the horrible details of the misfortune, it shocked Luci to discover that the two young men were Geneviève's nephews. "Why do you think that Aunt Lena is depressed and so irritable much of the time? How could any mother get over that kind of heartbreak?" Geneviève had questioned.

Not all stories in the column were as disheartening. Most of them reflected an orderly pace of day-to-day life. A bridal shower was given for Gertrude Meloche held in the Harrow Municipal Building forty years before. Lisette Pillon was the top of her class in No3B School in Malden fifty years previously. Mr. and Mrs. Achille L'Heureaux moved to their new home on Malden's fifth Concession twenty years earlier.

Luci found many of the stories amusing by the current-day standards and language. One reported that motorists in 1916 were obliged to observe a speed limit under ten miles an hour within the village. *Ten miles an hour was speeding?* Another stated: "Ross McBain disposed of his barbershop in Harrow." *Using today's language, this sounds as if McBain tossed his barbershop in the morning trash!*

As the evening wore on, Loretta Bondy was aching to give the details of the all-day family reunion she attended the past Sunday. "Why there were hundreds of my great-grandfather's descendants who came, and you can bet there was plenty of hubbub in that open pasture," she said. "You can't imagine the size of the barbeque and spread of salads and pies. And the activities! There were pony rides and a penny scramble for the children, foot races and ballgames for the men-folk, and a spaghetti eating contest for everyone." At that point, Loretta started laughing uncontrollably, forcing her to halt her tale for a full minute. Her giggling was infectious, and everyone on the porch joined in even though they did not know what they were laughing about.

Regaining her composure, Loretta continued to recount the saga. "Red sauce and noodles covered the contestants' faces, hands, arms, and even their hair. We all squealed until our sides hurt. And you should have seen Vic Pillon after winning the contest—he was as red as the Canadian Maple Leaf. After all that nonsense, we finished up with fiddle music and dancing on a huge wooden stage that Jack and Ted Bondy had built." Sighing, Loretta then added, "Oh my! The glow from the kerosene lamps strung above the dance floor and the moonlit sky made me feel like a romantic teenager."

Luci observed that the evening soirées focused on the community: stories, past and present, about local people and events, challenges with planting and harvesting the crops, fluctuations in prices for groceries and farm equipment, and occasions like graduations, weddings, and funerals. Rarely did they veer into issues outside those of Essex County.

This contrasted to her experience at home where she felt disconnected from the immediate community and where state and federal politics seemed to take precedence over local issues. Thinking about the phenomenon, Luci wondered if the well-being she observed was linked to social interactions that fostered feelings of belonging, acceptance, empathy, and safety. *Perhaps this is the reason Adele and Darla are at odds with Mother; they've never had the social support to establish positive relationships like these. What a beautiful and magical life here. I can never imagine a summer without Canada.*

Late into the evening, the guests left, and Geneviève, Marie, and Luci cleared away the empty beverage glasses and tidied and locked up before calling it a night. On the way to her bedroom, Geneviève put her arm around Luci, giving her a kiss on the cheek and whispering, "Big day tomorrow, dear. I can't wait to meet your air force cadet."

Getting into bed, Luci adjusted a thin cotton sheet to cover her, all that she needed in the summer evening. Lying still in the dark, she listened for the sound of the soulful ship horns from the Detroit River to lull her to sleep. Through her open bedroom windows, Luci welcomed a cooling breeze across her face, and she was content. Anticipating Barry's arrival in a few hours, a pleasurable jumble of thoughts floated through her mind. She felt uplifted by the reflections of the day that she wrote in her journal a few minutes earlier:

July 14, 1966, 11:07 pm

I am thankful for the relationships in my life because they help me live life fully.
I am thankful for Father Denis because he shows me how to be more open and less judgmental.
I am thankful for Uncle Ross and Aunt Millie because they are a perfect gift to share with Barry.

Chapter 17

Arthur

Luci woke early on Friday morning, July 15. With neither Geneviève nor Marie up, the house was eerily quiet. As Luci padded down the hallway to the bathroom, she sighed, grateful for a slice of solitude to prepare for Barry's arrival.

Opening the spigot in the sink, Luci let the water run until icy-cold. She had had a fitful night, and even her beloved freighter horns couldn't dampen her excitement enough to lull her into a deep sleep. Splashing the water on her face made her skin tingle, and the gentle towel buffing afterward gave her cheeks a creamy pink glow. Luci shook her head and ran her fingers through her hair, and looking in the mirror, she felt confident that she was in charge of the day.

She rummaged through her closet, looking for a smart, casual outfit and selected a green, yellow, and blue A-line cotton sleeveless dress that sat about two inches above her knees. After putting it on, she studied herself again in the mirror. *Not bad.* Completing her look, she pulled her hair back and fastened it with a large barrette at the bottom of her neck and slipped into a pair of color-coordinated sandals. Then, sitting on the chair facing the art deco vanity mirror, Luci carefully applied eye makeup and dusted a light coating of pink blush on her cheeks. Inspecting herself while dabbing a few droplets of the memory-making perfume on her wrists and behind her ears, she thought, *Hmm, looking and feeling bitchin'.*

Going to the kitchen, Luci halted at the open window at the top of the stairs, breathing in the fragrance of fresh-cut grass. Blue jays were squawking, and she could see the squirrels were up early, too, eagerly collecting dropped acorns from the old tree in her grandmother's backyard. *What great memories this yard holds: playing croquet with the Bouchard girls from across the street, feeding and petting grand-mère's cats, chatting with Dora over the fence, cutting rhubarb growing at the backdoor stump, and collecting fruit from the old mulberry tree for pie.*

* * *

Barry got an early start from Buffalo. He tossed and turned through the night, his mind restless thinking of Luci and anticipating holding her in his arms again. Crossing the bridge from New York into Canada and passing through Niagara Falls, Barry recalled the evening of June 10. *Little did I imagine that a month later, I would travel through the land of Lelawala and Thunder God on my way to be with the most fabulous girl I've ever met. Amazing!*

A couple of hours later, he passed through St. Thomas and then drove toward Lake Erie. There the two-lane road hugged the shoreline and passed through small towns where quaint summer cottages dotted the lakeside. Driving through the town of Leamington, a small sign that directed tourists to the Pelee Island ferry caught his eye. He remembered Luci telling him that the island was magical. "Can you imagine being in a place where there is no sound except for the breeze whistling off the lake? A place where there are no paved roads? A place where you can walk to wetlands, sand dunes, forests, and silky beaches all on the same day? It's as if time stands still on Pelee."

Barry recalled how Luci's eyes had sparkled as she told him about the butterflies on the island. "There's nothing so mesmerizing as seeing thousands of monarch butterflies stop on Pelee during their migration to Mexico. You can't believe how stunned I was one morning seeing hundreds of monarchs hanging on to the hollyhocks next to the cottage where we were staying. It was breathtaking. There were so many clustered that it was impossible to distinguish the stems from the flowers. As I went closer for a better look, the butterflies swarmed and surrounded me like a whirlwind of fairies. Then in a flash, they fluttered off without a sound." *Without a doubt, Luci with an i, someday we will make memories together on Pelee Island,* Barry thought as he drove past the ferry sign.

After Leamington, the road passed through picturesque villages interspersed with numerous small farm stands on both sides of the roadway. Luci had told him about these, but he never imagined there could be so many. "All along the lakeshore, there are lots of farm stands selling every imaginable vegetable and summer fruit and other items such as honey and maple syrup. Grand-mère and I have favorites that we visit two or three times a week."

Luci was right! Barry admitted. It seemed that every quarter mile or so, there was another small stand offering freshly harvested produce from tidy gardens that butted up to the edge of the road. As he drove through the pastoral countryside, Barry's thoughts wandered. *Life on this side of the border sure seems a heck of a lot more laid back than in the States.*

* * *

As the noon hour approached, Luci felt her stomach fluttering as fast as the sunbeams she was watching dance on the porch floor. Geneviève reached over from her rocker and patted her granddaughter's hand. "Ma Bichette, please relax, dear. He'll get here when he gets here. Save your energy to spend on him when he arrives. Live in the present, and you won't be anxious or worried."

Luci thought about that advice. *How brilliant of Grand-mère! If you live in the present, worries about the past or the future are impossible. No wonder people come to her every evening for her guidance.*

Sitting together on the front porch, grandmother and granddaughter lounged in the comfortable temperature. It had dropped twenty degrees from a sweltering and humid ninety-three two days earlier. Heeding her grandmother's words, Luci felt the tenseness in her shoulders evaporating. The jitters in her stomach began to fade, and she was able to listen to her grandmother's conversation.

Barry's upcoming visit kindled a feeling of giddiness in Geneviève. Her granddaughter's excitement was an electric bolt that recharged her spirit and made her feel young again. Long-submerged youthful memories of beaus and romances had flooded Geneviève's thoughts as she lay in bed the previous evening. *Aah, the taste of spiked punch and flirting with all those good-looking suitors at the holiday parties. And those sleigh rides in the bitter cold; the nuzzling that went on with my sweethearts under fur-lined blankets! And flying across the frozen ponds ice skating hand in hand with all those handsome young men. Oh, and in the summer! There were picnics, too many to count, along the lakeside or on Bois Blanc where I exchanged naughty innuendos and a lot more with my latest admirers.*

Reviving the intensity of her romances, Geneviève felt a closeness to her granddaughter, believing that Luci, too, would understand the passion she experienced as a young woman. She scooted her rocking chair closer to Luci, longing to confide stories of her youthful *affaires de coeur*, as she delicately called them.

"Oh, my dear, I'm reliving my old romances vicariously through you," Geneviève said in a breathy voice. "Anticipating Barry's visit is rejuvenating me! My memories last night made me so wistful I couldn't sleep. I turned on my bedside light, got out of bed, and went to my hope chest and retrieved mementos of those romantic times."

Luci pulled back in her chair and felt a flush starting to climb on her face. It was difficult imagining her grandmother in a relationship, much less one so passionate that it would still resonate after sixty years. But Luci's embarrassment turned to fascination, and she wanted to hear more but was uncertain how far she should probe.

Geneviève giggled and then shot Luci a sharp look. "Aah, I see you want to learn about my secrets! It will be so good to share some of these with you, and your grand-mère might surprise you!"

Leaning her head on the back in her chair, Geneviève lowered her eyes and took a deep breath. "Let me tell you about Arthur. Oh, was I ever over the moon for that man!"

Luci never heard Geneviève mention Arthur. But the poignant impact the reminiscence had was being revealed through her grandmother's facial expression. *What will grand-mère say?* It was Luci now who reached over and patted her grandmother's hand. "Grand-mère, if it's too personal, I understand."

Geneviève's eyes opened, and Luci thought they had started to glisten. "Oh, no, Ma Bichette," she said, shaking her head. "I must share this with you! You are right, it is bittersweet, but I've had a heavy heart for far too long. It's time to release this, and no one will understand it as much as you."

Luci could hear her own breathing as it got faster.

"I met him when I was attending business school in Windsor, and he was a student at Assumption College. He was so handsome—fine features, wavy hair, sharp blue eyes. Beyond his looks, though, it was his intellect that attracted me—and his humor, of course."

Geneviève learned over the chair's arm and closer to her granddaughter. "I always liked a man with a sense of humor, Luci. A man who has no wit is useless; remember that! Someone who can't make or take a joke raises a red flag. Relationships depend on people being able to laugh with each other. Humor helps us face setbacks, smooth over the rough spots, and put things in perspective." Geneviève paused and lowered her eyes, and her chest heaved as she took in another deep breath.

"Aah, yes, that's what I loved about Arthur. You know, in one of his letters, he joked that I was too stingy with my kisses!" she said. The remark tickled Luci's and Geneviève's funny bones, and they laughed like preteens until they were brought to tears.

Luci gave Geneviève an impish look. "Oh, Grand-mère, how could you be so unkind?" You can't hold back now, Grand-mère! What happened to Arthur?"

Geneviève cast her eyes toward the ceiling, a tear forming in her eye. "Arthur went on to medical school in Detroit. He was so sweet writing to me. He'd compose his letters in French and address the envelopes to Mademoiselle Geneviève Desjardins. Aah, it was so romantic; my heart still sings! Such memories make me blush with happiness, but they also make me downhearted. Can you understand that, dear? To have feelings of joy and sadness at the same time?" she asked, her lips quivering.

Luci sat mute. She sensed a verbal response was unfitting. What Geneviève craved was compassion and affection to reveal her emotions without judgment. Luci's silence was the answer her grandmother desired.

"After finishing medical school, Arthur practiced in Detroit for a short time before joining the American War Department as an army surgeon. He went to the most marvelous cities like San Francisco and Washington, DC. He traveled to exotic places like Japan, the Philippines, and Hawaii and brought me back the most wonderful gifts. It was unbearable being apart, and our letters were our sole consolation for relieving our loneliness and the pain of separation from each other."

Luci sighed. *Wow, that touches a chord! This explains why Grand-mère was so animated when she handed me Barry's and Chris's letters.*

Observing her grandmother, Luci was relieved to see a twinkle emerging in her eyes. Grinning, Geneviève crept her hand into the pocket of her shirtwaist dress and pulled out what looked like letters, tied neatly together with a gold ribbon. Luci's heart flipped, looking at the packet.

"See here, Luci," Geneviève whispered, patting the bundle as lovingly as she would a kitten. "These are some of the letters from my dear Arthur."

She paused, meeting Luci's eyes. "What do you think? Do you want to read them with me?"

Taken off guard, Luci's hand flew up to cover her mouth as her grandmother untied the ribbon as if it were pure gold. Clasping the notes between her hands, Geneviève caressed the cherished mementos with her thumbs as though rubbing them would resurrect Arthur's spirit. Carefully, she opened one of the fragile, yellowed envelopes and removed several pages of stationery. Even from where she was sitting, Luci saw the beautiful script of Arthur's hand. The lines of written words were straight and neat with capital letters highlighted in crafted swirls. Luci edged to the front of her chair for a closer look at the letter in her grandmother's shaking hand. *If the content is anywhere close to the beauty of Arthur's handwriting, then it must be amazing.*

USA General Hospital
Washington Barracks
Washington, DC

August 22, 1901

My Dearest Geneviève,

Was delighted to receive your most welcome letter this morning, and you see I am answering it at once. Am I not most prompt? No, we have no long Sundays here, in fact, no long days at all; just about right. And I imagine the Sundays at home could be made much shorter, if you were expecting someone shortly after dinner, or even as a guest for that very meal. Of course, then you and the someone would sit out under the trees, or, perhaps, even in the hammock. Of course, you would be well acquainted even to the extent of holding hands and exchanging kisses often. (You would have a good argument, also. I remember how you like to argue!) Well, it would be dark night before you realized it, don't you think? I know, on my part, it would, and I would enjoy it with you in the shadows where no one could observe us.

You asked me to tell you about my surroundings here. Well, Geneviève, they are most picturesque—you know it is somewhat hilly about here. I told you about the green, green, fields of Virginia, did I not?

The Potomac at Washington is divided in two by a long, narrow island called the Potomac Flats. It reminds me very much of Fighting Island and the Canadian and American Channels but has no such memories for me! Do you remember our last ride down the river to Bois Blanc on that memorable Sunday? I still have the two half tickets yet; I keep them as mementos of our particular time and memory making near the old blockhouse there.

All kinds of excursion boats are passing up and down here all the time, and these bring back fond memories when we were together. As I am writing the Str. Newport News *is on her way south to Newport News.*

So you are again the star attraction at school! I guess you must like it a little anyway, now don't you? At least I am sure the pupils are all pleased with their pretty brunette teacher. Now don't laugh, for I am most serious. My heart aches when I think of the lovely brunette teacher, and I cannot be near her.

About the photos, Geneviève, I intend to have some taken shortly and will certainly send you the first one, provided you send me one of yours. You will post it with the next letter, and believe me, it will occupy the most conspicuous place upon my desk.

You haven't been to Bois Blanc? You awful girl. Well, you must go over Sunday and have a good time. I will be there in mind, so think of me while enjoying yourself, and I will dream of you.

With Fondest Greetings, Your Arthur

With their cheeks wet and hugs and smiles between them, Luci and Geneviève read Arthur's letters until they reached the last one in the packet. Looking down at the envelope in her lap, Geneviève hesitated and could not open it. "It's best to stop now." Geneviève's shoulders slumped, and the heaviness in her voice left Luci wondering about the last letter's content.

As grandmother and granddaughter held hands, lost in their own worlds, a breeze from nowhere arose from the river. It blew up the street and passed through the porch screen as if it were the fleeting spirit of memory making of long ago.

"What happened, Grand-mère?"

"Interference, dear. Interference and control." She closed her eyes and rubbed both temples with her hands. "To explain is too painful."

Geneviève took the golden ribbon and retied the letters together. She rose from her rocking chair, leaned over, and gave Luci a gentle kiss on her forehead before returning to her bedroom and replacing the cherished packet in the chest.

Alone on the porch, Luci was struck by her grandmother's final explanation. *What does Grand-mère mean by interference and control? What possible meddling could obstruct such an incredible romance and love story that made her so unhappy?*

Chapter 18

Fort Malden

"What a darling little car," Geneviève said after the red Volkswagen Beetle pulled up at her home. Sitting by her mother's side on the front porch, Marie was less impressed with the foreign-made vehicle. "Nasty little thing," she remarked and turned her face.

Peeking through the living room windows and seeing Barry, Luci dashed out the front door and down the walkway, her heart pounding as hard as if it were a bass drum. When the two saw each other, the smiles on their faces and their warm embrace needed no translation. Geneviève and Marie, observing the reunion, were correct in their interpretation: young sweethearts unconcerned with the world around them.

"So cute! Oh, and a smile as sunny as an ear of fresh corn," Geneviève said.

Marie puckered her lips. "Mother, stop it! You sound like a teenager going ape over a movie star."

Geneviève waved her daughter off.

Barry took Luci's hand, and his brilliant eyes fixated on the girl of his dreams. "Luci with an i, you are cuter each time I see you."

Luci's cheeks turned lemonade pink, and she felt bashful as she studied Barry. This was the first time she had seen him out of uniform, and she eyed how his jeans and T-shirt defined his muscular body. *Boss!*

With recollections of Arthur's embraces fresh in her mind, Geneviève's eyes sparkled, observing the two holding hands and chatting as if the world around them were suspended. Her memory resurrected the smell of sweet lilac fragrances the first time she and Arthur strolled together along a lakeshore cloaked in a blazing sunset. Shaking her head, she broke the spell and brought herself back into reality.

Geneviève greeted Barry with a grandmotherly hug. Then, holding his face between her hands, she planted kisses on both his cheeks. Barry's blush highlighted his surprise; no one had ever welcomed him with such gusto, and he warmed to Luci's grandmother on the spot. But Geneviève did a double take as Marie greeted the young cadet with an embrace of her own. *What is she up to?* she wondered.

During the past two days, Marie had evaluated how best to react to her daughter's infatuation. It was undeniable that Luci's new acquaintance intrigued Ross, Millie, and her mother, even though they had yet to meet Barry. Marie realized if she displayed a hair's resentment toward Barry, her relatives would consider her a sourpuss. *His good looks, flashy smile, and easygoing personality will take them all in, and I'll be the ogre if I'm not as fascinated with him as they are.*

Marie's relations were unlikely to be either direct or harsh in chastising her for an indifferent or cold behavior. But Marie knew their spirited badgering would make her life more miserable than an outright argument. She imagined Ross's side remarks delivered with a shame-faced grin, "Look at that. Marie is as tight as a tic today." Or, Millie's cutting sarcasm enveloped in her obnoxious girlish chuckle, "She's as controlling as a queen bee in a hive." *It's beyond my imagination why I ever chose Millie and Ross as Luci's godparents*, Marie thought.

Witnessing her mother's effervescent performance, Marie knew she was correct in predicting Geneviève's response to Barry's visit. Her mother's sentimentality often wove itself into her front porch evening soirées. By custom, friends and neighbors enjoyed these informal gatherings as a safe place for exchanging friendly gossip. But recently, the lovelorn were also finding Geneviève a refuge to share romantic secrets and to solicit her advice.

Marie scoffed at Geneviève's attempts at playing an armchair psychotherapist and romanticist. Marie was a realist, however. She knew that her mother was not going to change her outlook toward a budding romance, especially when it came to her granddaughter. To survive the weekend, Marie thought the best she could do was to put on a pleasant face, even though Luci and Barry's relationship galled her. Attempting to shrug off her concern, Marie chided herself: *After all, I only need to endure this crap for forty-eight hours.*

Geneviève's living room of overstuffed chintz-upholstered furniture was an intimate environment that made people lower their guard. While predisposed to sentimentality in managing the love lives of others, dealing with her granddaughter's romance was another issue, and Geneviève reigned in her romantic propensity. Everyone chatted while sipping cold drinks, and Geneviève handled her exchanges with Barry as if she were an intrepid sleuth. If he passed her test, then she would open the throttle of romanticism.

Without embarrassment, Geneviève interrogated Barry with leading questions.

"Oh, so you are from Buffalo? I've never been there. Tell me, what do you like best about your hometown?"

"You know, I have a lot of brothers and sisters. Sometimes they drive me crazy, but we still have a good time together. What about your family, Barry?"

"This Air Force Academy is a mystery to me. Why did you decide to go there? What was important about that for you?"

"You may know that in Canada we are discussing universal medical care like that in Saskatchewan. What do you think about all these Great Society programs of your President Johnson?"

Marie and Luci had provided Geneviève with the answers to most of these questions, but this was Geneviève's way of verifying Barry's truth telling. "Liars always slip up," she said, and there was nothing Luci's grand-mère liked better than to catch someone in a fib. Geneviève had a genial disposition, but if someone lied to her, she would confront and pounce like an angry cat on the offender. Luci's academy cadet passed through Geneviève's grilling without so much of a scratch.

Barry had a roster of questions ready, too. Blending these into the conversation with the skill of a weaver at a loom, he queried Luci's grandmother about her Irish ancestors, and he compared her snippets with his similar ancestry. Barry asked Geneviève about her life as a farmer's daughter and early career as a teacher, but when he inquired about her opinion on the Quebec sovereignty movement, she blinked. *I didn't think any American was aware of those rumblings and political situation!*

Except for those who came seeking her advice, Geneviève's encounters with the younger generation involved superficial conversations. Barry's curiosity and knowledge fascinated Geneviève. *Luci's new boyfriend is different than the usual. It's refreshing to encounter someone intellectual but not so self-absorbed to prevent him from listening, observing, asking questions, and considering my responses. This young man reminds me of Arthur!*

With her interests satisfied, Geneviève jumped up and clapped her hands. "That's enough visiting! Let's get you settled, Barry. You'll be staying with Millie and Ross, and they're expecting you shortly."

Barry's eyes clouded; he was befuddled. *Who the hell are Millie and Ross, and why am I staying with them?*

Without giving Barry the space to question her plans, Geneviève explained the rearrangement and inserted a white lie or two. "Now, Barry, I know you'll forgive Luci's meddling grand-mère. I'm responsible for canceling your reservation at the Blue Heron. You see, dear, I could never be comfortable letting you stay with anyone other than one of my relatives or me. What kind of hospitality would that have been for Luci's new friend?"

Geneviève stopped and placed her arm around Barry's shoulder as he rose from his chair, but she had more to say. "I mentioned your visit to Luci's godparents, Millie and Ross, and there was a battle between us to see who would host you. I gave in to them for reasons not to concern you, and so there you are! You have a wonderful place to stay with two of Luci's favorite relatives." Then, she turned toward her granddaughter. "Luci, dear, now you go with Barry and get him settled with Millie and Ross, and then the both of you come over to Duffy's for dinner."

Given the situation, Barry saw one viable option: accept with grace. *It's undeniable that Geneviève is a determined woman. Without a doubt, Luci inherited some of her spunkiness from her,* he concluded. In the back of his thoughts, though, he wondered why Geneviève was not hosting him if hospitality was as crucial to her as she maintained. *What did she mean by reasons not to concern you?* Barry tried to erase a sinking feeling it might have something to do with Marie.

* * *

As Barry maneuvered the car on the narrow village streets, Luci painted a picture for him of her godparents' lighthearted inclinations and their eccentricities. Barry, though, was less inclined to learn about these than to gaze at Luci. *It's as if I were a bee drawn in by a flower. How did I get so lucky to find her?*

The car's stick shift and bucket seats weren't conducive for cuddling, but Barry didn't let these structural impediments thwart him. Between gear shifts, he reached over and pulled Luci's hand close to him, gripping it and placing it on his thigh. When she reciprocated with squeezes of her own, his heart did double time.

"Uncle Ross is a real trickster. You better watch out, Barry! I'm sure he'll pull something on you," Luci said.

"I thought you wanted to make a good impression on me. Now you warn me about these people? What am I in for?"

"It's innocent troublemaking—no big deal."

"Like, for instance?"

"Well, for instance, one afternoon Uncle Ross visited grand-mère's house. When she left the room for a few minutes, he unplugged the downstairs lamps from their electrical outlets. That evening, Grand-mère tried to turn on the lights, and of course, none of the lamps worked. As soon as she figured out what happened, she was furious with Uncle Ross. The phone wires that night were on fire, and Uncle Ross received a real tongue-lashing. Uncle Ross came by the next day with roses to apologize, but Grand-mère would have none of it. She threw the bouquet at him, took the broom out of the foyer closet, and chased Uncle Ross all the way to the street with it."

Barry's eyes widened. "You've got to be kidding me! That must have been a sight. I can't imagine your genteel grandmother doing something like that, or for that matter, your godfather pulling such a prank."

"Oh, you'd be surprised! Grand-mère has a charming personality, but forgiveness and mercy aren't her strengths. To this day, she throws that event up in Uncle Ross's face whenever she wants something from him. He'll never be able to do enough to make it up to her."

Whoa, spunkier than I thought, was Barry's updated impression of Geneviève. Then his interest turned to Ross to prepare for what might be coming his way. "Has he ever pulled any shenanigans on you, Luci?"

"Of course," she said. "The poor man can't help himself. One time, when I was four years old and sitting in my little rocking chair on Grand-mère's porch, Uncle Ross pulled a whopper. I kept pushing back and forth, trying to make the chair rock, but it would not budge. I glanced at Grand-mère and noticed her giving Uncle Ross, who was sitting in the back of me, a dirty look. I snapped around and looked behind me. Sure enough, I saw Uncle Ross's muddy boot on the rocker preventing the chair from moving back and forth."

Chuckling, Barry turned to Luci. "And so what did you do?"

"I jumped out of the chair, turned around, faced Uncle Ross, and gave him a scolding. It must have looked ridiculous, a four-year-old shaking her finger and reprimanding a fifty-something-year-old man, but I wasn't intimidated. He apologized, of course, and then pulled one of those gargantuan Tootsie Rolls from his pocket and gave it to me. But, unlike Grand-mère, I didn't throw the peace offering back at him. I accepted it straight away and told him that he should never pull anything like that again."

Barry turned to Luci and grinned. "So now I know the best way to placate you: have a large inventory of huge Tootsie Rolls on hand!"

Luci shook her head. "Not on your life! I'm not four years old anymore. You'll have to do better than that, Barry Callahan, if you ever want to make up with me!"

* * *

Leaving the village's residential area, they drove along the river road toward open farmland. A line of lake freighters on the waterway barreled toward Detroit. Living in Buffalo, Barry saw large ships as a regular occurrence. Now, he had difficulty keeping his eyes off them as they navigated the river's narrow channel. Observing the vessels in the confined passageway made them appear larger and mightier than in the open waters of Lake Ontario. Eyeing a wide shoulder of the road, Barry pulled the Beetle over to get a better view. More important, though, he wanted to be alone with Luci.

Securing the vehicle with the handbrake and turning off the motor, Barry rested his back on the inside of the car door and turned toward Luci, reaching for her hand. She swiveled in her seat, facing him, putting one leg under the other. Luci's dress hiked up a little on her leg, and her action wasn't overlooked by Barry. She caught his eyes looking down and was happy that he noticed.

They seized the time as if it were an ember on a cold winter day and hung onto each other's words and movements. They laughed and talked without feeling the need to impress or to second-guess. Amid the occasional drone of the freighter horns and whistle from the river breeze, Barry quizzed Luci about her trip across the continent, not wanting to miss any detail. He had heard the Canadian Rockies were more jagged and spectacular than the mountains around the academy in Colorado and pressed Luci for a description of their majestic beauty. And the glaciers! He wanted one day to see the ones that Luci described.

In turn, Luci was curious about Barry's field experiences and the things he had done since returning home. She sat glued to her seat while he described his flight experiences and how it felt being in a plane when it broke the sound barrier. He gave her an account of cutting down trees in the forest near his family's cabin to prepare firewood for winter. He described the magnificent views from the cabin's front yard of the rolling Appalachian foothills and wished that Luci could have shared that with him.

They were aware, though, that this was the prologue to what they desired the most. Communicating with anything but emotions would have diminished the moment. Barry feasted on Luci's riveting eyes, and they told him that she was as desirous of him as he was of her. Now, out of uniform, he was not constrained by rules about shows of affection in public, and he was ready to let loose.

It was a spontaneous, fairy-tale moment better than any romance novel. Moving closer, Barry placed his muscled arm around Luci's shoulders and another circling her waist and drew her close. Luci reciprocated, clutched Barry, and dissolved into his embrace. Rekindling memories of Fairmont Park, Barry's sensations went wild, taking in Luci's familiar scent. Luci's body heat radiated through him and strengthened his desire.

Breathing as if he had scaled a mountain peak, Barry released his pent-up passion so that each touch, smell, and reaction was magnified like a planet in a telescope lens. He brushed kisses on her forehead and afterward on each of her cheeks, allowing them to linger as if they were the overture to a symphony. Then he pressed his lips with intensity on hers. She responded. Her lips were moist and warm, smooth and tender. "Thank you," he whispered, nuzzling her neck and unfastening her barrette and running his fingers through her silky hair.

Luci looked into Barry's dark-rimmed, crystal blue eyes and was overtaken by her desire. She caressed Barry's face with her hands, pulling his head toward her and kissing each of his cheeks. Luci let the kisses linger before pressing her lips on his. "You're welcome," Luci whispered as she edged back and smiled at him, satisfied. Her lips parted in a sliver, and she closed her eyes and moved closer, issuing an invitation for more. Barry responded by giving Luci the most passionate kiss she had ever experienced.

Afterward, words were irrelevant. Barry restarted the Beetle and released the handbrake. Holding hands and glowing, they were on their way. This time, though, their emotions were as free as down floating in a breeze, and they felt as if their hearts had melded, two souls united on a most remarkable journey.

* * *

When Barry turned onto the country lane leading to the house, Sport gave the customary greeting, meeting the car and barking and running beside it as they sped up the driveway. Wagging his tail like a metronome set at one hundred beats per minute, he entertained them with his gymnastics as he cavorted and, like a master, avoided contact with the car.

"What a cool place, Luci, and look at that pond! It's so storybook! It's like something out of a painting from a hundred years ago," Barry said. "And check out that house!" The stone structure always inspired visitors at first sight. Sitting among a grove of oak trees, the old home, built from quarry rock, had two stories and was three thousand square feet. In its time in the area, the house was a mansion.

Luci gave Barry a sly look. "If you think that's marvelous, wait till you meet Uncle Ross and Aunt Millie. You're going to like it here, Barry."

Alerted by Sport, Luci's godparents rushed to the door and were outside to greet their guests before the car reached the house. Barry's first impression was that Millie and Ross were straightforward and unpretentious folks. Ross's six-foot blocky build and weather-beaten complexion were a testimony to a lifetime of outdoor physical labor. His worn denim bib-overalls and mud-stained boots were proof that hard work was an everyday companion. At five feet tall with refined features, a diminutive Millie looked doll-like standing next to Ross. She wore a simple, patterned cotton dress, and her natural curly and salt-and-pepper hair was pulled back in a bun. She had a flawless complexion and pink cheeks that she complemented with a cheerful smile. *Homey, rural hospitality,* Barry thought.

Alighting from the car with his duffle bag swung over his shoulder, Barry went to open Luci's door. Before formal introductions, Millie was at Barry's side and embracing him in a warm hug. Ross's greeting was a broad smile and a hearty handshake, the force of which accentuated his calloused farmer's hand. Ushering their guests into their home through the preferred side door, Millie shot a sly wink at Ross, indicating she liked the cut of the jib of the young man. Ross passed her a subtle nod, his eyes saying he agreed.

The aroma of baked treats filled the cozy room and reminded Barry of his mother's kitchen and made him feel right at home. Before any chitchat, Millie insisted on escorting Barry to his bedroom. They walked through the formal dining and living rooms and climbed a long, narrow staircase to a guest room on the second floor. Millie's friendliness was unmistakable. She had an infectious laugh that delighted Barry, and her unassuming questions showed an inquisitiveness suggesting interest, not nosiness, that he thought was charming.

"Now, Barry, dear, I hope you don't mind all my questions," she said while she raised the bedroom windows to catch the late-afternoon breeze. "Asking questions is the best way to learn about people. It shows you have an interest in them, don't you think? Don't worry if I haven't gotten around to ask everything. I'm just getting started, dear. We have a whole weekend ahead to get to know one another," she said while patting Barry's hand. Having Barry stay with her and Ross did not replace their son, but giving affection to someone else's boy helped soften the edges of Millie's torn heart.

"Come now, dear, throw that duffle thing you have on the bed, and let's have a chat around the kitchen table before you go off to meet Geneviève and Marie for dinner." As they retraced their steps, Barry wondered, *Is everyone always this nice in Canada?*

Millie and Ross fulfilled their reputation as a lovestruck and lively couple. Ross regaled everyone with tales of his sailing days on the Great Lakes and how Millie's spirited personality and good looks drove him to distraction. Millie made no bones about her youthful flirtations and the way Ross, in the end, won the day. His persona of the French Canadian Voyageur and ruggedness captured Millie's heart. "I loved his body," Millie stated, unembarrassed. Everyone around the kitchen table roared at her remark.

* * *

Geneviève had made dinner reservations at the town's most popular Friday evening eating spot. Located on the edge of the Detroit River and Lake Erie, Duffy's was a fixture in the area for over three decades. Part tavern, restaurant, marina, and hotel, it was the place to be and to be seen on weekend evenings. The combination of drink, good food, music, and dancing created a backlog of pleasure boats in the river channel waiting for a slip in the marina to open. As the evening wore on, the venue's large car lot filled fast, and vehicles spilled out on the surrounding streets for blocks.

When they arrived, the hostess directed Luci and Barry to where Geneviève and Marie were seated. They had a prime table with an unobstructed view of the Detroit River and Bois Blanc Island. This evening, the northbound ship channel toward Detroit was a busy thoroughfare for pleasure craft of all sizes, and a favorite pastime was guessing which millionaire owned what yacht. Besides the view, the boisterous laughter originating from the far side of the building indicated the tavern clientele were getting warmed up. *Sounds like a fun-loving group of people and right up my alley,* Barry thought.

As the foursome chatted and looked over the menu, a steady stream of Geneviève's friends stopped by the table, extending hellos and exchanging snippets of gossip. Their surnames—Deslippe, Meloche, and Ouellette—confirmed for Barry that Luci came from a tight-knit community of French descendants. Geneviève and Marie mixed French and English phrases with their friends, making much of what they said unintelligible to Barry. With each introduction, Luci's grandmother insisted on showering praise on Barry as if he were already her grandson.

"Oh, let me introduce you to Luci's friend, Barry. He's from the biggest Irish Catholic family in Buffalo. He was the top student in his class in high school and was the quarterback on the football team too. Can you believe that? He's always loved aviation. You know, he's a cadet at that new prestigious Airforce Academy in Colorado. We're all so proud of him. And he flies those big supersonic planes that go 'boom' when they hit the sound barrier. He'll be a general someday, I know it."

Geneviève punctuated her exaggerations using hand gestures that pitched her red-nailed fingertips as if they were a flashing neon sign. She was aware that most of what she said was an overstatement. But as an octogenarian, she felt that embellishments, dramatization, and eccentricity were her prerogative. She made her greetings tantalizing by expressing them in an undertone as if they were an earth-shattering secret.

Naturally, the introductions necessitated Barry offering perfunctory remarks to his new acquaintances and a round of handshakes. Aware of his capacity to charm, Barry used the combination of his broad smile and electric blue eyes to great advantage with every introduction. From time to time, he threw Geneviève a raised eyebrow and approving nod, letting her know he was in lockstep with her game, happy to be on her team. His acknowledgment sealed their bond as co-conspirators in the harmless caper.

Luci didn't know whether her grandmother's hullabaloo should embarrass or delight her, but Marie had no equivocation. *This makes me want to vomit. Her childish behavior disgusts me,* she bristled. But she held her tongue and tried to hide her snarl. As the subject of the attention, Barry basked in Geneviève's hyperboles and marveled at how she condensed so much and divulged it so fast to her friends.

When they were ready to order dinner, Geneviève fixed her gaze on Barry. "You must get the perch, Barry," she said, pointing to the item on the menu. "Duffy's has the best fish on the river."

Friday night fish fries of lake perch were a cultural tradition in Buffalo. Geneviève's meal suggestion, though, provided an opening for Barry to amuse her with family fishing stories on Lake Ontario. Though Luci knew these accounts, she still got tickled hearing them again, and the one she liked best was where Barry and his brothers fell overboard. For Marie, her pursed lips and finger tapping on the tabletop made it difficult for her to disguise her frustration with Barry's malarkey.

Geneviève, however, was up for the game. Barry's tales led to a friendly squabble between the two about which of the Great Lakes, Erie or Ontario, had the most and the best perch.

"We may not have more perch in Lake Ontario, but we sure have the tastiest," Barry said with a twinkle in his eye. Then he laid down a challenge. "To prove it, you have a standing invitation to come to Buffalo and —my treat—try the perch at Murphy's. It's the hottest fish fry in Buffalo."

"Oh, do I like hot," Geneviève replied, and she and Barry made it official by shaking hands on the deal.

Marie fumed silently. *How juvenile! Thank God they didn't set a date for the eating challenge; otherwise, I would have had to reassess my weekend strategy. How many more hours of this bullshit?*

Geneviève liked Barry's spirit and, glancing at her daughter, wondered, *What the hell is wrong with Marie? Why would anyone not like this young man? He's smart, sincere, handsome, and, like my Arthur, has a great sense of humor.*

* * *

After dinner, Geneviève and Marie returned home. With dusk settling and the day's hustle and bustle behind them, Luci and Barry meandered undisturbed, holding hands, among the bulwarks of old Fort Malden. On the banks of the Detroit River, the quiet park was the perfect haven. Once more, they were themselves, relaxed, and in total awareness of each other. There wasn't a need to strive to impress or meet anyone's expectations. Living in the moment without a wish or urge to change a thing satisfied them.

A soothing breeze flowed from the river and rustled through the tree branches above them, creating delicate crackling sounds as they walked by the old and imposing two-and-a-half story brick Hough house, nestled among the earthworks. Barry gazed at Luci's profile, and he brushed a lock of hair from her forehead that a draft of air had caught. Turning toward him, Luci looked radiant. The fading sun's rays bounced off her shining hair, highlighting a mixture of shades of brown, and her full lips accentuated a perfect smile. Her eyes, though, were the central feature that defined her beauty. *They are magnets that keep drawing me in. I am helpless!* Barry acknowledged.

"This time of day is my favorite here at the old fort. I remember, Barry, you telling me that you can feel the phantoms of generations past in the woods at your family's cabin. I feel the same way here," Luci confessed. Her eyes scanned the lawn, and it looked to Barry that Luci was observing events that took place there hundreds of years earlier.

Barry let the silence rest on the breeze and waited for Luci to continue. "So much has happened in this place. It's as if the earth is reaching out and pleading to us to acknowledge what has gone before. This is where General Brock and the Shawnee chief Tecumseh made their plan to attack the Americans and ultimately captured Fort Detroit during the War of 1812. My relatives supported General Brock, and there's a musket in Grand-mère's basement that was used during that war. Think of the energy of that time. I feel it whenever I am here or see that gun."

"The French Canadians supported the British against the Americans?"

"It's a complicated story," Luci said, and she tried to explain a Canadian perspective of the War of 1812 that was foreign to Americans. "The British and Canadians saw the war as unbridled territorial aggression. You know,

Thomas Jefferson said that the Americans could conquer Canada by doing nothing more than marching their troops over the border. But when the American army came across into Canada and looted and burned the small communities, the resistance solidified against them."

Barry's brow furrowed. He knew little about the War of 1812 except for the British invasion of Washington DC and some of the battles in New York State. He had not heard this viewpoint before. *Ask questions, listen, and learn*, he thought.

"You look surprised," she said.

"Actually, I'm flabbergasted by what you've told me."

"What do you mean?"

"I never gave much thought to Canada and the United States in war. Mostly it's shocking to hear you say we Americans burned and looted here. It causes me to question the one-sidedness of the history that I've learned."

Luci nudged Barry. "To enlighten you, expect a book on the War of 1812 from the Canadian perspective for a Christmas present," she said and then challenged Barry to race with her through the old fort's earthworks.

Later they inspected the mounted cannons and peered into the windows of old brick barracks before sitting down on a bench overlooking the river. "Look over there, across the water. That's Bois Blanc," Luci said, pointing out the three-hundred-acre island.

"I remember hearing your grandmother mention it at dinner. What's the name mean, Luci?"

"Bois blanc means white forest. When the French came here in the early 1700s, they gave it that name because the birch and beech trees made the woods look white. Today most people call it Bob-Lo—an English corruption of the French.

"But your grandmother didn't call it Bob-Lo."

"Umm, You have to remember, Barry, she's French! Grand-mère would never use a mangled English version of a French name."

Barry laughed, thinking back on the episode with Ross. "Well, I don't want to get in trouble with your grandmother, so I'll remember to call it Bois Blanc too. Now, tell me more about the Island."

"Well, no one lives permanently on the island now. A huge amusement park, like the one you talk about in Crystal Beach, has taken over the island. You'll see it tomorrow when we take a ferry over there. But Bois Blanc played a big part in settlement of the area. In the beginning, it was home to the Wyandotte and the starting point of the Great Sauk Indian Trail. That trail went all the way from here to the Mississippi River through Michigan, Indiana, and Illinois. I kinda know about it from stories in my family since some of my fur-trading relatives traveled that trail. But in the late 1700s, the island served as a strategic military location. The British used it to secure boat traffic going to and from Detroit to keep you pesky Americans at bay."

Barry groaned. "Am I the enemy now?"

Luci raised an eyebrow. "Well, it depends on how pesky you get!"

Barry grinned and looked way. "And I suppose there is more?"

"Yeah, there is, as a matter of fact! We have particular pride that the island served as a conduit in the Underground Railroad for American slaves fleeing to freedom in Canada. Not far from the terminal where we will board our ferry for the Bois Blanc, there is a historical marker commemorating this fact."

Barry smiled while rubbing his chin. "Luci, you continue to amaze me! You are a walking history book. Last month, you told me all about the history in your home area. Today, in a totally different geographic area, you tell me stuff that happened three hundred years ago. I'm not sure I could do as well with the local history of Buffalo."

Luci's eyes sparkled, and she added another detail to whet Barry's interest in Bois Blanc. Leaning closer to him, she said, "Bois Blanc has been a favorite of lovers for decades. You might say it's a lovers' lane on an island. Even Grand-mère had romantic dates there as a young woman."

"No way! Your grand-mère?"

Luci nodded.

"Well, in that case, I don't want to be the one who breaks any family traditions," Barry shot back. A raised eyebrow from Luci set down a challenge.

Turning abruptly, Luci pointed upriver. "Hey, look, Barry! There's the ship coming down from Detroit going to the island."

Barry followed Luci's direction. "Wow! That is some impressive boat." As the ship drew closer, Barry got a better perspective of the imposing three-deck SS *Columbia* ferrying partygoers to the Bob-Lo Amusement Park. Illuminated with twinkling white lights from bow to stern, the steamer looked like a floating Christmas tree. "Oh my god! It's another coincidence," Barry said.

"Huh? What do you mean?"

"That ship looks like the Canadiana that used to sail from Buffalo to the amusement park in Crystal Beach. I can't believe it. It could be a twin of that ship."

Luci gave Barry a vacant stare, beginning to wonder if there was something to the idea of coincidences after all.

"When you told me we would take a ferry over to the island, I wasn't expecting something that huge! I never had a chance to ride on the Canadiana because it stopped sailing about ten years ago."

"Oh, no. I'm sorry. We'll be taking a little ferry, called the Papoose, from the Canadian side, not that one. In Canada, unlike in the US, people don't believe that everything bigger is better," Luci said, adding a wink.

Barry frowned, playacting his letdown and ignoring her wisecrack.

"Have you been on that big one?"

"A couple of times. There's an enormous ballroom on the top deck with live music and dancing that gets the passengers revved up on the ride from Detroit. If you think the ship is massive from this view, wait until it gets closer and docks, and you hear its horn blow."

A few minutes later, Barry got a sample of the ship's blast. "Yikes," he yelled, covering his ears with his hands. Luci laughed back at him and brought his hands down into hers. The steamer maneuvered to moor at the landing, and pumped-up passengers lined the decks, waving to those on the shoreline. Welcoming the partygoers to Canada, Barry and Luci reciprocated their greetings with enthusiastic waves of their own.

Barry put his arm around Luci's shoulder, pulling her closer. He felt like beating his chest and announcing to the world he had the most beautiful girl in his arms. The lengths of their bodies touched each other, and Barry took in Luci's scent. No girl had ever had such a powerful effect over him. In the past, emotion and sex had fueled his excitement. Now, those feelings mingled with wanting mutual fulfillment and creating an enduring relationship filled with love, joy, hope, amusement, inspiration, and even awe.

Luci's head was spinning. Barry was a gift better than any dream could summon. He was fun and authentic and enjoyed life, and, most of all, he listened and communicated his thoughts, feelings, and ambitions.

Feeling Barry's touch sent goosebumps rushing through Luci like small electrical shocks. She liked it and wanted more. His sweet aroma, the heat emanating from his body, and the tickle of his warm breath on her neck aroused pleasurable feelings in places that Luci could never have imagined. She had felt passionate sensations with Steve and Brian, but this emotion was different. Now, the mood was amplified in joy and the power of love grounded in fulfilling mutual desires and well-being.

Nuzzling, they shared their innermost thoughts and planned their future. Lingering kisses and sensual caresses made their emotions feel as high as untethered balloons. And as the river lapped on the shoreline and dusk gave way to the waning crescent of the moon, they created memories in the shadows of the old Fort Malden.

CHAPTER 19

Bois Blanc

BARRY had a lot to think about on his drive back to Buffalo. He was overwhelmed. *What's happening?* he thought. His emotions were a pattern of jet contrails tangled together across the canvas of a bright blue sky. He was joyful, grateful, optimistic, and serene at the same time. In the past thirty-four hours, he concluded that his life had taken on more meaning than ever, and he looked toward his career with a renewed passion. *Luci will be by my side.*

When he returned home, Barry knew he would be bombarded with questions. His father and mother would limit their curiosity. His parents had four good-looking sons, and fleeting romances were typical. They were used to a girl being hot for a few weeks, but then there would be another in the wings to take her place. His mother would ask about Luci's family, what he saw and did, and his general impressions of the past two days. Even though Luci heightened Barry's interest enough for him to travel two hundred miles for a short rendezvous, there was no reason to suspect that this girl would be different from the rest.

Joe was another story! Barry figured his brother would pepper him with questions about anything to do with sex. *Sorry, Joe. Not this time, brother!* John was in the army and not around to ask questions. Robert, a teenager absorbed in his own summertime puppy love adventures, would not care about Barry's love life.

The question Barry dreaded, though, was the one his father never failed to ask. It was about rubbers. *Good grief, Dad!* Barry thought. But Connor threw his son a curveball, holding back the irksome question Barry anticipated. A shrewd judge of people, he understood Barry had turned a corner in his life. "What did the trip teach you about yourself, Barry?" asked Connor.

His father's question rendered Barry speechless for a moment. The words he mustered felt inadequate. "Wow, that's heavy, Dad."

Connor held his gaze. "I think your shoulders are strong enough to carry the load." Then he turned and walked away, leaving his son with the challenge.

What have I learned? Barry asked himself. *I've left the nest. I set and fly my own course now, answerable and responsible for my choices and their results. Yeah, Dad, that's damn heavy.*

* * *

The morning after he returned home, Barry was up early, though he hadn't gotten much sleep. Joe had been away for the night, and Barry had the luxury of being alone in his room with his thoughts. But, even so, he struggled until the wee hours of the morning trying to compose a letter to Luci. He assumed his words would gush like a deluge expressing his joy, gratitude, and love. But as he tried to describe his feelings, he knew no thesaurus in the world could help him. The wastebasket in his bedroom overflowed with crumpled writing paper.

Then, he stopped trying so hard. He gave himself a gift of silence, closed his eyes, and listened to the summer night sounds flowing through his open window. *It's incredible,* he thought. *The things you can hear if you focus and are curious without judging: a neighbor's dog barking, footsteps on the sidewalk, a rustling of tree leaves, the sound of a distant car's engine, the opening of a garage door.*

After a few minutes, he took out a clean sheet of paper and tackled the letter once again. This time, the words fell like leaves in an autumn wind.

* * *

Geneviève retrieved a bundle of correspondence from her post office box early Thursday morning. Between greeting acquaintances in the lobby of the building, she absently scanned the small stack of envelopes in her hand. There were some personal letters, one from Sam to Marie, and some bills. *Aah! A message for Luci.* She recognized its author by the postmark from Buffalo. As she fingered the letter, memories of Arthur ignited a wave of warmth, and she felt she might be blushing. Closing her eyes, her senses spun back to the smell of fresh-cut summer hay and the glorious summer days on Bois Blanc with her first love.

She roused herself from the revelry, and reaching the bottom of the bundle, she was surprised to see another envelope addressed to her granddaughter. The return address was from Luci's hometown, but the name was mysterious. *Hmm, who could S. Ciao be? Isn't "ciao" Italian for "good-bye"? Does Luci have other admirers besides Barry and Chris? Lucky for my granddaughter that I'm not as nosy or as narrow-minded as her mother,* she thought, smiling at the half-truth.

Geneviève knew Marie's weakness for prying and hated her behavior. Since she had been a child, Marie had been a busybody. Geneviève would have accepted Marie's propensity as inquisitiveness, an excellent characteristic in anyone, except that her daughter corrupted it with biases of what was acceptable and not. If Marie thought a behavior was objectionable, she used her knowledge as a means for power. In childhood, Marie tattled on others to gain the attention and the approval of her parents. In adulthood, she misused her gift of curiosity as a way to constrain the behavior of others and to control events. Her interference might gain the desired results in the short term, but it often backfired in the long run. More important, though, Marie's meddling often resulted in the estrangement of others, leaving psychological scars on them and herself.

In Geneviève's opinion, Barry's visit was a victory. Millie and Ross adored him and threatened adoption. Barry proved his mettle sparring with the twenty relatives who attended the Saturday night dinner. Most importantly, he passed muster with Luci's cousin Jack, the worst of the bunch. A loudmouth without a brake, Jack got under people's skins as fast as greased lightning with his pranks.

"Yep, Barry," Jack had said while tossing down another whiskey. "You're not faint of heart, that's for sure. You stand your ground well. And that's saying a hell of a lot coming from me!" Everyone who heard Jack's remark roared and gave thumbs up in agreement for the compliment paid to Barry and for Jack's opinion of himself.

Marie was good-tempered during Barry's stay, but she unleashed her frustrations the evening after he left. "It's too much too fast," she said to her mother as the two sat together on the front porch.

Believing it was better to let Marie unload her irritation, Geneviève withheld comment and bided her time. *One thing my porch soirées have taught me is that listening and forgoing judgment goes a long way in understanding the core concerns beneath a person's words.*

"It's obvious that they're infatuated with each other. Luci isn't old enough to get entangled in a long-term relationship. For that matter, neither is Barry," Marie said. "I bet his parents aren't too happy about this misadventure, either. He's got three years left at the academy, and God knows how much more training after that. I rue the day I allowed Luci to accept those stupid invitations from Sister Mary Catherine."

Geneviève half-heartedly concurred with her daughter. "I'm not going to argue with you about Luci's age and experience. I'm sympathetic to your concerns. In my era, limited career choices restricted women's potential, and early marriage was one of the few options."

Marie gasped, raising both eyebrows, and put down her cocktail. *Mother is agreeing with me?*

Geneviève rocked in her chair, thinking it best not to give advice but to get to the root of Marie's irritation. *It's a long way from infatuation to a lifelong commitment. What is beneath Marie's obsession with breaking up this relationship?* "What's the bottom line, Marie? What is it that you want?" she asked in a tone above a whisper.

"I want Luci to end this relationship with Barry!" *At last, I can say out loud what I think and not be condemned for it.*

Through years of listening to friends and relatives pour their hearts out, Geneviève knew when people affirmed what they wanted, it was not the whole truth. The real motivation lurked beneath their wish—the desire for control over events, people, or the future. Exposing the naked truth of a matter required uncovering the reason for control. Marie wanted Luci's relationship to end; she had not revealed what fanned that desire.

"Why is this important to you, Marie?"

"Aren't you listening? I told you, Mother. Luci is too young for an all-consuming romance. She has college and an entire life ahead. I don't want to see her get hurt."

"Getting hurt because of heartbreak? Marie, I've seen people fall in love, but it's not real or committed love. It's infatuation. It runs hot, and it burns itself out. I've even had a few of those hurts in my day. Do you wonder if this isn't a natural part of life's experience? A part of finding one's path? A part of taking responsibility for one's choices and growing up?"

"Should experiencing life mean ending up like Adele or Darla? I don't think so! I don't want to see Luci turn out to be like her sisters," Marie muttered.

"Luci has three sisters. Why do you fear she'll be like Adele or Darla? Why can't she wind up like Aimee?"

Taking a sip of her old-fashioned, Marie considered Geneviève's remark. "Okay, Mother, I concede your point. What bothers me is that he's in the service, that his family is so far away, and that we don't know anything about him."

Geneviève allowed silence to intervene before proceeding. Her intuition told her these were subterfuges. "Is there something else?"

Fear—that's what's at the bottom of this, Geneviève surmised.

Marie was at odds with herself. Underneath, she knew these were pretexts, but she wasn't ready to admit an unpleasant truth. Her inability to manage her own emotions and feelings of insignificance stoked her relentless need for control. She needed to bathe in the reflected glory of her children's successes to boost her self-esteem, and she wanted to ensure this through complete authority over her daughters. Most of all, she wanted her children to need her. If they were self-sufficient, where would that leave her?

Marie left her mother's question unanswered.

* * *

Returning home from her errands, Geneviève found her granddaughter on the front porch curled up in an overstuffed chair, engrossed in a novel. Giving Luci a knowing smile, she furtively handed the two letters to her. Luci's eyes widened, and not wanting to alert Marie to the correspondence, she tucked the envelopes between the pages of her book.

It is a good thing Marie doesn't pay much attention to the New York Times *bestseller list,* Geneviève thought, a slight smile crossing her face. *Otherwise, she would go berserk to learn Luci was reading a novel she no doubt would consider trashy.*

Tired from her errands, Geneviève lowered herself in her rocking chair next to Luci to rest. "I see you have a new book there?" she commented with a sparkle in her eye. She looked sideways to read the title of the work: *Valley of the Dolls.*

"Oh, is it as scandalous as the reviewers and my evening *soirée* ladies say? To be honest, I wanted a peek at it myself to see if it outdoes *Moll Flanders* and *Lady Chatterley's Lover*."

Luci blanched and stared at her grandmother. It wasn't that Geneviève was aware of the nature of the novel she was reading that shocked Luci. Instead, it was that her grandmother had read two of the more salacious books of the time.

"Grand-mère! You've read those novels?"

With a characteristic wave of her hand, Geneviève confessed. "Ma Bichette, of course, I have read them! Why are you so surprised?" she asked.

Luci blinked her eyes. "But . . ."

"It doesn't matter what generation you are born into, youth never changes. My young friends and I were as interested in sex as much as you and your chums are today. How else do you think we could endure procreating without having some fun doing it?"

Luci's mouth fell open. It was awkward envisioning her grandmother reading or thinking about anything verging on licentious behavior. But this also raised her curiosity about why such thoughts were uncomfortable for her and for her friends. She and Shelia had often giggled about the idea of their parents having sex and never considered that they engaged in it before marriage. *Do cultural and religious norms and taboos shape these feelings? Why do we deny our parents and grandparents the pleasures we want for ourselves?* But these questions prompted another question. *When parents tell their children that sex is forbidden or should be avoided, why shouldn't children ascribe the same condition to sex when it involves their parents?*

"But Grand-mère, *Lady Chatterley's Lover* was a banned book."

Geneviève shook her finger at Luci. "All the more reason to read it!"

Luci turned her head, unable to look at her grandmother in the eye.

"Ma Bichette, please don't act so stunned! My attitude and actions have nothing to do with youthful rebellion; they are grounded in a belief of personal freedom. Because some group or government bans a book doesn't mean its material has nothing valuable to teach us. Make no mistake, Ma Bichette, governments and narrow-minded groups ban books because they challenge and teach people something important. Banned books are bold and provocative and confront issues that certain segments of the population want to sweep under the carpet."

Luci's mind swirled as if she were in discussion with the Nerd group. *Grand-mère is spectacular.*

But Geneviève wasn't finished. "Banned books often question current social, political, moral, or religious ideas and norms. Society can never progress if groups of small-minded people deny others access to new information and ideas."

Luci rubbed her temple, uncertain about how to respond.

"Oh, yes, a book might attract us in the beginning because it is said to be shocking, but that's the author's come-on. We enjoy the book, at the start, superficially for that reason. But underneath there's generally a deeper message and something to learn. It's not the sex, violence, murder, or romance that keeps us turning the page. No, it's the clash of ideas that challenges our thoughts, biases, and behaviors. If we are lucky, it changes us for the better, and that is what makes a book worthwhile."

Geneviève let her thoughts settle on Luci and then said, "I've got a present for you. Wait here."

She lifted herself from her chair and hustled from the porch. Returning a few minutes later, Geneviève handed her granddaughter a book with an orange and black cover: a complete and unexpurgated copy of *Lady Chatterley's Lover*. "Read it, Ma Bichette, and learn."

* * *

Soft strains of Franki Valli and the Four Seasons played from the transistor radio on Luci's bedside table. She had saved opening Barry's letter until late in the evening as a child might do with a Whirley Pop, heightening the anticipation of what was within. Sitting on the side of her bed, her hand shook as she held the letter, gleaning new and deeper meaning from Barry's words each time she reread it.

> *Monday, July 18, 1966 – Buffalo, NY*
>
> *Dear Luci with an i,*
>
> *Here I am at 2:00 a.m., a lonely lover whose sole comfort comes from the cherished memories we made together a few hours ago. My desk is a witness to the completion of many term papers and homework assignments, but it has never been my partner in a confession of love. Can words convey the depth of my thoughts, rampant emotions, and gratitude to you? I'm uncertain they exist, and*

if they did, it's unclear that I could assemble them to explain how you have captured my heart and what you mean to me.

I'm no John Keats or Robert Browning, but my feelings are no less potent than their descriptions of love. Being "in love" is a passion like the flames of a blistering fire that race across the prairie. It's fierce and red, self-serving, and out of control. It feeds upon itself until there is nothing left. "To love," though, is a passion like the embers of a flickering fire that lingers within the hearth. It's gentle and glowing, crackles with surprise, and permeates the senses. It's warm and steady. It rekindles itself, and it endures.

With you, Luci, being "in love," is inadequate for me. No, I love you. You unexpectedly and beautifully transformed my life the evening you entered it. Because of you, my world flourishes in joy, compassion, amusement, serenity, and awe. I feel, for the first time, that I am entirely immersed in the bounty of life. I would be lost and hollow without you. You've made me complete. I can face any hurdle and accomplish anything with you beside me. Our time is just beginning, Luci, as we walk across the stepping-stones of life together.

For all of this and more, I seal my love with gratitude for our memory making. I send you a cascade of Bois Blanc Island kisses, placing each one where I know it will please you the most.

Barry

His last line evoked a flood of happy and sensuous memories of their time on Bois Blanc Island. Luci lay back on her bed, cuddling the sable-brown Bob-Lo teddy bear Barry purchased for her at the amusement park. The television advertising jingle "Take someone you love to Bob-Lo Island" had a new meaning for Luci. Closing her eyes, the smell of the damp ground, the fresh-cut grass, and the soft sounds of the river stroking the shore permeated her body.

She and Barry had played nonstop on the topsy-turvy amusement park rides, the Wild Mouse roller coaster and Rockets circle swings being favorites. But the most memorable was the ride on the park's carousel. Like the one in Fairmont Park, its horses were exquisite, hand-carved masterpieces. Music pulsed from the band organ that kept the horses on their pace. Luci rode a silver jumper with a golden mane. "You look every bit a forest princess as you did in Fairmont Park," Barry called out.

In her heart, Luci had wondered whether she was astride the same horse her grandmother rode during her trysts with Arthur on Bois Blanc. Flying on her make-believe steed with Barry by her side, Luci sensed the air still held the energy from those lovers of over a half century past.

Glad to catch their breath after the rides, Luci and Barry had strolled hand in hand to the southern tip of the island. Luci promised Barry to take him to a special place where they could enjoy the sandwiches and cold drinks they had purchased for a late lunch. There were many secluded spots on the island where lovers could roam and be undisturbed, far from the crushing crowd of thrill-seekers. But Luci selected this one because she knew its sense of history would please Barry—and she remembered something else special about it from Arthur's letter.

"What the heck is that? It looks like part of an abandoned fort!" Barry said.

"That's an old blockhouse from the 1830s. It was an extension of the Fort Malden defenses."

"Good God, this thing is sturdy," Barry said as he walked closer to examine it. "It's all square-cut logs and looks like white oak."

Luci gave Barry a gentle shove. "Remember, the British built it to fight off those annoying Americans."

"You do remember, Luci, that I am part of the American armed forces. I could be on a reconnaissance mission. Bois Blanc might not be safe in Canadian hands for long."

"Smart aleck!"

Barry gave her a poker face, grinned, and turned toward the structure and circled the building.

"This is in remarkable shape. Look at the line of gun slits on all four sides of the first and second floors. I guess the British were damn serious about holding on to this piece of real estate," he said.

Peeking through one of the slits, Barry saw narrow openings cut into the ceiling above. "That's curious. What the heck?" he remarked. "Hey, Luci, I've read about this before but have never seen it." He lifted Luci so her eyes could reach the narrow openings. "Take a look at those long slots in the ceiling."

"I see them! What are they?"

"Those are murder slits. They allowed the soldiers on the second floor to protect themselves. It made it easy for them to shoot intruders who came into the blockhouse."

A chill went through Luci's body as Barry lowered her to the ground. "Oh, that's creepy! I hate to think about it."

"Yeah, I agree. Like Lincoln said, 'There's nothing good in war. Except its ending.' So no more blood and guts. Let's split this place," Barry said, retaking Luci's hand.

Leaving thoughts of the blockhouse behind, they walked toward the lakeside, hoping for a different kind of memory making. Barry spread a blanket on the ground underneath a small grove of trees next to the shoreline, and he and Luci sat down with their luncheon sacks. A smile tugged on Barry's lips thinking of Millie's insistence that he take the blanket to the Island. "Barry, dear, young lovers never go to Bois Blanc without a blanket," she not so innocently said. Her meaning was clear, and what it suggested was on the minds of Luci and Barry since they had arrived on the island.

Barry's mood changed without warning, and he felt his throat tighten. "Luci, sometimes I am not sure if I made the right choice in going to the academy."

This stunning admission left Luci speechless for a moment, and her double take registered her surprise. "What do you mean?"

"Looking at those murder slits kind of threw me," Barry said. "I love planes and aeronautics, but I don't like the idea of killing. I guess you could call it a clash of conscience or a moral dilemma. I know I told you President Kennedy's remarks inspired me about the military's new role in shaping the world to be a better place. I hold on to that vision. But if I am truthful, I'm uncertain whether this is the right path for me."

Barry's comments sounded a familiar bell for Luci. *Wasn't Chris going through the same predicament? Didn't he sort it out by choosing a noncombatant role and reframing the situation?*

Luci didn't like giving advice, believing it generally provoked a defensive response. From her father, she learned that people don't want to be told what to do. "The best way to help people is to enable them to clarify a predicament," Sam said. "Ask questions or tell a story that opens up a person's imagination to see options. Remember, the best advice giver always bundled his guidance in a parable."

Unwrapping her sandwich, she began sharing Chris's story with Barry. "One of my Friday night buddies. . ." Luci began. She explained Chris's choice to enlist in the army and how he had recast the dilemma to fit his life's vision.

The tranquil setting with the river water glistening in the afternoon sun proved to be the perfect place and time for reflection. Barry relaxed; he was with someone he implicitly trusted. He absorbed Luci's narrative and thought about the message within it. "Luci, this is one reason I love you so much. You listen and understand. Your friend Chris sounds like an incredible person, and that is a great story. I've got a lot to think about, and you've helped me see some choices."

Barry drew Luci closer to him, his powerful arms wrapping her in a cocoon of tenderness and intimacy. His classic broad grin beamed across his face, and his blue eyes intensified, studying Luci's delicate features. "But this is the other reason I love you so much," he whispered before giving Luci an exquisite kiss on her mouth. He breathed in her scent, ran his fingers through her hair, and stroked and caressed her with his lips in every imaginable place she would allow.

That afternoon, Millie's blanket was put to good use in memory making on Bois Blanc Island.

* * *

Luci refolded and wiggled Barry's letter back into its envelope and placed it for safekeeping in the side pocket of her suitcase in the closet. Sitting on top of her bed, Luci studied the other letter resting on her bedside table. "S. Ciao," Luci said aloud and then chuckled. *Shelia and her shorthand. What does this mean?* In another time, Luci would have ripped the letter open, anxious to figure out Shelia's meaning of assigning the Italian word for goodbye as her last name. Now, though, she hesitated. As Shelia would say, *I'm suffering from Barry Glow, and I don't want to let it go.*

After a few moments, Luci unsealed the envelope and removed her friend's note. As her eyes scanned the document, Luci's mood changed abruptly. Its contents were devastating. Things between Shelia and Bob had bombed. Now, Luci understood her friend's shorthand. *"Ciao" means goodbye to Bob.*

That news, though, was not the worst. Shelia was in a mess. "A repeat scenario of Darla's story," Luci mumbled, her vision blurring with tears.

How Luci wished she could be with Shelia to comfort her and serve as a sounding board. She knew, though, that as much as she may want to offer words of advice, there was nothing she could do to provide help. Like Barry's quandary, this decision was so personal and life changing that giving guidance would serve to compromise her friend's autonomy. In the end, freedom of choice, while sometimes a burden, is a responsibility that rests wholly with the individual. Luci sat down and, her hand shaking, began a letter to Shelia.

Thursday, July 21, 1966, 11:00 p.m.

Dear Shelia,

I just read your letter and had to respond right away. I am sorry I'm not with you in person to be a sounding board, help you grieve, and silence the vicious inner voices . . .

Part II

1984–1986

CHAPTER 20

Mourning

It was a dark, cold, damp morning, November 15, 1984. The clouds were so thick even the smallest ray of sun couldn't penetrate the late autumn sky to shine on the walnut casket descending in the ground. The Knights of Columbus, the pallbearers, were dressed in full regalia: red, purple, and white lined capes, gleaming silver swords, and black velvet and ostrich-plumed chapeaux. They stood out in stark contrast to the dismal surroundings of the bare trees and brown grass of the Catholic cemetery in the Ontario countryside. The pomp and ceremony would have been to her liking: an overflowing crowd at the rosary and visitation at Sutton's funeral home, the ostentatious three-celebrant High Mass, Gregorian requiem chants performed by the diocesan choir, and a lengthy funeral cortege stretching for two blocks. Marie could not have planned the event better if she had done it herself.

Luci, Adele, Darla, and Aimee stood together, separated a few feet from the rest of the mourners. Now grown women, they lived within driving distance of each other in Southern California. Adele and Darla had homes within the Inland Empire area. Aimee had a medical practice in Santa Barbara, and Luci lived in San Diego. After years of conniving and controlling her daughters' lives, Marie, in the end, achieved one of her most significant aspirations: all her children lived near her.

Many of the funeral-goers had a cursory connection with Marie. Some were alumni of Geneviève's evening *soirées* and came to the funeral out of respect to the grand matron. Others were cousins or distant relatives who remembered Marie from the old days. But after living thirty years away from her birthplace, many who knew her well lay in the same cemetery that was her final resting place. Geneviève, Millie, Ross, and even Sam had died before her. *Cherished memories and secrets of the olden days are slipping away*, Luci thought as the priest shook the last sprinkles of holy water on Marie's casket.

For the sisters, the days surrounding their mother's funeral resurrected childhood recollections. Eating perch at Duffy's Tavern, watching the massive freighters navigate the river channel, walking past the limestone library, and meandering through Fort Malden transported them for a few hours to a bygone era. The funeral played out in places associated with childhood memories and family lore. Suttons, the mortuary, saw to the arrangements for every family burial for decades. The old church, Sainte Jean Baptist—the site for family weddings, baptisms, and funerals over the past 150 years—was the location where the marriages of Lucinda, Geneviève, and Marie took place and where the solemn Masses for their funerals were conducted. In the graveyard, named the same as the church, the graves of family members since the 1830s could be found. These places were so embedded in family tradition that people often sensed odd feelings of inspiration and happiness there, thinking these were the expression of family spirits.

While the nostalgic thoughts summoned recollections of a cherished period for the sisters, they triggered sad emotions as well. Each asked herself, *Would life have been better had we stayed? Would Adele have married a better and more stable provider? Would Darla have married her first love? Would they all have had a better sense of place?*

* * *

After the reception for the mourners, Luci drove her sisters to the airport to return home. By choice, over the years, the three older girls suppressed memories of their birthplace as a way of coping with their sense of loss and homesickness. They did not want to tarry longer than necessary after the burial for fear that the feelings being resurrected would haunt them. Adele confided to Luci the day before the funeral, "After we moved to California, I lost a sense of belonging. I always felt I was straddling a line, one foot on either side and not embedded anywhere."

Luci stayed on for two days after the ceremony. Besides arranging for Marie's name and dates of birth and death to be added to those of Sam's on the tombstone's brass plaque and hosting a luncheon the day after the funeral for relatives and friends, Luci wished to disconnect from her regular life. She wanted time to grieve: to be free from commitments, to-do lists, and phone calls. Most of all, she wanted to be in a place that could give her comfort.

Of Marie's daughters, Luci was the one who retained the most connection to the area. She described her visits to Canada as *going back home*, making it clear where her heart resided. A continuing and close relationship with Geneviève and Millie and Ross over the decades fostered and nurtured her feelings. But there was something more potent than these ties that kept drawing Luci back: it was the memory of the summer of 1966 and Bois Blanc Island.

* * *

Returning from the airport to her hotel room at Duffy's, Luci collapsed in bed, exhausted. The past two months had been draining. Marie's last stages of metastatic uterine cancer required extensive care. It was the same diagnosis that had taken Geneviève, and Luci and her sisters often wondered if this might be the end in store for them as well. But considering this eventuality was one more reason Luci tried to live in the present and enjoy each moment. Achieving equilibrium in her life, however, was a continuing challenge. Unrealistic expectations and demands from work and family were like invasive weeds, but Luci pushed back and prevented them from overcoming her.

Unlike her sisters, Luci had no spouse or children who required her attention. She had lovers, but she did not allow them to dictate how she should live. The one in her life who had a modicum of influence was Dickens, a handsome twenty-pound Boston terrier. His name was a good fit, Luci thought. The pooch had a gentlemanly style like Charles Dickens but could also be a rascal with his playful antics. Dickens made his mistress laugh, and he and Luci had a special relationship of mutual affection and loyalty that other pet lovers understand.

Over the last months of their mother's life, Luci and her sisters took turns relieving Marie's live-in caregiver. It was fortunate Sam had planned well, and there was enough money to cover Marie's medical expenses and nursing care. Other resources, the girls discovered, like Medicare, were not enough to cover all outpatient chemotherapy or long-term care and professional at-home care. In her social services work, Luci understood the enormous gaps in a safety net for healthcare services. "We have a non-system in healthcare," Luci said as she witnessed catastrophic medical expenses financially devastating families and sending them into bankruptcy.

Luci's family was among the lucky ones, primarily because of Sam's resources. Even so, the nest egg their father put aside was wiped out by the time of Marie's passing. As Luci looked at her parents' last bank statement and their depleted finances, she wondered, *In the end, what does life boil down to?* Many times, Sam had counseled Luci and her sisters, "Take advantage of the present. After all, it's the only thing that you ever truly have." Tearing as she looked at the ledger that revealed the extent of her parents' drained assets, Luci bit her lower lip and closed her eyes. *Pop's wisdom has never rung truer.*

The family's home would be sold. The T-Bird, Sam's jewel, was parked in the garage, a sad reminder of better days. As much as Marie had kicked up a fuss over her husband's purchase, she did not have the heart to sell the car after he died. Holding on to the vehicle allowed Marie to imagine that Sam would come back at any time to his cherished "Bird." Throughout her life, Marie ruminated about her choice of a husband. Sadly, it wasn't until after Sam's death that she comprehended the depth of her husband's understanding and love for her. After his passing, the words of Emily Brontë haunted her, and she realized, *Without Sam, my universe has turned into a "mighty stranger."*

Disposal of the real estate was in the hands of an executor. *Thank goodness, my sisters and I don't need to deal with the legal issues that go along with probate,* Luci thought. But there were still personal effects that required sorting out: family memorabilia, photographs, letters, and books. There were clothes, dishes, and furniture requiring disposal or distribution among the siblings. The T-Bird would go to a nonprofit for auction. An art gallery in Palm Springs, where Marie's work was known, would relieve the family of her paintings stacked in her studio. Luci and her sisters wanted everything removed from the home before the Christmas holidays, and they chose the week after Thanksgiving to face the challenge of clearing out a lifetime of accumulated possessions.

Tonight, after Marie's funeral, though, Luci was not thinking about any of this. All she desired was sleep. Tomorrow she would visit with relatives at the luncheon and devote the rest of the afternoon to grieve in her own way.

* * *

Luci was unsure whether it was fatigue or the desire to be by herself that caused her anxiousness at the start of the luncheon. Her mind wandered to the old days, and she found it difficult to focus. Her anxiety produced bursts of prickling sensations across her skin that made her fidget. Chatting with cousins, aunts, and uncles, Luci smiled and nodded. But she was only going through the motions of being present. She was off-kilter. *I'm surrounded by a whirlwind of sound, yet I feel shrouded in a blanket of silence and loneliness.*

It was Luci's cousin, Jack, the person who had teased Barry years before in Millie's kitchen, who snapped Luci out of her muddle. Jack's instincts were as sharp as a razor, honed from decades of acute observation in negotiating business dealings. His penetrating gaze shooting from his steely eyes could make even the most skillful deceiver crumble. Nothing got by Big Jack's notice. That's what made him a natural in discovering others' vulnerabilities and leveraging these to his advantage. Sometimes, though, he used his skill to help others.

Jack stood across the room, scrutinizing Luci. Strolling up to her side, he leaned in close and, in his low, rough voice, whispered, "Come and join us, Luci." Startled, she looked at him and then gave him a knowing smile.

Luci was thankful for Jack. She loved that bear of a man who knew her better than she understood herself sometimes. During her summer visits, Luci would spend several days with her uncle and his family of ten boys and two girls on his large farm. Luci got a kick from the "crazy dozen" as her uncle referred to his family. At mealtime, it was each child for him or herself, and Luci learned that fact fast during lunch when she was seven years old.

Not liking something on her plate, Luci turned toward the head of the table and told her aunt, "Yuck, this doesn't taste good. I don't like it."

Looking through her black-rimmed glasses, her aunt shot back, "Luci, you don't have to worry about it. Jack just ate it."

Luci snapped her head and stared at Jack, who sat next to her. With a wily grin and scrunched nose, Jack returned her look as he swallowed the offending piece of food. *Lesson learned!* Something about the incident, though, drew the two cousins close to each other, and they remained friends throughout the years. Now, Jack took Luci's hand and pulled her into the present.

It was a remarkable reunion. The atmosphere was raucous and chaotic. Everyone was living in the moment, laughing, joking, nudging each other, and telling tall tales and recounting reminiscences. Combined with good food and ample drink, the high-spirited gathering was woven together as well as the best-crafted textile. Geneviève would have adored the ruckus —Marie not so much. Most of all, though, the family had given Luci a gift: a lesson of being present and creating memories that could not be taken away.

* * *

The luncheon proved the best prelude for Luci's time alone. She needed a respite to help drown out the unhappiness of watching her mother suffer from her wretched disease. Marie's pain, weakness, and wasting away were hard for her daughters to bear. The worst was hopelessness; everyone knew there was nothing any of them could do that would change the inevitable outcome.

Marie had her faults. She was controlling, self-centered, stubborn, and distant. But Marie's daughters were realists; they came to grips with her flaws, and, for the most part, tried to forgive her transgressions. Through their own life experiences, they recognized that context contributed to defining a person. Environment and life circumstances don't excuse bad behaviors, but they can explain them. As a result, Marie's imperfections did not override her daughters' feelings of empathy or compassion for her as she battled her illness. After all, she was their mother.

It was another cold and dreary afternoon. The wind had picked up from the river, enhancing the chill and making it more biting than usual. Luci wrapped a bright woolen scarf around her neck and slipped on a pair of lined leather gloves. Her navy double-breasted coat, worsted slacks, black boots, and a felted red beret would, she thought, keep her plenty warm.

Leaving Duffy's, she walked up Dalhousie Street and past Gore Street to the central part of the village. Seeing familiar places elicited memories that warmed Luci despite the cold wind needling her face. There was Moffat's drug store on her right side. Raising her head, she sniffed and thought she smelled the comforting odor from the old-time pharmacy reaching out to her. Vapors from the medications Mr. Moffat made with pestle and mortar comingled with the scents of liniments and ointments, creating a pleasant aroma that had felt soothing to Luci as a child. This is where Geneviève purchased exotic elixirs for one ailment or another. Luci recollected the small bottle of paregoric made by Mr. Moffat that her grandmother had stored in her wooden medicine cabinet. If Luci had an upset stomach or jittery nerves, she remembered how Geneviève dispensed the little green drops, which tasted like peppermint, into a glass of water and gave it to her. *How things have changed*, she thought. *Today, people would be hysterical at the thought of giving a medication laced with opium to a child. Funny, somehow, my generation survived!*

Luci put her hand to her mouth, trying to suppress a chuckle as she passed the town's two banks. They were on opposite corners at Dalhousie and Richmond Streets, and their physical position was a bold advertisement to the townspeople of the competition that existed between them. She recalled the lighthearted arguments each summer between her mother and grandmother about which of the banks was the better place, the Bank of Montreal or the Dominion Bank of Canada. They never settled the dispute. *Perhaps,* Luci supposed, *they're still disagreeing about the matter and driving the angels to distraction.*

The post office, further up the street and in the middle of the block, was an unpretentious building. In Luci's opinion, it was not an adequate replacement for the original sturdy two-story red-brick edifice filled with banks of gleaming brass postal boxes in its lobby. Even though the older building was more classical in design, it couldn't compete with the newer one's unique place in Luci's memory. Tears started to well in her eyes, recalling the letters from and to Barry that traveled through the nondescript structure. Luci's hand involuntarily reached over her chest. *Oh my! How my heart aches, wishing I could receive those again.*

With teardrops staining her cheek, Luci turned and walked further, passing the old movie theater on the corner of Richmond and Sandwich Streets. *How many films did I see there? How many bags of popcorn did I devour with my cousins and later with Brian? Brian!* She had spoken with Brian at her mother's visitation at Sutton's funeral home. He was as good-looking and charming as he was twenty or so years ago. And the way he hugged her revealed that the memories they had made together years before were as precious to him as they were to her. *Respect and caring are emotions that last,* Luci mused as thoughts of her connection with Brian warmed her heart.

Ambling in dreamland, Luci found herself facing the front of Geneviève's home. She winced when she saw that the old oak tree in the front yard was gone—cut down, perhaps due to disease. Its thick foliage had safeguarded the porch and its inhabitants for decades from the blazing sun's rays. *What a shame! The tree lent such a noble character to the grounds.* A shiver went through her body as if she had lost a friend. *I loved hearing the rustle of its branches from the river breeze creep as comforting as a lullaby through my bedroom window at night.*

The porch, though, was still intact and screened. It was closed now, of course, due to the cold weather. After all these years, Luci sensed the place still retained the energy from the secrets revealed there and the memories it helped to create. Standing motionless, she cocked her head and instinctively put her finger across her mouth. She thought she detected Geneviève's fruity voice cross-examining her guests while her rocker creaked, marking time. Luci shifted her eyes and felt the intensity of her grandmother's gaze and the comfort of the light touch of her hand. She had kept the volume of *Lady Chatterley's Lover* that Geneviève had given her. It served as a reminder of her grandmother's open-mindedness that strengthened her own perspective about the destructive power of bias.

And how could I ever forget the Lucinda stories I heard on that porch? How could I forget the gift of Lucinda's wisdom that has been my north star and guided my life? In the end, what is life's meaning? Luci asked herself, thinking of the words from Lucinda's journal:

> *A flower begins by taking a seed from one who has gone before, and at its end, it provides a seed so another can start. The meaning of the flower is not in the taking and giving. Its purpose is in the quality of the bloom that it nurtures to beautify the world. I have received, and I have given. The meaning of my life is the bloom that I have become.*

Something from the old days, though, continued to haunt Luci: the bundle of letters from Arthur. Luci had the packet, still held together by a golden ribbon, and kept them tucked in a desk drawer at her home. From time to time over the years, she retrieved and read the bittersweet correspondence. Now, standing on the sidewalk on the empty street, the memories of Geneviève's recitation of Arthur's love notes rolled through her mind, overcoming her with nostalgia and puzzlement. *Oh, Arthur!* Luci whispered, her eyes cast down. *What was the interference? Will the reason ever be disclosed?*

Luci let out a gasp, startled from her thoughts by a tap on her shoulder from behind. Luci turned, and her eyes focused on the middle-aged woman standing before her. "You know, that old house is haunted," the stranger said, pointing her finger at Geneviève's home.

Luci peered back at the gossiper, a smile flowing across her lips. "I have no doubt about that. It probably is!" Then, turning on her heel and rebuffing the busybody, Luci walked down Murray Street toward the river, her reminiscences not yet concluded.

* * *

Luci left the most poignant recollection for last: Fort Malden. *How the riverfront has changed*, she reflected, viewing the treed landscape of the old fort. The Hough house was still there and had not changed much, which was comforting. But the foliage, trimmed and contained, looked artificial; before, it was wild and natural. Now, designated walkways directed visitors around the ramparts; before, she and Barry tramped through the earthworks and slid down them like children. In front of her, there was a concrete riverwalk that guided walkers and runners along the shore; earlier, there were rustic and narrow pathways enticing young lovers to stroll holding hands.

Nevertheless, the manicuring and modernization could not destroy the resilience of the old fort's spirit. The fortification's life force emanated as strong as ever and rose from the earth and battlements like a quivering earthquake. The power of General Brock and Tecumseh, the soldiers, the French settlers, and the First Peoples, still cried out demanding acknowledgment. *They will not be denied,* Luci comforted herself. *Time marches on and changes things, but it cannot eradicate the imprint of energy stamped on a place. Energy does not die. Its vibration, perhaps redistributed, continues. Memories are similar. They do not die; they are the waves that flow throughout a lifetime.*

It was a different season, but Luci's memories, seared in her mind and engraved on her heart, were not diminished. July 15, 1966. She recalled the soothing breeze flowing from the river and Barry's gentle touch as he pushed back a lock of her hair from her forehead. She shuddered now, not from the cold but from pleasurable feelings like those she had experienced then. Retracing her walk with Barry across to the river's edge, she found a bench to sit on. Closing her eyes, her recollections were crystal clear.

Barry's touch sent goose bumps rushing through me like small electrical shocks, and the warmth of his embrace made me dissolve into his arms. His sweet aroma and a wisp of his warm breath tickled my neck, arousing the most pleasurable feelings in places of my body I could never have imagined.

Looking across to Bois Blanc, the island was silent. No lighted steamships were speeding down the river with joyous travelers. Rattling rides, the smell of cotton candy, and the carousel music were hibernating, resting comfortably, waiting to reawaken in summer. Millie's blanket! *I remember the feel of it, soft underneath as Barry cuddled and nuzzled and kissed me with his warm lips on every available part of my body.*

Her eyes misted. *What happened, Barry?*

CHAPTER 21

Transgression

LIKE a tornado, 1984 came from nowhere, without warning, and was devastating. Sam's death on January 13, 1984, was a shock to everyone who knew him. How could a small wound, a spider bite, cut down a man as robust and resilient as Sam so fast? Two days after the injury, he had minor flu symptoms but discounted these. Instead, he looked forward to his weekly poker game with city politicos, businessmen, and influencers. It was not in Sam's character to permit a slight case of the flu to divert him from an evening of fun and acquiring the latest local gossip and business scoops.

Sam's symptoms turned serious the morning after the gathering. He arrived disoriented at the emergency room with a raging fever, rapid heartbeat, and shortness of breath. Deterioration was swift. Within seventy-two hours, he succumbed to an infection that spun out of control and left his body powerless in the face of septic shock. Like a forewarning, Sam had often predicted, "At the most unexpected time, I'll meet my match, and death will sneak up from behind and get the better of me."

Sam's passing was an irreversible loss to the structure of the family fabric. His strengths of perspective and open-mindedness were his bedrock, and he wove these into a resilient tapestry that withstood the stresses of the ebb and flow of family dynamics and conflicting personalities. Without his presence, sustaining a bond between his wife and daughters would be difficult. With Marie's death a few months later, the family never had the chance to test their tenacity in accepting each other's foibles and pulling together without Sam's fortitude and strength.

* * *

Luci arrived ahead of Adele and Darla to tackle emptying their parents' house. To no one's surprise, Aimee was too busy with her medical practice to pitch in and help. Marie's little darling, with narcissistic-leaning characteristics, was never around when needed. "Exactly like Mother," Darla had said.

Luci stood outside her childhood home, eyeing and contemplating the familiar. Hired landscapers had manicured the lawn and flowerbeds, and she saw that Ida, Marie's longtime housekeeper, had opened the window shades in preparation for the girls' visit. Turning the key in the front door lock, Luci's eyes teared. *How often have I done this without understanding that someday it might be such a lonesome act?* Stepping across the threshold, Luci was engulfed by emptiness, and she realized the dwelling was a shell of its previous self. In the house's abandoned state, it seemed unholy to enter it on her own. As sadness crept through her body, Luci backed out and waited on the stoop for her sisters.

When Adele and Darla arrived, the three women entered the home together as if it were sacred ground. They tiptoed down the corridor that years before they would have had no hesitation in walking through. Without warning, Darla halted and looked down, stroking her foot across the polished sienna-colored tiles and broke the silence. "This is a feature of the house that Mother considered one of its gems."

Adele chuckled and raised an eyebrow. "Remember the hullabaloo Mom carried on, insisting that these be authentic Mexican tiles, Darla? She drove Pop nuts dragging him all through the county before she found a place that could import these."

Darla nodded, and the sides of her lips crept up. Luci was a toddler when Sam and Marie built the house, and her sisters' memory was a fact she knew secondhand. At times, Luci felt her parents had two families, one with her siblings and one with herself. Adele, Darla, and Aimee were close in age to each other. They had inside jokes, experiences, and memories, and it was hard for Luci to relate to these. It was not intentional, but Luci often thought herself more an outsider than part of the family whenever her sisters shared their recollections of an earlier life. Their nostalgia was as profound but, in many ways, different from Luci's.

"Yep, that was Mom, driving everybody crazy. Demanding her way and getting it too. It didn't matter whether the outcome was good or bad," Darla said. She turned on her heel and walked on alone without allowing her sisters to respond. Luci and Adele threw each other glances, but Adele understood the reason for Darla's caustic remark better than Luci.

Of her daughters, Marie's interference in Darla's life left the worst trail of damage. Marie's meddling involved a young man named Bennett Jordan, BJ for short. He and Darla met at a party when Darla was sixteen. For Darla, it was not an instant infatuation, but Bennett had an attraction that drew her in. He was five years older, of Anglophile heritage, and was Protestant. All three of those characteristics, Darla surmised, would rate him a failing grade in her mother's eyes.

Nonetheless, the six-foot-two, blue-eyed university student with a cockeyed smile and disheveled, wavy chestnut-colored hair intrigued her. At their first meeting, Bennett said that he planned to be a teacher, which, in Darla's mind, was a dull profession. She would have preferred something more ambitious like a lawyer or more romantic like a Canadian Mountie. But Bennett was cute and had a jocular way about him, so she gave him a chance.

By contrast, Darla transfixed Bennett. Her sultry and fox-like dark eyes, thick shoulder-length hair, and full sensuous lips, accentuated by the bright cherry red lipstick she wore, charmed him. She was sassy and flirty. She excited and challenged him, and he liked a tease. The girls Bennett had hung out with were conventional and too straitlaced for his liking. Darla was a bundle of zest and fresh air and what BJ wanted. In the first few minutes after they met, he targeted her as his heart's desire.

Two months before the family's departure to California, BJ proposed to Darla, and she accepted without a second thought. During their two-year relationship, Darla realized ambitious or romantic careers did not substitute for a man who was engaging, humorous, and exciting and who made her the center of his attention. Together, they were a ball of energy. They liked it best when they were on the move: going to dances, parties, and the movies; enjoying the nightlife and big bands in Detroit and necking on the top deck of the Bob-Lo Island steamers during the moonlight cruises. Darla viewed life as an adventure as much as Bennett, and they were a locomotive on a fast track.

Sam thought Darla and BJ made a good match. He liked Bennett. He was personable, smart, and empathetic, and he had grit. Sam knew Darla could never be happy with a man who was not playful and adventurous and self-confident enough to make her the middle of his universe. Bennett had the right combination of these traits, in Sam's estimation. The religious and age differences between BJ and his daughter did not trouble him in the least.

Marie's feelings were otherwise. She had a laundry list of barriers. Bennett was not a Catholic. Darla was too young to make a lifetime commitment. The difference in education between the two would create challenges in the marriage. *Don't I understand that, given my own circumstance?* Marie often felt the discrepancy in goals between herself and Sam rested on the difference between their educational levels, and she projected her theory onto Darla and Bennett. Marie's last objection was the issue of geographical separation from her daughter. Where did the move to California leave Darla if she married Bennett? *Not with the family!* Marie concluded.

Through a well-planned and contrived interference, Marie got her way. Bennett's rejection left Darla confused and hurt, resulting in grief, a lack of belief in herself, and feelings of unworthiness that led her down a vulnerable path. Darla would wait over a decade before unearthing the reason for Bennett's abandonment and her mother's role in it.

* * *

As the three women looked around the home, the furniture, curtains, pictures, treasured art pieces, books, rugs, and personal effects were still harmonized in place. But the home's warmth and vitality had disappeared as fast as its former occupants. Even the enclosed patio, the home's stunning retreat, was silent, void of songbirds or the delicate sounds of splashing water from the fountains in the ornamental pool.

If one could personify a room, it was the kitchen so loved by Sam. For over three decades, Sam's trusted and agreeable companion offered him an escape from mundane stressors. It was here Sam applied his imagination and creativity in dreaming up and executing new culinary concoctions. The place did not pass judgment on his recipes, or how he sautéed a dish or dressed a pork roast, or if he sang Italian ballads off-key. Instead, like a steadfast ally, it joined forces to fulfill him.

Luci and each of her sisters had special memories of the place. Part confessional and part therapist office, the kitchen was where they felt safe to huddle with their father and share their joys, successes, failures, worries, and aspirations. "Food is a comfort to the heart as well as the stomach,"

Sam often told them. Allied together, Sam and the kitchen provided both to his daughters.

Within the confines of the kitchen, Adele had shared regrets over her missteps into an ill-conceived marriage. Later, it was where Sam had empathized and had given her the emotional support she needed for ending the relationship. Here was the table where Darla sat with Sam and shared her grief over her breakup with Bennett. A few years later, it was where she confessed her unwed pregnancy and where her father gave her his unconditional love, understanding, and guidance. In the warm and cozy kitchen, Aimee shared her joy of acceptance to medical school and celebrated her graduation with a medical degree. In this room, while making omelets, Sam encouraged Luci to take a risk and ask a boy from Buffalo to dinner. It was also where Sam comforted Luci over her unexpected and unexplained parting with the same young man.

Now, though, the kitchen was forsaken. It, along with Sam's daughters, had lost an irreplaceable ally.

* * *

By midafternoon, the sisters wanted a break from going through "clutter," as Darla referred to the house's contents. Sorting family papers and mementos and determining what to keep and what to dispose of from their parents' belongings drained them physically and emotionally.

Darla went to the kitchen to make coffee, and while scouring the pantry for a snack, she saw something that gave her a sudden pause: an unopened package of chocolate-covered French biscuits. She reached in, removed the box from the shelf, and opened it. As she placed the delicate cookies on the familiar Depression glass plate, flashbacks of afternoon treats as a child flooded into her consciousness.

Letting her mind drift, Darla smiled at her reminiscences. *Mother would arrange tidbits on this plate and have them ready for us after school.* Her mouth watered, thinking about the cookies. She could taste the sweet, thick coating of chocolate on each cookie, accompanied by glasses of warm milk in winter and a cold beverage in spring. Then, of course, the kitchen was not in this place; it was in their home in Canada. That house was so unlike the one where Darla stood now. It was old-fashioned, not modern. It was cozy, not pretentious. The red-brick bungalow had a small kitchen with a breakfast table where the girls had sat munching the treats Marie prepared. The house was in a little township, not a former citrus grove. It was equidistant from the Detroit River, the girls' Catholic elementary school, and the family's parish church. Here Darla and her sisters felt safe and walked everywhere unaccompanied. *It was a good place to grow up. How I long for those happy times when Mother seemed different*, Darla thought. Blinking her eyes, Darla left her memories, and taking the plate of cookies and coffeepot to the dining room table, called out to her sisters, "Coffee is ready."

* * *

By the week's end, the women had the house cleared out. Instead of holding an estate sale, they preferred to donate most of the items to those who were in need. Volunteer staff from a variety of charities packed and removed the furniture and general household items. It was poignant watching their parents' cherished things leave the house so unceremoniously. *What would Pop have thought of that?* Luci wondered, her eyes blurring. Without a doubt, he would have had a down-to-earth retort, but Luci was at a loss for words to identify one.

The nonprofit group took Sam's beloved Bird for auction, promising the proceeds would go to programs for disadvantaged youth. Medical bills had depleted most of Sam and Marie's estate. But the sale of the home and consignment of Marie's paintings provided each of the daughters a small inheritance. Sam, no doubt, was smiling, knowing that he had helped his daughters financially along their way.

Each sister identified items with special meaning. Luci took family pictures, letters, diaries, and mementos going back several generations. She promised to catalog these, make copies of items of interests, and donate the originals to the local historical society in Canada. Darla took most of the extensive library her parents had accumulated, and Adele collected other family heirlooms. Aimee was sent sculptures and artwork. "Leave it to Aimee! She'll take the items she thinks have the most financial and prestige value," Darla said with a sneer.

* * *

Luci had scheduled a luncheon date with Shelia the day before the keys to the home would be turned over to the realtor. Adele and Darla had offered to sort through the remaining items and give the former high school chums a chance to catch up. Even though the geographical distance between Luci and Shelia was not far, in-person visits were infrequent. Luci was hungry for a few undisturbed hours to rehash old times and catch up with her girlfriend.

Shelia had gotten through her rough patch with Bob; it had not been easy, but she persisted. Afterward, she blossomed. It was as if her confrontation with choice and the exercise of autonomy increased her self-reliance and confidence. She amazed her parents, but not her Friday evening movie pals, by being awarded a full college scholarship through her graduate studies. Now, she enjoyed the status of a full-time research associate at a state university, specializing in entomology. "Yikes, a bug doctor," Luci had kidded her friend when Shelia received her doctorate.

Driving to the restaurant, Luci recalled her euphoria the July evening in Canada, eighteen years earlier, after reading Barry's passionate letter. But then her joy vanished as she read Shelia's letter. *How things have changed in these past years! Back then, I thought life was linear. All you needed for a perfect future was to connect the numbered dots and presto, like in a child's activity book, an ideal life would emerge. Crazy!* Luci thought.

Luci's life experiences and career as a social worker told her that things were not that simple. "Life's more than a dot-to-dot picture experience," she advised colleagues and clients in her social work practice. To her university students, she elaborated in academic terms. "Life and human behavior comprise a web of interactions and relationships that influence each other. We should look at life as derived not from the sum of its dots, or events, but as a complex system of interacting elements. We cannot evaluate events and behaviors in isolation from each other. Every challenge, action, or problem is the product of the synergy among numerous influences, many of which we might not be able to isolate or define. Be careful, then, before you judge," she warned.

Driving along the familiar roads in her old hometown, Luci assessed the truth of her mantra applied to her own and Shelia's lives. *God! The dot-to-dot picture thing sure didn't work for either of us,* she thought, remembering the content of Shelia's letter so many years before.

July 15, 1966

Dear Luci,

Boy, I wish you were here! Have I ever screwed up! I found out that Bob has a wife and a kid!! Can you believe it? The real reason he came to live with his sister was for a trial separation. What an SOB! How did I find out? He told me. I guess I should be happy he didn't pack up his bags and disappear on me. Anyway, the trial separation is over, and he's decided to go back to his wife in Georgia. His reasons are not worth putting into a letter. But I wouldn't have him now even if he did divorce his wife. Once a guy lies to you, odds are he'll find it easier to do it again.

I feel betrayed and stupid, Luci. I know that you and the Nerd gang never thought Bob was right for me. There were so many red flags, but I didn't pay attention to them or, better said, I didn't want to pay attention to them. I'm so embarrassed and ashamed; this has shaken my self-confidence. I wonder if there is anyone out there who will love me or that I can trust again.

It's been a rough few days, but that is not the worst of it. I'll wait until you come home to tell you all the details. I wish you were here with me and could help me make some other decisions. You always have a good way of looking at things and solving problems, and I feel that you'd never judge me.

Having thought through my options, I'm not conflicted about my decision, but having you here would make me feel more secure. I hope things will be straightened out after this, and I can get on with my life. Next week, I'm visiting TJ. Sean, Chris, and my sister Colleen are going with me.

Hugs, Shelia.

Bob's deceit was grave enough, Luci remembered thinking. But it was the last sentence in Shelia's letter that made Luci's stomach churn and raised the most concern for her friend. Reading between the lines, TJ meant Shelia was going to Tijuana. There was one reason an eighteen-year-old girl like Shelia went to TJ in 1966. It was evident to Luci that her friend was going for an abortion.

In most states, abortions for the physical or mental health of the mother or in cases of rape or incest were unavailable or difficult to receive in the safety of healthcare facilities. Luci knew all too well the dangers of illegal abortion, regardless of where performed. Botched procedures leading to severe injuries to reproductive organs, incomplete abortions, life-threatening hemorrhages, or infections that might lead to septicemia and death were not uncommon. Connie, a friend of Darla's, had gone to TJ. The result was an incomplete abortion leading to a severe infection that could have cost her life. Connie was fortunate. She had a sympathetic local family doctor who treated the dangerous post-abortion complications in his office. But the physician's admonition was stark: "Never do this again! Next time I might not be able to save your life." That warning was one that Luci never forgot.

It was not until Luci had returned home that she learned the details of Shelia's plight. Sean had found out about a leaflet, developed by feminist activists, that was circulating in the San Francisco area and furnished a list of Mexican abortion providers. Given the reputation of the notorious TJ abortion mills, *The List* was an attempt to ensure that women seeking help would be seen by trustworthy providers. Nothing, however, could be considered safe in an underground environment. Sean, Chris, and Colleen accompanied Shelia to ensure her safety and to help disguise her as a tourist. Border agents were quick to notice individuals who did not fit the visitor profile and arrest them—two boys with their girlfriends going for a day's lark in TJ would not raise suspicions.

As soon as she finished reading Shelia's letter, Luci responded with her own that day.

Thursday, July 21, 1966, 11:00 p.m.

Dear Shelia,

I just read your letter and had to respond right away. I am sorry I'm not with you in person to be a sounding board and help you grieve and silence the vicious inner voices.

I am comforted that you have good friends accompanying you on the upcoming trip. Sean and Chris are bulwarks of strength, and my respect and love for both know no bounds. It's good that Colleen is going along too. I wish I were there to hug you all.

I am with you in spirit. You are correct to say that I would never undermine your freedom in making your own decisions by criticizing them or giving advice. You are a woman who is resilient and capable of choosing the right direction for yourself. I am here as your friend to encourage and back you in making your choices, not to judge them.

Know I support you from afar and please write and tell me how I can help you. I will be home soon, and then you can let everything pour out; I will be an open vessel.

Love, Luci

As she wrote the letter, Luci was grateful for the wisdom of the Friday evening Nerd group. For them, the question of abortion was not taboo to explore. They argued over the topic many times throughout the past three years. Luci's high school religion classes treated the termination of a pregnancy as a moral evil. Catholic women who received an abortion were *latae sententiae* or automatically excommunicated from the church. That sounded horrific to Luci, an attempt by mortals to repudiate, on their own, God's love by excluding one from the sacraments that they most needed.

The group did not worry about holding opinions contrary to the church. They reasoned that excommunication was a censor for not following the rules. It prohibited one from receiving the sacraments; it was not—nor could it ever be, they believed—separation from God. "To place a sentence on a person for choosing an action without evaluating the conditions surrounding it is absurd and arbitrary," Sean had argued. "If abortion is murder, why aren't all murderers automatically excommunicated? For that matter, all child murderers? Sounds like a double standard for women."

Paul disapproved of people using rules as scapegoats to excuse their own wrongdoing. "The act of blind obedience to rules when they are morally or ethically wrong is the graver sin than the challenge to them. Acting in fear of or to please an external entity isn't being moral."

"Law and morality aren't necessarily the same," Sean had asserted. "Because something is legal, say like slavery was when our country was founded, doesn't mean it is moral. On the other hand, something illegal, like selling liquor during Prohibition, doesn't make it automatically immoral."

Looking back on these discussions, Luci recalled a statement Chris had made the evening he revealed that he was enlisting in the army. "You cannot contract out responsibility for exercising your conscience to religion, government, or other authority. To mindlessly follow authority thwarts one's autonomy. After all is said and done, you are accountable for your choices. Those who believe that following the rules will excuse them from moral responsibility are living in fantasy land."

Thinking about July 21, 1966, Luci realized that Shelia's exercise of conscience and autonomy fueled her own insight that life was not a dot-to-dot picture experience. *Life is too rich and complex to boil it down to a linear pathway that follows a series of rules and prescriptions.*

* * *

Late in the afternoon, Luci phoned her sisters. "Hey, Darla, Shelia and I are hanging out for a while longer. I hope that you and Adele don't mind handling a little more of the work without me," she said.

"Us? Mind? Just call us Saints Darla and Adele! And, by the way, we will be staying up and wringing our hands and making sure you make your curfew."

Luci laughed. "Go jump off the nearest cliff. And don't hold dinner for me either."

Darla looked at Adele after she had hung up the phone. "What a relief. This gives us time to figure out how to tell Luci about what we found today. What a picture! Mother's deceit is as clear as any landscape she ever painted."

Because of the age difference between Luci and her two older sisters, Adele and Darla served neither as guardians nor companions to their youngest sister. But despite this, two forces influenced each of their lives. The sisters were united in viewing their father as an advocate and regarding their mother as an adversary. When it came to a threat by their mutual challenger, without hesitation, they rallied in support of each other.

Adele uncorked a bottle of white wine and poured a glass for her sister and herself then slammed the bottle in the middle of the circular kitchen table. "There's a lot more where that came from," she said. "Thank God Pop made sure the place was stocked with wine and liquor. After we finish with this, we have the hard stuff."

Darla threw back her head and took a gulp from her glass. She was an emotional cyclone with no desire to hold her feelings in check. Even gazing through the kitchen windows at the colorful bougainvillea and tranquil garden setting could not quash the fire burning inside her. "I am pissed and feel eviscerated. How could this shit happen again? I forgave what she did to me. But this—this reignites all the painful memories I tried to forget."

Adele lowered her eyes, unable to look at Darla. "I don't get it."

"What don't you get, Adele? Mother was manipulative, controlling, scheming, and cunning. She was always right. Her judgment was final. She had to win. It didn't matter what the consequences were for anyone else," Darla said, pounding her fists on the table, her body shaking.

"Oh, I get that, Darla. What I don't understand is why she did these things to her own daughters."

"How does that matter now? We can't turn back the clock and retrofit her behaviors. Conjuring up explanations for her actions is a waste of time. It doesn't change what she did. It doesn't resolve the immediate problem," Her cheeks stained by tears, Darla got up, grabbed a tissue, and sat back down at the table with her sister.

"I'll agree we can't change the past," Adele said. "But at some point, we have to understand what made Mother tick. Don't we owe that to ourselves so we don't propagate the insanity? Don't we have to reclaim our lives from this sickness of resentment?"

Darla was in a hot-blooded superstorm. Her body was on fire. Resting her head with closed eyes between her hands, she focused on her breath, counting to ten, doing whatever it would take to bring herself under control. "You're right, Adele. Agonizing over past abuses isn't the path. But before thinking about forgiveness, we have a problem to resolve now—should we tell Luci?"

The sisters debated back and forth, "Should we or shouldn't we tell her?"

"We're emotional wrecks, and we've had a lot to drink," Darla said and let out a heavy sigh. "We're in no condition to dump this on Luci tonight, and besides, it would be thoughtless of us to ruin the good time she had with Shelia today."

Adele refilled her wine glass, furrows on her forehead. "I think that the best thing, Darla, is to share your story with Luci in the morning. I'm sure she will make the connection, and then we can put the evidence before her."

They stared at each other, appalled by the other's appearance. Both looked like zombies in a horror movie. Their skin was drained. Their eyes were rimmed with dark circles, and their hair was disheveled from strokes of anguish. They were so infused with numbness that there were no tears left to shed. They had their plan. They hugged each other goodnight and were in bed before Luci returned from her visit with Shelia.

CHAPTER 22

The Bug Doctor

Luci and Shelia planned lunch at an upscale bistro close to Shelia's home. The restaurant was not far from the air force base, and the drive to meet Shelia brought up bittersweet memories for Luci. The familiar roads were the same that she took on June 13, 1966, and her breathing quickened as she passed the freeway exit to the base. Luci inhaled, and her head buzzed. The fragrances of Wind Song perfume and the cologne Barry wore melded in a romantic bouquet that seemed as real in the present as it was the first evening they met.

It had been several years since Luci and Shelia had shared a freehearted conversation. There had been many phone calls between them, but those couldn't suffice for the intimacy of a face-to-face visit. Since high school, both women had experienced setbacks, but in the long run, each had succeeded in creating a flourishing life.

When her relationship with Bob disintegrated, Shelia skipped the denial and bargaining stages of grief and went straight to the anger phase. At first, she was enraged at herself for getting sucked into a superficial romance and getting pregnant. Working through her anger, Shelia shifted her perspective. She stopped excusing her behavior with the self-deprecating phrases "I was wicked, stupid, or undesirable." Instead, she accepted the choice for what it was, and while she could not change it, she believed she had the power to prevent a similar one.

Shelia halted fantasizing about her relationship with Bob, conceding that he could never have been a trusted companion. Their interests, motivations, and dreams in no way could ever be synchronized. Her anger empowered her to work through her grief, and bit by bit, she acknowledged that she deserved better than Bob. Her journey of hope was not a short one. To be sure, there were many bumps and lessons learned along the way, and the path was a continuing process.

During lunch, Shelia talked about her life as if recording a memoir. "Yeah, I broke up with Chuck. He had a workplace fling, and when that didn't work out, he showed up one Sunday morning, literally, at eight o'clock on my front stoop, pleading to come back."

Luci flinched, trying to imagine the incredible sight.

"Yes, Luci, he rang the damn doorbell and was standing on the front steps at eight o'clock in the morning. His girlfriend had kicked him out."

Luci raised a brow. "What an a-hole. What did you do?"

"I told him he was a dick and that choices have consequences. In this case, he proved untrustworthy. My choice was not to live in doubt and anxiety with someone who was undependable. Period, end of the paragraph, and I shut the door in his face."

After her divorce from Chuck, Shelia concentrated her energy on her children and career. She set her sights on finishing a doctorate she had started years earlier, specializing in entomology, hence the tag "bug doctor."

"You know, Luci, going through the fiasco with Bob taught me a lot. Breaking up is traumatic, and it's a foolish person who underestimates its repercussions. With Chuck, I ditched the what-ifs and sidestepped the anger and angst. I didn't allow self-pity, second-guessing, or rage to overshadow my life. I hired a therapist who helped me boost my willpower to move ahead in a positive direction. Every day, I found something to be grateful for: my health, my children, my friends, a sunny day. I concentrated on good things. I believed that a happy future was something I could create in the present and *voilà!* Here I am with a new husband who adores my three children and me, and a career that is going gangbusters."

Luci smiled, acknowledging her pride in her friend. "You have such tremendous endurance and optimism."

"My dear," Shelia said after finishing a bite of her BLT sandwich. "Pat yourself on the back for your accomplishments. You made it through tremendous losses and got a PhD like me. Every day you contribute by working for social justice causes you always believed in. I'd say that's grit!"

"Thinking about it, I do feel good about my achievements, and I don't underestimate them. I guess my strength comes from acting on my sense of fairness and helping people get an equal chance. But you know, there's a bump in my road that never goes away."

Shelia's eyebrows drew together in a mixture of frustration and compassion. In every face-to-face visit that she and Luci had, the same topic would bubble up during their conversation.

"I get it, but I don't get it, Luci. Look, I work with insects all day. I like them because they don't have emotions or at least ones that I can detect. You deal with people's reactions all the time in your work. Luci, can't you apply the empathy and kindness you have for others to yourself? What's underneath your feelings with Barry? It doesn't seem to be anger or denial. And why do you obsess over the loss? What's at the bottom of this?"

Luci inhaled and raised her head, eyes scanning the wall. Shelia had nailed it! *No, it isn't anger or denial. It's a web of self-blame and guilt I've constructed around me.* Luci stumbled for the words to answer her friend. "What's the root of it? All these years, I have been in the dark, not knowing what happened. My finger has been pressed on the ruminating button, trying to shine a light on what went wrong, and it's driven me nuts. I've let my inner critic, Doris, live in my psyche and pop up whenever she damned pleased, admonishing me with 'What did you do?' and laying a guilt trip on me."

Shelia gave an affirmative nod. *Doris!* She recognized Luci's old nemesis. "I know all about Doris. Her twin sister tries to hit me up, too. But I enjoy squashing her like a bug," Shelia said, pounding her fist on the table.

Luci shook her head. "I see you haven't lost your sense of humor or theatrics."

"All kidding aside, Luci, what's the deal?" Shelia pressed.

Luci sighed and ran her hand through her hair. "Shelia, I've acted like an unquenchable two-year-old asking "why" and then answering the question by placing fault on myself. The truth is that I don't know what led to the breakup with Barry. One day he's committed, considerate, and consumed with sizzling romance; the next day he's vanished like *poof* into thin air."

"May I butt in with my perspective?"

Luci shrugged. "You are going to do it anyway, so yes, butt in. You've fired up my curiosity."

"Look, uncertainty has clouded your perspective. In this fog, you have dreamt up undeserved conclusions about yourself. Resolving the unknown is not under your control, but you can control the guilt trip and stop it in its tracks. Substitute *bad me* by thinking *lucky me*. Think about the good times with Barry. Concentrate on that and use it to enrich living now."

Luci let Shelia's advice settle, then she smiled. *Sage guidance*, she thought. "Psychiatric Help, The Bug Doctor Is In. Five Cents, Please!"

Shelia rolled her eyes and called the waitress over. "Another margarita, please."

Leaning across the table, Shelia covered Luci's hand with hers. "Luci, I've embraced the belief that there are no second chances in life. Trusting that things in the past might have been better if this or that had happened is fooling yourself. And, putting faith in the future, hoping to find a better life without making the present as fulfilled as possible, is cheating yourself."

Shelia waited to see if her words hit their mark. Luci's eyes were downcast, but she returned a nod, and Sheila got to her point. "I pity those who give up their freedom or cave in to adversity because they hope fulfillment will materialize in the future or in an afterlife. I made a choice eighteen years ago, and I assumed accountability for my actions. If I concentrate on living a good life every day, I don't have to rely on hoping whether I have enough brownie points at the end of it. The life I'm leading now, today, is fulfillment enough."

A frown formed on Luci's face. "That's heavy stuff. Are you discounting the importance of a future or an afterlife?"

"I neither count on nor discount the future," Shelia answered. "All I'm saying is that by leading a good life in the present, the future becomes immaterial."

Luci took in a deep breath. "Okay, so tell me about this good life. I'm puzzled. What does that mean? Sounds like a cliché, and definitely something you wouldn't expect a *bug doctor* to say."

"Hah! We've reeled the movie backward twenty years, arguing like we did with my brother and his nerdy friends?"

"Yep, the game is on. And by the way, your margarita has arrived."

Taking a long sip from her refreshed cocktail, Shelia was up for Luci's challenge. "It is simple. Having a fulfilled life depends on three things."

Luci held her hand up. "Hold it there! Now it's a fulfilled life? What the hell happened to the good life?"

Shelia smirked. "Don't go getting all academic on me, Doctor Luci! Good life and fulfilled life, they're the same in my book. The terms are interchangeable. Let me finish, will you?"

Both women laughed. Ragging on each other brought back good memories of their teenage years with Sean, Chris, and Paul. *How those conversations would drag on!* Luci remembered them now more with fondness than the frustration she sometimes felt at the time.

Shelia threw her friend a saucy look. "Here's my simple summary of the good and fulfilled life. Satisfied now?"

"Yes, dear, we've got the semantics clarified. Please continue."

Sheila fortified herself with another swallow of her margarita. "To be fulfilled, I need meaning or purpose in my life. Translated, this means serving something bigger than myself. To put it bluntly, the world doesn't revolve around me; it centers on making the world better. So I do bugs! I study them and their relationship to human beings and the environment. I make the world a better place by the work I do. I make contributions by discovering new methods of protecting crops and livestock, looking at ways insects can benefit people or be used to inhibit disease. This work gives meaning to my life."

Luci looked in the distance and cleared her throat. "Without meaning, I suppose there isn't much hope, is there? I encounter this with many of my clients. They haven't found their meaning, so they can't make sense out of their lives or see their own self-worth." Luci looked back at Shelia. "I can't help wondering if there is a connection between having a purpose in life and general well-being and even health. What do you think?"

Shelia sat back, her fingers tapping the table. "There is a connection, Luci. That's what I'm trying to tell you! But there's more to a fulfilled life than that. I have to enjoy what I'm doing. I could work with bugs all day, but if I don't enjoy it, what's the point? To lead a good life, I must love what I do. I mean enjoying something so much that I can't wait to get up in the morning to get started. It means getting so lost in what I'm doing that time stands still. I know people consider my work with insects boring. Let me tell you, though, when I'm in the research lab, the outside world stops. My work energizes me. And I bet you feel that way in what you do too," she asserted.

Luci leaned forward, resting her elbow on the table. "Yes, I do! I am on fire working on public policy that helps the disenfranchised. One of my most satisfying times was helping my congressional representative on the Social Security Reform Act and testifying before a committee in the House of Representatives. Wow, what an adrenaline rush that was."

"Oh, do I remember that! You were on the local television news. Say, whatever happened to that cute congressional staffer you worked with?"

Luci waved her hand, brushing Shelia off. "Aah, he was handsome, but not for me long term. I'd say his work engaged him, and he had a purpose, but he wasn't much fun. Too intense for me."

Sheila winked. "Decoded: not good sex."

"Can you stop it!" Luci slapped the table and then waved her finger at her friend. "Get your mind out of the gutter. I see some things never change."

"Great segue, though. It leads right into the last thing rounding out a fulfilled life, and that's having some pleasure. There must be enjoyment if you're going to have a good life. You need to feel comfortable and be joyful in your relationships with people, and, for good measure, throw in great sex too. Now that sounds comforting!"

They both roared at Shelia's last remark as if they were teens again. "Do you suppose," Luci whispered, cupping her hand, "that Sister Mary Catherine would consider a fulfilled life sinful?"

"Perhaps, but what the hell do we care? How naïve we were back then," Shelia cracked.

"Think about the stress we endured trying to navigate the imaginary line between venial and mortal sins. It seemed we were always fearful that we would be going to hell if we crossed over into the dangerous big sin territory." Luci cringed, shaking her head in bewilderment as she recalled the *sin papers* handed out in religion class that listed the mortal sins in all capital letters.

"Speak for yourself, dear!" Shelia said, taking her margarita glass and toasting Luci. "The good life dispenses with all that nonsense—little and big sins and worrying about the future, hell or otherwise. I can lead a moral life for its own sake. I won't need any bargaining chips for the future, whether it means in this or the supernatural world."

Luci finished up her strawberry daiquiri and plopped the glass on the table. "You know, I feel like I'm talking to Sam right now, Shelia. Pop always found some excuse for expounding upon Aristotle's virtues and the importance of creating a habit of each. There are so many connections between what you've said and my dad's advice. In his folksy way, he'd say 'Lead a virtuous life, and you'll never be uncertain of your next step. You won't have to question or second-guess your motives. You will be free.' I hadn't talked to Pop about that for a long time. You've brought me back to recalling good times. I guess the bug doctor is worth the five cents," Luci said, rolling her eyes.

* * *

Returning home past midnight, Luci turned the key to the front door with trepidation and laughed to herself: *Old habits die hard.* But at the same time, she was saddened. No Marie. No Zeppie. No Sam. Her previous life felt a world away. *Had it ever happened?* she wondered as she walked down the familiar corridor to her old room.

CHAPTER 23

Secrets

Luci woke refreshed the next morning, revitalized from her visit with Shelia. Tumbling out of her girlhood bed, she threw on a pair of jeans and a light sweatshirt emblazoned with a George Orwell quote: "Orthodoxy is Unconsciousness." Its appropriateness never failed to amuse her; after all, it was 1984.

Strolling into the kitchen, Luci found the room buzzing. Darla had coffee brewing and the kitchen table set. Adele was fussing over the ingredients of an omelet concoction and had fresh-squeezed orange juice ready like Sam would do.

"Hey Sis," Darla called out as she went to pour Luci a cup of coffee. "How is Shelia doing with that new husband of hers? Is she still messing with her bugs?"

Luci gave her sisters the rundown, catching them up on the latest news and gossip. But Adele and Darla weren't posing their usual nosy follow-up questions, and this set off Luci's alarm bells. *What's up with them? They seem preoccupied.*

"It looks like you two made progress in sorting things. I feel sort of guilty not being here to help. I know, though, I'll get over that fast," Luci said.

"I have no doubt about it," Darla replied as she placed the steaming cup of coffee before her sister and slid a small pitcher of cream toward her.

Darla's comeback didn't squelch Luci's sixth sense. *Something is quirky. Those two are hiding something.* She hit her sisters head-on. "Did you two find anything interesting prowling through the old trunks and dusty file cabinets, like maybe a windfall of cash? Do you remember the freezer full of money and that second marriage certificate Bruno's family found when he died? Find any fun stuff like that?"

Adele let out a high-pitched laugh and tossed Darla an anxious glance. "Sorry, no cash, or at least nothing we would tell you about."

"A lot of memories reawakened, and old wounds reopened," Darla said.

So I was right. They did find something. "Are you two going to let me in on the secret—or should I say secrets in the plural form?"

Adele brought over the omelets and a platter loaded with roasted potatoes coated in pesto and Parmesan cheese, pan-fried Roma tomatoes, and charred crusty bread.

"Jeez, you're like Pop, Adele, trying to fatten us up. Remember how upset he was that we were so slim?" Darla asked.

Adele stretched her arms wide open. "Pop always said that a good woman is an armful. And would he be pleased to see us now."

"Speak for yourself, dear," Darla said. "My figure is still curvy and catches the right glances."

Adele rolled her eyes and joined her sisters at the table, serving herself a large portion of the potatoes. "What about the day Pop came home with Ronnie Ingles's advice to give us a gin and tonic before dinner to increase our appetites?"

Darla shook her head. "Oh, was Mom furious that he gave us cocktails before dinner. Did Pop try that on you too, Luci?"

"As it happened, he spared me the aperitif ritual since my figure was perfect," she said and added a mound of potatoes to her plate as well. *Distraction—they're trying to change the subject. I'll play along.*

"Okay, smarty-pants, what was that story about Pop getting you drunk?" Adele asked.

Luci shrugged and suppressed a smile. "What story?"

Adele narrowed her eyes.

"Oh, that story!" Luci replied.

"Yep, that's the one. Cough it up," Darla said.

Luci hung her head and faked surrender. "That story. It happened when I was eighteen; the summer I met Barry. Pop took me to a late-afternoon party at a new office of one of his business friends. There was a table spread with all kinds of food, but what attracted me most was the centerpiece. It was one of those crazy punch bowl fountains that had champagne tumbling out from everywhere. Well, you know our dad—he was busy yacking with everyone and not watching me. Long story short, I was drinking the punch and getting drunk and having a great time talking with Mr. Guidici and Mr. Neri. At some point, Pop notices and says, 'It's time to go, Luci.' We made a fast exit, and Pop drove us to the Stater Brothers supermarket parking lot. You know, Pop didn't swear much, but I remember him saying, 'Holy shit, Luci. You are damn drunk. I can't bring you home to Marie in this shape. We'll have to stay here for a while until you get sobered up.' So we spent the rest of the afternoon there until I could at least walk a straight line."

While Luci's siblings howled in unison, she slid her finished plate to the side, fed up with the cat and mouse game her sisters were playing. "Okay, those were some of the good times. What reawakened memories and reopened wounds yesterday?"

Adele and Darla looked sideways at each other. They knew the time for telling the truth had come. "I don't know, just some stuff we found," Darla said.

"Stuff? Like what kind of stuff? Did you find papers, accounts, checkbooks, diaries, birth certificates, letters?" Looking at her siblings' faces, Luci knew she had struck close; Adele and Darla were terrible liars.

"Oh, no," Luci muttered. "You found a marriage certificate. Pop was married to someone else before Mom, like Bruno. Was it a girl in Italy? Or perhaps you found love letters from Mom's secret lover?"

Adele giggled uncontrollably. "Luci, you get a gold star for imagination! Mom, for sure, is turning in her grave."

"It's time for some wine. Adele, don't you agree?" Darla asked.

Luci did a double take. "We're drinking wine at ten thirty in the morning? You two dare to talk about my fantasies! You both are incorrigible."

Testing her sisters, Luci sauntered to the pantry and pulled out a bottle of Chianti. With her free hand, she opened a cupboard and grasped three wine glasses by their stems. Adele retrieved a corkscrew from the island drawer, uncorked the bottle, and poured each a glass of the Chianti Classico. *Oh God, are we actually doing this?*

The two older sisters had their strategy: lead with an unknown and eye-popping fact that would lay the groundwork for the real exposé.

Adele shook her head. "You don't know how close to the truth you came, Luci, dear," she said and paused to let the tidbit sink in. "We found a couple of bundles of letters tucked away in that old Lane chest in mother's studio. You know the one that she kept locked. We had a devil of a time finding the hiding place of the key."

Memories of Arthur's letters to Geneviève flooded Luci's mind. *Was there a secret love in Marie's life too?* "Come on and spill the beans! Did Mother have a hush-hush relationship before she met Pop?"

Adele shrugged. "Not exactly—more like a relationship when she was with Pop."

Luci froze. Adele saw that nugget caught her sister unexpectedly. "Don't go fantasizing, Luci. We don't believe there was anything physical involved, more emotional and mind stuff."

"Holy crap!" Luci said, covering her mouth with her hand.

Darla nodded toward Luci's wine glass. "Take a drink, a big one, sweetie. Mom might have had more spark in her than we gave her credit for."

"Oh, stop, Darla," Adele said. "Don't be so dramatic. We don't want to mop Luci up off the floor, do we?" Then she and Darla laughed in unison to relieve their tension.

Luci stretched in her chair, feigning boredom at her sisters' antics.

"Do you want to hear about this or not?" Adele asked, snapping her fingers in front of Luci's face.

Luci slapped her hand on the table. "Of course, I do. Will you get on with it, Adele?"

"Remember that confessor of hers? You know, Father Kelley, who got under Pop's skin."

"No way!" Luci said.

"Well, oh, yes! One bundle of letters we found was from him. They start from the time we moved to California until the fellow croaked a few years ago."

Adele's animosity was evident. How the relationship between their mother and the priest started wasn't known by the women. Adele and Darla remembered Marie attending religious retreats conducted by the priest during their preteen years. Also, they recalled that Marie visited Kelley at his parish residence between the structured spiritual programs. After the family's move to California, the relationship, unknown to them, had continued via letters.

Luci stirred her coffee, eyes cast down. "I guess that's not surprising."

"What do you mean, not surprising?" Adele asked.

Darla folded her arms across her chest. "You don't think it's weird that a married woman continues a long-distance relationship with some priest, who her husband happens to hate? It isn't like there weren't advisers here if she needed one."

"I'm not saying the relationship was good or bad. I'm saying that it's not startling that it continued by mail since Mom saw Kelley every summer we visited Grand-mère."

The kitchen was as quiet as a tomb.

"Mother continued seeing Kelley for years? Did Pop know about the meetings?" Darla asked, breaking the silence.

Luci went mute. She realized she had said more than she had wished. Her sisters stared at her, and Luci could not meet their eyes, feeling like a two-year-old child who had misbehaved and had gotten caught.

"So Pop didn't know about these visits over the years?" Adele asked, recoiling from the table, her voice cracking like thin ice.

"This is conflicting for me," Luci said, looking from sister to sister. "To my knowledge, Pop didn't know."

Adele and Darla sat stone-faced. "Is that so?" Adele's eyes narrowed, signaling Luci that she had better continue.

Feeling queasy but relieved of an obligation put on her as a ten-year-old, Luci burst out with the truth. "I remember one particular time when Mother visited Father Kelley. Grand-mère said to me, 'Under no circumstances do you tell your father that your mother saw Father Kelley.' To be truthful, that freaked me out."

Adele hit back. "And what made that time different from the others? What was freaky about it?"

"That time, Mom had to take a bus and travel for several hours to Father Kelley's parish. I forget the town, maybe Hamilton, but I do remember that she stayed overnight at the rectory."

"Oh, barf!" Darla said and turned her head.

Luci's not to blame. After all, she had nothing to do with this tomfoolery, Adele thought, and her tone softened. "Grand-mère approved of all of this?" she asked.

"Oh, no, she didn't approve one bit. Grand-mère gave Mother a severe scolding, and she refused to give Mother her the car. But you know how pigheaded Mother was—she went anyway but took the bus."

"Did you ever tell Pop?" Darla asked.

"Pop never brought up the subject of Father Kelley with me, but I felt deceitful, anyway. I don't know what I would have done had he asked me a direct question about what I knew of these meetings."

Everyone sat without uttering a word, each lost in her thoughts, sizing up the situation. Even the wine wasn't sufficient to diminish the sisters' shock at the revelation.

Luci broke the silence. "Did you read the letters?"

"Damn right, we read them," Darla said. "She was so bloody intrusive into our lives. We didn't hesitate to poke around into her secrets, even if after the fact."

Adele elaborated on what they found, but she expressed puzzlement. "It's weird that the letters contain no spiritual advice at all. On the surface, though, they didn't include any romantic stuff either. It was sort of like friends writing to each other about day-to-day activities. My gut told me, though, that the contents contained sub-messages."

"The letters made my skin crawl," Darla said. "Given the secrecy, and Pop's and Grand-mère's distaste, I'd say the guy was a manipulative son of a bitch. He saw someone who was insecure and vulnerable; he knew her private struggles, and he took advantage of his position of power. Don't I know about that! Who is to say if anything physical happened? What does it matter? In the end, it was dishonest."

"Don't you believe people have a right to privacy when it comes to personal issues that involve counseling, therapy, or spiritual advisement?" Luci asked.

Darla's stern expression answered Luci before her sister opened her mouth. "They do have that right, as long as it's balanced with the rights of others. In this case, the arrangement feels underhanded. It was unfair of Mother and Grand-mère to put you in such a vulnerable position. That is what is indefensible."

Luci had to agree with her older sibling. She got up and hugged Darla, consoled that someone, even though it was nearly three decades later, sympathized with her situation.

Afterward, no one spoke. Luci was thankful the secret was out in the open and that she was relieved of the burden. Luci knew she was not responsible for her mother's behavior. But Doris had spun a web that made Luci feel complicit. Luci was grateful to Sam. Whether he suspected a continuing relationship or not, he never subjected Luci to choosing sides by probing her for information on her mother's activities. That was the wisdom, compassion, and self-assurance of Sam.

Taking advantage of the interlude, Luci dialed back to something Adele said earlier. "You mentioned a couple of bundles of letters, Adele. Was there something more that you found? I can't think of it getting any weirder."

Oh, crap! Here it comes, Darla thought. "Do you know the whole story about my engagement with Bennett, Luci?"

Darla's question came out of the blue, and Luci wondered, *Is there something they discovered in the old trunk about Darla and Bennett? What's it got to do with the letters from Father Kelley?*

"I know that you were engaged, and for some reason, the two of you broke up. I never knew the reason, except for a few comments Mother made from time to time." Luci refrained from providing more, although her mother's words rang in her ears. "That Darla was too flirty. Bennett found out she was fooling around on him, and he dropped her like a hot potato."

"Oh, I bet she came up with some doozies to conceal her deceit. I don't need to hear those. Knowing them would make me more teed off than I already am."

Seeing Darla's clenched fits and fearing that her sister might break down, Adele stepped in. "Bennett Jordan was a great guy, and I was jealous of Darla for having landed such a catch. Pop liked him, but Mom had a list of objections a yard long. BJ was too old for Darla, he wasn't Catholic, Darla was too young to get married, Darla would live far from her family if she married BJ, and blah, blah, blah."

Luci frowned and looked toward Darla. "Couldn't those issues have been worked out?"

"Of course, they could have! But more to the point, those weren't my concerns; they were Mother's fears. It was my life, and BJ and I had addressed most of the issues anyway. Age difference, of course, we couldn't change. But he was ready to convert. We agreed I'd go to business college after we married, and he didn't oppose moving to California and leaving his family. It was all nonsense on Mother's part."

Luci glanced at Adele for confirmation. "That's all true," Adele said, nodding. "I overheard Pop arguing with Mom calling her anxieties irrational. He was severe with her, saying her actions were too controlling and unhealthy."

"What an understatement!" Darla said, and no one in the room disagreed.

Luci looked between her sisters for an answer. "What happened? What caused the breakup?"

"Plain and simple, Mother's need for control and her talent for deceiving and manipulating caused the breakup. Sometimes, I have more pity than hatred for her. Being so controlling must have been a hellish way to live," Darla said.

"Well, what the hell happened?" Luci asked, looking at Adele.

"Mother executed a series of well-planned actions based on a lie: she told Bennett that Darla was two-timing him."

Luci shot her sisters a disbelieving look; her mother's words about Darla's flightiness pounded in her head. *Were these lies?* Recovering, Luci posed the obvious question. "Didn't Bennett try to confirm this? Get in touch with you, Darla?"

"Did he ever!" her sister answered, her voice trembling and tears burning her eyes.

Adele reached over and clasped Darla's hand, and Darla took a hard swallow. "He wrote letters to me, but Mother intercepted them. She returned the letters to him unopened with *Return to Sender* blazed in capital letters across the envelope."

Luci sat shocked, biting her thumb, stupefied at the revelation.

"In those days," Darla said, "people didn't make long-distance phone calls often within or across country borders. Even so, Bennett did phone, but Mother took the call and told him the lie that I was running around on him. Bennett went to talk with Grand-mère, but Mother fed the same lies to her, and unknowingly, Grand-mère reconfirmed the lie to him. Bennett later said that it was Grand-mère's validation that cinched it for him. He believed her, but Grand-mère was an unwitting accomplice to Mother's deceit."

Luci sat perplexed. "Darla, didn't you wonder why you hadn't heard from Bennett?"

"I did," she cried, her face contorted. "I wrote letters, but I never got a response. Then the double deceit came. Mother intercepted my letters. When I didn't receive responses, Mother told me Bennett had phoned her, told her he had another girlfriend, and that he couldn't face telling me and blah, blah, blah. I believed every word Mother said. I've kicked myself repeatedly for trusting her. I could never imagine that my mother could be that manipulative." Darla stopped to recover her composure. "After I thought Bennett jilted me, I self-destructed, and the rest is history," she sobbed.

The silence was deafening. Darla's face was blotchy, and her lips quivered as she forced herself to go on. "I felt betrayed, undesirable, and unlovable. I felt as if I had lost myself. I was vulnerable and fell for someone else's attention. I engaged in self-destructive, risk-taking behavior, and got pregnant. I don't know if I can ever get over the trauma of betrayal, but I'll be damned if I'm going to spend energy being angry at a dead woman. I refuse to give her that control over me."

Luci sat dumbfounded. She was familiar with stories of romantic breakups. Besides her loss of Barry, Luci had heard similar accounts during counseling sessions with her clients. She understood the trauma they felt. But there was something more nagging her. The question about the second packet of letters remained unanswered. *How do the letters fit in Darla's story?*

"How did you confirm this, Darla?" Luci asked. "Do the letters you found yesterday corroborate Mother's actions?"

Darla sighed and lowered her head and continued in a whisper. "I was talking on the phone with a former girlfriend from our hometown a couple of years ago, and she let it slip that I had jilted BJ. You can imagine how astonished I was to hear that, and I grilled her about what she had heard. My friend told me that the rumor mill had it that I was two-timing Bennett and was returning his letters to him. My girlfriend knew where BJ was living, so I got his address, and I wrote to him."

"And what happened?"

"This time, my letter wasn't intercepted. I'm surprised that Bennett didn't throw it in the trash, but he read and answered it. He confirmed what we've told you in a letter to me, and I approached Mother about it. Of course, she denied everything and said she always knew BJ was sly, but I had the proof Mother was the liar. BJ kept the letters with 'Return to Sender' written across the front of the envelopes, and he mailed them to me."

Luci's eyelids quivered, and she felt her heart fall. The story was hitting too close to home, and the puzzle pieces were starting to fall into place. Luci felt as if she were a character in a fantasy novel. *This can't be true! But deceive once, and it works; deceive again, and it works.* Luci recoiled, and a feeling of nausea overcame her. *Could Mother have played the same scheme a second time?* Luci shook her head back and forth in a sweep of denial.

"I'm afraid my story may have been repeated," Darla said in a whisper as she handed a bundle of four letters to Luci. "We found these yesterday in the chest in the studio."

Luci looked down and sifted the items through her hands. Two letters were addressed to her in Barry's handwriting. The tops of the envelopes looked as if they had been slit with a letter opener. From the postmarked dates, she knew she had never seen these. The other letters were addressed to Blackhorse Road on the familiar red stationery she used for writing to Barry. They were stamped but not postmarked. *The letters were never mailed.* Luci was stupified before realizing what had happened. *Oh, no! Mother must have retrieved my letters from the mailbox before the mail was picked up.*

Sliding her fingers across one of the envelopes, she recognized the shape of a keepsake carefully placed there years earlier. The object slipped into her hand, and Luci bit down hard on her lip to suppress a wail. *It's the key—the key to my heart I sent to Barry*, she cried inwardly. The fusion of tension, regret, betrayal, anger, and sadness in the room was enough to explode a bomb.

Luci's eyes went vacant. "Did you read these?"

"No," Adele said. "We wouldn't intrude in that way. We were uncertain how to proceed after we found the letters. In the end, we felt it was best not to propagate the deceit; it was time for it to stop once and for all."

"You did the right thing," Luci murmured, casting her eyes downward and staring at the letters and the key clutched in her hand. Tears welled in her eyes, causing the address, 181 Blackhorse Road, on the envelope to blur and become unreadable.

Chapter 24

Final Goodbye

It was his twenty-first birthday, October 13, 1967, and Barry opened his academy mailbox hoping that a greeting card from Luci was waiting for him. Scanning the contents, he saw there was one from his little sister, another from Carole, an old girlfriend in Buffalo, and one from Ross and Millie. But the familiar red envelope that encased Luci's letters was not there. He shook his head, and his fingers fumbled closing the mailbox. *What's gone wrong? Why has Luci rejected my letters and returned them unopened?*

During Barry's furlough the past summer, he and Luci created memories that surpassed even those of the previous year. Barry's mother had corresponded with Marie to smooth the way and arrange Luci's visit to Buffalo. Between letters and a few phone calls, Breana and Marie struck up a warm relationship, their concern for their children a mutual interest binding them.

While not controlling like Marie, Breana was a mother too. She had her own reasons for measuring up this young woman who had captivated her son for over a year. Maintaining such a long relationship was unusual for the Callahan boys, although there were a few girls who kept "tagging along," as Joe put it. Marie's duplicity, though, was masterful. *It never makes sense to create a fuss with another mother. After all, I may need her as an ally in the future or, in the worst-case scenario, she could be my daughter's mother-in-law,* she considered.

At the beginning of his summer vacation, Barry made the drive from Buffalo to Canada to bring Luci back to meet his family. While in Canada, Barry stayed with Ross and Millie, who were ecstatic to host him again. The three had remained in contact through occasional correspondence, and they formed a bond over the intervening months. The more Millie baked and cooked for Barry, the happier she seemed, and this year Barry worked with Ross, helping with farm chores. Ross appreciated the camaraderie of having another man at his side and was glad to have one who was strong and not afraid of work.

"Oh, Barry! Oh, Barry!" Geneviève cried, scooting out the front door when Barry pulled up to her house. "You've come in that darling little car again. Maybe you'll take Luci's grand-mère out for a spin this time?" she flirted and planted a kiss on each of his cheeks. "Come in, come in, we have so much to catch up on." To Geneviève, Barry seemed more beguiling than the year before. His shoulders looked broader, and his hair had taken on a creamier butterscotch tone. *Why hadn't I noticed those slight dimples that make his smile dance? Oh, and those blue eyes! Aah, I see why Luci is infatuated.*

Marie was aloof, giving Barry perfunctory greetings and a cold hug. It was a hard thing to pin down, but from time to time, the faraway look he'd catch in Marie's eyes made him feel that there were two parts to her. One was present in the flesh, and another was in a time warp whirling somewhere else. *She is distracted by something*, he thought. Even Marie, at times, felt as if she were outside her body. She was not happy; she was scheming.

* * *

Luci made a hit with Barry's parents and siblings. Fifteen minutes after meeting Luci, Joe took Barry aside. "You are a lucky dog! She's a dish," he said, and little Norah immediately adopted her as a big sister. After a year of college, Luci's maturity grew beyond her young years, and her sophistication and level-headedness were not lost on Barry's parents. They liked her. She was fun-loving and playfully haggled with Barry and his brothers, but she could also be serious and voice her opinions. Her apprenticeship with the Nerds prepared her to move between quick and sassy comebacks and thoughtful rejoinders. *She has convictions,* Connor thought, and he admired that.

Barry's broad smile, ringing voice, and spontaneity showed his thrill being with Luci. His fondness flashed in his eyes that stuck to her like glue. He was attentive, insisting her choices come first, and at the end of each day, he showed his thoughtfulness by giving Luci gifts of his gratitude. One evening he produced a small stone-cut seal figurine representing dreaming and imagination. Another time he surprised Luci with a handwritten poem, and the final evening, he gave her a bouquet of pressed flowers gathered from a meadow that held special memories for both of them.

After returning from his mailbox, Barry sat in his dorm room, perplexed. His mind drifted, recalling how carefree he and Luci were when they drove from her grandmother's home to Buffalo. They got an early start on their trip, arriving at noon at the point of land cut in two, the scene of Barry's tale of Lelawala. He remembered Luci's wild-eyed expression as she viewed the spectacular Niagara Falls and cuddled up to him. "They're awe-inspiring," she cried out right before she dared him to pick her up in his arms like Thunder God. He flashed a smile and obliged, swinging her around until they were dizzy and laughing out of control.

They went on the Maid of the Mist boat tour that challenged the waterfall white water, dodged massive rock formations, and got them drenched to the skin. The crashing roar of the falls rocked the earth in stereophonic sound and made Barry and Luci feel like they were living the fantasy of Lelawala and Thunder themselves.

Barry took Luci to Cazenovia Park, and here they made new memories strolling on rustic paths and crossing languid streams. They soared on roller coasters, walked through the midway, and rode the carousel at Crystal Beach Amusement Park. But it was the three-day stay with Barry's family in the Appalachian foothills where the magic potion of Luci and Barry's relationship settled into simmering and lasting love. Lazy walks through the forests surrounding the family's cabin and late evenings spent snuggling by the dying embers in the fire pit allowed them to understand and appreciate each other and gave them the privacy to create dreams of their future together.

On her last day at the cabin, Barry surprised Luci with a packed picnic of chilled wine, cheeses, fruits, and ham sandwiches made on crusty French bread. Barry had sworn to Luci that they would eat in a hidden meadow that was the most mystical in all New York. "You're going to feel the Irish fairies," he had promised her.

With Barry carrying the food and a blanket in a backpack, they walked holding hands for a mile down a narrow, mud-puddled access road that skirted and then went beyond the Callahan property. The infrequently used dirt road dwindled to a pathway, and when it ended at the edge of the forest, Luci gasped. Barry had not exaggerated the beauty of the panorama. *What a* Sound of Music, *top of the world experience,* Luci's emotions screamed. Looking at Barry, her surprise registered, and she sang out, "This is my meadow place!" In front of her was an expansive field whose undulating borders were formed by tall timbers; beyond that, a forest extended over thousands of acres. Barry kicked back and laughed as Luci ran open-armed through knee-high grasses and a medley of shocking pink dames rocket, violet fireweed, and delicate white meadowsweet wildflowers.

They nestled their blanket on the soft meadowland and were as carefree as the floating clouds above them. They sipped the sparkling wine and indulged in lover's banter and caresses amid the meadow's colorful glow and the warm sunshine. Lying together, Luci took her finger and traced the top of Barry's nose, and her gentle touch moved further across his lips. She loved the splash of light freckles across his cheeks, the slight dimples when he smiled, and the cleft in his chin, almost unnoticeable. Barry rolled over, facing her, and looked as if he had found a pot of gold. "The entire canvas," Luci said, "reminds me of the romantic scene from the movie *Spenser's Mountain.*"

"My idea exactly," Barry agreed. As gentle as the meadow grass bending in the breeze, he put his arms around Luci and drew her closer to him. "But unlike James McArthur," he said, "I'll be careful and not get my backside sunburned." Except for the woodland creatures, the two lovers had the meadowland to themselves as they shared kisses that tasted as sweet as whipped cream on their lips.

* * *

Saturday, the day after his birthday, Barry was single-minded. *I must talk to Luci.* After Luci returned home to California in September, his letters were going unanswered. Worse yet, they later were sent back to him unopened, with "Return to Sender" scrawled on the envelopes. He was befuddled. There was no explanation for Luci's behavior, and Barry was more concerned about her welfare than feeling spurned. *If she were ill, wouldn't Marie or Sam get in touch with me? Things don't make sense!*

Barry had little opportunity to phone Luci. Outgoing calls during the week were forbidden, and phoning on the weekend was limited between mandated activities. But in his last letter to Luci, Barry promised he would phone her the day after his birthday.

It was a Saturday, and the line of cadets waiting to use the payphones was long. Barry waited for thirty minutes until a phone was not in use. He pulled a handful of quarters from his pocket, guessing he had enough for a two-minute long-distance call. He dialed Luci's number, paid the amount requested by the operator, and waited for the connection to go through. After ringing several times, the phone was answered, but Barry was not pleased—it was Marie. He greeted her with small talk, but his heart raced. He had one and a half minutes left before the call would automatically disconnect, and he got to the point.

"Is Luci home, Mrs. Bartolino?" he asked, holding his breath.

"Oh, of course, Barry. You haven't called to speak with me," she replied in a honeyed voice. "Um, I'm afraid she isn't here now. She's out with some of her friends."

"Do you know when she will be back? When would be a good time to call?"

There was a long silence. Barry knew something was wrong.

"Is Luci sick, Mrs. Bartolino? Has something happened to her?" he asked, his voice starting to crack.

Marie's tactic was to be direct but sound sympathetic. "Barry, I know Luci has returned your letters, and I guess that's what you are calling about." She paused, and as if she had x-ray eyes, she saw Barry's mouth drop, registering his surprise and embarrassment that she should know something so private. "There's no way to sugarcoat this, Barry. You should know there is someone else. You may even know of him. His name is Chris," her voice dropped . . .

Barry stood speechless and disoriented, his emotions acting against him. His knees started buckling, and his head began throbbing as his brain synapses fired in all directions. He tried recalling everything that Luci told him about Chris. *She and Chris were exchanging letters, but they were friends, not lovers. Chris was part of the Nerd group. Chris enlisted in the army. This can't be. What has changed in the last three months since we were together?*

Regaining his equilibrium, Barry shot back. "Yes, Mrs. Bartolino, I know about Chris, and Steve, and Sean, and Paul." Reeling off the names of Luci's friends, Barry thought he might throw Marie off her game if she were trying to shock him.

Marie maintained her pace and calm. "I know this may be difficult for you, but Luci and Chris are more than friends. In fact, Chris has proposed, and Luci has accepted."

If Marie had punched him in the gut, Barry could not have felt worse. "I find that difficult to believe," he said, instinctively putting his hand to his middle.

"I'm sure that you do. Luci is sweet, and giving bad news isn't her strong point. Barry, believe me, I pleaded with Luci to have a frank talk with you last summer. But Luci said she couldn't find the words to tell you that she was falling in love with Chris; she couldn't face seeing you heartbroken. Barry, I apologize for Luci. I don't excuse her behavior, but that's the truth of the matter."

Barry leaned against the wall by the phone, shaking inside, but Marie had more to dish out, and she dug the knife in deeper. "Barry, she's known Chris for years but you for a short time. I'm sorry, but it's best to tell you this now and not drag it out. Calling and sending more letters won't change the situation. You are a nice young man, and Sam and I wish you all the best. I'll tell Luci you called and leave it up to her if she wants to contact you." Then the phone went dead.

Barry felt his blood starting to boil and his face beginning to turn hot. He started to imagine conspiracies designed to keep him and Luci apart. Instinctively he conjured up his first impressions of Marie as being two-faced. *I don't believe that witch for a second. She has something to do with this*, Barry snarled under his breath.

Slumping, Barry wandered down the long corridor from the payphones back to his room. He sat at his desk with his head in his hands, trying not to jump to conclusions. *These aren't actions in line with Luci's character! I can't accept Luci two-timing me. If I can't talk with Luci, I know someone I can trust to get the facts.* That evening Barry wrote to Ross and Millie. Deep inside, Barry felt that there was no truth in Luci's engagement, but he was unsure of what to suspect.

* * *

Thursday, October 19, 1967

Dearest Barry:

Ross and I were so happy to get your letter, but we were saddened to hear about the breakup between you and Luci. To be truthful, we can hardly believe it ourselves! We thought the two of you were a perfect match.

We didn't know anything about this when we sent your birthday greetings. But earlier this week, Geneviève told us the terrible news. We don't know anything about this Chris fellow, except that he has been a friend of Luci's for several years and is in the army now. Geneviève mentioned that he has been pursuing Luci for a long time; apparently, he was sending letters to her while she was visiting Geneviève. But Luci never talked about him to us, which is odd.

We don't know the best advice to give you, keep pursuing Luci or leave it alone—you alone can make that choice.

Ross and I think the world of you. Do not be a stranger to our home. We will keep in touch, and we sincerely hope you will do the same. If we hear any different news on the subject, we will write to you without delay.

Hugs,

Millie

Barry's heart dropped after reading Millie's letter. He crumpled the note and pushed it aside, then opened another one—it was from his mother. Breana letters were infrequent since Barry started his third year at the academy. Her son had adjusted to the school's routine, and he did not need as much emotional support now. Besides, he had Luci's letters to buoy his spirits, she reasoned. Breana's note was succinct and sympathetic, but as devastating as Millie's.

Thursday, October 19, 1967

Dearest Barry:

I received a phone call from Marie last week. She told me that you and Luci had broken up, or I guess, more to the point, that Luci is

> *engaged to a local boy. You hadn't mentioned anything about this in your last letter to me, so Marie's call with this news surprised me. You know Marie and I connected last summer in making plans for Luci's visit. Even though I thought she was a little highfalutin, I think she's a sincere and attentive parent, and I was happy that she thought enough of me to call.*
>
> *More important, though, Dad and I are concerned about your feelings and your reaction to this turn of events. We liked Luci, but it's the people involved in a relationship that must make the final choices.*
>
> *I won't meddle. You are an adult, and I trust your good judgment and level-headedness and recognize you can make your own decisions. That said, breakups are painful; I should know because I went through a few of those myself before landing my great catch.*
>
> *Know that Dad and I are here to listen and support you and help you in any way we can.*
>
> *Love,*
>
> *Mother*

Angry, Barry crumpled that letter, too. He felt cornered. *Coincidence? In Fairmont Park, Luci told me that random acts appeared like coincidences. Should I take her word for it now?* His mind still buzzed with thoughts of the intrigue and plot-making that could be keeping Luci and him apart. He loathed the line in his mother's letter that sided with Marie being an attentive parent. *Controlling is more like it*, he steamed.

Regardless of Marie's chumminess with his mother, Barry thought it offbeat that she phoned Breana to explain her daughter's personal life. *Good grief, who does that kind of thing*? The timing of Marie's contact with Geneviève also seemed odd. *Everything fits as tight as a rim to a tire, and it is too damn flawless. Then again, who would plan such an offensive strategy? Who has a mind that perverted?* What pestered Barry more, however, was how to reconcile the difference between the person portrayed by Marie and the courageous, honest, and caring girl he knew. It all did not jive. He was pissed. He shook his head, got up from his desk, and went for a run. He needed to clear his head and steady his emotions.

* * *

For the next few weeks, Barry mulled the question of whether he should pursue the relationship. *When does ruminating over what could be, conjecturing intrigue, judging, and assigning blame need to stop? When does persistence become harassment?*

He reflected on his and Luci's long discussions about choice and the importance of living in the present. She always said a person has three options when faced with a decision: be complacent, accept the situation, and endure it; pretend everything is fine and live in a fantasy world; or find a solution to overcome the obstacles and get what you want. *What do I really want? How can I know the hurdles if I don't know what I want?* were questions churning in Barry's mind.

Barry's relationship with Luci made him feel happy and fulfilled. Their values and aspirations, he thought, were as tight as woven fabric. Their romance, Luci confided, was "as sizzling as fireworks shooting beyond the universe." The memories they created, Barry believed, were filled with the playfulness of a three-year-old, the thrill of a roller-coaster ride, and the complexity and loveliness of a symphony. *But if the relationship is falling short for Luci, how could I be happy with that? How can a healthy and fulfilling partnership sustain itself under those conditions?* he asked himself.

Barry assessed his choices. *I can roll over and accept the situation and feel like a damn victim by blaming Luci for being two-faced. I can live in a fantasy world and keep pursuing her, or I can deny that the last eighteen months ever happened. On the other hand, I can act and overcome the obstacles to get what I really want.*

Barry chose to free himself by answering the question, "What do I want?" *I want to live in the present. I love Luci, and I want her to be happy and fulfilled. If Chris gives her this, then that's what I want too. But what are the obstacles?*

Barry confronted the obstacles: ego, judgment, and blame. Putting his ego in the driver's seat to prove the relationship was right or to view Luci's decision as a rejection would destroy his self-esteem and confidence. Making a snap judgment about Luci's actions, getting angry, and placing blame on her would trap him in the past. Barry reminded himself that Luci always said, "Living in the present helps us opens our hearts so we have greater room for gratitude, kindness, and love."

The first evening home on Christmas furlough, Barry sat at his desk. In the solitude of his room, he wrote Luci a heartfelt letter thanking her for memories that would last a lifetime. The next day, he slipped his final goodbye into the postbox.

Chapter 25

Christmas Miracle

Luci closed the front door of her girlhood home for the last time. A chapter of her life was finished. But as the next one began, the ghosts of the past were already slithering on its pages.

She opened the door of her 1976 royal blue 280-Z sports car and fell into the driver's seat, exhausted. Sitting with eyes closed and rubbing her forehead, she recalled when she first purchased the vehicle. Sam was all over the car. It was right up his alley, and he showed off his driving prowess taking Luci for a spin around the tight curves of the Lytle Creek road. With windows wide open and the eight-track blasting oldies, he roared, "This will be a classic."

Marie, on the other hand, had scoffed, "What kind of car is that for a professional woman?"

Luci fired up the Z, drove down the driveway, and headed toward Riverside. There, she took the freeway to Santa Ana and afterward the interstate toward San Diego. At Riverside, she had deliberately passed the exit to Highway 395, even though it would have shaved off fifty miles of her trip. A former two-lane and curvy road, the route was now a freeway, but the accident that occurred on it over a decade ago would always haunt her. After the car crash, Luci refused to travel the route again.

* * *

Whizzing down the freeway, Luci's thoughts turned to the events seventeen years ago that had brought her and Chris together. At the time, a riptide had caught her, and Chris was the lifeguard who threw her a lifesaver.

When communication ended with Barry in the fall of 1967, Luci was confused, depressed, frustrated, dejected, grief-stricken, and pessimistic. Her inner critic, Doris, found a welcoming camp in Luci's psyche and set up her tent, determined never to leave. The troll dug in and dished up a heaping platter of self-doubt, guilt, and blame, diminishing Luci's confidence and leaving her feeling worthless. *What did you do? How could you fall for his baloney? Why did you compromise yourself? How could you be so stupid? Why would anybody love you?* "My heart burns as if it is being seared by red-hot molten steel running through it," Luci had confided to Shelia.

It was late Saturday afternoon, October 14, 1967, in the kitchen of her home, where Marie broke the news about Breana Callahan's phone call that morning. Luci knew now, though, it had all been a lie.

"Breana called this morning," Marie said to her. "She had some disappointing news."

What does she mean "disappointing"? If someone is hurt or sick, that's sad or unfortunate, not disappointing.

Confused, Luci asked, "What do you mean, Mom?" Then she saw Marie pressing her lips and knew what was coming next was not good.

"Oh, Luci, I hate to tell you this. There's no easy way to say it, dear. Barry is getting engaged to a local girl from Buffalo during the Christmas holidays." Luci turned white and, on the verge of fainting, slipped into a kitchen chair.

She choked, struggling to find her voice. "That's impossible!" A million questions swirled in her mind, but Luci mumbled the two making the most sense at the moment. "Why didn't Barry tell this to me? Why did Breana call you and not me?"

Marie walked over and put her arm around Luci. Prepared with her invented explanations, she shot them out at breakneck speed. Barry felt too awful to tell her. Barry let the situation get out of control, and he couldn't face Luci. Marie could break the news to Luci better than Breana. Breana was disappointed in Barry, but there was no use in sending letters, making phone calls, or trying to break up the engagement.

Luci sat openmouthed, feeling embarrassed and betrayed. She moved off the chair, walked toward the doorway, and wandered down the hall to her room, bewildered. She fell across her bed, grabbed her pillow, and put it over her face, crying and trying not to jump to conclusions. *This isn't like Barry! I can't accept that he could be untrustworthy. Who can I talk with? What can I do?*

As the days passed, Luci had an unsettled feeling. Her intuition nagged at her, thinking that things did not jibe. *I can't believe my assessment of Barry could be that wrong. This behavior is out of step with the person with whom I fell in love.*

Like a phantom, Geneviève's phrase from years past leapt to Luci's mind: "It was interference." *But what could be the interference?* she'd wondered. Luci began to imagine conspiracies designed to keep her and Barry apart. Instinctively, she thought about Marie and her need for control, but her mother had never disparaged Barry to her face. *Yes, he plans on a military career, which mother doesn't like, but don't his religion, Irish heritage, education, and potential make up for that assumed flaw?*

The intrigue Luci's brain devised was a step too far for her to consider. Yes, Marie was domineering, but Luci was unaware of any underhanded behavior to break up a romantic relationship. The one other conspirator Luci considered was Breana. *But that doesn't make any sense. There's no motive for her to want Barry and me to break up,* she reasoned.

Looking at the situation, it remained elusive as to why Barry would forsake her. *What did I do? What clues along the way did I miss that Barry was unhappy? How could I be so wrong? Am I that unlovable that someone would dump me like this?*

Sam hated seeing his daughter in such a depressed state, and Barry's turn of character mystified him too. However, he assessed the two sets of facts available. Barry had stopped writing to Luci, and Breana provided Marie with the explanation. *I always told Marie to stop her fussing because the odds are that long-distance relationships fizzle out.*

But a dark thought crossed Sam's mind, thinking about Marie's interference between Darla and Bennett. When Marie told him of Breana's phone call, Sam shot his wife an admonishing look. "Don't you dare, Sam! I know what you're thinking. I learned my lesson. I had nothing to do with this."

After Marie shared Barry's letter with Sam eighteen months earlier, there was no evidence that she had pried again. Even Sam could not bring himself to believe that Marie had obstructed once more.

* * *

Sam helped Luci put together the pieces of her shattered life and climb out from the hole of personal criticism, what-ifs, and imagined deceptions. "Bambina, you have choices," he reminded her, and Luci took his advice. What she did not know was that she and Barry were on the same path of renewal and asking themselves the same question: "What do I want?"

Over the weeks, she struggled to ferret out the strengths of courage, judgment, and perspective to help her weigh options and make sense of her world. She resurrected thoughts about the perseverance and resilience of Lucinda McCormick and how her role model used these to design her future. It was far from easy for Luci to surmount the hurdles in her way: self-doubt, anger, pessimism, and despair. She had many bewildering, tearful, and anxious episodes that were hard to control. She reflected on Shelia's advice: "Go ahead and indulge in a pity party, but make sure you don't partake of it forever. Like all parties, Luci, it has to be short and end."

I can decide to choose to accept the situation and feel victimized. I can opt for fantasy, pretend the past year and a half never happened, and metaphorically run away from it through denial. On the other hand, I have the power to act and overcome obstacles to get what I want. But what is it that I want?

* * *

As he had planned, Chris enlisted in the army in 1967. His Friday night pals accepted his decision, even though they were unhappy about it. Each promised to write to him and send care packages. But it was Luci's letters that he desired the most.

To the Nerds' surprise, things worked out as Chris had planned. He finished basic training at Fort Ord in California and afterward went to Fort Sam Houston in Texas for pharmacy technician training. Unlike many of his cohorts who were sent to Vietnam after their medical training, Chris received an assignment at the army field hospital in Heidelberg, Germany.

A short furlough during the 1967 holiday season before shipping overseas was fortuitous for Luci. Although she did not believe in coincidences, Chris appeared on the scene at the pinnacle of her grief. As Luci's most ardent cheerleader, he helped her choose to act and put her life back together. He soothed Luci's wounds and replenished her spirit and showed her how to make sense of her world.

It was two days before Christmas when the dark clouds started to part. "I'd like to take you to a special place for midnight Mass," Chris said.

"But I don't feel special right now."

"I know. That's why I want to take you somewhere special."

With a half shrug, Luci accepted Chris's invitation. On Christmas eve, they drove the empty backroads bordered by citrus groves and vineyards until they turned onto a long, private roadway. Rounding the last curve of the narrow drive, an unpretentious chapel, nestled into the quiet foothills outside Riverside, appeared before them. The sky was crystal clear, and there was not a sound to be heard. As Chris helped Luci from the car, she looked up and marveled. "The stars are dancing across the sky, Chris. This is the most peaceful sight I've seen in a long, long time. But where are we?" she asked as she continued to scan the sparkling display.

"At a seminary," Chris replied.

Her eyes turned to Chris. "A seminary! You're not planning on becoming a priest, are you?"

Chris chuckled. "No way I'm thinking of being a priest, Luci. Hell, that's the last thing on my mind when I'm with you," he said with a playful DeLuca wink.

Luci stared at Chris. The line from his letter that she had pushed to the back of her mind now became apparent. *I don't want them stealing your heart and preventing you from returning to a guy who loves you the most,* she remembered him writing.

Not ready to admit Chris's feelings, Luci gave him a friendly punch on the arm and her standard line. "Chris DeLuca, you think every girl will fall for your pretty face."

"Got that right!" Then he took Luci's hand, and together they walked up the stone path to the chapel.

Chris delivered on his promise. *This is a special place,* Luci thought, when she walked into the dimly lit chapel. It held no more than one hundred worshipers, and its intimacy and simple architecture challenged the need for ostentatiousness. The High Mass, rich in symbolism, melded with a chorus of vibrant voices and gave Luci the gift of serenity she craved. Worry and recrimination evaporated as Luci shared the kiss of peace with Chris and the other churchgoers. *Something mystical has happened*, Luci thought. *Maybe it's because I don't feel alone now.*

After Mass, they returned to Luci's home, and Marie, true to form, was up to meet them. "Merry Christmas," she said. But as she turned to walk down the hallway, she could not control the impulse of adding, "Be sure you but don't stay up too long."

The couple looked at each other and returned knowing smiles. Then they walked to the living room and sat together in front of a crackling fire and nibbled on an odd combination of Christmas eve snacks that Chris had brought.

"You are a nerd, Chris DeLuca," Luci teased.

"What?" he scoffed, nudging Luci.

"Roasting marshmallows complemented with a glass of wine! I'd call that nerdy."

"You don't know about the finer things in life," Chris said as he offered Luci one of the sugary, charred treats.

She accepted the mushy offering and stuffed it into her mouth, and when Chris gently wiped the vestiges of sticky stuff from her cheek, their eyes met. "I know, Luci, you are going through a rough time, and I am sorry about that. How can I help?"

Luci gazed away and then turned and faced Chris. "I don't know if anyone can help."

"May I share a story about my loss?" Chris asked.

Luci returned a blank stare. "Okay."

"When my father died, Luci, my grief was so overwhelming that there were no words in any dictionary that could describe my feelings. People kept telling me, 'Give it time. It will lessen.' I asked myself, 'How can caring and loving someone lessen over time? How can a person's loss be lessened?' The truth, Luci, is that love and caring don't diminish. To reduce my emotional pain, I needed to find ways to honor my father even though he wasn't with me anymore." He paused and looked at the flickering embers in the fireplace.

"So what did you do?"

He turned his head back and met Luci's gaze. "I looked for new ways of including my dad in my life. Of course, I couldn't have talks with him or ask for his advice. But I could remember the talks we had and the advice he had given me. I show my love for him by pursuing my dream to eradicate cancer. I show my feelings for him by being grateful for the times we shared and recognizing that he helped me be the person I am."

Words of loss from Lucinda's journal rose in Luci's consciousness. Now she understood the wisdom of her grandmother.

> *I remembered the songs my mother sang to me. I held her prayer book during church services, knowing I was fingering the pages she had touched. I took one of her delicate, laced handkerchiefs and safely tucked it among my belongings. This tiny piece of cloth gave consolation to me, just as a locket of hair provides comfort to a lover.*

Tears welled in Luci's eyes, and she reached over and embraced Chris and held him tight. "Chris, you are my Christmas Miracle," Luci whispered in his ear. "You've given me the gift I needed most."

During the following week, Chris's story churned in Luci's mind and helped her make sense of her world. *Ruminating and deconstructing the past can't change the present; that behavior hurts no one else but me. I must use my energy cherishing the times I spent with Barry that gave me happiness and fulfillment. I want to live in the present with an open heart so that it fills with gratitude, kindness, and love.*

Luci knew now that the obstacles of self-criticism, doubt, wrath, and depression were self-induced. Barry had nothing to do with any of them. She was in control and could either inflict these feelings on herself or neutralize them. *What I want is happiness for Barry and me. If our relationship, as fulfilling as it is to me, isn't making him satisfied, then how can I be happy?*

Luci took Doris and her tent and all her baggage and pushed her off a cliff. Then, on New Year's Eve, she wrote Barry a final letter expressing her gratitude for the meaning and memories he gave to her and to say goodbye.

* * *

In the summer of 1968, Luci visited Chris in Germany during his furlough. Marie went into apoplexy over the trip, contending it was immoral for a girl to be traipsing around Europe alone with a boy. Chris was paying for the expenses, and Luci was not about to bow to her mother's control. During her relationship with Barry, she walked on eggshells around Marie, trying to mollify her about spending time with Barry. Like dealing with a petulant child, the giving was never enough for Marie. Luci was not about to repeat her reticence.

Chris and Luci romped through Europe on Eurail passes. They started in Heidelberg and branched out to Italy and France. They took in the famous cities of Paris and Florence, but the places they most enjoyed were quaint villages off the tourist-beaten paths.

The Tuscany and Emilia-Romagna region felt like home to them both. This was where Sam was born and Chris's grandfather too. There, carefree, they drank Campari cocktails in the afternoons sitting in small-town squares. Melding with the locals, they roamed through the open markets, and they joined religious processions that weaved through tiny stone-paved streets celebrating the patron saints of the medieval towns. They marveled at cathedrals built in the Middle Ages that were part of the via Francigena, the route that the pilgrims and the Crusaders took that led to Rome. They hiked along pathways enjoying picnics of wine, crusty bread, cured meats, cheeses, and olives. Their affinity, intimacy, and passion grew as they created lasting memories.

Chris proposed to Luci in the central nave of the Romanesque Cathedral of San Donnino in a small Italian town, and Luci accepted. Nothing in Luci's imagination could have made the proposal more romantic or meaningful. As Chris took Luci's hand and kissed it with the gentleness of a feather fluttering in the breeze, she had chills that accompany true love. They stood, hand in hand, alone in the majestic twelfth-century church as an island unto themselves. Fresco painted walls, sculptures, and soaring columns and arches were their witnesses. Luci's realization of Chris's inner beauty had budded long before. But it was in this moment that the bloom matured, and she truly understood the loveliness and essence of his being. As Luci gazed at the cathedral's ceiling overflowing with paintings of saints and scenes of miracles, she smiled. *Miracles, indeed! My Christmas Miracle.*

A year later, after Luci's college graduation, she and Chris married, surrounded by family and close friends in the cathedral where Chris had proposed. Marie had realized her wish. Her daughter was marrying a well-educated Catholic boy, who would be soon leaving the military, and who would be bringing Luci back home to her. And Sam was Sam. "What's not to like with a handsome young man named DeLuca?" he asked.

After Chris's discharge from the army, he and Luci moved to La Mesa, a sleepy San Diego bedroom community. They choose a condominium on the top of Grossmont Hill, whose selling point was the marvelous view it had of the California sunsets. There was enough money from the GI Bill, Luci's scholarship, and their graduate research associate positions to pay for Chris's graduate work in chemistry and Luci's in social work.

To say Chris and Luci were happy together would be an underestimation of their relationship. Still debating "stuff" like the old Nerd days, Luci and Chris joked that they fit together like a hand in a glove. It wasn't the house on fire love story that Luci shared with Barry, but it sparkled with fun and romance and was solidified on a foundation of similar values. Over coffee on Saturday mornings, the two lightheartedly made up similes and metaphors about themselves: *Drawn to each other as butterflies to blossoms*, and *Happy and wacky as clowns at a birthday party*, or *Frisky as colts at play*. Together they danced in the moment.

Seven months after moving to California, a roaring funnel cloud raced across Luci's life and flattened her to the ground. A drunk driver on the curves of old highway 395 stole all this magic away, robbing Luci of her beloved Chris.

As he had done before, Sam supported his daughter with love and perspective. But it was Luci who found the courage to face the obstacle of loss and chose to believe she could bring about a good future. In her worst moments, late in the night, she was drawn back to the evenings on Geneviève's front porch and to the Lucinda stories. *What defines a person*, Lucinda had said, *are not one's financial or physical attributes or beliefs. Instead, it's the choices one makes in surmounting life's challenges.*

Lucinda's philosophy was Luci's North Star. Its glow guided her thoughts in tamping down her inner critic, Doris, and boosting her courage, gratitude, and love in facing her challenge. "It's not a fleeting pleasure that creates happiness or meaningful memories. Instead, it is choosing to use one's strengths in worthwhile work and being with the people you love," Chris had once told her.

* * *

It had been a warm day, above the average temperature for that time of the year, reaching about seventy-three degrees when Luci left her childhood home. As she approached the skyline of San Diego, she took the Point Loma turnoff and maneuvered the Z to the hallowed ground of the military cemetery.

Parking the car, Luci bowed her head and waited before walking toward the spot that was chiseled in her memory. Rising up before her, the gravestones stood as straight as the soldiers they honored. Aligned in perfect geometric order, they spanned the gentle slope to the edge of the cliff. Fading fast, the sun's rays played peekaboo with the branches of the Torrey pines before the shadows settled across Luci's forehead in a delicate pattern. She was alone in the cemetery, running her hand over the top of Chris's military grave marker.

Mother couldn't let it rest, she whispered to Chris. *I never thought it possible for someone to reach from the grave and tear your heart out, but she has accomplished that in spades.*

Her vision began to blur, and Luci could feel pain overtaking her chest as she clasped her hand over her heart. *Seventeen years ago, Chris, you were my Christmas Miracle. You rallied around me so I could gain my equilibrium and sort things out. You helped me understand that other people's decisions are not a reflection of me. You supported me tenderly and let me grieve my loss of Barry. You never exploited my vulnerable situation or manipulated it for your own benefit. You were my rock, and you patiently helped me navigate the stepping-stones to gain back my self-worth and identity. You are my forever love; no one ever can take your place. How I wish you would appear, breathe your strength into me, hold me in your loving arms, and be my Christmas Miracle once again.*

* * *

Luci returned to her home in an emotional lockdown. She had picked up Dickens from the pet sitter, but even her frisky Boston terrier couldn't budge her from her depleted mood. With Darla's story and the newfound evidence, Luci could, without reading the contents of Barry's letters, sketch a portrait that revealed betrayal. The previous day, she had lacked the energy and heart to read them, and her sisters hadn't pressed her to do so.

Luci went into her bedroom, removed the envelopes from her oversized purse, and placed them on her dresser. Barry's were the ones on the top of the small bundle, hers on the bottom. Taking the first of Barry's letters, she rubbed her fingers across the address on the envelope, the same ritual she performed many years before. She raised the letter to her face and inhaled to see if there was any of Barry's familiar scent left to it. Gazing down, the handwriting was as recognizable as it had been eighteen years earlier.

Luci clutched the letters to her chest and then placed them back on the dresser. She went into the living room and phoned an associate of hers, a trained counselor like herself, and made an appointment for the next day.

CHAPTER 26

Facing Fear

THE next morning, the light on Luci's answering machine was flashing, and reluctantly, she pushed the button to scan the messages. Darla and Adele had called, but she would phone them later after meeting with Pat. There were calls from the university and the clinic, but those would hold. *I'm on leave, and I am not dealing with work issues now. There are responsible people in the department and the counseling center, capable of making decisions without me.*

After breakfast and a walk with Dickens around the perimeter of Grossmont Hill and her condo complex, Luci headed her 280-Z toward La Jolla. "Lucky Pat," she often teased her colleague. Luci lived in a middle-class community, unlike high-end La Jolla with its ocean views, quaint eateries, and boutiques.

Forty-five minutes later, Luci pulled into the driveway of Pat's low-level ranch home and walked to the side of the house where the counselor turned life-coach had her office. She removed the wooden mallet by the door from its holder and tapped the chimes to announce her arrival. The beauty and energy of the bells' vibrations coursed through Luci's body, and she could feel the healing process begin.

"Hi, Luci," Pat said, giving her client a hug.

"Thanks, I needed that."

"My intuition told me you did," Pat said as she put her arm around Luci's shoulder.

They moved into Pat's office that overlooked a manicured garden with a breathtaking view of the ocean and coastal islands beyond. Luci halted, drew in a deep breath, and let her eyes scan the vista. *I know I've come to the right place*, she thought, reassured.

Luci had given Pat an earful during their phone conversation the previous evening. "I'm falling into a chasm of anger and hate. It's dark and cold here, and I can't see a way out," she had cried.

Now, the coach and client sat across from each other in stylish and comfortable turquoise mid-century armchairs, and Pat got right to the point. "What do you want to walk away with at the end of our session today, Luci? What would the outcome look like?"

"I am incensed and maddened," Luci said. "I want to unload my rage and pain. I want to walk away without these burdens and find balance."

"How would it feel to do that?"

Luci choked up, her voice quivering. "It would be freeing. I'd feel that I'm not a victim. I'd know that I had slipped off my mother's yoke of control."

Pat gave Luci space and waited, letting the five-second silence lift some of the weight from Luci's shoulders. "What's the real challenge for you?"

Luci didn't respond, and Pat made no attempt to fill the gap.

Lowering her eyes, Luci answered in a hushed tone, "Forgiveness and compassion for my mother."

"Hmm, that seems like it was a hard thing for you to acknowledge. What's difficult here?" the coach prodded.

* * *

In twice-weekly hour-long sessions, Pat put Luci in control of the agenda and her life. Pat was Luci's champion, supporting her on the pathway that Luci would design to find fulfillment and balance. "You are creative, resourceful, and whole, Luci. You are capable of finding the answers; you can make the choices and take the actions you decide on," Pat assured her client in their first session.

The coach pressed Luci in her discovery process with powerful questions.

What are you concerned about?
What's the bottom line?
Do you have all the facts?
What's the obvious thing to do?
If you had no fear, what would you do?
Have you had a similar situation?
What worked then?

What ideas do you already have?
What do you want to do?
What do you want?
What do you need to know?

The last question struck Luci with the force of a lightning bolt. It broke the impregnable fog and let the clarifying sun come through. "I need to know more. I need to know what Barry thought," Luci asserted. "I've drawn inferences, but I haven't verified them. I haven't opened and read the letters. I don't know what's in them."

"What's holding you back from doing that?" Pat asked.

Luci struggled. Her throat clenched, and she rubbed her clammy palms together. "It's dread. I fear that Barry thought I deceived him and cared so little for him that I would abandon him. Most of all, I fear to learn that he suffered. That would break my heart."

The coach pressed, "If you had no fear, what would you do?"

That question stopped Luci dead in her tracks.

* * *

September 29, 1967, USAFA

Dearest Luci,

I went to my mailbox this afternoon, and there was another letter that I'd written to you that had "Return to Sender" written across the envelope in capital letters. This is the second letter I've received like this. At first, I thought I made an error in writing the address; but that wasn't the case. Then, I considered the letter was undeliverable because you and your parents weren't living at that address anymore. But I quickly discarded that thought as being totally unreasonable.

So here I am, perplexed. Is there something wrong with the US postal system, are you sick, or is there is some other reason my letters are being refused? I know in my heart you'd never reject my messages. Another strange thing is that I haven't received any mail from you. Perhaps you're swamped with your college classes?

If there is one thing I know about you, Luci, it is your courage. You'd never run away from speaking up if I had done something to upset you; that's not your style. That's why this silence between us doesn't make sense.

What sustains me in all the craziness and stress at school is dreaming of our memory making this summer. Recall Spenser's Mountain, the best meadow in all New York State, and the place we spent our last afternoon together? I don't think either of us will ever forget! Do you think we embarrassed the birds and bees and other critters there?

I cherish our lazy walks through the woods. I yearn for nuzzling with you around the flickering embers of the fire. I know you are the one for me; I hope I am the one for you!

One of my strengths is optimism, and I believe that there is a good reason my letters are being bumped back to me. If I haven't heard from you on my birthday, I will call you the next day, on Saturday, October 14.

Love, Barry

After reading Barry's letter, Luci focused on the vast desert-like canyon that lay beyond her living room picture window. Stroking Dickens, curled next to her in the oversized chair, she closed her eyes and sadness tore at her heart. It started to make sense, the pieces falling into place as effortlessly as those of a toddler's wooden puzzle. Marie had opened Barry's letter, and in doing so, she knew beforehand the time that he would phone that Saturday. Luci thought back to that day. *No wonder she encouraged me to go on the day trip with the hiking club from school. She wanted me out of the house!*

Although Marie's scheme was pathetic, there was one aspect Luci found humorous. *I bet Mother came close to a meltdown reading about the Spenser's Mountain meadow.* Luci laughed aloud as she created an image of her mother pacing and tearing at her hair. Then another chilling thought occurred to her. *How long had Mother been reading Barry's letters? Had she read Chris's letters too*? she asked herself and felt sick at the thought.

As the facts crystallized and the plot unfolded, Luci agonized thinking of the lines of Barry's letter. "If there is one thing I know about you, Luci, it is your courage. You'd never run away from speaking up if I had done something to upset you; that's not your style."

Luci crumbled in uncontrollable sobs, and grief cut through her heart like shards of glass. Even though she was faultless, Luci's inner critic, Doris, dredged up old feelings, making her feel she had let Barry down. "You didn't try hard enough. You should have called Breana. You lacked the courage to fight for your autonomy."

Luci's mouth went dry, and her pulse raced when she picked up Barry's last letter. She held it in silence, tears welling, and dreaded reading its contents. She was tempted to burn the letter. *Do I have the courage to read his last letter? Will I be able to deal with his incriminations, anger, bitterness, contempt, and, most of all, his hurt? How can I possibly hold out hope for his understanding when everything told to him was a lie? How could he understand when he didn't know the truth?*

The question "*If you had no fear, what would you do?*" played as an endless loop in her mind.

December 16, 1967, 181 Blackhorse Road

Dearest Luci,

I phoned your home a few weeks ago, and you weren't home. But I spoke with your mother, and she told me that you are getting engaged to Chris. I'm not surprised that you might fall in love with Chris. I remember telling you one time that I thought your friend, Chris, was an incredible person.

Marie phoned my mother, too, and confirmed to her what she had told me. Marie said that phone calls were useless and that any letters I sent, you would return. I pray that you open this one, at least.

There's no use trying to hide my sadness that our relationship has fallen short for you, Luci. But how could I possibly be happy if you are not? You always spoke about choices. I could put my ego first and try to prove the relationship was right and to continue pestering you. I could choose to be angry and place blame on myself or on you. Those are things I do not choose to do. I know my life will not be the same without you, and I grieve that I've lost my best friend and confidant and my lover. But I am reminded that you always said living in the present helps us open our hearts so we have room for gratitude, kindness, and love.

This is my gratitude letter to you, Luci. Love will always be in the present tense, not the past tense in my feelings for you. You are the girl I love, and I am grateful for the memories we created. They were as thrilling as a roller-coaster ride, as comforting as a mountain meadow, and filled with an intimacy that had no limit. You once said our romance was as sizzling as fireworks shooting beyond the universe. I'm holding on to those fireworks as my shooting stars, and I thank you for them.

I want to live in the present. I love you, Luci, and my biggest wish is that you be happy and fulfilled. If Chris gives you this, then that's what I want, too.

May your path through life, Luci, be strewn with abundant love and roses.

Always madly in love with you, Barry.

Luci doubled up, covered her mouth, and let out a primal scream. There was a cacophony of thousands of swords clashing and echoing in her head. She rocked in her chair, hugging herself, trying to rouse a flicker of comfort. *There is no doubt left in my mind that Barry was the kind, generous, compassionate, and wise person I thought him to be.* The thought was double-edged. It consoled her, but it ripped her heart to shreds to think she had believed a lie for almost twenty years that came from a person she should have been able to trust.

CHAPTER 27

Forgiveness

FOUR days before Christmas, Luci and Dickens headed north on a five-hundred-mile road trip to Carmel-by-the-Sea. The quaint European-style village had been on Luci's list to visit for years. Now, she thought, it was the ideal getaway, a place where she could find space to acknowledge her hurt and repair it with forgiveness. They cruised along on the interstate at eighty miles an hour with Neil Diamond blaring on the eight-track and Luci singing along. The steady beat energized Luci and synchronized her mood with happy times in high school and with Barry. "The healing power of vibration dials down stress and turns up optimism," Sam had always said. At the moment, Luci could not have agreed more with her father.

"Are your ears hurting, Dickens darling?" Luci asked the Boston terrier occupying the passenger's bucket seat of the sports car. From his mournful eyes, the pooch shot her one of his "you got to be kidding me" looks. Luci glanced sideways at him. "Okay, we'll lower the volume." Afterward, Dickens curled up and settled down for a nap.

Luci's coaching sessions helped her come to grips with her emotions of betrayal, anger, and resentment. Still, she knew resolution was a long road ahead. "It's a wise counselor who recognizes when she needs help," Luci told her graduate students. She was thankful now that she had the humility to follow her own advice.

How can people be resilient and healthy if they are unforgiving and hold on to anger, resentment, and thoughts of revenge that trigger stress? she wondered. With her psychology background, Luci knew that if she didn't find forgiveness that she would pay a high price.

"Mentally, I have forgiven Marie," Luci had told Pat. "But I know that making a decision to forgive and saying you forgive isn't enough. That won't remove the anger and bitterness I have. I need to move to a deeper level to eliminate my rage and animosity. All this ruminating about what might have been must stop. I need to detonate and blow up Doris like a bomb to rid myself of these crazy feelings of guilt."

Luci knew the coping strategies to use to resolve her negative emotions. Indeed, she had used many of these methods with her clients who had similar situations. For Luci, however, there was no possibility of accepting an apology from Marie or witnessing her remorse. Nor was it feasible to receive restitution or resolve what could have been.

So what comes next? she asked herself. *This time, the lifesaver can't be Chris or Pop. It must be the gift of time in calm surroundings to allow my heart to open and find forgiveness.*

* * *

The one-bedroom, A-frame cottage Luci rented was nestled among the serenity of Monterey pines in the coastal hills not far from the village center of Carmel. Floor-to-ceiling windows welcomed soothing sea views into the living room and the loft bedroom above it. In the evenings, Luci and Dickens cuddled before the fieldstone fireplace, its embers flickering until dawn, and they fell asleep to melodic ocean sounds slipping through the loft window.

Each morning, a chorus of jeers from Blue jays awoke Luci, and as she padded down the stairs from the loft, she saw deer peeking through the living area windows. During the day, Luci and Dickens hiked the trails in Big Sur. From her vantage point, she watched sea otters at play and sighted clouds of vapor expelled by the gray whales on their migration to Mexico. Nature's palette, fused with the gift of time, began unlocking her heart and making room for gratitude, kindness, and love.

Luci's journal, her constant companion, helped her confront her feelings of injustice and bitterness. Reflection came naturally, but deriving meaning from the process ground as slowly as the repetition of a waterwheel's millstones. Little by little, a profound awareness surfaced from the click of the gears. *Preoccupation with my mother's betrayal offers me no benefit; it is unhealthy and robs me of autonomy.* It took several journal entries before her thoughts on forgiveness began to take shape.

December 22, 1984, Carmel-by-the-Sea

I walk blindfolded in a dense forest. It's damp, cold, and silent. I am alone; even the rabbits, squirrels, birds, and deer are circumventing this unsettling place. I creep and stumble, trying to locate the first steppingstone to forgiveness. What is forgiveness? I don't know yet. It is as arduous to catch as an elusive fairy.

December 23, 1984, Carmel-by-the-Sea

Why do I wear a blindfold? Why do I walk in such an unfamiliar territory sightless? Before I can walk toward forgiveness, I must find the path that leads to it. How do I discover it without knowing where to look? How can I look without seeing? How can I see when I have shuttered my eyes?

December 24, 1984, Christmas Eve, Carmel-by-the-Sea

A homemade quilt is draped around Dickens and me as we sit together. In front of us, the fire is a chemical combustion: crack, bang, pop! The flames licking the logs bring to mind the elusive forgiveness fairies. They are here one moment and gone the next, fluttering by so fast that they are impossible to touch. But, as I eye the dancing ensemble, I ask myself, Have they left? Are they laying low among the embers? Are they grasping a draft and swirling upwards to the chimney and enticing me to come along for the ride?

I am playful tonight, and I'm tempted to frolic with them. I can't soar blindfolded, though! The lure for freedom is so tantalizing that even with trembling hands, I choose to remove the covering that veils my eyes. Perhaps the forgiveness fairies aren't elusive after all if I observe open-eyed and allow my curiosity to surge.

December 25, 1984, Carmel-by-the-Sea

It's evening again. Hiking on the trail this afternoon, I remembered Sam's advice: "Be thankful, Luci. It changes your world." I once told Barry that I was going to keep a "thankful journal." I forgot about that, but I am going back to fulfill that promise made so long ago. Tonight, I am thankful I've made the decision to forgive my mother's betrayal because it's a step toward freedom. I know deciding to forgive is no more than the beginning of the journey.

For real forgiveness, I must follow the forgiveness fairies and the pathway to self-awareness and compassion.

December 26, 1984, Carmel-by-the-Sea

Sitting on the cottage deck this morning, I looked across to the ocean. The precision of the whale blows, I thought, would make the iconic Trevi Fountain envious. Like geysers, they reminded me of the fairy-flames curling themselves around the fireplace logs. It's another sign the forgiveness fairies aren't deserting me; they have persistence, and they wait untiring until I am ready to follow them. I am grateful for Dickens because he brings humor into my life. I am thankful for the gray whales because they've given me new insights. I am grateful for my sisters because they gave me the truth.

December 27, 1984, Carmel-by-the-Sea

I caught a forgiveness fairy and hung on for dear life! Like a hummingbird, she fluttered before me, daring me to follow her contrails for a ride. I took the bait! We whizzed through the forest path, and the place was no longer cold, damp, and unforgiving. Woodland creatures scurried everywhere. Delicate flowers caught the sun-rays as they played hide-and-seek with tree limbs. I could see the lane was clear, its edges marked by ferns rippling in the gentle breeze. The path to forgiveness will guide me to freedom. I will be nobody's slave! I am thankful for this cozy cottage because it gives me serenity. I'm grateful for my father because he gave me wisdom. I'm thankful for the sunset because it awakens my appreciation and enjoyment of beauty.

December 28, 1984, Carmel-by-the-Sea

I keep asking myself what is forgiveness? Forgiveness is not pardoning. It is not overlooking or justifying my mother's transgression and the hurt her actions caused. I am relieved that I don't have to condone, excuse, reconcile, or even forget her behavior to forgive her. What is forgiveness? The nuggets were there all the time in Barry's last letter; forgiveness is choosing to reject resentment and embrace compassion.

I've read Barry's last letter a dozen times, and today was the first I saw how the pieces of the forgiveness puzzle fit together. As I studied his words, I stepped away from being a participant in the account. This allowed me to view the narrative with a learner's mind and not an emotional one. I could observe Barry's actions as a student might, with curiosity, and as if I were witnessing a demonstration in forgiveness conducted in a graduate course.

Or I could imagine how the Nerd group might handle this hot potato. Oh yes! I'm laughing at the scene. Sean, of course, would make it a Socratic seminar, asking the rest of us probing questions. Then, in a professorial style, he would reiterate our answers in bullet point fashion.

"How do you suppose the process of forgiveness began for Barry?" Sean begins. We all stare at him!

Chris stammers, "Before he can forgive, he must acknowledge an injury, right? At least, what he believes is an injury? If there isn't a belief that an injury occurred, then there's nothing to forgive."

"Do you believe there was a transgression that required forgiveness?" Sean challenges.

"Hell, he lost his best friend, for goodness sakes! He feels hurt," one of us barks.

Paul cuts in. "But the hurt isn't what Barry believes is Luci's transgression—the hurt is Barry's reaction."

"Oh, come on, Paul," Shelia exclaims. "The wrong is a betrayal. She's not honest with Barry. She didn't confront him. That's the transgression."

Sean probes us harder. "Do you think Barry showed emotions that people, on the whole, display after someone has committed an offense?"

Then one of us wants to look super smart and says, "He does because he says he feels hurt. But I think he was angry at one point too. He alludes to it in the letter. He says something about his ego; if he let his ego take over, then he would blame Luci. He doesn't want to do that."

"So how does Barry move beyond those emotions of blame, hurt, and anger?" Sean asks, pushing us to think deeper.

I take the bait. "He makes a decision to forgive."

"Is that enough, to say he has forgiven? Will it remove the negative emotions?" Sean challenges, his eyes looking right through me.

"No," answers Chris, and he elaborates. "Barry gets over his negative emotions by replacing them with understanding and compassion. He shows empathy by putting himself in Luci's position." I'm listening to my beloved in this play scene and think, *how discerning and wise you always are Chris!"*

"And what is that perspective?" Sean challenges again.

Someone pipes up. "Barry realizes Luci isn't happy in the relationship. If Luci isn't happy in the relationship, and it's not fulfilling, then it would be crazy, wouldn't it, to make her continue in it? Wouldn't that be bullying a person? Would Barry like that for himself?"

Sean presses. "So that's the insight, the ah-ha moment when he puts himself in Luci's shoes?"

"Yeah, that's when he identified and understood her situation. I think he demonstrated empathy. His understanding removed the negative emotions," Chris confirms.

Sean digs deeper. "Isn't Barry pardoning and excusing Luci's behavior when he shows empathy? Should he pardon her?"

Paul thinks he has all the answers. "Empathy has nothing to do with pardoning someone, and it doesn't excuse her behavior. Excusing someone means an injustice didn't happen given specific circumstances. For instance, you're excused from not showing up to work because you are sick, or you are excused from injuring someone if it is in self-defense. Empathy isn't about excusing or pardoning. Empathy is being able to explain someone's actions from their perspective."

Not satisfied, Sean persists and pushes us to contemplate further. "To forgive, do you need to pardon? Do you need to receive restitution? Do you need to reconcile with the person who has hurt you?"

"No, Barry didn't pardon or excuse Luci's behavior, and he certainly didn't receive restitution. I don't know how he could be compensated for his hurt anyway. Make her pay money or something?"

Shelia glibly adds. All the Nerds roar at her last comment, including Shelia.

"What about reconciliation. You know, make up and shake hands, and all of that?" Sean speculates.

"Barry didn't reconcile with Luci," is Chris's immediate reply. And then he justifies his position. "That was clear in his letter. Forgiveness is about abandoning resentment, anger, bitterness, not about having to reestablish a trust relationship with someone. You can forgive someone but not be buddy-buddy with them again."

"So what was the outcome for Barry, do you suppose? At the end of this, what did he walk away with?"

We are silent for a minute and have to reflect.

Then I say, "Barry walked away with giving the gift of forgiveness. He opened his heart, and in doing so, he filled it with gratefulness and kindness. Barry released the burden of negative emotions and replaced them with positive ones. He saw meaning in his memories, and he saw he still had a purpose in life."

What a tsunami of a revelation! Barry revealed the forgiveness pathway in his letter! I have a choice. I can wallow in ego by insisting that I'm right that Mother was vindictive and unfair. Egocentricity results in anger and bitterness and is never resolved. That makes me a victim and holds me hostage.

I can say "I forgive" and hope that time will run its course and that the bitterness will disappear like magic. That thought is ridiculous!

On the other hand, I can walk the forgiveness path and let it transport me from resentment and anger to empathy and compassion. This is what I choose.

Pondering her mother's behaviors, Luci came as a learner, not a judger, and as a forgiver, not an accuser. Writing in her journal, she grappled with what her mother must have felt and experienced.

December 31, 1984, Carmel-by-the-Sea

The way I can follow the forgiveness fairies and harness their energy and love is to cleanse myself and empty the darkness within. I open myself to a white light and let it course through my body. My pen is the instrument that allows my understanding to flow and dissipate the darkness so that it never returns to overshadow my world.

Control for Mother was a defense for her own powerlessness and low self-esteem. To believe in herself, she thought she needed to exercise control by manipulating her children and others.

She desired to live in the shadows through her children, directing them to accomplish what she couldn't achieve. In this way, she could feel accomplished and fulfilled. Controlling Adele, Darla, Aimee, and me and succeeding in making us conform to her rigid belief system, gave her the feeling of self-efficacy.

Had her life been overcontrolled as a child too? Was she recreating the same emotional stress in her children that she felt as a child? I don't know; those questions are unanswerable. But how unsatisfying her life must have been when her desire for total control overshadowed everything else. It made life a constant struggle, filled with stress and disappointments.

I acknowledge the injury Mother did, and I don't excuse her behavior. I don't ask for retribution or reconciliation. Instead, I forgive her by releasing my resentment and embracing compassion for her own suffering. I am grateful for the forgiveness fairies because, through them, I have reaffirmed a purpose in my life and reclaimed my autonomy, regardless of the injury I incurred.

I end my thoughts with thankfulness. I am thankful to Barry because he has shown me the path to forgiveness.

Luci closed her journal. There was one line in Barry's letter, though, that she could not shake. "You'd never run away from speaking up if I had done something to upset you; that's not your style." She embraced the hope that one day she could lessen the pain of that line.

The clock in the A-frame chimed midnight: 1985, another year and another beginning.

CHAPTER 28

Hope

BARRY hit the gas pedal of the rental car, propelling it along the back roads of south-central Wisconsin. The region's geography reminded him a little of western New York State, and the day's temperature was what he might have expected on Hartsville Hill in early June. *But the sky*, Barry thought, *is not as magical. It is not the vivid blue of New York's southern tier, and it is missing the fluffy clouds I love watching.* Barry smiled. *Nothing beats the Appalachian foothills of New York*, he said to himself, pushing the accelerator to its limits. He loved speed; after all, he used to be a pilot.

The countryside's serenity from Madison back to Chicago's O'Hare Airport provided a welcome respite. After two demanding work-filled days, the short trip gave Barry the space to resurrect happy memories. "June 10, 1966," he murmured out loud to himself. *Today is the twentieth anniversary! After all this time, I can remember that street dance as if it happened yesterday. Every aspect of it is etched in my mind.*

Barry had graduated from the Air Force Academy and afterward went to flight school. Of his time as a pilot, a year was in combat in Vietnam. Like his father, Barry rarely talked about his wartime service, and he often sought refuge from his memories by drinking alone. When his brother Joe asked Barry about these episodes, he would repeat their mother's phrase, "Some things are better left unsaid."

As much as he loved flying, Barry found that the regimentation and hierarchy of the military were far from what he wanted for his life. Fitting into a command structure that awarded conformity but not innovation was stifling, not unlocking, his potential—he wanted to flourish, not just survive. But it was more than these constraints that nagged at Barry. His confession to Luci on Bois Blanc was a frequent companion: "I love planes and aeronautics, but I don't like killing. I guess you could call it a clash of conscience or a moral dilemma." Meeting his required service obligation of eight years after he graduated from the academy, Barry resolved his quandary by resigning from the air force.

A few months after leaving the military, he and his wife divorced. "On the face of it," he joked to his brother Joe, "Carole liked the uniform better than she did me," and within six months, his ex-wife married another air force officer.

Eleven years after the divorce, Barry was still a bachelor. He had graduated from law school and passed the New York Bar, and had a position as a civil rights attorney. His career was intense but exciting. He worked long hours and traveled frequently, but he felt more alive than he could ever have imagined. Two days before, he had wrapped up attending a conference on civil and human rights in Chicago and decided on a side trip to Madison to meet with colleagues who had worked for the passage of the nation's first statewide gay rights law. Now, he was heading to Chicago to catch a late evening flight home to Buffalo.

Today's anniversary date was always bittersweet, mixed with good memories and doubts about how his relationship with Luci ended. He often thought about skipping over the border to Canada and looking up Millie and Ross but then had second doubts. *What would I accomplish?* He did not ruminate, but an inner voice told him never to lose hope that the uncertainties surrounding the breakup would some way be revealed.

Today, Barry concentrated on the memory making he had created with Luci. He was grateful to have had her as a confidant for confessing his career uncertainties. Their conversation on Bois Blanc helped him recast and look at his moral quandary from a different perspective; in the end, it influenced his decision to leave the military. Believing in choice gave him the strength to choose a new path and legacy. When it came to his obituary, he wanted it to say he was a person of courage who spoke up for what was right and who fought to give everyone a fair chance.

Without question, Barry had meaning and purpose in his life now. His work engaged him, and each time he pushed progress ahead on equity, he felt a sense of mastery and accomplishment. Barry had a circle of good friends and a vibrant social life. After his divorce, he had several relationships, and they filled a void of intimacy up to a certain point. But Barry had yet to find romance with someone with whom he could confide everything or for whom he would do anything. He wanted a partner whose absence from his life would be a misery. Barry's brother Joe thought he was a tireless romantic, but Barry persisted in being hopeful that he could find a *Luci* again.

When Barry crossed the border into northern Illinois, it was early afternoon. A few miles down the rural two-lane highway, he saw a small directional sign: Woodstock – Historic Square and Downtown, Next Right. *Why not?* he thought. *I like history and have time to kill!*

He made the turn and drove a few blocks through a residential area, surprised to find streets rich in Victorian architecture. Everywhere he looked, there were delightful examples of Queen Anne, Second Empire, and Victorian shingle-style homes, each gussied up in their painted best. Smaller and classic English-style cottages were sprinkled among the large Victorians that lent variability and kept him curious as to what might be on the next block. The place was real Midwest, with youngsters riding their bicycles, jumping rope on the sidewalks, and running through front yards. Thoughts of his childhood summers in Buffalo spent playing with neighborhood friends rushed to his consciousness. When he saw children playing jacks, cards, and board games and reading books on wraparound porches that extended across the front and the sides of their homes, he felt right at home.

From nowhere, the historic two-acre square appeared. *This place is frozen in time. Turn of the Century Americana,* Barry marveled. *This looks more like New England than the Midwest!*

A large tree-shaded park with a manicured lawn sat in the middle of the square. Wide brick-paved streets, each a block long, bordered the four sides of the park, and each was flanked with old buildings housing commercial enterprises. Restaurants, women and men's clothing and shoe stores, banks, barber and beauty salons, a hardware store, and even an old-time pharmacy were included among the jam-packed businesses along the square's perimeter. The place buzzed with people, and it took Barry some time to find a parking space on a side street. Leaving his car, he was curious to explore what seemed to be northern Illinois' best-kept secret. *It feels good to stretch my legs, and I could not have found a prettier place to do it.*

Strolling along the sidewalks, Barry peeked through the windows to gain an idea of the wares the businesses sold. He made a dead stop before an imposing old opera house and ventured to take a look inside. *There are so many interesting angles to this place,* Barry thought, after he discovered that Paul Newman, Geraldine Page, and others were among the summer stock players at the old theater during the 1950s. *And who knew?* Orson Welles grew up here, and the creator of Dick Tracy, one of Barry's comic heroes, did his creative work in this small town.

Barry noticed a shop with the sign "Read Between the Lynes," that lured him in. *A great play on words for a bookstore—must be the owner's last name,* he surmised. He was surprised when he walked into the store. It was larger than its outside appearance suggested, and it featured a café section providing coffee, sandwiches, pastries, and ice cream. Even though the town looked turn of the century, the bookstore was keeping pace with current trends of independent booksellers by enticing customers to extend their stays. He liked the place.

After purchasing a *Chicago Tribune* and ordering a sandwich and coffee, he sat at a small table at the window overlooking the square. As he ate, he worked the newspaper crossword; afterward, with a second cup of coffee, he sat back and enjoyed the impeccable postcard scene before him. *There couldn't be a better place for my June 10, 1966, reflections. I'll never forget how my heart raced the evening I first saw her—the lighted streets, my palm tree fiasco, the slow dances, and her fragrance that made me go wild.*

Voices coming from a separate room off the central area of the store interrupted his thoughts. He turned around to look and saw a steady stream of people going into an anteroom. The commotion was enough to pique his interest, and he got up and walked over to the cash register to pay his check and find out what was going on.

"Looks like a lot of people are coming in. What's happening in there?" he asked the friendly clerk waiting on him.

"Oh, yes," she replied, taking his credit card. "There's an author's book signing and presentation this afternoon."

"Is that so? Must be quite a novelist to attract this kind of crowd in such a small venue."

"Oh, she's not a novelist. I don't know how you'd categorize the book—kind of half memoir and half self-help book, maybe?"

"It must describe a fascinating life to draw this audience. Have you read the book?" Barry asked.

"Oh, yeah! It's cool!"

"How is it cool? Tell me about it," Barry asked, flashing the clerk his signature grin as he signed the credit card slip.

"It's about a California girl growing up in the 1960s who has a meddling mother who destroys her love affair. The mother has some big hang-ups, and her lies break up the couple's relationship. Even though it's not a novel, it reads like one."

Nah, it couldn't be, he thought. *The 1960s, California, love affair, meddling mother.*

Disregarding his silence, the clerk went on. "You must have heard about it. There's been a buzz on television over it. The title is *Blackhorse Road.* Do you know it?"

Barry felt the blood flowing out of his face. His knees started to buckle, and he clutched the counter to steady himself. "Yeah. Yeah, I guess I do know it, now that you mention it."

"Well, would you like to buy a copy? There are still a couple of tickets left for the author's presentation and signing too."

Regaining his composure, Barry handed his credit card back to the clerk. "Yeah, sure, I'll take a copy and a ticket."

"Hey, are you all right? You look like you've seen a ghost."

Barry returned to the small table and sat down to recover from his shock. He tried to comprehend what was happening. His heart and adrenaline were firing faster than the fighter planes he had flown. He broke into a sweat, and his palms were clammy. On the one hand, he was ecstatic; on the other, he was afraid. He took the book in his shaking grasp and ran his eyes over the summary on the back of it.

> *It's the turbulent mid-1960s, and Luci, an eighteen-year-old Southern California girl, is on the quest for self-determination and new beginnings. Three powerful forces influence her values: the grit of her Irish great-grandmother, Lucinda McCormick; the philosophy of choice of her father, Sam; and the 1960s ideals of equity and altruism. But potent foes thwart Luci at every turn. Her budding romance with a handsome United States Air Force Academy cadet sets the stage for conflict and deception that last for two decades. A betrayal set into motion by someone she should have been able to trust plunges her into despair. When Luci discovers how her autonomy and her love affair were hijacked, she struggles with anger and bitterness. But from a surprising source, she finds a forgiveness path that restores her well-being and hope and, in the end, faith in herself.*

Her words synchronized with events familiar to him. "There is no doubt now," he said under his breath. His mind raced back to his phone conversation with Marie revealing Luci's impending engagement. *Marie's phone call to my mother and her message to Luci's grandmother about Luci and Chris were skillful and abhorrent. There was no engagement at all! My intuition was right; I never should have trusted Marie,* he seethed.

Barry was one of the last to arrive in the presentation room, and he took a seat in the back. Even from this distance, Barry's eyes did not deceive him. His heart took a dive down to his knees. *She wore a simple but chic outfit that separated her from the rest of the group and screamed sophistication. She is still beautiful and breathtaking.* Barry closed his eyes as Luci introduced her story, comforted in hearing her voice once again.

> *The cranky engine revved as the driver shifted gears, and the military bus crawled forward exiting the air force base. Along a narrow and dark roadway, the vehicle increased its speed and left the MPs at the gate standing immobile and mute in the glow of the rising moon. Drifting through the open windows, the Southern California desert air blew like pixie dust across the faces of the thirty young women headed home from the street dance. A few hours ago, they were preening and adjusting their bouffant hairdos, reapplying creamy pink lipstick, and placing the last twirls of mascara on their eyelashes to prepare for a street dance with cadets from the elite Air Force Academy. Then, the atmosphere buzzed with gossip, chatter, laughter, and anticipation. Now, the glimmering night sky created the perfect backdrop that lulled each into a contented silence to fantasize about the handsome men they had met.*

"This is the beginning of my story about love and betrayal and a journey toward empathy, compassion, and forgiveness. It is also a story of choice —my choice to be inspired by the resilience of a great-grandmother, the values of a father, and the wisdom of a spouse. But in the end, it is a story of how a letter of gratitude from an address on Blackhorse Road reminded me to open my heart to love and kindness."

Barry listened spellbound to Luci's story. It was not until now that he realized their first meeting was as emotional and meaningful for her as it had been for him. As Luci proceeded, it was difficult believing that he played a principal role in what sounded like an invented tale. His feelings were a geyser of hot emotions: anger, frustration, bitterness, loathing, disgust, and sadness. These, however, cooled as Luci guided her audience in the embrace of choice and gratitude, the themes she had rendered familiar to him twenty years before. His eyes misted as Luci read aloud his last letter and explained its lifesaving effect in putting her on the pathway to finding forgiveness.

Barry rubbed the bridge of his nose, his head down with tears burning his eyes. *This is surreal. Is it a dream? Can I hope?*

After the presentation, the questions the audience asked spanned the continuum from superficial to profound.

Why didn't you phone Barry?

Why did you trust your mother?

Why didn't Barry try calling you again, do you suppose?

Aren't you excusing your mother's behavior?

Did you try to locate Barry after you found out your mother's deception?

Why isn't restitution enough for achieving forgiveness?

Why is being thankful important?

What's the biggest lesson you learned?

What was your hardest challenge?

How do you continue to forgive?

In each case, Luci responded thoughtfully, many times posing powerful questions to the inquirers, helping them sort out the answers to their own queries. Throughout the sixty-minute exposé, Barry sat still, desiring to go unnoticed. The last thing he wanted was to burden Luci with the emotional shock of seeing him when she was in the spotlight.

After the formal session finished, the audience lined up to have their books autographed. Unlike twenty years earlier, this time Barry stepped to the end of the line but kept Luci within eyesight. *Wow, she was worth the wait*, he said under his breath.

His turn came, and as he wished, he was alone with Luci. She was looking down when she reached out to take his book. She hesitated. A frown passed over her face. The outstretched hand in front of her seemed oddly familiar. She raised her head upward, gasped, and sat paralyzed in disbelief. Her eyes locked with Barry's in a powerful bolt of recognition.

"I never gave up hope," Barry whispered.

"Neither did I," Luci replied.

* * *

Discussion Questions and Resources

Values, beliefs, and life philosophy form the backbone of *Blackhorse Road* characters. Book reviewer, Gayle Scroggs, PhD, PCC, suggests that "The exceptional self-awareness that the characters show is what stands out in *Blackhorse Road.*"

What are your reactions to the following quotes and inner thoughts from the characters? Do you agree with the opinions, beliefs, or philosophies that they espouse? Would the story outcome have changed for the characters if they had held different perspectives? Are there contradictions between what the characters championed and how they acted? What contributed to the conflict between the characters and the successes or the failures of their relationships?

* * *

Lucinda—Chapter 1: *What defines a person are not one's financial or physical attributes or beliefs. Instead, it's the choices that one makes in surmounting life's challenges.*

Lucinda—Chapter 1: *Acknowledge the goodness in life for there you will find happiness. Live in the present for there is the path to a worthwhile life. Seek out your options for there you will discover the best choice.*

Lucinda—Chapter 1: *In the end, what have I given? A flower begins by receiving a seed from one that has gone before, and at its end, it gives a seed so another can start. The purpose of the flower is not to receive or to give. Its meaning is in the quality of the bloom that it nurtures to beautify the world. I have received, and I have given, but the essence of my life is the bloom that I have become.*

Luci—Chapter 1: "Conformity may make life seem more comfortable. But blind obedience, in time, frustrates and disappoints us. It is conformity that robs us of our hope and deprives us of improving ourselves and creating a better and fairer world."

Sam—Chapter 2: "You have three options when you hit a brick wall and can't get what you want. You can be complacent and accept the situation and endure it. You can live in a fantasy world and pretend everything is fine. Or you can persist and find a way around the wall."

Marie—Chapter 2: *Is the short-lived thrill of seduction worth the cost of losing self-determination and social status?*

Sam—Chapter 2: *Lying once makes it easier to do it the next time and the time after that. Deceit has a funny way of propagating until it finally destroys the thing it was attempting to protect.*

Sam—Chapter 2: "I survived the Depression by being hopeful and grateful. These are the two most powerful virtues a person can have to get through life."

Marie—Chapter 2: A world of self-scolding for not measuring up plagued Marie, and she subjected her family to common refrains of doubt and self-rebuke. "I should have attended the university. I wasn't good enough to marry into society. I should have pursued being an artist. I could have done better."

Marie—Chapter 2: "Sam, we left a tight-knit group. Communities like that give people a sense of place, set boundaries, and check people's actions. You think twice before breaking the rules."

Sam—Chapter 2: "Following the beliefs and rules of a specific faith is not what matters. What counts is how people morally conduct their lives."

Adele—Chapter 2: "Mother never learned from her frustrating experiences. Instead, she replicated them with us. She intensified the behaviors that stymied her autonomy and self-determination. In the end, Mother couldn't break the family's cycle of control. Had she thought to balance her disappointments with the positive things in her life, she would have been a lot happier."

Luci—Chapter 4: *I won't be tied to a person whose religious fervor outstrips common sense or targets people because of their doctrinal beliefs.*

Sean—Chapter 5: "Making people anxious through irrational fear," Sean said, "diverts their attention from real problems. Such tactics allow authoritative people to take actions that many times are not in peoples' best interests."

Sam—Chapter 6: "Given the relevant facts and the chance to think things through, most people are smart, creative, and resourceful enough to make the right decisions."

Sam—Chapter 7: "Energy wasted on the past doesn't produce much for the future."

Connor—Chapter 8: "Time and place shape a person."

Sam—Chapter 9: "Pull the cinch too tight and the horse bucks."

Sam—Chapter 10: "Don't make snap decisions, good or bad, about someone. Before forming an opinion, figure out what makes a person tick."

Sam—Chapter 10: "Understanding what motivates people," Sam always stressed, "is a circular process. Listen to what people say, observe their behaviors, ask them questions, then repeat the steps."

Connor—Chapter 10:" If you don't know people's experiences and what they are thinking and why, you can never learn how they feel or what matters to them. To have a real relationship with someone, you must understand them. To understand them, you have to ask people questions and listen to their answers."

Luci—Chapter 11: "What I mean is that we shouldn't spend our energy wondering if hidden messages lurk in unexpected events or if they are random. Isn't it better to be curious about the event itself and not the why of it? Explore the novelty and the opportunities that something presents to you?"

Luci—Chapter 12: *Undeniably, seeing different perspectives helps people increase their knowledge and tolerance. Respecting divergent viewpoints is as vital as having overlapping values in a relationship.*

Sam—Chapter 13: "Using money as the foundation for independence won't save you from your own downfall."

Sam—Chapter 13: "Life's a journey," Sam told his children. "You get to pick the highway, the destination, and transportation. You choose the provisions available on the way. You make the decisions. In the end, you are answerable for your actions, looking out for your best interests, and completing the journey."

Luci—Chapter 13: *No, Barry Callahan, I wouldn't allow any boy to steal my heart, including you. I will only give it freely to the one I genuinely love.*

Sam—Chapter 14: *Finding a companion to complete oneself is absolute rubbish; people fulfill themselves by being who they are and knowing and leveraging their strengths.*

Luci—Chapter 14: *Relationships are fundamentally based on trust,* she reminded herself. *Lying to Barry, even with good intentions, is not the path to intimacy.*

Luci—Chapter 14: *Wallowing in self-pity is a waste of energy. Pessimism robs people of their freedom. It closes your mind to possibilities and opportunities. It makes you a victim of your own behavior.*

Chris—Chapter 15: "To be honest, deep inside, I'm afraid. I'd be nuts if I weren't. But if I allow fear to rule my life, I will never feel the joy of experiencing or accomplishing anything."

Chris—Chapter 15: ". . . You know, there's that old saying, 'Better safe than sorry,' but I like saying 'Safe but sorry.' I think my version is better. I don't want to end my life, Luci, dwelling on all the should-haves or could-haves that I didn't do because I was afraid."

Chris—Chapter 15: "I want to be inspired in life—feel real stuff like love, joy, gratitude, and pride in my accomplishments. These are the things, Luci, that make a person happy."

Barry—Chapter 15: "If you are going to get what you want in life, you have to have a contingency plan in your back pocket."

Geneviève—Chapter 16: *If you want to change people's behavior, it's best to give them a plausible option.*

Luci—Chapter 16: *What is it between mothers and daughters? What causes toxic behavior and one-upmanship? Is it because the earlier generation had fewer opportunities and less freedom than the next? Or is the clash between what is permissible and not due to mothers trying to protect their daughters from making the same mistakes that they made?*

Luci—Chapter 16: Thinking about the phenomenon, Luci wondered if the well-being she observed was linked to social interactions that fostered feelings of belonging, acceptance, empathy, and safety.

Geneviève—Chapter 17: "Live in the present, and you won't be anxious or worried."

Barry—Chapter 19: *I've left the nest. I set and fly my own course now, answerable and responsible for my choices and their consequences.*

Barry—Chapter 19: *It's incredible,* he thought. *The things you can hear if you focus on the present and are curious without judging if a sound is good or bad: a neighbor's dog barking, footsteps on the sidewalk, a slight rustling of tree leaves, the lonely sound of a distant car's engine, the opening of a garage door.*

Geneviève—Chapter 19: *One thing my porch soirees have taught me is that listening and forgoing judgment goes a long way in understanding the core concerns beneath a person's words.*

Geneviève—Chapter 19: "Because some group or government bans a book, dear, doesn't mean its material has nothing valuable to teach us. Make no mistake, Ma Bichette, governments and narrow-minded groups ban books because they challenge and teach people something important. Banned books are bold and provocative and confront issues that certain segments of the population want to sweep under the carpet."

Barry—Chapter 19: *Being "in love" is a passion like the flames of a blistering fire that race across the prairie. It's fierce and red, self-serving, and out of control. It feeds upon itself until there is nothing left. "To love," though, is a passion like the embers of a flickering fire that lingers within the hearth. It's gentle and glowing, crackles with surprise, and permeates the senses. It's warm and steady. It rekindles itself, and it endures.*

Sam—Chapter 19: "Ask questions or tell a story that opens up a person's imagination to see options. Remember the best advice giver always bundled his guidance in a parable."

Luci—Chapter 20: *In the end, what does life boil down to?*

Luci—Chapter 20: *Respect and caring are emotions that last,* Luci mused as the memories of her connection with Brian warmed her heart.

Luci—Chapter 20: *Time marches on and changes things, but it cannot eradicate the imprint of energy stamped on a place. Energy does not die. Its vibration, perhaps redistributed, continues. Memories are similar. They do not die; they are the waves that echo throughout a lifetime.*

Luci—Chapter 21: "Life's more than a dot-to-dot picture experience."

Sean—Chapter 21: "To place a sentence on a person for choosing an action without evaluating the conditions surrounding it is absurd and arbitrary."

Paul—Chapter 21: "The act of blind obedience to rules is the graver sin than the challenge to them. Acting in fear of or to please an external entity isn't being moral."

Sean—Chapter 21: "Law and morality aren't necessarily the same."

Chris—Chapter 21: "You cannot contract out responsibility for exercising your conscience to religion, government, or other authority. To mindlessly follow authority thwarts one's autonomy. After all is said and done, you are accountable for your choices. Those who believe that following the rules will excuse them from moral responsibility are living in fantasy land."

Adele—Chapter 21: "But at some point, we have to understand what made her tick. Don't we owe that to ourselves so we don't propagate the insanity? Don't we have to reclaim our lives from this sickness of resentment?"

Shelia—Chapter 22: "With Chuck, I ditched the what-ifs and sidestepped the anger and angst. I didn't allow self-pity, second-guessing, or rage to overshadow my life. . . Every day, I found something to be grateful for: my health, my children, my friends, a sunny day. I concentrated on good things. I believed that a happy future was something I could create in the present."

Luci—Chapter 22: *No, it isn't anger or denial. It's a web of self-blame and guilt I've constructed around me. Luci stumbled for the words to answer her friend.* "What's the root of it? All these years, I have been in the dark, not knowing what happened. My finger has been pressed on the ruminating button trying to shine a light on what went wrong, and it's driven me nuts. I've let my inner critic, Doris, live in my psyche and pop up whenever she damned pleased, admonishing me with 'What did you do?' and laying a guilt trip on me."

Shelia—Chapter 22: "Resolving the unknown is not under your control, but you can control the guilt trip and stop it in its tracks. Substitute *bad me* by thinking *lucky me*."

Shelia—Chapter 22: "Luci, I've embraced the belief that there are no second chances in life. Trusting that things in the past might have been better if this or that had happened is fooling yourself. And, putting faith in the future, hoping to find a better life without making the present as fulfilled as possible, is cheating yourself."

Shelia—Chapter 22: "I pity those who give up their autonomy or cave into adversity because they think fulfillment will materialize out of thin air in the future or in an afterlife," Shelia asserted. "I made a choice eighteen years ago, and I assumed accountability for my actions. If I concentrate on living a good life every day, I don't have to rely on hoping whether I have enough brownie points at the end of it. The life I'm leading now, today, is fulfillment enough."

Luci—Chapter 22: "I can't help wondering if there is a connection between having a purpose in life and general well-being and even health. What do you think?"

Sam—Chapter 22: "Lead a virtuous life, and you'll never be uncertain of your next step. You won't have to question or second-guess your motives. You will be free."

Luci—Chapter 25: *I want to live in the present with an open heart so that it fills with gratitude, kindness, and love.*

Chris—Chapter 25: "The truth, Luci, is that love and caring don't diminish."

Chris—Chapter 25: "It's not a fleeting pleasure that creates happiness or meaningful memories. Instead, it is choosing to use one's strengths and experiences in worthwhile work and being with the people you love."

Pat—Chapter 26: "You are creative, resourceful, and whole, Luci. You are capable of finding the answers; you can make the choices and take the actions you decide on."

Pat—Chapter 26: "If you had no fear, what would you do?"

Barry—Chapter 26: *But how could I possibly be happy if you are not? You always spoke about choices. I could put my ego first and try to prove the relationship was right and to continue pestering you. I could choose to be angry and place blame on myself or on you. Those are things I do not choose to do. .. I am reminded that you always said living in the present helps us opens our hearts so we have room for gratitude, kindness, and love.*

Luci—Chapter 27: *How can people be resilient and healthy if they are unforgiving and hold on to anger, resentment, and thoughts of revenge that trigger stress?*

Luci—Chapter 27: *What is forgiveness? I don't know yet. It is as arduous to catch as an elusive fairy.*

Luci—Chapter 27: *Tonight, I am thankful I've made the decision to forgive my mother's betrayal because it's a step toward freedom. I know deciding to forgive is no more than the beginning of the journey. For real forgiveness, I must follow the forgiveness fairies and the pathway to self-awareness and compassion.*

Luci—Chapter 27: *I keep asking myself what is forgiveness? Forgiveness is not pardoning. It is not overlooking or justifying my mother's transgression and the hurt her actions caused. I am relieved that I don't have to condone or excuse, reconcile, or even forget her behavior to forgive her. What is forgiveness? The nuggets were there all the time in Barry's last letter; forgiveness is choosing to reject resentment and embrace compassion.*

* * *

Several resources were used to describe historical places, eras, and background in this story. For the curious reader, a partial listing of these is posted to the author's website at www.MeridaJohnsAuthor.com

About the Author

Hailing from Windsor, Ontario, Canada, Merida Johns grew up in Southern California and has lived throughout the United States from coast to coast and border to border. She intertwines the history of time and place with stories about the human experience and shows how ordinary people tackle challenges, live though sorrow and betrayal, struggle with doubt, and act on their aspirations to achieve positive relationships and flourishing lives. Her stories are learning lessons where awareness, curiosity, and imagination transport the reader to the most unexpected places.

Made in the USA
Monee, IL
07 July 2020